WAR OF
THORNES

Eva Thorne Book Four

Lorel Clayton

LC Books

This is for everyone who, like us, prefers to live in other worlds.

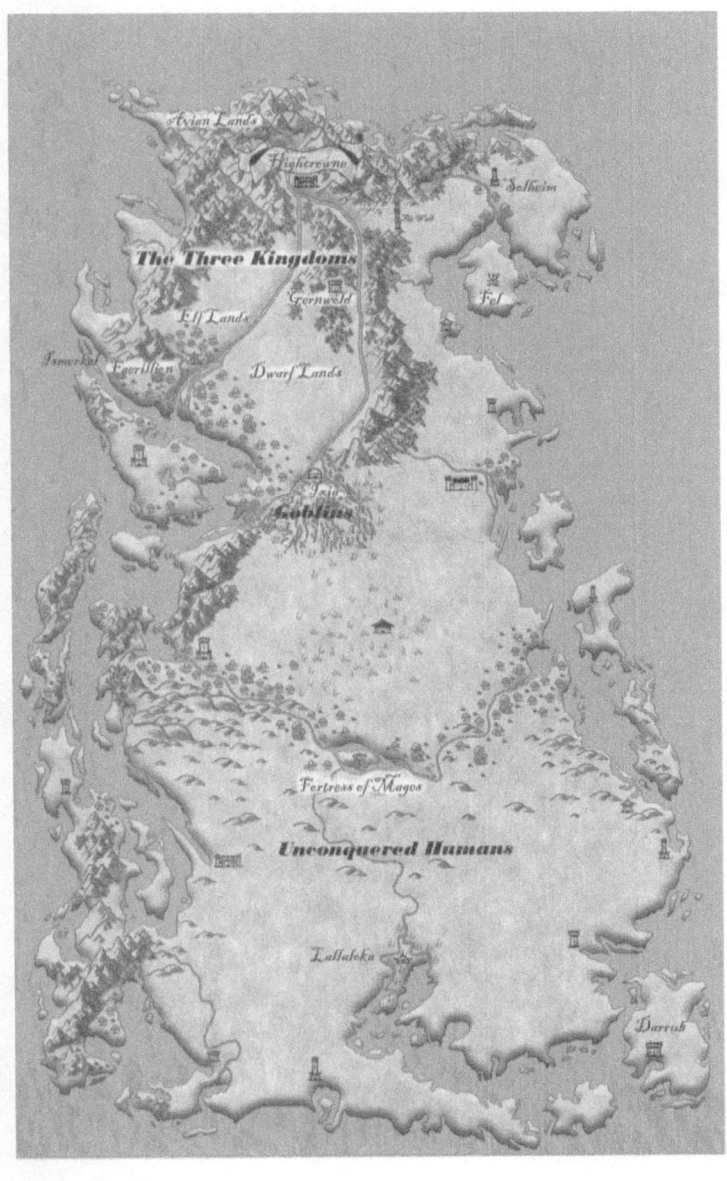

*No one can be trusted. Get jaded enough and you
learn you're the most untrustworthy of all.*

—Eva Thorne

1　HUNTED

O range light seeped through the gaps between mountains, staining the mist in the valley below, like watercolor seeping into paper. There was no sign of the army come to kill us, but I knew it was there.

Our companions—even Conrad, an abomination of my own creation—had gone their separate ways, leaving Thane and I to evade the enemy that stood between us and my home.

I didn't mean the home where I was born, not Solheim where the Dead God reigned.

My mother was high priestess of the rite that had summoned the god and destruction to our world, so she could rule over the dead. She had promised my soul in payment to seal the bargain, but I was nobody's sacrificial goat. She couldn't have me.

"We go right through the middle," I told Thane.

I was tired of running. We'd been skirting the edge of the valley for days, hiding from patrols, killing if we had to. I didn't do the killing, and not from any conviction that bad guys could be reformed. No, I wanted the bad guys dead, but I wasn't the one to do it. Not out of squeamishness either. Quite the opposite. If I grew too fond of killing, I was certain to become my mother.

What daughter hasn't struggled and failed to avoid becoming what she hates most? Still, I couldn't afford to give up the fight.

Lili of Solheim was the worst person in existence, if you could call her that. She was a lich, a dead thing held together by force of will. She worshipped Death, commanded Him. But I had a leg up on the ladder to damnation—I was Death's promised bride. Everyone would pay the price if I became like her.

The Dead God's armies blanketed the human realms to the south like the orange fog before us, ripping away souls and carrying them to the afterlife, leaving animated shells behind to swell the ranks of His armies even further. There were more dead than living in those lands now. Only one refuge for humanity remained: The Three Kingdoms and its capitol, Highcrowne. My true home.

I wanted its familiarity, wanted it more than any-thing. Maybe I could find the old Eva there? I didn't recognize the person I'd become.

The god harvested souls, and it seemed He wanted His bride to do the same. I hungered for the lives around me, aching to breathe them in and consume them.

That's why I shouldn't kill.

"I believe in you, Eva, but going through the middle of Lili's troops?" Thane shook his head.

"Think about it. Fharen fooled my mother, stole the First Soul out of her hands without her knowing. You have the same power."

I picked up a pebble. "You can place a glamour on this stone and make it look and feel just like the First Soul. We can tie it to a horse and let it go. Meanwhile, we walk right past everyone, with the real relic con-cealed by another glamour. Us along with it."

"You're relying on me a lot," he pointed out.

"I trust you." My voice didn't waver as much as I feared it might.

He'd been the enemy once, but Thane was a com-plicated being. And 'being' was probably the best term for him. He had no body of his own, but the one he was currently inhabiting, Fharen's, had magic that could be very useful right now.

"I'm not sure I can trust me. Lili's ritual gives her command over the Dead God until the bargain is ful-filled. Until you are sacrificed to Him, He's trapped and must obey her. That means she could have power over me. She could command me to kill you."

The other complicated thing about Thane was him being part of the Dead God, a portion of His spirit, wandering about possessing bodies. It was a long story. In a sense, he'd betrayed Himself for me. Romantic—and scary as hell.

"Then we stay away from Lili. She never sees us. It's a big valley."

"And a big army."

He was right. As the fog cleared, we saw the entirety of it, stretched like a fungus over the landscape. Dwarves mostly, as the risen troops could not violate the divine Compact that kept them out of the Kingdoms. The enemy camp was farther east than last time we looked, either headed back into Dwarf Lands or shadowing us until their hunters caught me.

Lili's army had been even bigger before a third peeled off to besiege Illul Faellion. Princess Hilja and hordes of scheming elf royals were holed up there, too busy fighting among themselves to do anything about the lich-led soldiers banging on their gates.

The army felt like overkill for little old me, as I was sure the werewolves in the hills and soldiers on horseback would catch us soon enough. We saw or heard them wherever we went. Thane's glamour kept us hidden, but how long until a determined mage penetrated it?

We should go where they weren't looking.

"And see there," I pointed at the silver ribbon of water, one section bristling with tree-sized masts. "There are boats on the river. We steal one and give our feet a rest. The horses' hooves. Whatever."

He sighed. "Alright."

I read souls, Thane's easier than anyone else's, and I knew he wasn't convinced, but he'd try for my sake. He knew I was a city girl and living wild was taking its toll. Living in fear of dying was the real drain. I wanted this over. One way or another.

He cupped the pebble I'd given him in one hand and then passed the other hand over it, like a street magician doing a parlor trick. The stone suddenly flared in my soul sight.

The flash of power turned from white to inky black, as he replicated the miasma of the First Soul. It was a relic from the time of the earliest gods, their failed attempt at crafting a soul. They had created *something* else instead. Unlike most souls, which shined liked stars in the black of the Void, the relic was beyond black. It absorbed all light and hope and left only despair. Anger. Greed. At least that's how Thane described it.

To me, it was a siren. It called me to embrace my hunger, to revel in power and fear nothing. Let others fear me.

"You've copied it perfectly," I said, unwilling to touch the pebble now.

The relic was dangerous. It made me think terrible things, but it was supposed to be a tool, a key, something I could use. Somehow. If only I could figure it out. I needed help. I needed to get home.

"If it convinces you, it will convince anyone." He put the enchanted stone into his horse's saddlebag.

"How do you do a glamour like that?" I asked. It seemed risky, copying something so evil, and I hoped I was wrong about how he did it.

"It is risky," he said, answering my thought.

We did that often, he and I, communicating without words. We both had soul sight. It was more than reading minds, it went deeper than thought, and was more truthful. It also made it hard to hide anything from one another. Without it, I would never have trusted him. He was the enemy after all.

Thane's soul sight had changed him. While hunting me down and preparing me for the last step of Lili's sacrificial rite, he had built a deep connection with me. That connection worked both ways and made him change his allegiance.

Some things about him would always be alien, though. He only cared to help my friends and Highcrowne because I cared. He felt the world through me. There was no love in him for it otherwise.

"How risky is 'risky'?" I persisted.

"A glamour is essentially a reflection. It can be a fear, a dream, an image, but it must first exist in someone's mind to be given form. The relic's image—

the blackness you see, its compelling power—all of that exists in your mind, Eva, so I reflect it onto this stone for Lili to see as well. The risk is I reflect too much, that she sees more of your thoughts, or worse, guesses this is a glamour because it does not match how she perceives the First Soul. I do not know her mind, so I cannot be sure the illusion is perfect."

"All I need is a distraction, not perfection." I took the saddlebags off my horse, cautious as the mount's eyes flashed white at me. The beast's silken brown coat shivered at my touch. Horses didn't like me much, and I didn't like them in return. "Get," I told it.

"Lead it to the plain," Thane chided. "There is little for it to eat here among the rocks."

People he didn't love, but animals he did. Strange man.

Even as he chastised me, he slapped his own mount's rump and said, "Go."

"You're shooing yours off."

"Mister Gardens will be our decoy." He indicated the fake relic in the animal's pack. "If he will leave my side. Go!" Thane repeated.

Thane had named Mister Gardens after my favorite fictional detective, but I still didn't like the beast.

My horse, which I rode when necessary, and unwillingly I might add, looked eager to be away.

"Why not this one? He'll make a good dinner for the wolves hunting us," I said.

It eyed me angrily and raised a hoof, wanting to stomp me no doubt. My glare put it on its best behavior again.

"No," Thane said. "Gardens will do his duty."

It didn't look like it to me. The stallion continued to follow us like a puppy, no matter how many times Thane pushed it away with a pained expression. Finally, he stopped and put his forehead against the animal's cheek, speaking in elvish.

I spoke elvish, but this was a dialect I didn't know. It made my skin tingle. The words carried power, strange and unlike the chill of Solhan necromancy. This power was akin to sunshine, a breeze carrying the first scents of spring.

Gardens snuffled Thane's face. It looked like a kiss, and then the horse bolted. He climbed into the hills and was soon out of sight.

"What was that?" I asked.

"An understanding. I spoke to him and told him why it was so important he obey. Elves disdain the old ways, lowering themselves to speak with primitive beasts, and so Fharen never used that language. None of them do anymore. While I become those whom I inhabit and know everything they know and feel, I am not them. I like the old language, and I like the beasts they—and you—deride, for they are pure and uncomplicated."

Thane surprised me every day. I liked it.

Some men you could gauge in an instant, but Thane's soul was vast, his personality formed from all the people he'd possessed and the experiences he'd had in foreign lands. He seemed innocent and naïve at times, dangerous and seductive at others.

I kissed him to surprise him back.

I'd grown serious ever since my sister died and after what I did to Conrad. We hadn't shared a carefree night of passion since before we faced Harbinger. There was something about danger that lowered my inhibitions, though, and we were about to do something very dangerous.

His cinnamon taste drew me in. I pulled away from the kiss before I was lost in distraction. There wasn't time. "You ready?" I breathed.

He nodded, but I sensed his hesitation.

"This will be fun." I smiled wickedly to convince him.

"You sound like me now. Only I'm immortal and you're not."

"Mortality doesn't make me an invalid. You wanted to know what life feels like? It's scary and dangerous, because it can all end in an instant. Fun. Like I said." I set off down the game trail we'd been using, knowing he'd follow.

I dragged my horse along, not needing to speak its language to sense it would have preferred to go with Gardens.

I was glad to have the creature for once, using its reins to steady me. There was a shakiness in my gut that made me want to throw up. My legs trembled with each step. I'd hoped to trick myself into bravery, but it wasn't working.

When we reached the valley floor, my false confidence vanished completely, and I stopped. The army had seemed unreal from the ridge, but up close I couldn't make out the horizon for all the tents, uniforms and sharp weapons obscuring the view. Dwarves bred faster than rabbits, with ten males to every female, and the army's ranks were swollen with recruits.

They weren't trained for war though. The Three Kingdoms had been at peace for centuries, and you could see it in the soldiers' eyes. None of them knew what they were doing, and the officers drilling them looked almost as nervous. They'd been hoping for a chance to finally be soldiers, but theory was one thing, reality another.

I pulled back from reading their souls. It was automatic, like breathing, but I didn't know if they could detect when I did it. We couldn't afford to be caught, so I struggled to control the ability that had crept up on me along with other disturbing powers. They surfaced when I first absorbed my sister's soul and grew with each one I devoured after.

The monsters and I looked a lot alike some days.

Thane assured me devoured souls were purified, not lost. They continued to the Halls of the Dead. No permanent damage. Except to me.

Thane removed my horse's bridle and released the mount near other horses belonging to the enemy cavalry, which were staked out on the periphery to munch the thinning grass.

If anyone was watching, the mare would have appeared out of thin air, Thane's glamour no longer hiding her. Fortunately, the guard on duty snored noisily.

Many elves used glamours, but I'd never encountered anyone as powerful as Fharen, the Elf King. If Thane hadn't acquired the king's abilities when he acquired his body, I wouldn't dream of doing what we were doing now.

Not that my hand didn't stray to the hilt of my sword from time to time. I wouldn't kill, but there was a head-knocker on the handle of the Ashur if I needed it.

We wended our way past sharpened stakes, ditches and other defenses. What would dare attack this place? Maybe it made the nervous soldiers feel better?

I wasn't familiar with how armies worked, but this one looked busy. Soldiers marched in formation or swung weapons at posts painted with elfish silhouettes, while others worked at repairing armor damaged in the recent battle against the elves.

The werewolves, the dozens who survived anyway, were practicing too. They had a manikin with pointed ears they took turns pouncing and savaging.

"I don't think they're all hunting me," I whispered.

Thane laughed, and I shushed him. "Don't worry," he said. "My glamour hides our voices along with our presence. And of course, they are not all looking for you, as delightful as you are to hunt. They are preparing for war."

"Illul Faellion is the opposite direction. I assumed they were chasing us."

"The river leads other places."

"Highcrowne." I got it. I'd hoped home would offer refuge, and surely the Avians, with their ancient knowledge and power, could protect us, but they'd soon be surrounded, trapped by invaders. If I didn't hurry, I'd be trapped outside the city, unable to find the answers I sought within it.

A wolf growled and twisted mid leap, turning back to sniff the wind.

I froze. "Does it smell us?"

"We are concealed," Thane repeated, although he didn't sound as certain as I would have liked.

Another wolf tore through a nearby tent and jumped the one who'd been on the alert. They fought, rolling in the mud, their snarls making my hairs stand on end.

Thane sagged. He had dark circles under his eyes, and I realized the glamours he was maintaining were taking their toll. Not only had he kept us hidden for days already, but now he was hiding our sounds and scents even, as well as the glamour he maintained at a distance on Gardens and the fake stone. Not to mention hiding the real one, even from me.

I'd almost forgotten about the First Soul, which was the point. Now it stirred. Thane furrowed his brow, struggling to shield it again.

The First Soul was a twisted mistake that shone darkness instead of light in the universe. It corrupted and controlled, maddening mortals and gods alike. Thane could only cover it with illusions, like a silken scarf over an oil lamp, and those illusions burnt away whenever the relic was determined enough.

I was its Keeper. It was my job, not Thane's to quell it, but I hesitated.

Beads of sweat formed on Thane's brow, and I sensed a stirring in the distant command tent where my mother met with her generals. Werewolves and soldiers would not kill us as quickly as she would. She was the true danger, and now the relic would give us away.

I spoke to it in my mind: *Hush. I don't want you stolen by her. You want to be with me, don't you?*

You never speak to me anymore.

I'm trying to get us to safety, to a place where I can be yours.

You lie. I know your feelings. It meant Thane.

Mortal passions cannot compare to you.

No, for I offer more than you can imagine. There is no need to run or hide. I will give you power this pathetic world has never seen. We shall tear the Dead God to shreds. We shall make all the enemies you flee quiver in terror. Give yourself to me, and I will be all you need.

It shoved images into my head. I saw the army around us dead at my feet. My mother's head bowed— before I cut it off with the sword I'd inherited from her, and her soul infused the blade with the echo of yet another death. Her powerful soul would feed me and *it*.

The relic was all I would ever need.

"Yes." I reached for the First Soul, clutching at the pouch on Thane's hip where he kept it from me.

"Eva." Sweat poured off him in rivulets now. He took my hands in his strong grip. "Stop talking to it. Look at me. Look at me."

I gazed into his eyes. Pale blue, not Solhan white. Fharen was half-elf and half-Solhan, but he usually used his impressive power to maintain a glamour of pureblood elf perfection. Thane hardly looked like King Fharen at all. He was my Thane. In his eyes, I saw the one I loved. His golden soul was the antithesis of the relic's black blight, and I clutched at him like you would a railing when you've nearly fallen.

I let the First Soul's visions slip from my mind and fade like a dream.

When I was in control again, I nodded. Thane relaxed his brow, and I felt the tension in him ease.

The relic tortured him in its own way, and we seldom had a day where it did not intrude.

I couldn't allow that thing to warp me. It was supposed to be my key to stopping the Dead God. I needed to learn how to use it, and that's why I needed to reach Highcrowne soon.

Lili had used the First Soul to summon the Dead God into the world, but she had listened to the relic too much, or maybe it had listened to her? I don't know whose idea it was originally, but they both wanted the living crushed beneath their feet.

I sensed she remained in the tent, undisturbed by my battle with the First Soul. She still didn't know we were here. Good.

I could veer over and confront her, of course. Demand the knowledge I needed, use the Soul to compel answers from her.

I quashed that thought as a dangerous one that would leave me vulnerable to it again. No.

Uncle Ulric would know what to do. I was certain of it.

I had tried dream walking to speak with him, but it hadn't worked. Highcrowne was in turmoil, and I feared he was dead. But there was no justification for that fear. My uncle was a powerful Asheen, one of the nine who had ruled Solheim. My own lack of skill was likely to blame. I'd find him and learn what I needed to know. That was the plan.

Why did I bother to make plans?

We were halfway across the valley, almost to the river and the possibility of a boat to carry us to Highcrowne faster than Lili's army could march, when I felt something new.

I had clamped down hard on my magical senses to keep the voice of the First Soul out of my head, but another voice pressed into my mind and screamed for my attention. I couldn't resist, not even a little.

Eva... Thorne, it said over and over.

It knew my name. Its silent voice seemed to call from a nearby tent, and I had no choice but to step inside.

"What are you doing?" Thane followed without waiting for my reply. I couldn't explain it anyway.

I moved deeper into the gloom, and my Solhan eyes adjusted to the darkness. The interior was richly decorated: silks hanging from poles, embroidered carpets beneath my feet.

A lone vase drew me. It was displayed on a nondescript table, it's eggshell blue ceramic polished to a glossy shine, the neck elongated like that of a crane. The tent was large enough to hold a dozen vases on plinths, but there was only the one.

I knew what it was. Life echoed within; the fading warmth of a soul long separated from its body.

Uncle had more soul jars in his small study. What was so special about this one? How could it compel me?

As soon as I touched it, I knew it was a mistake.

Lili jerked into full attention. I felt the shift in her. She knew some intruder had entered her personal tent. I dared not read any more from her, else she might guess it was me.

"Soldiers are coming," Thane hissed.

"I know." I knew before I heard the shouts and rattle of dwarvish chainmail.

I grabbed the jar, which was small enough to carry in one hand, and ran. Sensing where my mother was, I shifted our vector to stay as far away from her as possible.

Lili was a powerful necromancer, but she couldn't counteract elvish glamour. The soul jar vanished from her senses, hidden along with us in an illusion of Thane's creation. She was confused, shouting commands to "find it." And then she realized another soul was reading hers.

"Oops." I really wished I'd learned more control. At least not been so tempted to eavesdrop.

"Lili knows it's us," I warned Thane.

He gave me a look but didn't say more. He was busy, fighting to hide us from an alerted army. Werewolves stopped their play and sniffed the breeze, muscles taut as war horns howled their brassy commands.

We reached the riverbank, only to find the masts we'd seen from the hills were attached to broken wrecks grounded on the shore.

When the army first swarmed this valley, the merchant captains must have wisely fled before any useful vessels could be commandeered. Their quick thinking was our doom. The current of the Serpent's Ribbon was too strong to navigate without slave-rowed ships with banks of oars, sophisticated sails, or a steamboat.

Dwarven troops had begun building more. Piles of trees cleared from the lower foothills were stacked along the shore, some skeletal hauls taking shape, but none were finished. The soldiers who had been sawing and working them now donned armor.

We were hemmed in on all sides. Lili was sure to track me down before we could return to the hills. I had no choice but to swim—and I really wished I'd learned how.

A few row boats were intact, rocking against the side of the dock. Better than swimming. Barely. Boards creaked as we moved, despite all the shrouding glamours we wore. I settled on a bench and grabbed the oars.

I winced from a splinter and had a flashback to the last time I rowed a boat.

"Allow me," Thane said, taking the oars instead. He must have remembered too. Then he gasped and stuck a bleeding thumb in his mouth. The hands he'd borrowed from Fharen were as soft and delicate as only a pampered king's could be.

I laughed. "Splinters aren't so funny, are they? I have a higher pain tolerance than you. Allow me."

I rowed for a while, fighting against the current until my stomach muscles ached, and I couldn't hide my discomfort anymore. Thane took over then, his hands wrapped in cloth, and I despaired when his efforts did not get us any further upstream than mine. We were still within sight of the dock.

Our only hope was to throw my stolen treasure over the side and let it be carried downstream. That might distract Lili.

I reached into my pack to feel for the blue jar I'd hidden there. It had quieted, but as soon as I touched it, I heard it again. Like a vibration moving through my hand and up into my skull, it took hold of my muscles and wouldn't let me get rid of it.

I couldn't throw it away. Even if I could make myself, part of me didn't want to. I needed to know how it could control me, why it knew my name—my true name.

2 UNQUIET

It was bad enough I had the First Soul whispering in my head, now this too?

Thane frowned. "I recognize that expression. Is my glamour slipping? Do you hear the relic?" There was sweat beading on his brow from either the rowing or all the concentration on magic or both. He was much more than a man, but he had his limits.

"No, don't worry. Stay focused on what you're doing. I'm listening to the jar. I hear my name. What else does it know about me?"

"It's talking to you? Throw it away, Eva. Into the water right now. That was Lili's private tent. That thing belongs to her, and it cannot be good. I served Lili for years, reporting to her whenever I passed by

Solheim, and I never knew her to eat or sleep or leave the throne she erected in the inner sanctum. All she needs is power. The fact she has a personal tent, with one occupant—that jar—is disturbing."

"You said it: all Lili needs is power. So, I have to know what power this jar gives her. Maybe we can use it? Besides, it would be unwise to let anyone else have it. It knows my name."

"A lot of people know your name. You are a Thorne."

"My true name."

Solhans, fairies, and many other races believed power lay in true names. Solhans used them to control souls. Even the most unskilled practitioner could wield the power of a great necromancer over a soul chained to them by invocation of a true name. Others believed names granted wishes. Someone could not rest once you called their name, not until they fulfilled your desire. Fairy tales were full of such stories of compelling gnomes and spirits with a name.

I believed in all those things, but I'd never had to worry about keeping my name safe before. I never knew it. Only Lili did.

The fact she hadn't used it against me probably meant it was all superstition. Or, perhaps she'd already invoked my name when she sold my soul, and my hand in marriage, to the Dead God?

Whatever the reason, she had told the soul within this jar my name as well. At least I thought it was my name, because it started with 'Eva' and ended with 'Thorne' and had two other names in the middle. And whenever it whispered those names, I couldn't dream of setting it down. It *had* bewitched and compelled me to obey.

The First Soul would be jealous.

Thane stayed quiet. He'd inhabited Erick and so carried the knowledge of one of the greatest Solhan necromancers. He understood why the jar was important. He also didn't bother to ask my name, because he knew I'd never tell him. He kept up his struggle against the river's current and left me to my questioning without further argument.

"Why did you call me?" I asked the jar. I felt stupid talking out loud, but I worried my internal voice would connect to the wrong mysterious, dangerous relic in our possession. One cursed object at a time.

Eva... Thorne. That's all it said, over and over.

Frustrated, I stuffed it in the bottom of my pack, muffled in clothing and dried provisions. See how it liked being ignored.

"You could throw it in the river," Thane suggested again, as if the thought had never occurred to me.

Then, for a moment, I wondered if he meant the First Soul? *Not until I'm done with it.*

It heard my stray, traitorous thought and flared to life.

Thane cried out in pain, and the glamour shrouding us disappeared.

One of the soldiers posted along the bank spotted us and cried out, "Ahoy, you in the dingy! Make yerself known before we sticks an arrow in ye."

"Lili will see us too," I warned.

"I know, but I can't contain...It hurts!" Thane screamed, hands clutching his temples as though his mind was about to explode.

The dwarven soldier on the shore notched an arrow, and more came out of nearby tents to stand beside him.

I took the oars again and heaved, rowing as fast as I could, allowing Thane time to recover. I knew I should intervene in his struggle with the Soul, be a proper Keeper and force it to obey, but I didn't know how anymore. Whenever I tried sweet talk or reason, it seduced me with dark dreams.

"Eva," Thane gasped, tears streaming down his cheeks.

With my soul sight, I saw the relic's black miasma. It was like inky tentacles, wrapping themselves around Thane and trying to swallow the bright light of the man I loved.

"Stop!" I ordered, but the Soul didn't listen.

Scores of soldiers stood along both banks now, arrows drawn. I heard the growl of a werewolf close by, an excited, hungry sound.

Thane, despite his agony, managed to summon a glamour again. The soldiers' expressions turned from focused to confused when we vanished from sight.

They released their arrows anyway, seeking to strike us even if they couldn't see us.

Projectiles hit the river all around, sending out expanding ripples, and two struck the boat with a dull *thunk*. The dwarves needed more practice. Of course, one of the arrows hit a hairsbreadth from my left knee, so we'd been lucky.

I was more worried about the werewolf.

Surprised dwarves went flying, shoved aside by the preternaturally strong creature as it homed in on us. I sensed Lili close behind. She couldn't penetrate the glamour, but it had been down long enough for her know I was here.

I'd changed my mind. I was more worried about her than the wolf.

I rowed so fast that instant calluses formed.

Thane spoke an incantation in that old elvish dialect he'd used with the horse, his words clipped, as he struggled through the pain of the relic's punishment.

Are you punishing Thane or me? I asked it.

It didn't answer.

One side of the river erupted in vines, ensnaring the archers. Thane waved a hand, and the other bank was likewise choked in brambles. Trapped soldiers cursed, while others drew swords and tried to cut them free. The werewolf jumped over the top of it all and landed in the water, paddling like a dog right for us.

That's when I realized we were not invisible after all: the boat made ripples in the water. The creature could pinpoint exactly where we were.

"Damn it." I needed the First Soul.

I'd used it to boost my magic before, but each time it got harder not to listen to its suggestions. I worried I wouldn't be controlling it—it would control me. But time and doubts were luxuries I didn't have now. I'd pay the consequences later.

I extracted the gem from Thane's belt pouch—he was in too much agony to stop me—and blew a kiss across it, stirring the dark mist shrouding its crystalline surface, until my breath became a black gale that tore across the river, creating ocean-sized swells.

The werewolf was pushed back on a wave of water several feet high, and our boat sped up the river.

Thank you, I told the Soul, which was as heavy as lead in my hand. *Now release Thane. Please.*

You wanted to throw me away, it said, venom in the voice that scratched at the back of my mind.

I didn't mean it. I'm sorry.

See what would become of you without me.

It sent me visions so real, I feared the wolf and Lili were upon us this time. I felt its wet fur pressed against my face, its teeth tearing into my stomach, and I couldn't do anything to stop it, because my mother was there, freezing me in numbing darkness, just as she had frozen my arm with her necromancy. I was helpless. Then the Soul came to my rescue, obliterating her and all the creatures who wanted me dead. Everyone, especially that traitorous Thane who'd suggested I give up its power.

"No," I said, shaking my head to clear it of the First Soul's warped visions.

Using it, even speaking to it now, was worse than playing with fire. It wanted to turn me into something I didn't want to be—but which I could too easily become.

Thane clutched his head, fighting to maintain the concealing glamour and hide the First Soul's voice from me, but it fought him as it never had before. I had to do something.

I cast back to when I first tamed the relic. I stole it from Leviathan, an ancient monster who could swallow me in one bite. I had been too terrified of that creature to fear the Soul then. So, when the First Soul wrapped me in its black, suffocating miasma of evil, my first thought, strangely, was of all the evil people in my life who I nevertheless loved. The Soul craved such unconditional love above all things.

I took a breath and thought of Ilsa, who I'd lost. Of Ulric and Nanny who I could not reach. But the one I feared for most of all was Little Viktor. If I did not find a way to stop this war, my nephew and everyone I cared about would die.

"Help me," I begged the Soul. "I swear I will never throw you away. I will protect you as fiercely as I protect them."

I fed it reassuring emotions, real emotions I summoned from memory. I imagined the relic as my nephew when he was an infant in my arms. I'd been so terrified of the small creature back then. I worried I'd break him, worried he might spit up on me or worse, cry as he had at Nanny, but he didn't. Vikky lay serene in my arms, and I realized how perfect his little nose and fingers, how wonderful he smelled. I lifted him to my face, breathing him in.

Calm, I cradled the First Soul—a diamond-like crystal the size of my fist—and said, "Hush."

I tried to recall a lullaby, but all I could think of was the prayer of reverence I'd been taught as a child: "Darkest Soul, bow to me as I bow low...."

The relic fell asleep in my hands. Its inky black tendrils released Thane and collapsed down into a blanket covering itself.

I held my breath, afraid to break the spell, and slipped it back into its pouch on Thane's hip. As my fingers released it, I heard it say, *You swore.*

Thane ceased his struggles, instantly free of pain, and he snapped a powerful glamour into place to conceal the Soul from me again.

Its voice was silent, its dark aura gone, leaving only crisp, morning light behind. It slept—for now.

Thane furrowed his brow at me. I'd taken too many risks: going through the heart of Lili's troops, stealing the soul jar, and then this. I'd played carelessly with the relic when I first found it, but since then I'd learned how stupid I'd been.

"Well," I said, trying to downplay the near miss, "at least we won't be werewolf dinner tonight. Back to rowing." I kept going, mostly to occupy my muscles, so my brain wouldn't drift into dangerous waters.

But this was me we're talking about.

We'd been pushed miles upstream and out of danger, yet, regardless of how gentle the current, we were going against it and would never reach Highcrowne this way. First order of business was to steal a real boat.

We found said boat in a rats' nest. Water rats. Freshwater pirates and smugglers who trawled the length of the massive river that ran from the Avian mountains, past Dwarf Lands, to empty into the sea near Illul Faellion. Their steamers choked one riverbank, some three deep. They had plenty to spare.

I daresay, they weren't too welcoming when we rowed into their tumbledown port. Not the right kind of welcoming, anyway.

I tried tying the dingy to the dock, but the thick poles were covered in black tar and too slippery to hold on to. I grabbed the creaking pier, hoping to climb up and tie off from steadier ground, when massive hands as oily and grimy as the pole grabbed me and hauled me up.

"Weeell," the man drawled. "What do we have here? A pretty little thing come to keep me warm?"

The way he ran his hands over me was an improper greeting for a lady he'd only just met. I wasn't a lady, so he'd regret it even more.

Thane scrambled up beside me, leaving the dingy to float away unmoored, and looked ready to tear the man apart.

I held up a hand, stopping him mid-lunge. "Allow me."

I continued the movement and reached behind me to draw the Ashur from its sheath. Its shining, serrated teeth were reflected in the smuggler's black pupils.

He grabbed for my sword arm, but I dodged his meaty fist and sliced from below, severing his belt and trousers, but not penetrating flesh. His pants hung around his ankles. I'd cut close enough to his man parts that he went pale and dropped me to clutch them protectively.

I let the half dozen friends of his who'd crowded in to watch see my weapon.

"Now," I said, allowing the chill tone of a Solhan to creep into my voice.

I paused, assessing each in turn—a filthy, drunken bunch who looked too stupid to realize the war was coming their way—and gave them time to take in my white eyes and pale skin. A few stared at the gray flesh of my left arm, the one that was dead if not for the necromancy I'd managed to cast to animate it.

One pirate gulped.

I smiled. "Which of you gentlemen is willing to volunteer their ship to give us a ride home?"

"None of us will part with our livelihood," the one holding his private parts said. Seemed he loved his ship more than his manhood. Stupid, just as I'd first surmised.

"We're not thieves," Thane said, "no offense to present company, and so we're willing to pay for passage." Thane lifted a heavy pouch full of coins that hadn't been there a moment ago. He poured a few gold and silver coins into his hand. Fae illusions. If only I could do glamours. Oh, the tricks I could play.

There were greedy murmurs, a pink tongue licked greasy lips, and they pressed closer. Now they were interested.

"We are headed to Highcrowne," I said, and they took a step back again, leaving the one with his pants down.

He shambled off but didn't manage to get far enough away before I said, "Perfect. We're already acquainted. I'm ready to go now."

"There's an army headed this way," I warned the onlookers, "so I recommend none of you remain here." I had no love for criminals, but anyone alive deserved a chance to stay that way.

"It'll take days yet for those land-locked dwarves to finish their ships," one of the scoundrels said, spitting chaw in an arc that went over his companions' heads and hit the water. "We'll scatter through the tributaries long 'afore they gets here."

"But Highcrowne," the one with his pants down chimed in, "is not a friendly place these days. We're liable to get killed goin' there." He looked back at his mates for support, but they'd already drifted away. They returned to the shacks that lined the wharf, crowded with the sounds of drunken men, loudly celebrating the end of the world.

"I can assure you," I said, "I am even less friendly than Highcrowne and even more certain of getting you killed, if you don't do as I ask."

He had his pants up now, and his poker face didn't reveal the emotions and thoughts roiling beneath the surface. He was thinking about the knives hidden on his body, wondering if he could best me if he weren't caught off guard. Maybe when we were asleep on his boat? It was five nights to Highcrowne, plenty of opportunity to slit our throats. He'd like to have his way with me too, but safer to slit my throat first.

It was not a pretty vision, but the curse of being able to read souls meant I got to know some people more than I'd like. It was usually the sick ones, those so disturbed that my magical sight could penetrate their unshielded chaos.

"Fine," he said, evil plan fully formulated. "It's this way."

"Thank you." I followed, Thane guarding our backs as we climbed across slimy decks and out to a rusting steamship.

It had a single pilot's cabin up top, no bigger than the smokestack that took up most of the deck. Cargo was kept below decks, hammocks hung between the crates wherever there was room. Most crew slept on deck in the weather until they could get their ill-gotten gains to shore.

Sometimes, I had flashes of people's entire lives when I read them. This man's was one endless sequence of violence, followed by boredom, followed by desires that led to more violence, starting the whole cycle over again. Predictable. Except for the flashes of thoughts he had about Thane between thoughts about me. I'm not sure which disturbed me more.

"Perfect," I said, concealing my disgust. "You can operate this ship alone, can you not?"

"No, I need more people. And the captain. This isn't my ship. I'm just the helmsman. I can go back and fetch them if you wait here." There were five other crew members, I knew, all ashore drinking. They'd try to kill us faster than this one, and he felt more comfortable killing in a pack.

"I think not. Thane can stoke the boilers below."

The pirate, who was called Loch, blinked, wide-eyed for a moment, before nodding. He imagined locking

Thane in the engine room, while he had his way with me tonight. Kill Thane and whatnot later. Maybe he'd even keep the ship, get a new crew upriver, and become captain of his own rusting kingdom. Another evil plan hatched. He smiled. "Sounds good."

"I'm sure it does to you."

Loch showed Thane what to do with the engine. Thane was a quick learner and soon had the boilers stoked, the steam pumping, and pressure modulated—I was learning the terminology—all to get the propeller spinning. I preferred the silent beauty of a sailing vessel, but this ship was human, in all its grungy, loud, modern goings-on.

I'm not old fashioned, more like sensible. What use was a metal ship on the water? It would sink twice as fast as soon as it got a hole in it. Typical Southern nonsense. I would be glad when were rid of it.

Loch didn't object to me following him everywhere, confident in his plans. I knew how chaotic his thoughts were, and I preferred to keep a close eye on him.

He unmoored the ship and took up the helm. We steamed upriver as the sky turned pink and purple.

Another day closer to home. Another day still alive.

Loch asked for payment, even though he planned to take whatever else we had hidden away after we were dead. He held Thane's conjured silver for a long while, before licking his lips and putting it away, not knowing it would vanish with the dawn.

The stars were brilliant that evening, wherever I could see them between puffs of noxious black smoke from the chimney. The ship ran on coal and smelled of Highcrowne winter.

"Sure you're not feeling a bit tired, milady? There's plenty of bunks down below, with us running this on a skeleton crew." He chuckled at that, picturing mine and Thane's skeletons rotting at the bottom of the river after he'd dumped us.

"No, not tired," I repeated. I don't know how many times he'd asked. I didn't tell him Thane and I could go days without sleep. It was a Solhan thing in my case, or necromancer thing, hard to say. It was a divine thing in Thane's case.

I also didn't tell Loch he was toying with the incarnation of Death and his bride. Let him keep his evil dreams a while longer.

"I can take over," I said.

It was well past dawn, and the man was slumped against the helm, rocking back and forth, so I was getting seasick.

"I see how you spot the deeper channels now and can avoid the shallows. I'll take good care of your ship, don't worry," I added.

I pried his hands off, and he slumped to the deck, snoring loudly.

I made sure we were on a relative straight stretch of river and tied off the helm with ropes set up for just such occasions where little navigation was required.

I heaved and shoved and dragged the man to the small plank that stuck off to one side, permanently nailed into position. Planks were required on pirate vessels for sport, I presumed.

I thought about his evil plans, all I'd seen in his soul, and I wanted to cut his throat in revenge for what he planned to do to me. I longed to rip the soul from his dying carcass and shred it into little pieces until the man he was now was no more, until he was reborn as innocent as a babe.

But that was Death's job, refining souls in His crucible until the impurities were burnt away. Not mine. I didn't want this power He'd given me, didn't want to judge the souls who passed before me or even see them as I did. It was more than anyone would want to know.

When I found a way to use the First Soul to send the god back to where He came from, I'd force Him to take this power from me as well. I didn't want this knowledge, didn't want this temptation to murder and judgement. I wanted to be Eva again.

I rolled Loch off the side of the boat and laughed when he spluttered awake.

"Shore's that way." I pointed. "Set foot on this deck again and you'll be the one with his throat cut."

I drew my Ashur and watched him swim, cursing, to the far bank. I didn't put the weapon away again, or tell Thane, until we were miles upriver and he came out looking for something to eat.

"This stomach is gurgling louder than the steam pipes. I must feed it something." Sometimes Thane seemed put out by the limitations of a physical form.

"I saw some tinned meats and barrels of water through that hatch. Help yourself."

"Where's Loch?" he asked, looking around. "Will I wake him if I go down below?"

"Nope."

"You threw him overboard." Thane had soul-reading ability too. But I think he simply knew me well.

"We don't need him. You're running the engine; I'm steering the ship. He was useless. And creepy."

"You should have killed him while you were at it. His absence would make the world a better place."

"I know it, but I'm on the wagon. Start with one sip and soon I'm ripping out souls and guzzling them down so fast I could never return to polite company."

I suddenly remembered Nanny setting up tea and biscuits on doilies in the parlor. The tea was noxious and the biscuits hard as stone, but it had looked pretty. Ilsa always sat there, prattling to Uncle about her ideas for the business. I'd roll my eyes and go up to my room while she played house.

I'd never see Ilsa with her lace gloves and pinky finger sticking out ever-so-properly again. She'd always been there, and now she wouldn't be.

Thane put his arms around me, and I stiffened. "It's not your fault. All of this was done to you, and we will undo it."

"Except what was done to Ilsa."

"It was her choice. You let Loch live, and that was your mistake. All you can do, moment to moment, is make a choice and live with it. Didn't you tell me that is what made life worthwhile?"

"And scary as hell."

"Not as scary as knowing you are steering this ship. I've seen you row. Not to mention that time you tried to drive your uncle's motor carriage."

I laughed, remembering. "You saw that?"

He nodded. Thane had been with me almost as long as Ilsa. He was my shadow, sent to retrieve my soul for the Dead God. I was glad he'd changed sides. I was glad he knew her and all of it. I had the strangest feeling I wouldn't survive the battles that lay ahead, so I wanted someone left behind to remember.

"Eva," he began.

I shook my head. "Stop listening in and stop trying to make me feel better. You already have. Now, go eat! I can hear your stomach too." I shoved him in the right direction. "And bring me back some dried fish."

Having survived Nanny's cooking my whole life, I could eat anything.

He obeyed and left me to the quiet of the river. The engine chugged away below deck, but up top there was enough of a breeze and the cries of birds to cover the sound. I smiled as I steered the boat I'd pirated from a pirate.

We travelled for days, losing time in an elvish port looking for coal. The place was nearly abandoned, the stragglers left behind more frightened of the dwarvish army downstream than the smugglers had been. The coal bins had been emptied, but I scavenged enough dregs to make do for the rest of the journey.

We slept or ate as the need arose, and as we made our way upstream, summer grasses gave way to autumn trees. The mountains were always a season colder than the plains. I was certain to be tasting winter again soon.

I lay on the deck, overhanging trees providing passing shade as we moved slowly against the strengthening current. It was nice to relax, watching Thane in the midday sunlight as he steered the ship. His long, raven hair glinted blue and was a beautiful contrast to his fair skin. I was seeing lots of skin. Lots of flexing muscles too. I sighed.

It wasn't Thane's body I cared for—it was only borrowed—but him. His soul. I couldn't stand Fharen's face, but as soon as Thane's soul stepped inside that cruel shell, it was transformed into something beautiful.

I liked the way he smiled at me, in between course corrections. No one had ever smiled at me with such contentment. He didn't want anything more from me than this. I led him around, and he followed, with a reasonable amount of questioning, but without doubts. He believed in me, and because of that, I believed in myself more than I ever had before. There was someone on my side for once.

I was going to need it.

"If you were anyone else, I'd have gotten you killed by now, you know?" I stretched out on the deck. Without snow, the autumn days in the valley were hotter than Highcrowne summer, so I wasn't wearing much, just an elvish camisole that came with the outfit I took when I left the palace. It was lacey and revealing, and I revealed a bit more by lowering one strap ever so slightly. "That's what femme fatales do."

"You read too many mysteries." He looked at me, which had been my intent—and he kept looking.

"Maybe it's a good thing in your case. Because I, also know the femme fatale is supposed to be irresistibly seductive." I tossed my hair, and the other strap slipped down.

He absently tied off the ship's wheel, never taking his eyes off me, and lay on the deck beside me. I'd been using my discarded gown as a layer of protection against the grimy surface, but he spread out on an algae-stained patch of rotted wood without a care.

"Eva," he breathed as his mouth found mine. He had to take his eyes off me then, but his hands caressed me instead, taking me in with a different kind of sense.

It was strange how, when our souls entwined, I could feel what he felt, know what he knew. It was an out of body experience.

I was pure consciousness, drawn to the sun-bright warmth of him, peripherally aware of how his fingertips made goosebumps form across my breast in a wave, and aware of how cold my skin felt to him. I didn't want to be so distant from it all, I loved the being that was Thane, but I also loved what he could do with the body he controlled.

I focused on his maddingly gentle touch, the taste of his tongue, the softness of his lower lip against my teeth.

"Eva," he said my name again, and I smelled cinnamon.

How could a soul carry scent? Somehow his did, that of a cinnamon smoke so intoxicating I wanted it to fill my lungs and permeate my pores, to stain me forever. His voice was the one that had invaded my dreams for long as I could remember, whispering to me of love and longing. Now that voice promised more.

As much as I tried to enjoy the moment, to focus on sensation and forget thought, his soul was wide open to me, and mine to him. I sensed his concern for me, the worry that I had not yet recovered from Ilsa's loss—or Conrad's.

There can be no recovering, my soul whispered to his, but I choose to live. I will not join the dead.

We made love slowly, quickly, gently, roughly. Over and over, eating or drinking when we needed, laughing and crying, until the light vanished, leaving us to stare in wonder at the stars.

Thane talked of his adventures in Darrub and of the time he stood against the Dead God's hordes in the form of a minor warlock manning the Fortress of Mages. He'd seen the war from the opposite side for the first time, and it shook him.

I didn't let him dwell on war, for we'd see it again. I told him about Viktor and Duane and the laughing, carefree days of childhood. I hadn't experienced the same grand adventures, but I paid attention to details, the little moments in life that made it so precious, because they were ephemeral.

This was one of those moments.

I wished I could stay with him, drifting on the river forever, but the river was not the world, as much as I wanted it to be.

I slept, for what would be the last time for a long time, and that next morning, I saw the signs of Lili's army behind us.

On a straight stretch of river, I glimpsed a distant, white wall of sails. Lili's newly built ships had been sped along with her own brand of magic. She was catching up.

And the wolves—they had no need of boats.

Half a dozen raced along the banks, smudges of black, gray or brown fur against green foliage. They kept track of us by our ship's stray puffs of smoke, or the disturbance its keel made in the water, neither of which Thane's glamour completely concealed.

The creatures darted ahead, then they looped back and stopped. They watched us with glowing eyes, tongues lolling from cavernous mouths edged in sharp fangs, as though this chase was a game for them. Maybe it was.

"Don't use the relic again," Thane warned.

I tore my gaze away from them. "I hadn't planned to."

"You didn't plan to before. You could have killed that first wolf who swam for us, torn out his soul rather than summoning a wave. Why didn't you? Why don't you kill these ones?"

Thane knew my deepest fears, so the only reason he spoke about this now was to remind me of my mistake. I knew he meant to keep me from making another one, but I had never liked lectures. All it did was annoy me.

"You know why. Every soul I take, I see their whole lives, and then I snuff it out. I can't do that again. I won't do that again."

These wolves had been dwarves not so long ago, living ordinary lives. I'm sure they never dreamt they'd be soldiers on the wrong side of a war that was meant to end the world. None of this was their fault.

"I know you so well, yet you are a puzzle to me, Eva." The way he said my name always made me shiver, and I forgave him his prodding. He did not ask me to kill again.

We stayed in the middle of the massive channel. Whenever any dared to swim across, Thane summoned vines to strangle them and pull them under. Werewolves were resistant to magic, not to plants or drowning, and he reduced their number by two.

I cringed at the necessity of their deaths, but it didn't affect Thane like it did me.

He attempted to kill any that came within range of his conjurations. The surviving wolves learned, cutting an ensnared comrade loose whenever Thane cast his vines on land, and staying out of the water to avoid drowning. They kept their distance too.

We stopped sleeping, and our carefree moments were lost to memory. The coal for the steam engine was almost gone, and, despite Thane's warning, I began to think about calling on the First Soul again.

At last, we reached our destination. The canyon walls that had contained us for miles, rising so high they left only a narrow river of sky above to mirror the river below, finally widened to reveal snowcapped Avian mountains. At their base perched Highcrowne.

I was home. And bringing death with me.

One werewolf had caused so much destruction before I left. What misery would an army of them and dwarves cause? Lili would destroy everything I loved, all that was left, if I didn't find my answers here, and soon.

3 HOMECOMING

One side of the canyon had been graded down to form Highcrowne's port, cut into alcoves for docks, warehouses, and shipyards. Thane said not even Darrub had engineered on such a scale.

A switchback road led up one cliff face, wide enough to accommodate the miniature locomotives that hauled cargo to and from the hundreds of ships that passed by every year. Donkeys, people, elves, humans, and dwarves usually hiked the steep path on foot, and I'd done it myself a few times. It was murder on the calves.

The airship dock perched on the clifftop. Dirigibles moored there as often as ships in the riverport.

I recalled the dock master's office and the screaming hordes arguing over fees and complaining about missing cargo. It was chaos, and the living heart of the Highcrowne.

At least, that's how I remembered it.

The greatest city in the world was deserted. The Docks District was silent, empty. The only ships moored were a few small cutters, their masts splintered by something huge. I couldn't imagine anything doing that except a very angry grall.

Jorg. My heart constricted, wondering where he was, where everyone was. Only ghosts lived here.

A mist hung over the water, softening the sounds of our steamship and adding to the haunting atmosphere.

"Perhaps they evacuated?" Thane said.

"Where to? This is the last refuge. The last." I smothered a sob and leapt to the dock, ran over rattling boards, hit solid ground and kept running. I made it a third of the way up the zig zag road before my legs burned and my chest tightened. I stopped, gasping.

Thane followed, driving a little steam train. He'd mastered the boiler on the steamship, so the locomotive was simple enough for him. He rode on a seat behind the engine, feeding the fire tiny scoops of coal. It's diminutive size and the way Thane sat astride it, suavely, with an air of a hero come to the rescue, made me laugh. And then I cried.

I hated tears, despised them, and so I cursed the noxious smoke from the locomotive, blaming it for them.

Thane knew better, but he didn't say a word. He patted the seat behind him, and I climbed aboard.

The engine moved slowly up the steep incline along its track. A high seat back kept me from rolling down the mountain, and the slow pace gave me a chance to recover.

My mind conjured many comforting explanations for the quiet, but none that I truly believed.

"Thanks for the ride," I told him when we reached the top. "No one would have left this impressive piece of machinery behind. I'm sure they're all inside the city, celebrating some festival I'm not aware of."

"Of course," Thane chimed in. "They must have heard of my—Fharen's—defeat in Faellion and be doing just that. The Elf King was always a right bastard. You think it will be funny if I put on the glamour with the golden hair and stride in, saying 'surprise!'?"

"I think it would be funny, for about five seconds. I prefer you like this. My Thane." I wrapped my arms around him, breathing in his scent, feeling his soft hair against my cheek. I knew once we saw whatever lay ahead, everything would be different.

Hold onto the precious moments, I reminded myself.

Howls echoed off the canyon walls. Some close, others farther away. A sad symphony, it was as though each wolf despaired of ever seeing its pack again and so cried out to them, joining their voices across the distance. I would have felt sorry for the creatures if they were timber wolves, but these were the cries of our pursuers, the closer scouts telling those in Lili's army where we were,

"We don't have much time," I said, stating the obvious.

The fog turned to drizzle, and Thane pulled up his hood. I noted how he adjusted it, creating shadows to conceal his features.

"No one will recognize you," I assured him. "If anyone's alive to see you, that is. Without Fharen's golden glamour you look like a Solhan."

"Elves will know." He didn't lower the hood.

The rain intensified, and I thought about my travelling hat, which I'd left behind in the boat. No going back for it.

We reached the city gates and found them shut. Hope rose in me. Live people tended to worry about gates and walls more than the dead. I shielded by eyes against the drizzle, trying to see.

Arrows struck the ground in front of us.

"Off with you, rabble," an arrogant voice shouted. "No more human refugees allowed. Leave or die."

"Captain Uanal?" I said. The joy I felt was not characteristically associated with the silver-haired Captain of the Marketplace Guardhouse. He'd thrown me in prison and questioned me once, and I tended to hold grudges about such things.

My smile seemed to disturb him too. "Dear gods. It's 'Detective' Eva Thorne." He sounded like I was the nail in his coffin. "You, especially, go away."

"I'm coming in." I banged on the huge, wooden gate, and a small door opened on the side. A nasty looking elf soldier with a scrunched nose and furrowed brow leveled his sword at me.

"The Captain said go away."

Now, I've never been one to listen to authority, especially when said authority started negotiations with threat of violence. I did take a step back, which he might have assumed meant retreat, but he was in for a surprise.

It was never good to meet violence with violence—you had to up the ante. What everyone in Highcrowne feared was necromancy, and so I summoned green fire in my hand and held it out like a gift.

The startled elf took a step back, so there was even more distance between us.

I couldn't do much more than a pretty light show, else I risked waking the relic, but I did bring out my Ashur and leaned on it, letting the green magic arc and dance along its scabbard to great effect. The carvings of tormented souls and slain enemies in bas relief along the length of bone sheath were disquieting to anyone close enough to see them, and the dread aura of that green fire was enough to chill those too far away to appreciate the full effect.

"I knew it," Uanal said from the catwalk above the gate.

He leaned on the battlements lightly, as though distaining the need to physically touch anything in the filthy city he'd been tasked with guarding. I didn't know why he was being so prissy. The outer wall had been completed only last spring, and so the stones were still crisp and free of lichen and other creeping things that tended to grow during Highcrowne summer.

"You're far from the Market District Guardhouse, Captain. The Outskirts, and my house, lie a stone's throw behind you, and so if you'd be so kind as to let me go home? The weather grows unpleasant."

"You evade the question, Miss Thorne."

"I didn't hear you ask one."

"You are a mage, and an illegal necromancer I suspect. You lied about that as well as being an emancipationist."

"I have no idea what you're talking about. Besides, city laws seem such petty things these days. There's an army of dwarves and werewolves, not to mention real necromancers—the Asheen liches of Solheim—coming down the river right behind me. Let me in already."

While I often enjoyed toying and verbally sparring with Uanal, my urgency was real. I'd seen Lili's army in action against Fharen's forces, and I knew closed gates wouldn't deter her as much as they did me.

"No one gets in or out, by order of the Elf King."

Thane sighed. He'd been hanging back, allowing me my fun, but it was clear where this was going.

Thane lowered his hood and donned Fharen's usual glamour along with it. One moment he was the dark-haired, half-Solhan, taller than me and thick with muscle; the next he was the shorter, golden-haired and golden-skinned full elf, King Fharen.

"Your Majesty?" Captain Uanal was confused, not because he doubted the glamour—elves must smell one another or pick up on other cues to compensate for shifting appearances, a necessity when everyone shrouded themselves in illusions—the captain was confused because he never expected to see the Elf King with me.

"I wish no one else to know of my presence here." Thane mimicked Fharen's commanding tone perfectly. He was the Elf King now. Fharen's soul was buried somewhere deep inside, subsumed to Thane's greater being, watching helplessly. I smiled a little at that thought.

Uanal nodded, and Thane turned the glamour off, returning to his natural form. I sensed the Captain was even more confused by the realization his king was half-Solhan.

The gates opened, and we walked inside like we owned the place. At least one-third of it, which Thane as King did.

More guardsmen crowded around us, desperate expressions on their faces. Uanal forced them back.

"What is your command, my liege?" the Captain asked.

Thane and I shared a look and a silent communication. We had no idea what to do. People couldn't abandon the city, for there was Lili's army to the west, enemy dwarves to the south, and Solheim to the east.

I thought of the north, but the Avian mountains were impassable, and Highcrowne was as far north as it was possible to go. We and whoever remained in the city were stuck.

The only hope was to learn how to control the First Soul and shut out the Dead God. I didn't think it worth explaining all that to Uanal. Neither did Thane.

"Continue to guard the city against attack," Thane said. "I will communicate new orders when the time is right." He managed a reassuring air of authority, despite such a vague statement, and the soldiers seemed mollified. They resumed their posts with determination.

Uanal narrowed his eyes at me. "Be wary of this one, Sire. She is slippery."

"Oh, I'm well aware of that." Thane gave me a raunchy grin, and I elbowed him in the ribs.

"Come on." We'd lost enough time getting through the front door. I still had to find my uncle.

I stopped by my house, as it was on the way, and the eerie silence was creepier than ever. Where was the bustle of human merchants turning their noses up at me? Where were the servants, goblins and street cleaners? I checked the bookstore first, but the door was locked, the windows boarded up.

Somehow, my keys were still in my belt pouch. They had rusted from saltwater and other adventures, but I managed to open the lock. "Kali?" I called.

No answer.

I climbed the main stairs and went through the house calling names. No sign of Kali or Nanny. I found Jorg's things in the basement, but no grall. A seven-foot-tall mountain of muscle and tusks was hard to misplace.

"Where is everyone?" I didn't get an answer.

Thane opened closet doors and cupboards, joining in the search. I knew he was not as hopeful as me.

I should have asked Uanal, but part of me preferred the search to knowing the reality.

Had they been shipped to Faellion? Had we watched them die in Fharen's service?

The real news about Highcrowne and the world beyond was always to be found in the common room of Karolyne's Café. I learned more from mercenaries and travelling merchants while I was working there than any of the half dozen, agenda-laden newspapers that circulated the streets. We went there next, a dread feeling building in my stomach like pooling lead.

Karo's place was boarded up too. That didn't surprise me. What made the hairs along my arms stand on end were the messages left by vandals in black paint: *Collaborator. Traitor!*

I ran to Uncle's house, sinking to my knees as soon as I got there.

LOREL CLAYTON

It was burnt to the ground.

The home where I'd grown up, where Ilsa, Viktor and I had played—it was gone.

4 FIRE AND ASH

I picked through the ruins, reminded of the time I'd searched the warehouse fire for clues to the monster bombing Highcrowne. I hadn't realized then it would be a literal monster.

But the objects burnt and buried in ash here weren't nondescript pallets of cloth and merchant goods. These were my family's things. Uncle's annoying mechanical clock from the south, Nanny's old china and silver sets, Ilsa's wrought iron bed. I found a pile of charred toys from the attic I'd forgotten about. Buttons Bear was missing an eye even before the fire put out the other one. Viktor's rocking horse.

"Viktor," I whispered. My brother's death still felt like a fresh wound, but what cut deepest now was

Little Viktor. I had vowed to protect him. Where was the boy?

Thane put a hand on my shoulder, and I shrugged it off.

"I need to know what happened." I fought back tears, useless things, calling on Solhan stoicism.

And I reached out for souls.

If my family had died here, I wanted to know. After three days, all human and Solhan souls were summoned to the Dead God's side, and this fire looked older than that, but I had to try.

I sensed residues of life, like those that clung to my Ashur. These were ancient and tied to relics that had adorned the shelves of Uncle's office, the effigies in the shrine, the necromantic tools hidden in what had once been Morgan's room. There were no recent dead, and no soul jars either. Uncle must have had time to get away, to get Little Viktor away, if he had time to take them.

I sighed, relaxing my soul sight, but the blue jar in my pack stirred to life, whispering my name again.

The First Soul whispered too. *Kill all responsible*, it told me. *Destroy them.*

I put hands over my ears, as if that would shut out temptation, and focused on the more innocent voice of the soul jar. At least it didn't want me to kill anyone. It seemed energized in this place, as though struck by lightning, and whispered more names than mine. It knew my brother's true name too. It knew Ilsa's.

"Who are you?" I asked it. What power had Lili captured, and how could I use it to help those I loved?

It did not reply. Unlike the First Soul, the jar was not alive. It was but an echo, a ghost, looping forever in memory like some regret, repeating its accusations until you grew sick of it.

Thane waited patiently, and that bothered me for some reason. He read me so well, but he didn't understand fear of death and loss as a true mortal would. It did not exist for him. The Lands of the Dead were more familiar to him than the world of the living.

Fury filled me, and I stood, saying, "We keep looking. They are alive. Somewhere. I know it."

"I wonder who did this?" Thane picked up a scorched silver frame. The photo within was gone. "Captain Uanal? The Guard? Fharen has no memory of this, but he seldom concerned himself with the 'little' things. He ordered the conscription of humans but did not care how it was achieved."

I clenched my fists. "Maybe, but the rest of the city is intact. Uncle had a lot of enemies. Perhaps they seized an opportune moment to strike. You go question the Guard, see if they know anything about this, because if I see them, I'm liable to kill them, even if their only role was not putting out the fire fast enough."

"We shouldn't separate. We don't know what the First Soul will do," he warned.

"Give it to me."

"No."

I tore the satchel off his belt. "You can maintain a glamour over it at a distance, right?"

"Yes, somewhat."

"Then we'll be fine." I headed for the Warehouse District.

"Where will you search?" Thane sounded worried, but this was my turf, and I didn't need a chaperone.

"I'll find you," I called back, loud in the silent streets.

Truth was, I only had two places left to look for answers. Duane was my last resort, and he wouldn't speak freely with a stranger around. Bell was the better bet, as she was the one who kept most of Duane's crew alive, so if anyone had survived it was her. Of course, she had no love for elves, or half-elves, as Thane appeared to be. Yet another reason I was better off alone.

When I reached her workshop—ours, actually, as I was part-owner—there was nothing but a smoking crater where her shack used to be. It looked like a bomb had gone off. I knew she kept dynamite in the icebox, so that could have been what happened.

Another dead end.

Then I noticed, barely visible through the maze of junk she used to keep intruders away, that the main workshop was intact. It was harder to see than usual, because it was buried beneath exploded scrap metal and other debris.

I knew where the traps were. I wended through them and stopped at the door, delaying the inevitable. I was afraid she wouldn't be on the other side. That there was no one left.

Hesitation saved my life.

"Don't touch the latch," a voice whispered from below my feet. I looked down through the grate of a trap door. A petite blonde smiled up at me. Her worn leather goggles were covered in soot and other less recognizable residues.

"Bell." I sagged with relief.

"Come on down." She raised the hatch, and I descended the ladder to a secret room I hadn't known existed.

"What would have happened if I touched the door?"

"Boom." She illustrated with hand gestures and sound effects. It was even more impressive with her hair dyed a fiery red and pig tails bouncing around in sync with the simulated destruction.

"Lucky you were here to stop me."

"Not luck. My people heard the commotion at the City Gate. What were you, of all people, doing hanging around with the Elf King?"

"Why do you have people now?" I countered, trying to deflect her curiosity, but I should have realized it was hopeless.

"You do know what Fharen did? What your friend Uanal and all of them did? Kali saw it coming before any of us. She told me to leave with her, and I wished I had."

"She's safe?"

"Probably the only one. Hiding in the hills with Jorg's family. Elves came for the refugees first, then us gutter rats. Ulric turned on us. He sold us out to protect his own skin."

"Don't tell me you burned down our house?"

"I wished I had, but I didn't join the bucket brigade, that's for sure."

I clenched my fists. "Little Viktor…"

"He's safe. Don't worry. Everyone hates your uncle and Duane. I would never let anything happen to the others."

"You know where they are?"

"Those traitors vanished, but Nanny and Vikky are safe," Bell repeated. "I'll take you to them."

"Wait a minute. Traitors?" People wrote the same thing on Karolyne's shop. "Why do you suddenly hate Duane?"

"Because that hoity-toity elf-lover took Ulric's side too. He turned on his own kind. It's because of him the streets are empty, our people imprisoned or fled. He's the worst of the lot."

That was the biggest surprise of all. Bell had always been devoted to Duane, against all common sense, and to hear her so against him was strange. Just what had he done?

I asked for more details, about Karolyne too, but she said, "Enough. Time is precious these days."

I had to agree with her. I was getting side-tracked. Lili's army was coming, and I needed to focus.

"Do you know where Morgan is?" I asked. Bell might spit on Ulric's name, but she wouldn't begrudge me wanting to find Morgan. He would know where to find my uncle and the answers I needed.

"This way."

The underground room turned into a tunnel with a low ceiling, so I had to stoop to walk. It was narrow, with flaming lanterns a little too close to my hair for comfort. She stopped, and I barreled right over her.

As we disentangled ourselves, she touched my Ashur and then snatched her had away, like it burned her. "I see you still have that creepy sword. I hope you're here to fight."

"Fight what?"

She gave an exasperated huff. "That's why you're talking to Fharen and Uanal, instead of killing them. You're ignorant as usual. The elves."

"I've heard about Fharen's camps." In fact, I'd seen the abominations he'd created from enslaved humans, but I didn't want to mention that horror. It would only make Bell more furious, and she was already worse than I'd ever seen her. She'd never liked elves much to begin with. Neither had I. But something had tipped her over the edge to outright malice.

"You don't know the first thing. But don't let me describe it to you. You can talk to Little Viktor."

That awakened new fears. What had happened to Vikky? But she wouldn't say anything more. Bell had turned cruel, making me worry. Whatever she'd faced these past months had hardened her.

I didn't waste any more time or air—it was thin underground and full of musty odors—on fruitless conversation. She led us a circuitous route through old mining tunnels, dug by dwarves in ancient times, before they ever built shops or houses above ground. These were the catacombs, where the Avians first gave them sanctuary. Now it was sanctuary for humans.

The tunnel opened into an underground hall full of people, hundreds of them. Smoke from cookfires hung from the shallow ceiling, and I coughed so badly I had to get down on my knees. Tents and bedrolls, washing lines, and tubs of water took up all the space. I walked, hunched, through people's living quarters, over old men asleep and past women peeling tubers or washing babies.

Children wrestled on bedrolls and ran around beneath tent ropes and any spare space to stretch their legs. Bell stopped before one of the children, and it took me a few long seconds to recognize Little Viktor. He was so thin.

"Vikky." I held out my arms.

He stopped and cocked his head, looking at me strangely. He seemed taller too, more gangly, and his front teeth were missing. I wanted to punch whoever had done that to him, until I realized he must be seven now and they were supposed to fall out. How could a few months apart feel like a lifetime?

"Aunty Ilsa?"

No wonder he was so distant. He thought I was her. How could he not tell? Had I changed too?

"No. It's Eva."

He relaxed then and ran to me. His hug was fierce and brief and raw, and just what I needed, but he pulled away sooner than I liked.

"Have you seen Uncle 'Ane?"

I shook my head. From the sound of it, if Bell had her way, Duane wouldn't be visiting any time soon.

"What happened?" I asked. "Where's Morgan and Nanny and Uncle?" I wanted to know about Karo and Jorg too, but I thought I'd already overwhelmed him, and I'm sure none of my friends mattered to him.

"Nanny's cooking dinner and Morgan is fighting the enemy. He wouldn't let me go along, but now that you're here you can tell him to let me. I know how to use a sword." He brandished the stick he held. The boys and girls behind him mock-battled each other, and he was drawn back into the fight.

I called his name a few times to regain his attention. "I mean, what happened to the house? How did it burn down?"

He shrugged. "I was in the Outskirts school. Guards dragged us out and put us in cages. We was to be slaves like other humans from the south, they said. I was scared, but I shouldn't have been. Morgan and Uncle 'Ane came and got me. Wish you'd been there too, but it worked out."

I felt a pang that I hadn't been. I'd been busy, but it didn't feel like a good enough excuse.

"We didn't save all the children," Bell pointed out.

"But Duane helped, he fought them. Vikky said so."

"At first, 'til he told them he'd work for them. Showed them a better, more efficient way. Sure, he got them to leave the kids alone after that, but he caught parents instead."

I couldn't believe it. Then again, maybe I could. Duane was ruthless, and I'd once suspected him of murdering Viktor. I was angry then, and I was angry now. I've learned I can't trust my judgement when I'm like that. I do stupid things. So, I pushed the anger down deep and focused on the bigger picture.

The past wasn't important. Duane wasn't important.

"Take me to Morgan. He will know where Uncle is."

Bell shook her head. "Morgan isn't too happy with Ulric either. Your uncle is the one who set the slave brands on the people Duane captured."

Now that didn't surprise me at all.

"I'm not seeking him out for hugs and grins. I'm trying to end the war."

"Then fight for us. We might be able to use a dark, evil necromancer—if she's on our side." Bell fingered whatever weapon she had stuffed in her pocket, and I knew I frightened her. I always had, but now there was good reason.

"The necromancers are what we have to worry about. There's an army on my heels led by the worst of them, the Dead God's chief general."

"Risen?"

"Liches. Plus, dwarves and wolves that can do plenty of damage on their own. I've seen it."

"Werewolves." Bell trembled, and I remembered how the creatures we'd faced in the mountains terrified her.

She'd been unconscious most of the time, so it was my turn to say, "You don't know the half of it."

"I'm fully aware of what we face." A familiar figure stepped out of the shadows; his skin dark enough to be shadow still. The white hair and Darrubian accent gave him away though.

"Aguragas." I didn't bother to glare. I pulled my sword and struck.

He hadn't been expecting the attack, but he was quick. He dodged, pulled a hidden blade and held it up in friendly warning. It was friendly for him, because he was such an effective killer that blade in hand meant I could be dead already.

"What are you doing?" Bell intervened. "He's one of us!"

"He's the reason Conrad is dead."

I'd played my part, but Gas was the one who betrayed us and turned Conrad over to my enemy. Of course, Conrad was nothing but another guardsman to Bell.

"He's done nothing but help us." Bell put a hand on my sword arm. I shrugged it off.

"It's not for free. There'll be a price." I didn't take my eyes off Gas.

"They're all on my side, Eva, you heard her. You are too. You just don't know it yet." Aguragas sheathed his dagger, so I sheathed my sword.

This wasn't done, but I felt time ticking away. Or maybe it was one of the bombs Bell always kept in her belt pouch. Either way, I felt buried alive in this underground tomb. Gas made the place uninhabitable.

"I have our best interests at heart, Eva," he said. The way he kept using my name annoyed me, because he made it sound like I was a pet he had to soothe. "It was unfortunate about that guardsman, but you betrayed me first."

"Enough. I don't want to hear another word from you—Aguragas," I made it sound like a disease, "and if I see your tongue wag again, I'll cut it out. Or die trying." I knew I couldn't best him in a fair fight, but neither of us would fight fair.

Gas knew better than to try more sweet arguments on me, so he kept his mouth closed. I wanted to wipe the arrogant smirk off it still.

Bell didn't know when to shut up: "Eva, hear him out."

"No. Show me to Morgan now, and then I'm gone. But take care of Vikky. Don't let him get pulled into any of Gas's insane crap, or I'm coming back for you too." I let the green fire I'd showed Uanal arc between my fingers.

Yes, the First Soul hummed. *Yes.*

Bell took a frightened step back.

I'd find Morgan myself. I turned and fought my way through the crowded space, avoiding the muck and filth with practiced ease. I'd grown up in the Outskirts, and this kind of shanty town was not new. Humans had always been stamped down. I was about to do some stamping of my own and change things.

I got lost when I reached the edge of the cavern. There were several tunnels leading off at an upward slope. Any of them could go to the surface.

"Morgan is with General Moore's group. They're raiding an internment camp in the Smith's District," Bell said, coming up behind me. I hadn't frightened her away after all.

"There are camps there?" That was almost the Central City. "Which tunnel?"

She took off, and I followed. The Bell I knew would have chattered or pestered me to explain myself. This new Bell was quiet. I was the one who broke down first and said, "I mean it. Gas can't be trusted."

"I'm sorry about Conrad. I don't know what happened, but Aguragas saved my life. I trust him."

"Duane trusted him once too. See how that ended up."

"Pretty well, until Duane turned against his own people. I hated his business dealings with elves, cozying up to Princess Hilja. Disgusting."

"Hilja's not all that bad."

"You an elf lover now too?" She appraised me, but not with a joking sparkle in her eye. The new Bell was almost scary. The pigtails ruined it though.

"You're an idiot. The elves are idiots, same with Gas and the Upside Down Party."

"Party?"

"Long story. The point is, we need to stop fighting among ourselves. Death is coming."

"Can't He come for the elves? That'll solve all our troubles."

"He will, but at the end of the world when it's too late."

"I never understand half the things you say."

"Likewise."

She led me to Morgan in silence. Not just because she was grouchy at me, but because Morgan was in the middle of 'enemy' territory, as Vikky and his pint-sized soldiers called it.

The Smith's District was transformed. Barricades, made from magically summoned walls of thorns, blocked access to the gates and stairs that led to other sections of the city.

We emerged through a sewer grate. Dwarves had sewers at least. They were not clean, and disgusting to skulk through, but walking the streets of the Outskirts on a summer's day was worse. We had relied on muck-rakers, not drains and sewer rats.

'Had' was the operative word. The Outskirts was gone, aside from Bell's underground band of refugees, and the dwarves were now the ones interred. Whoever hadn't joined Gypsum's forces or fled back to dwarven lands fast enough ended up a prisoner. Their homes were just out of reach, on the other side of iron fences, magically summoned thorns, and spiked walls.

I thought the conditions Vikky and the others were living in was bad, but this was worse. Thousands of dwarves had been shoved into the Smith's District ass to elbow. No latrines, no water, no tents.

Why hadn't they gone underground like humans had? Had they tried to escape and failed? Bell complained about Ulric and Duane's methods, but part of her must know she and the others were safe because of their collaboration. The alternative was worse.

"I thought, with Gas spewing all his Upside Down Party, humans-only rhetoric, you wouldn't be helping dwarves." I was kind of proud these were the people she and Morgan were fighting for.

Never think the best of people.

"I'm not. Let 'em rot in here. There's nobody on our side, Eva. Dwarves turned against us, elves too, and the Dead God is a comin' as you say. Throw some of these between Him and us. Morgan is here to steal weapons and stir up trouble. It's easy to toss a few stones—or throwing knives—and trigger a riot. Let them go at each other's' throats and leave us in peace."

Where was the Bell I knew? Nothing and no one was recognizable anymore.

I wasn't staying, I reminded myself. Find Morgan, find Ulric, then get out of here. When the Dead God was no more, everyone would stop being so afraid. Everything would work out.

That's what I told myself.

My mental mantra did little good as we slunk through the shadows. Dwarves saw us, but they were so tired and beaten down, flesh hanging off their bones, few stirred enough to raise their eyes to us.

I felt like Death Himself walking among this latest crop, scythe ready to harvest them. Their souls lingered so close to the surface, pushing at fragile shells. One more cough, one more fever, one more day without food: it would take little to set them free.

I fought down the green glow that rose in my palms, fought down the urge to release them.

They could not wait for grand plans and for me to save the day. Every single one of these people needed saving now.

By the time Bell found Morgan, I was seething.

Then he shushed me. I hadn't said a word, but he put his fingers to his lips, probably knowing me well enough to know I never kept quiet for long. I was too furious to speak this time, though, and he took my quiet for obedience.

Morgan was the sword master who'd trained me. My uncle's manservant, right hand thug and all-around obedient slab of muscle. I'd listened to his wise counsel over the years, quoted him and relied on his lessons for survival more than a few times. The closest thing to a father I had. I respected him—but I didn't respect what he was doing here.

He wasn't alone. A few Southerners were with him. I could tell by the tans they'd carried into High-crowne's eternal winter that they hadn't been in the city for long. Their armor was strange too, more leather and less plate. Judging by their blonde hair, they probably came from the central kingdoms, same as Bell's ancestors.

One of them was clearly in charge. His armor was finer, his blonde beard better groomed, and he had the straight spine of a military man. Yet, he used the tactics of street urchins and thieves.

The Southerner whistled, and on that signal, his soldiers stormed the guard tower.

I'd been too busy glaring at everyone to notice the elves so near. As soon as they heard the clamor of weapons and armor, they shot arrows enchanted with fire runes or Avian goo into the darkened mass. These weren't unarmed dwarfs, though, and the arrows bounced off the Southerner's shields, briefly illuminating a tower emblem. The Fortress.

They came from the Fortress of Mages? Why no magic? No warlocks?

Nearby tents and straw bedding caught fire. Avian goo spread across the flagstones or stuck in the links of chainmail, glowing bright enough for the daftest archer to sight on. When an arrow hit, the effect was catastrophic. Two of the southern soldiers disintegrated into ash.

"Idiot," I whispered, pushing the nearest soldier aside. I think he was surprised at my strength. A good shove was more in the technique, start low and push up, throwing them off balance and using their own momentum. He tumbled into the muck, washing away glowing ooze and probably saving his life.

Not that he thanked me. He cursed and drew his sword.

Morgan stepped between us. "Continue with the plan. She is mine to deal with."

For half a second, I thought Morgan wanted to fight me, but he turned away and clenched his blade between his teeth. He clambered up the side of the guard tower, using the smallest seams between planks, and reached the top in seconds. The elves' shouts were quickly silenced, probably by Morgan's blade across their throats.

Bell climbed up just as nimbly and joined the fray. Those two made quick work of the elf guards, while me and the heavily armored Southerners were left below staring slack-jawed at their cruel efficiency.

When they were done, Morgan and Bell tossed down swords, bows, and flasks of goo in a rain of plunder. I snatched one of the flasks before it hit the mud and exploded or worse.

After the stolen weapons and armor were gathered and passed down into the sewer, Bell shouted out, "Die elven scum! Long live Queen Gypsum!"

The elves in the guard tower across the square heard her, and the dwarves huddled in the intervening space were too slow or weak to refute the battle cry in their name. Arrows fell like rain, and then some dwarves found strength to scream. The loudest cries were those of children.

I punched Bell in the mouth so hard she spit blood all over the shiny armor of the Southern leader behind her. She hadn't expected that. I hadn't expected her to have grown so heartless.

Morgan frowned.

The Southerners seemed unsure if I was an enemy or an ally, the way their hands hovered on their sword hilts. They seemed to be looking to Morgan for direction, but he was sending me the "not right now" warning look.

To hell with it.

"These people are dying. Stop playing your revenge games over their corpses and start helping them, damn you. Damn all of you." Green fire flared to life across my palms, urging me to action.

The Southern leader leveled his weapon at me. Bell paused, fist in the air. She wanted to hit me back, but I scared her.

I could feel their fear, but the dwarves' fear was greater.

Who knew why the elves kept them in this weakened state? Did they enjoy their pain? New slaves to torment? All I knew was it had to stop. Every side had to stop.

I didn't know how to use the Avian goo I'd grabbed, but I knew how to wield the magic that arced between my fingers like lightning. I knew how to reach past flesh and mind to the naked soul beneath.

But for me, it was 'on' or 'off'. No half measures.

I reached out to the elves firing arrows on innocents—and ripped out their souls.

I instantly regretted it. I didn't want to be a killer, as inevitable as it seemed.

I chose to try another way.

I lacked discipline. That's what my godmother, Olyve, once said. It was that lack of discipline that hurt people and made me feel like a monster. So, this time, I focused my will and used it, rather than raw anger, to guide the green fire that stretched between me and them. That energy dug into the guards, coring them like an apple, but I stopped digging before it was too late.

White, ghostly lines of force stayed attached to their bodies, even as their souls hovered over their tumbled corpses. Part of me didn't want to stop. Part of me wanted to breathe in their lives, consume them. Sweat beaded on my cheeks, but I held my hunger in check.

"By all the gods!" A Southern soldier fell to his knees, muttering some prayer of protection.

"Well done, Eva," Morgan said, his Solhan upbringing making him appreciate the power required for such necromancy.

Bell simply ran away.

At least I'd made everyone stop. Hadn't that been the point?

The elven soldiers were dead for only a few heartbeats. I knew from reading other souls I'd seen fall in battle that the moment of death stretched into an eternity of reflection. It was the threshold before the Lands of the Dead, where lessons were fully learned.

I forced each soul back into their bodies. I should say 'coaxed'. Their ghosts were frightened and confused, and each one required soothing words from my soul to theirs.

"You can live again," I told them. "Go back but remember why this happened. Remember the pain they feel."

I read souls easier than books these days, and the sufferings of all the dwarves before me were writ large. I let the elves feel their pain. I let them fully realize what they had done here. And when they settled back into their bodies, they woke up screaming.

I went over to a wounded civilian. The old dwarf looked vaguely familiar, perhaps a shopkeeper I'd seen around. An arrow protruded from his side.

Killing came more natural to me than healing, so I asked the Southerners, "Do you have someone who can help them?"

Morgan bent down and placed a hand over the old dwarf's wound. Green light shone, and then he ripped the arrow free. The dwarf screamed. Morgan placed both hands over the gash, and a few moments later it was healed. I had no idea Morgan was as skilled as my uncle at such things. He moved to the next person.

All the Southern soldiers did was stare at me, their blades drawn.

"A Solhan necromancer," their leader finally said. "It's because of those like you the Fortress of Mages fell. You spare elves, help dwarves, and stop us from doing what we came here to do. I don't know whose side you're on. Your friends seem confused too. Why shouldn't we kill you now?"

"Because you can't." They must be blind or stupid. "Stay out of my way and you'll be fine."

"Eva." I recognized the voice, despite how weak and far away it sounded. I was glad for the distraction, else there were about to be a few Southern ghosts, and my hunger for souls had been awakened. I wasn't sure I could abstain from devouring these ones.

"Reginald?" I found him holding Bert.

"He's not good." Reginald's hand was clamped over a wound in Bert's neck, an arrow shaft framed by the bloody 'V' of fingers.

I waved Morgan over. "This one. Now."

Bert's once sturdy frame was shrunk, wizened and frail from starvation. If he'd had more blood to lose, he would have died quicker. As it was, his shriveled veins released only a trickle, so Morgan had time to remove the arrow and seal the ragged hole left behind.

I saw Bert's ghost hovering above his body, sensed his desire to rest. So many fragile shells around me, his had broken. I forced him back inside. I couldn't heal, but I could do that much. I could help him fight.

"You've survived all this," I told him. "Don't give up now. Things are changing for the better, starting today."

And he lived.

Reginald held him, keeping his head above the mud, as I accompanied Morgan on his circuit, attending each wounded prisoner. Whether they'd been shot this day, beaten yesterday, or tortured the day before that, they were all wounded.

When we were done, Morgan was exhausted. I knew he didn't approve of helping those who could easily turn into the enemy, but he did it for me.

All I could do for them was offer a hand to hold, a whispered command to their souls to 'stay'. Most slept after I passed. The effort of living was all they could manage.

"Stay here and protect them *all* this time, instead of trying to get them killed," I told Morgan. "Really, I have no idea what's happened to you, to everyone in Highcrowne. This is madness, and it ends now. It all stops. Understood?"

Instead of his usual half smile, Morgan gave me the look he often gave my uncle. He bowed his head, obedient as any servant.

Was I just another powerful Thorne in his eyes now? So be it. I turned my question into a command: "Tell me where Ulric is."

"I cannot, Mistress."

So much for obedience.

"All our lives depend on it," I said more softly, but I did not make it a plea. Never show a Solhan weakness. Isn't that what Morgan taught me?

He met my gaze, and the pain in his eyes was not weakness; it was fuel for anger. "Ulric would not tell me. After he began working with the elves, setting marks for them, he shut me out. I don't know where he is."

It was true then. Ulric, and probably Duane, were traitors.

I'd asked what I'd come to ask. I knew I should keep searching—in the Central City, all the way into the grall-infested Avian mountains if need be—because, traitor or no, Ulric had answers I needed.

But I'd already stayed too long. I'd gotten too involved. I had no choice.

Too many people I cared about were hurt or hurting, and if they didn't kill one another soon, Lili would finish things for them. Only a united Highcrowne had any chance of stopping her.

I should have taken the First Soul and gone straight after the Dead God. I should have let the relic's whispered promises of victory tell me how to defeat Him. I should never have come home.

Because now, I would have to do something about all of this.

I went to the nearest barricade, a makeshift wall of iron, stone and wood, and unleashed green claws of force. My Solhan power came easily when I was furious, no need to draw on the relic, even though it hummed joyfully in my mind as I destroyed the fences that separated dwarves from their homes.

See how much better the direct route, the First Soul said. *See how much better to attack. Listen to me—let me in—and we can do so much more.*

"Shut up." I was in no mood for sweet talk, and it quieted. Maybe it was content for me to be angry and power-hungry, a step closer to the temptation it offered.

Thane, I called silently, stretching out my soul sense to find him.

Eva, are you alright? The touch of his soul to mine, even stretched across the city, warmed me. He was brighter than the weak autumn sun halfway up the sky, and so I steered toward him.

I'm coming to you. I told him. The elves must be stopped.

I'm in the Central City. I know what they've done.

I shook my head, and the elvish guards I passed thought I was warning them. They'd seen me rip apart the barricade, saw the glow of necromancy pulsing in my fists, and they stayed back. They need to pay.

Governor Walz says he followed my orders precisely. Fharen's orders. This is my fault.

No scapegoats. I say all perpetrators, highest to lowest, need a share in the reckoning.

Retribution can wait, Eva. Death evens all scores. What about Ulric? Where is he? What happened to the plan?

I didn't answer. The plan was changing.

5   RECKONING

I didn't know who Governor Walz was. Highcrowne had never had a governor as far as I knew, but I didn't really care. It was good to have a name to shout as I banged on the ornate gates leading to the Central City.

"Open up! I'm coming for you, Walz!"

Most humans were hiding from the Elven Elite Protectorate, and here I was clamoring for the attention of those same EEP Guards. It startled them, but they quickly recovered.

"Take her," a lieutenant with a white plume of rank on his helmet ordered. He probably had his own perfectly functioning hands, but the job of officers seemed to be to delegate tasks that involved touching.

I held out my wrists and let them manacle me. "I hear you have a Mark-maker who can enslave me. Where is Ulric Thorne?"

My little game was interrupted too soon when the gates squealed open and Thane stepped out. The EEPS were unnerved to see their newly returned King.

"Ulric is missing, which is all I learned," Thane said, continuing the conversation without a pause. "That's why the humans left in the city haven't been harvested for the new army."

"Morgan doesn't know where Ulric is either," I said. "But it doesn't matter anymore."

Thane raised an eyebrow in that way I'd come to find distracting. I couldn't just blunder my way through things when he was around. He called me on it, and I was forced to explain. Of course, I didn't have to do that out loud with him.

Soul to soul I showed him my memories.

He saw the human camp, with Little Viktor and hundreds of others squeezed inside underground warrens, and he saw the dwarves, who would have found such wretched conditions a paradise compared to their own.

Thane did not see the living world the same way I did. My reluctance to feed on souls, to kill my enemies, it was a beautiful mystery to him. Nevertheless, he felt whatever I felt.

When we joined together like this, our souls became entangled. He had no way to shield himself from the raw emotion coursing through me—and he was not as restrained by morals as I was.

Thane turned and beheaded the nearest EEP.

I hadn't seen him draw his blade. He wasn't fast, I knew he was no sword master, but he had Fharen's magic, which included glamours that could hide his actions. That's how he'd struck before anyone noticed.

The elves were shocked. I'd never seen the arrogant bastards grovel. All five guards fell to their knees and put their foreheads against the flagstones, helmets rolling loose, plumes waving in supplication.

One brave officer spoke up, asking, "Have we displeased Your Majesty?"

"Don't get me started." Sometimes Thane borrowed my mannerisms when we'd been so closely linked. He even spoke in Solhan. In elvish, he added, "Do not speak to me until I summon you. I will be in private council."

They mistrusted me now. Solhan words on the Elf King's lips?

Suspicious looks from beneath lowered brows, pupils peeking at me uncomfortably from the corners of their eyes. My palms still glowed green, my anger fuel for the grim light, and the elves looked at me the exact same way Bell and the Southerners had.

At least they could all agree on one thing—evil Solhan necromancy in the hands of Eva Thorne was something to fear.

I didn't care what they or anyone thought. But I did care about putting my city back together and keeping it safe from the madness within and the death charging at us from without.

We entered the Central City without interruption, the guards keeping a wide buffer around their erratic king.

"Tell me you will behead this Governor Walz too," I said.

"I cannot kill them all for you, Eva, else there will be no one to defend the city when Lili comes, and I now see that is what you want. Even more than defeating the Dead God."

"There's no point if everyone I care about is gone. Do you realize how few humans there are? The slaves scattered throughout the Elf Lands can hardly be called human anymore, and with Illul Faellion under siege, there's no guarantee they'll even survive. This is the last refuge. How many people do you think were crammed in those underground halls and sewers? Hundreds? Thousands? They are all that's left, as far as we know. We can't rely on elves to defend them, not when they've been killing them. We have to do more."

"What?"

"You're the king now—you tell me."

I wanted the elves responsible to pay for what they'd done, but I tried to control that fury, and the green light emanating from my hands grew dimmer.

Thane was right about Highcrowne needing all the defenders it could muster.

There were other methods besides force to unify the city: coercion, diplomacy, authority. Those things should be unfamiliar to a refugee from the Outskirts like me, but I'd seen them used all my life. By Uncle, the powerful Solhan Asheen turned gangster, and by the Three Crowns. I happened to have the most powerful of the Crowns in my hip pocket. Not that I had pockets, but you know what I mean.

"Let's start with this," he said, reaching out.

With Thane's touch, the manacles fell from my wrists.

He took me by the hand. His warm fingers entwined with mine, dispelling the anger coursing through my veins, like mist evaporating in the sun's heat.

He led the way through the Central City, and it was new to me. Always Gypsum had been my escort here, the guards reluctant to let me through. But now, when we crossed the gardens, the trees and ivy turning red, gold and orange, I didn't have elves everywhere I looked turning up their noses at me. They saw the Elf King and immediately dropped their eyes. They bowed or curtsied, holding the pose until we passed. It was like being able to stop time, to freeze everyone around us, and enjoy the view. Just the two of us.

And me, the First Soul added. *I could give you such power in your own right. Take what you deserve, Eva.*

It wasn't going back to sleep. Fighting and killing had fueled it.

"Such pretty elves, with pretty glamours, anyway," I said, my anger rekindled by the relic's reminder. "I can see how their manner makes you forget their crimes. The one responsible for all this at least will pay. Now."

"It was Fharen, and he has. I feel him trapped inside me, screaming to get out, and it is possibly the worst justice imaginable. Being so powerful and now so powerless. If we're to defend Highcrowne, Eva, there is politics to consider."

"Politics? Really?"

"Fharen is—I—am not all-powerful."

I shook my head. "I don't want you to ignore the cries of Fharen's victims like you ignore his. I want...."

The First Soul showed me visions of the pretty elves decapitated like the unfortunate EEP outside, their red blood blending with the autumn leaves. Their heads were like stones littering the ground, and Fharen's was among them.

"I just want..." I struggled against the visions, pressing my fingers to my temples "...I just want the relic to shut up."

He kissed me then, and it felt like the summer sun had come out. Just the two of us in the entire universe again. My killing fury eased.

"My King," a smooth-voiced royal said, intruding on our interlude.

I looked him over. Shiny boots, pressed pants, impeccable waistcoat. He kept his head properly bowed, eyes on the ground, but there was an irreverent smile on his lips.

"Who are you?" I asked.

He stiffened, addressed by an inferior race in his mind, and he did not answer.

I felt my hackles rise, and the First Soul stirred again.

Stay calm, I told myself and it. Was this to be my struggle every day, every moment? Unable to allow myself to feel angry, for fear the relic would twist my thoughts and desires? Is this how Lili became so warped?

"Governor Walz," Thane said, "let me introduce you to Eva Thorne."

This time I was the one who stiffened. The relic practically chuckled in my mind, knowing how much I wanted this stranger dead.

Instead, I held out my hand to the governor, and with his King watching, he had no choice but to kiss it.

"Milady." Walz's voice was as refined and civilized as could be, and his irreverent smile flattened into a serious expression. He turned to Thane. "Your Majesty, I have summoned the war council as requested. We await you."

"I've changed my mind. Summon the full Crown Assembly. Ask Queen Calka to attend, if she will listen to the Elf King anymore."

"Very well. When should they expect your address?"

"When I'm ready. Tell them to wait while I confer with my new advisor, Miss Thorne, in private."

"Advisor?" Walz did well to hide his shock and disgust; only a cloud of it crossed his dark eyes.

I noticed a scar near his nose, a few wrinkles around his mouth and across his forehead. His blond hair was sandy, not the perfect golden color of most. He was one of the purists. Elves who spurned glamour in favor of true superiority earned through blood and deeds.

Thane, in contrast, kept his golden glamour firmly in place. The likes of Walz would not appreciate his half-Solhan nature.

The governor was not alone. Two more purists flanked him, the muscled sort of elves who went wyvern and dragonling hunting for sport. I'd seen their kind strutting between the Central City and the Docks many times, wagons filled with their grim trophies. I preferred the obsequious elves we'd passed earlier to these ones.

The purists showed their King no disrespect, but I saw into their souls. They knew Fharen wasn't a pure-blood like them. They knew about his glamour. And they believed an untainted branch of the royal tree should rise to rule the elves—after humans, dwarves and all the lesser creatures of the land were kindly exterminated by the Dead God first. They had no desire to defend anything but themselves.

Politics indeed.

Thane and I didn't need to go anywhere to confer in private. It was already done. Whenever our souls merged, our thoughts did as well. But I was grateful for any excuse to get away from them before I killed them.

We made our way into the palace, and they trailed us. It felt like predators were stalking me, looking for a weakness.

Won't they be surprised by the real predator here? The Soul chuckled in my mind again.

I ignored it and studied the gilded architecture around me.

I'd seen the mausoleum wing, also known as the Dwarf King's quarters, on my last trip to the palace. Okay, my only trip, but I tried to act more worldly than I was. I had never been to the Elf King's wing before, and it made everything else look like a peasant hovel.

There was marble, gold, silk hangings, along with more marble, more gold. Let me just say some things, like carpets, shouldn't be gilt. There can be too much of a good thing, and the result was tacky. It gave me a headache.

The world is made of give and take, rough and smooth, quiet and clamor. The undiluted mass of 'rich' without 'poor' illustrated exactly what was wrong in the Three Kingdoms: Elves had no space in their world for compassion.

I glared at guards, courtiers and nobles. They didn't notice my disapproval, because they all bowed to the man they thought was their king. If they figured out Thane was not who they thought, this plan would come crashing down worse than the first one had.

We strode past advisors or hangers-on, it was hard to tell which, who shifted from foot to foot waiting for an audience. They must have heard the king was on his way. Thane strode past them without a word, leading me to an antechamber separated from the throne room by thick doors. Wards meant to prevent magical intrusion were carved into the oak.

"Wait here," Thane ordered Walz and his minions.

They halted and bowed politely, but another advisor, a patchy-bearded elf who wore a glamour to appear older and wiser than he was, sidled over. "Your Majesty. If I could have a word?"

Thane shut the door in his face.

This could be fun.

When we were alone, I asked, "Why is Governor Walz so important?"

It would have been faster to merge our souls again, but something about the wards etched into the door made it hard to focus on magic. Even Thane's glamour had dropped, and I heard the whispers of the First Soul in my mind. It was listening too.

"Much has changed in Highcrowne since the war broke out. The Avians have not been heard from, and the dwarves not turned against us or imprisoned, as you saw, have been killed, leaving only Fharen to rule the Three Kingdoms. In name. In fact, the elves rule, with all their usual Parties and politics at play."

I groaned. "I saw enough of that in Faellion to see where this is going. Crazy."

"Exactly. Governor Walz is the main power in Highcrowne, not loyal to Prince Gallan's faction but aligned with it. He has his own agenda and enough supporters that King Fharen must cater to him, whether it be a title or internment camps. Fharen was focused only on bodies for his hybrid soldiers, on defeating the Dead God no matter the cost. Like Gallan's Peace Party, Walz's Isolationists would prefer a new Compact with the Dead God. One that leaves elves—and only elves—safe."

"Not good enough for Lili. Never going to happen. So, he's the one I need to kill to get vengeance for Reginald, Bert, and the rest?"

"When this is over, if you wish it." Thane did not blink at threats of murder.

I did. I blamed the First Soul for turning my thoughts to blood again, but I worried it was all me. I was Solhan after all.

"We must defend this city," I said, "even if it means letting Walz draw breath another day."

"Very well. And Ulric?"

"I'll discover how to use the First Soul. I haven't given up."

"And if this defense fails and Highcrowne falls—you will continue to Solheim and face the true enemy?"

I nodded. I knew that's where we were headed in the end, but it was a shock to hear him say it aloud.

"We won't fail," I said. "I saw into your thoughts earlier, and I know you have hope for Highcrowne. So, share the details. What's the strategy?"

The war room featured a massive table that looked to have been carved from gold, surrounded by brocade chairs meant for generals and aides. One chair was a throne, which had to be Fharen's. Thane drew my attention to a layer of glass too perfect to be hand blown that covered the table. It reflected the ceiling at present, and candlelight made crystals dangling from the chandelier sparkle.

He leaned over and gazed into Fharen's reflection, saying, "Mirror, show me Highcrowne and the Serpent Valley."

The mirror clouded, like a white fog had rolled in beneath the glass. The image shifted and revealed a dragon's-eye perspective of the lands. I'd been in a dragon's clutches once, so I recognized the view.

"There she is." I pointed to a line of ships sailing up the Serpent's Ribbon. Lili's forces were midway through Highcrowne valley. We had no more than a day.

"And here. And here." He indicated a line of wagons, horses, and foot soldiers moving along the partially destroyed rail line between Highcrowne and Gernwold. "Fharen tore up the track when Gypsum took control of the dwarves, but even without locomotives bringing them to our door, the land is clear and level enough to allow an army to march quickly. They will be here even sooner."

The other place he indicated was off the map, to the east.

"Mirror, show me the wall," I said. It wouldn't obey me, so Thane repeated the command. The magic viewing device couldn't discern some other soul riding around inside Fharen, but it could tell I wasn't an elf? Typical.

When the eastern wall was visible, I saw the mass of undead soldiers. They were like ants from the vantage of the map.

"How did you know they were there?" I asked. "Shouldn't the Dead God be moving them to attack from the south, through the swamps, now that the Fortress of Mages has fallen? The wall is impregnable."

"Nothing is impregnable."

He was right. The wall was merely a symbol—the magic of the Compact was our true protection.

Thane couldn't read my soul in here, but he knew me well enough to guess what I was thinking.

"The Dead God will attack from the south as well, but He cannot cross the border of the Three Kingdoms in either place unless the Compact is broken, or until He is freed at Solheim. Compact or no, none of the lesser gods can stop Him once He fully enters this world."

"That's only if I die and He takes my soul," I said. "Then my mother's spell will be complete, and He will be freed to destroy whatever he wants. Not going to happen. Let's just worry about Lili and Gypsum's dwarf army. But, once again, how did you know the Dead God's plans at the wall?'

"I do not sleep. While your mind wanders in dreams, my soul wanders through bodies. Those I have inhabited before are easiest to find, although anyone weakened or marked is vulnerable. I learned of Solheim's strategy from the priest of Fortune who is with Lili now. I commanded him to join her, to be my eyes."

I smiled. "How clever you are. Okay, besides me not dying, what else can we do to protect Highcrowne? There's ships and a land army to stop." The First Soul could do it, but I did not like how its whispers became hungry at that thought.

"I'm not sure we can," Thane said. "Not alone. Fharen's second slave army isn't hatched, and there are few real soldiers in Highcrowne, mainly city guard and Elven Elite Protectorate. With the dwarves and humans turned against us or imprisoned, there's fewer guards as well."

I stiffened, replaying what I'd heard. "There's another crop of slaves?"

Thane pointed to the valley near the wall. "More of those giant flowers we saw in Faellion. Fharen planted most of them here, thinking he'd make a hole in the wall and attack Solheim directly—if they worked as he hoped."

"I'd say they didn't. He was nearly captured, and most of his army retreated to Illul Faellion."

"They hatched prematurely. Not that I'm defending his actions, but I do know what the plan was. Fharen believed their sacrifice would help defeat the Dead God in the end. He believed the humans were the cause of all this and, so, should be the solution. Like the half-Solhan he was, he placed no blame on Solheim. It was their Imperial right to attempt domination, just as it was his."

"'Royal privilege' Hilja calls it. You keep talking about Fharen in the past tense." I guessed what he was thinking, but I wanted him to say it.

He reached for my hand across the mirror. Our fingers touched over the image of Gernwold, and he smiled with the face I'd come to consider Thane's rather than Fharen's.

"I need a body," he said. "I could take any evil man's and feel no regret, knowing I would stop him from causing others pain. Why not this evil man? I could live a life with you in this form. You could grow used to one face, and I would always have this hand to hold yours with. If you will you have me?"

"Yes," I said without thinking.

Only after the word was away did I wonder what he'd really asked, and what I'd agreed to. Not being able to read one another's souls had major disadvantages. Like confusion. Once we survived this battle—and the next—then I supposed I could worry about specifics.

He smiled wider, and I smiled back. It was automatic again.

"King Fharen was never my favorite person," I added, "but what becomes of him if you stay?"

"I have already lingered long enough that his resistance has dwindled. His soul is like a smothered coal within me, capable of burning bright again but on its way out. If I stay, I will send his soul to the Lands of the Dead."

"Does he suffer?"

"Not anymore."

"Then it's a more merciful death than many would say he deserves. Good."

While Fharen should pay for creating the abominations, for enslaving humanity, for whatever role he'd played in the atrocities the dwarves had just experienced … I didn't want him to suffer. At least, I didn't want to crave the suffering of others anymore. It damaged me more than it hurt them.

I turned to the mirror map, trying once again not to get derailed. Thane's smile made it particularly difficult. "So, My King, how do you recommend we defend your city?"

"The Avians must intervene. Legend says they have considerable magic, which has kept the Kingdoms safe for millennia. That's the legend. No one knows what they can really do. That's why I want an audience with Queen Calka."

"I've seen one fly and talk cryptically. That's about it."

"If Calka chooses to help, they may be all we need, but we must plan for the worst. Highcrowne was built for a siege, although it has never seen one, so we must seal off the avenues opened for mercantile traffic and make it defensible again."

"A few of Bell's bombs could help with that. I think she secretly prefers destruction." If I could get her to talk to me, let alone help.

"We still need mages and soldiers to defend the city. Without the dwarves, I have less than half the soldiers I need to man the walls and half of them are civilians. Even including the fops in this court, such as those who call themselves generals, it's not enough."

"You need the remaining humans and dwarves," I said. "They're not in great shape, so I'm not sure they're capable of helping, or that they'd want to."

"What's the alternative?"

There was no place left for humanity to flee. I knew it, but they might try the high mountains rather than fight. Humans had done the dirty work of Highcrowne for generations, the garbage heaped at the feet of the royals, pushed to the Outskirts. Was there any reason for them to care where they eked out a living? And after how the dwarves were treated, they might prefer being turned into werewolves.

Despite everything, Highcrowne was my home. Theirs too. They needed to believe if they were to fight for it. And to believe in it, they needed to matter.

"I have an idea," I said, "but it needs more work."

He nodded and stepped back from the scrying mirror.

I interlocked my fingers with his, feeling the tension in his grip.

"These are all 'possibilities'," I pointed out. "Tell me your real plan. You know I'll read you as we soon as we step outside these wards, so why hesitate?"

"Because you will not like it. As I said, Fharen has planted an army already. We must simply wake them up. They've had months more to mature than the last batch, and you saw how their poison was so effective against werewolves. They could stop Lili."

"No." I let go of his hand.

"It would be a mistake not to use them."

"It was a mistake to create them. I sensed the soul of the creature controlling them. It is more alien than the Dead God. All those people sacrificed to it, changed, controlled. It's wrong."

"There is no saving them now that it is done, but they could save us. They could save your friends. Your family."

Were there no other options?

I recalled Little Viktor's face, smiling and wanting to fight elves. Then I imagined it caged inside plant flesh—or shriveled and dead, like Lili's. That's what would happen if we failed.

"Alright," I said, quietly. "If it comes to it, we evacuate the city, flee to that valley, and you can wake those monstrosities up. But we try all other possibilities first. All."

"Agreed. If you can get the humans and dwarves to fight for the city, it may not come to that."

"I'll do whatever it takes to convince them, but you know what I need to offer them? Freedom. True freedom."

"I'll give the Crown Assembly no choice."

"And Governor Walz?"

"Once we defeat Lili, he is no longer of use."

I nodded. "Good."

So, this was politics. Murders calmly planned, alliances made with abominations, evil done out of expedience for a greater good. Was it worth it?

It never is. The First Soul's knowing laugh mocked me.

A few hours later, royal advisors, lords and ladies, and everyone else of 'importance' who had received King Fharen's summons waited in the Crowns' Hall.

The buildings in the Central City seemed to be in a contest of one-upmanship, but this was the worst yet, probably because it served all three rulers. This was where laws affecting all the Kingdoms were decided. It was purportedly the largest structure ever built by mortals. I couldn't see the ceiling. For all I knew there were Avians perched up there, watching.

The seats at ground level were more sparsely populated than I expected.

"I assure Your Majesty all present in Highcrowne have assembled," the chief advisor said when Thane asked.

Maybe there were elven nobles off fighting Lili's forces and protecting lands near Illul Faellion? Or, maybe they had decided to take a sailing trip around the world? Some of the large galleons could stay at sea for months, a good way to wait out the war.

I suspected quite a few of the empty seats belonged to Matriarchs. I heard the missing dwarf royalty had fled to Gernwold during the armistice when Gypsum first declared for the Dead God. Gypsum was a queen with no real title to justify it, so my guess was they hadn't escaped imprisonment. We might have more allies, if only we could free them.

One set of chains at a time.

I sat in the front row, which was empty but for Walz and his two shadows, and whispers spread across the half empty hall like snowflakes in a storm.

"Is that his lover? Here?"

"Ilsa Thorne," others replied to questions I hadn't heard.

I was not my sister, but as much as I wanted to stand up and tell them to shut the hell up, Thane had impressed on me the importance of diplomacy. I'd already pushed the bounds sitting so close to the governor.

"War is on our doorstep," Thane said from the only occupied throne on the dais, recapturing everyone's attention.

Except for mine. The two empty thrones to his left distracted me like a buzzing fly.

King Rutgard was gone, thanks to my mistakes. I thought of the assassins' token Aguragas had given me and which I'd thrown back in his face. Another mistake it turned out. Had someone else taken on the task of assassinating the Avian queen? Was that why she hadn't come to help?

Elven politics kept Fharen from being a dictator, but so did those empty chairs. They were a reminder that he was only one voice, one power among many— unless they stayed empty forever.

I sensed Governor Walz eying Fharen's seat and wondering where he could toss the other two.

Thane could read souls as I did, and he looked into the governor's eyes as he spoke.

"These walls have often heard our debates over what to do about the Dead God. You know my position is to hunt Him down, but many gentlemen and ladies of court, who I shall not name, delayed me at every turn for short-sighted reasons. I see most of these unnamed nobles are not even here, for they have already realized what I am about to say. Delay has brought us to ruin."

He let his words echo, allowing them to sink into the stone walls and statues and benches.

I knew there were plenty present equally to blame, but none dared speak. His audience was rapt, breaths shallow, as they lowered their gazes in deference to their king.

And he was their king. My Thane was hidden, wearing Fharen's mask completely. It chilled me.

When the silence had gone on long enough to please him, Fharen said, "No arguments this time? Yes, you've all heard the scouts' reports. The generals have all peered into the mirror of the war table.

"All the legions of Gernwold and the Dwarf Lands are on the march, and the ships bearing down on this city do not carry Faellion silks. They carry death.

"The dread liches of Solheim are no myth. They are deadly real. Illul Faellion is besieged by them.

Gernwold is controlled by them. And their queen, Lili of Solheim, the right hand of the Dead God is here to claim our corpses."

"They've come for the humans, not us." Finally, someone dared speak. It wasn't Walz, but the governor didn't look surprised a puppet of his had opened its mouth. The speaker looked at the governor repeatedly for support as his voice trembled. "Turn the humans out, throw them to the wolves, and we will be spared."

"That's not going to happen," Fharen said, and I saw a flicker of my Thane behind his sapphire blue eyes. "We defend this city and all within it—it belongs to all of us. We do not surrender."

He normally never wore a crown, but with a gesture Fharen summoned his bearers, and they dressed him in a snow fox robe, placed the golden elf crown upon his head—although it was more white diamonds than gold—and placed the similarly jewel-encrusted wand of kingship in his left hand.

When the gravity of the moment was heavy, he stood and stared above the heads of the crowd, saying, "I decree that all hostilities within Highcrowne proper are to cease. I call an armistice and demand peace negotiations with the human freedom fighters. Resident dwarves are to have all property returned to them, with compensation from the treasury for pain and suffering, on the assumption that all who remained here in the city were loyal to the Three Crowns and not traitors, unlike those who fled to Gernwold. I also decree that all prisoners not found guilty of a crime ratified into law before my assumption of sole command of Highcrowne are to be freed."

The assembled elf nobles were on their feet, shouting outrage. The last had effectively freed all political prisoners and illegally marked slaves created since elves took control. And peace negotiations with human vermin? These were not Fharen's usual sort of decrees.

His quiet voice cut through the clamor with the sharpness of a silver blade, "I'm not finished."

Fharen was King not only due to birth and political acumen. Other nobles might stake a claim to the position, many of them with purer blood, but Fharen still ruled because of his very real power.

He might not control every political faction, not have every general in the Kingdoms loyal to him, but anyone within his reach of his glamours felt it.

Those who shouted suddenly screamed, clutching their faces. I saw into their souls and knew they experienced real pain: the feeling of their eyes being burnt out. The one who had spoken with trembling voice now huddled on the floor, his mind plagued with images of icy hands and skeletal terrors reaching for him through the snow.

When you can confuse minds, stimulate senses, make someone feel entombed in a musty grave or cast onto a desert island all alone, all without touching them, and when you could place each noble assembled in the Hall into their own private hell—that was some real power.

They didn't stand a chance. Dissenters bowed, some in tears, until Fharen relented, and then they collapsed onto the floor.

Only Walz kept his eyes level, unaffected, his demeanor unmoved. The governor had real power of his own.

6 FRIEND OR FOE?

"Solhan necromancy," nobles whispered in the corridors afterward. They hushed when I swept past.

They were right, indirectly, but I wasn't the reason Fharen was behaving so strangely. They didn't know about Thane.

Courtiers who once flocked around Fharen now flocked around me, believing I was the true power to be appeased. It was amusing having elves grovel for once. I was seeing a whole other side of them.

It wasn't my spells to blame for Fharen's behavior, but those who craved power sensed it in others. They knew I was worth something.

Solhans were reviled for bringing the Dead God into the world, but everyone here remembered it was Solhans who had achieved it. Many thought I was one of Lili's liches in disguise, controlling Fharen. I didn't have that kind of power, but I was able to read them like an open book. Whether they wanted to curry my favor for their own survival, or to gain power in the Dead God's court, they all thought they could manipulate me.

The First Soul protected me from the nobles with glamours akin to Fharen's. I felt it when they tried to cloud my mind, felt it when the Soul smacked them down. It added to my mystique.

Glamours weren't a panacea. Those impervious to most magic were immune—like werewolves. Otherwise, Gypsum's army would not have defeated Fharen in the first place. He'd never have been driven to sell his soul to the Dead God, getting Thane instead. That meant Thane couldn't command the enemy to surrender, unfortunately. A shame. It would have been simpler.

I waved away servants and courtiers, offers of bouquets, jewels, even the loan of a luxurious bedroom brimming with soft cushions. I hadn't slept in days and couldn't anytime soon.

"Bring me a sandwich or something and fix the soles on my boots." I stopped in the middle of the hallway, took them off and tossed them to someone who looked like a seneschal, an officious overseer of slaves.

My favorite boots had worn thin over the last weeks. The socks were not in good shape either, so I tossed him those too. I squeezed my toes into the thick carpet woven of silken threads. It felt good.

"The cobbler has until I reach the door," I said.

The seneschal ran off with my things, terrified of what I'd do if I had to step outside barefoot on icy flagstones. Fortunately for him, the palace was huge, and it would take me a good half hour to reach the door.

To the remaining hangers on, I barked, "Get out of my sight."

"I must insist you talk sense into His Majesty," a general pleaded. "Treating with the dwarves and humans, taking down the fences around the camps ... it will leave us vulnerable to saboteurs."

"I'm not naïve," I said, "and neither is King Fharen. Guardsmen should escort the dwarves to their homes for 'protection' until all of this is over. Except Reginald and Bert and the others I put on that list I gave one of you. Them I trust, so treat them nice. Did you gather food and treasure for my negotiations with the humans?"

"That was the seneschal you asked," the general said. "He's busy with your shoes, I believe."

"Well someone damn well better gather it soon, because an angry mob of people is far scarier than mother-loving dwarves."

"Yes, milady." The general hurried away, grumbling under his breath.

I thought I'd have a moment of peace, but there was one sycophant left.

"Make it two sandwiches," I told him.

Finally, alone. I took my time walking to the front door. I wasn't trying to give the seneschal and cobbler an easier time of it, as I wasn't feeling that kindly toward elves, but I needed a moment to breathe.

Scary how naturally I bossed people around. I blamed the Thorne in my blood, something I'd hoped to bury. I didn't like taking charge, because it meant I was responsible if this went wrong, like if we released dwarven saboteurs, or Gas's cronies were free to terrorize the city from within while Lili attacked from without. But I had to risk it.

There are times you have to make the damn bread yourself, even if you suck at it, because no one else will, and you're starving. I sucked at analogies, but that's how I felt. Like I was out of my depth but still had a better shot at getting it right than the idiots around me. It was up to me to make friends and get everyone to cooperate.

Me, making friends? Another shocker.

Except for Gas. I could never play nice with him. The gold I'd asked for was to buy him and his assassins off.

Bell and Morgan I could reason with, thus the food for the refugees. Bell wouldn't forgive the elves, and neither could I, but I hoped it was enough inducement to work together for a time. There was no choice, really, not with Lili's and Gypsum's army bearing down on us.

That was about as much planning as I was capable of. I'd have to wing it from here.

When I reached the main door, the seneschal was waiting, breathless. He had my boots, new socks, and a long coat for me.

"Milady."

"Just in time." I put them on, enjoying the softness of the fur lining on the coat, and then stepped outside.

Time to get on with it.

The EEPs at the gate eyed me warily but gave me a wide berth. It was when I left the fortified Central City for the contested streets I worried.

Captain Uanal and a few guards waited to escort me, but I shook my head. "No. You stay here until you hear from me. Elves in tow will get me killed faster than opening Bell's fridge." She usually kept dynamite in there, but the elf captain had no idea what I was talking about.

Uanal, at least, hadn't started treating me different. He gave me a long-suffering look. "Miss Thorne, you have no idea what those madmen are capable of. Southern mercenaries, assassins, mechanoids rampaging, bombings: That is but a taste of what we've been dealing with."

"You weren't me." I held up my dead left arm, gray and lifeless except for the willpower I expended to make the fingers move. Just like I'd controlled Conrad's corpse. I was one of the necromancers Uanal had always feared. "Sounds like my usual crowd. See you later, Captain. Leave this to the professionals."

I couldn't resist adding the last bit. He had told me the same thing whenever I butted into one of his investigations.

"Very well, Miss Thorne. If you shall not rely on wisdom, then I cannot help you."

I nodded and set off across the center of the now empty market district. I was less confident than I appeared. I was about to face my friends and former associates, but that didn't make them any less deadly.

When I reached Bell's place, an automaton blocked the hatch to her tunnel.

She knew how creepy I thought those things were. Shaped like a human, they were molded from bronze and powered by Avian goo. At least this one looked to be, as the runes etched over its 'skin' glowed green with liquid magic. It looked like the ones she had been building in her workshop, but instead of being equipped with a shovel, it had an axe. And not the type for chopping wood. This was the type any executioner or dwarven war hero would be proud to use.

"Bell?" I didn't know if she could hear, but I pushed on. "Listen. I know it looks bad, me hanging out with elves and Fharen, especially. You know how much I hate that scum. I've ranted about him more than anyone. Only, and this is just between us and, well, your machine here. And I guess whoever else might be listening in. But fine. This isn't the same Fharen we know and hate. This is...."

I stopped.

Bell would be even more distrustful if she knew it was Thane. After all, he had trapped her in enchanted sleep and kidnapped her as a bargaining chip to get me to serve the Dead God. That was the old Thane.

I'd paused too long. A tinny voice came from a speaker set in the automaton's throat. "Go away. Stick around and you might get hurt. Go back to your elf lover. I knew you had to be just like Ilsa deep down."

I wanted to be furious, but thinking of my sister left a hollow ache in my chest, rather than the burning anger it once triggered.

My voice was calm when I said, "Ilsa is dead."

"You hoping to copy her on that front too?"

Enough already.

"I always liked you Bell, so here's some advice. Bitch doesn't suit you. If I were anything like Ilsa, I would have destroyed the world already. We wouldn't be having this conversation. I'm not exaggerating even a little bit. Stupid doesn't suit you either. I know it doesn't, because you're the smartest person I've ever met. A temporary truce with the elves buys us time and a chance to defend this city from the army bearing down on it. The elves are ready to sacrifice you all, because they're scared and blaming humans, when they should be blaming me. This is all on me. I'm trying the best I can to save you and Vicky, Nanny and the rest. I don't need an argument—I need a friend. I need the old Bell to help me figure this all out. Please."

Silence. The automaton stared at me with iron eyes.

I fingered the First Soul through the fabric of its pouch.

You don't need her or any of them, it whispered.

"Come down. You alone." It was a man's voice on the speaker.

"I am alone." Unless you counted the relic.

I'm always here. Waiting.

The automaton lowered its axe and moved aside. I bent down to open the hatch at my feet and then thought better of it. Stupid to expose my neck that way. I wrenched the weapon out of its grip and tossed it into Bell's junk heap. Then I climbed down.

More automatons stood in the narrow tunnel, like beams supporting the dirt ceiling. They stretched as far as I could see.

Bell had been busy. Some were powered with magical goo, but most hissed with escaping steam. They felt warm and smelled of coal, the boilers in their bellies gurgling away like living things. She'd created them just as she dreamed: machines without magic, built from human ingenuity. Only these were not the workers I'd seen sketched on her blueprints. Instead of pitchforks and hammers, they wielded spears, axes or swords. These were soldiers.

I didn't think Bell would harm me, but Gas was pulling her strings, whispering in her ear. He might.

I crept past the gauntlet of metal sentinels, holding my breath, my gaze locking on one sharp blade after another. Sweat trickled down my forehead into my right eye, and I blinked.

I saw metal shift, a sword glint in the torchlight. I instinctively borrowed power from the Soul to wrap myself in a protective bubble of force, shoving the nearest mechanoid aside. It slammed into the wall and caused a rivulet of dirt to pour from above.

I moved faster, not wanting to be caught in a cave in. I only made it worse, toppling every automaton I passed.

The relic whispered to me, *I can protect you, you see? Yet, there is so much more we can do. Machines are nothing compared to me. I know you desire what I offer.*

"Who doesn't want power to defeat their enemies? At least those of us with a lot of enemies. But, what's the price?"

Unity.

"What?"

The Soul went quiet, and the barrier around me vanished. Taking away its gift just to show me it could.

The toppled automatons struggled to regain their feet as beams shifted. More soil spilled into the narrow tunnel, choking me, and I ran.

I hated confined spaces at the best of times, and my terror grew as dirt smothered the wall torches with a sound like the hiss of snakes. I was in a grave, being buried alive.

I couldn't recall how I'd shielded us from the explosion at the temple. More lives than mine had been at stake then, and I'd reacted on instinct. Instinct abandoned me now.

With my last lungful of air, I mumbled into the dirt, "I do need you, but we do things my way."

The First Soul exalted. *Agreed.*

Its protection surrounded me again, gave me air, and pushed earth and stone aside until I found my way to the ladder and climbed up.

I paused on the top rung, catching my breath.

I'd made a deal with the relic I knew I'd regret, but it wasn't the first or last such deal I'd be making in the name of survival.

I was greeted at the hatch by Bell, who was furious.

"You buried them deliberately! It will take hours for them to dig themselves out. What's your plan? Call the elves to attack while we're vulnerable? Well, we're not vulnerable. We can still fight even without most of my automatons."

I dusted off my clothes and shook the dirt out of my hair, giving myself a moment to calm down before I got into a screaming match.

"From my point of view," I said, "you were trying to kill me with shoddy tunnels and axe-wielding monsters. I didn't mean for that to happen, Bell. Think. You know me. What's gotten into you?"

"Some sense. I should have seen it sooner: humans in the Outskirts, dwarves in the Market District, and elves living it up in the Central City. And you Solhans weaving your webs here, there and everywhere. It wasn't humans who brought on the Dead God, although we get blamed for it. It was your kind. Ilsa whispered in Fharen's ear telling him to enslave us, and now you've taken her place as his whore."

I slapped her. So much for not losing my temper.

It stung my hand, and her face went red in an instant. She rubbed her jaw, before getting in a final, verbal blow that knocked the wind out of me. "Maybe you're the real enemy."

I knew Gas had seeded these ideas in her mind, his fingerprints were all over it. Racial divides, half-truths, and convenient enemies were his wares. I never thought Bell would buy it. She was too smart. But then again, didn't I often wonder the same things myself? Was I the enemy? A true Solhan at heart?

I shook my head, arguing with myself as much as her. "No."

There was a flicker in her eyes, relief I had denied her accusation. Part of her still wanted to believe me, and I knew there was hope.

"The real enemy is the one who set all this in motion," I said, "the one who opened the floodgates, and she is coming here. You want to hate someone? Hate Lili of Solheim. You want to destroy something to fix this all? Destroy her army. Now is your chance."

Her gaze bored into mine. "You really know who did this? How to stop it?"

"I do. What do you think I've been up to since you last saw me? Investigation—and trying to stay alive. I really am sorry about the automatons, and I'll help dig them out. We'll need them."

"We." She turned down the corners of her mouth. "You're not talking about you and me and the survivors here. You're talking about elves."

"And dwarves, Avians, goblins, gralls, trolls, and even abominations. Anything and everyone who can fight Lili. We can always go back to fighting one another when this is over."

Hate was too alluring to resist, I knew. Could she redirect hers?

She didn't agree or commit to anything, but she did step back and let me walk a little further into the room.

The Southerner, General Moore, plus Gas and Morgan were gathered nearby at the entrance to the cavern. More armed automatons stood behind them, blocking the way. Did they plan to keep me from my family?

I fought to keep my anger in check, knowing it's what they all expected, what the First Soul wanted.

I held up my hands. "I come with gifts. All the barricades are coming down, and there's free food for everyone being distributed across the districts. You're all pardoned and free to go home. Leave or stay, you'll be left alone by the guards, as long as you stop trying to kill them."

"And we're to pretend they never killed us? Our friends and families? Turned them into slaves?" Aguragas said, and Bell nodded agreement.

"As I recall, Gas, you don't have any friends or family in Highcrowne. Or anywhere. And you've enslaved plenty of people in your time, so don't sound so indignant. You have no right." I glared, but instead of intimidating him, as it did most sane people, he smiled, as if we'd shared an intimate moment.

Despite our truce, the First Soul whispered to me every chance it got of how sweet revenge would be. *Aguragas killed Conrad. How freeing to remove him from existence, like all your enemies? What joy to walk in the dust of a world where there is no one left to do you harm...?*

Because there was no one left.

That's where that thinking led.

It was a lesson everyone here needed to learn, but they'd never listen. People were dumb. You could shout wisdom at the top of your lungs, but change came from personal pain and experience.

"Aguragas speaks for me," Bell said, arms crossed. "He may be alone in this world, but so am I. So is Daniel here, Gormless, Grim, all my crew. You Solhans," she looked at Morgan and me both, and I could tell Morgan disliked being included, "not to mention your lover, Fharen, and the rest of his stinking kind made sure of that. So, you can take your peace offerings with you to hell."

Bell was clearly at the pain stage and had not yet processed it into experience.

"But, a chance to resupply would be useful," General Moore said, reasonably.

"The food's probably poisoned or drugged. I won't risk a bite of it." Bell spit. "You came after the harvest, Daniel. They took people from their homes, branded them as slaves, and carted them off who knows where, never to be seen again. They want the same for us."

"We can take precautions, check the supplies," Morgan said.

"I knew you'd take her side the first chance you got," Bell retorted. "Why are you even still here, Solhan? Go kiss elves and be made welcome. Go kiss the Dead God too."

Go to the Dead God was an old Solhan curse. Bell probably didn't know that, but Morgan circled his heart, and Aguragas smiled again to see more lines and separations being drawn. Did he thrive off chaos, or was this his idea of fun?

I let Bell vent her bile at me and everyone around her, while I kept calm. The First Soul's whispers were louder than any shout, and if I could resist them, I could resist her pained logic.

When she looked ready to storm off and take Gas with her, I said, "You're going to kill Vikky, and that kid with the muddy hair, and the girl with goggle marks like yours I saw him playing with earlier.

"This isn't about what's right," I continued, "it's about surviving the rest of today, tomorrow and the day after that. When children can sleep in their beds, unafraid death will come at any moment, then you can take your dagger and go slitting throats in the night to gain your revenge. Don't be so freaking selfish."

"I'm not the one who's selfish," Bell countered. "I want humans to not only survive but come out on top. Elves and dwarves don't care about us, so why should we look out for them?"

I wanted to call her an idiot, but it was more important to convince her than label her. I dug deeper, for the real reason I'd gone to my enemies instead of my friends first.

"No one can stand alone," I said. "And no one is 'them' unless we are all them. I'm not human. My

people are outside those walls, Solhan liches and necromancers. With your way of thinking, I should go join
the Dead God and the forces about to burn
Highcrowne to the ground. By your way of thinking, I
should kill you all right now."

A few hands drifted towards the pommels of daggers and swords, until I added, "Lucky I don't think
like you."

"We've never really agreed on anything, Eva, and
now's not the time to start." Bell kept walking, Gas
blowing me a parting kiss.

I sagged. Maybe I should have called her an idiot.
At least it would have felt better than having my attempt at persuasion shot down.

Only General Moore and Morgan had heard me.

"I was never against you, Eva," Morgan said. "I
only hoped you hadn't learned to be such a true
Solhan. Tell me what you want me to do."

'Solhan' was what I always feared being, so
Morgan's words hurt. I didn't flinch or show that he'd
wounded me, because he was right. I was strong and
merciless when I needed to be.

"What I want you to do is fight for Highcrowne," I
told him. "All of it."

Morgan looked at the Southerner. That meant the
general was in command. I noted Bell's automatons
hadn't followed her, so were they under his control as
well?

"I do not know you, Miss Eva Thorne, and I do not know if you can be trusted," General Moore said.

Shot down again. My brain whirred, trying to come up with better arguments. Was everyone stupid or mad?

"However," the Southerner continued, "I recognize power when I see it. My friend and brother was a warlock, the most powerful man I ever met. He was able to kill anyone he chose, anyone who slighted him, with a flick of his wrist. He punished when he needed to, but he never killed when he didn't have to.

"I see such power behind your eyes. The same restraint. It is a mark of courage and self-discipline I respect, even if I know not if you can be trusted in the long term. But, for now, I will call you ally.

"The Fortress has fallen, the lands it once protected overrun by our own dead. Between the northernmost reaches known only to Avian kind and the river of Lyss in the far south, whose denizens allow none to pass, Highcrowne is all that remains. I will stand with you to protect it, so we can all survive another day."

The general was better than me at speeches. I saw why people listened.

He held out his hand, and I clasped it.

"Of course, I have never fought side by side with a woman before. Or even had much contact with them at the Fortress. Your hands seem far too soft."

I smirked. "Just had to ruin it, didn't you? And I was starting to like you, Daniel."

He laughed.

He and Morgan led the way. Automatons shifted aside, and Vikky ran up to me. "You came back!"

He had noticed I was gone. That felt good. I gave him a hug.

Nanny was there too, her ancient face wrinkled into a permanent scowl. "I'm finally run out of my own home and living in the mines like you always wanted. Hope you're happy."

"Yes." I'd even missed her screeching voice. "Because we're going to get our home back. Pack your things. We go now."

"It might be safer for the civilians to stay here until the fighting is over," General Moore said.

"First of all, there are no civilians. We need everyone. Vikky can put out fires or sound a warning if he sees anyone coming toward the house, and Nanny is one of the deadliest necromancers around. She trained Ulric. She'll be fine."

Nanny's smile was like sunshine. She even gave me a pat on the cheek. "That's my Eva."

7 THE CALM BEFORE

Surrounded by some of the same Southern soldiers who had seen me rip out souls, I felt twitchy, but not as twitchy as they were.

We were in General Moore's quarters, a shack built of discarded wood and metal supported by the shell of an ancient dwarven building. It was thickly constructed, not to keep out the weather, as there was no need in the cavern, but to provide privacy for discussions such as these.

I explained the defense strategies Thane and his advisors had come up with when I was in the palace.

General Moore listened throughout and then nodded. "Elves are not as foolish as I was led to believe. Calculating and immoral, but war brings out the worst in everyone.

"Call in the outer pickets and clear the tunnels." When General Moore gave his skittish soldiers an order they listened, spines straight, eyes never straying from him.

"Everyone goes to the Red Precinct bridge," he continued. "It and the harbor are the weak points, but we'll be able to take down a large chunk of the enemy if we destroy that bridge. The elves can hold the main gates until we're free to reinforce them. I want real soldiers on the walls between as well. These werewolves sound unpredictable, and the dwarves from the camps are too weak to do much good. They and our civilians can provide support."

Within minutes of the general giving his commands, everything was in motion. Sergeants barked orders, the camp was packed, and weapons distributed, although most people had no more than tools and pieces of wood, much like Vicky's toy sword, to protect them if they were attacked while carrying water or pitch to supply the walls.

As humans and Solhans packed up camp, ready to return to the world above and fight for the dung heap they called home, goblin street cleaners, the usual denizens of the caverns crept back in, happy to see everyone go.

"And don't come back!" one shouted with a raised fist. The goblin had emerged from a shadowed crevice I hadn't thought big enough to hold him. It looked like there were tunnels within the tunnels, and more goblins poured out.

A female, although it was hard to tell the goblin sexes apart, wearing a rag dress and a real gold nose ring paused to pet the cavern wall. "Me poor lichens. Took long time to grow, and now they's eaten! Me mushrooms, picked too. Shoo!" she told me.

I held up my hands. "Don't look at me. I didn't eat them. Where were you all hiding?"

In answer to my question, a huge, long-limbed troll pulled itself out of the crack in the wall and said, "In the sewage drains. Murky, disgusting places even your kind shy from. Teeming with indigestible goblins. Nothing but rats and garbage to eat." He appraised me in a lustful way, although not the type of lust I was used to. "Looks like my luck has improved. Hello, juicy."

I took a step back. Trolls were dangerous at the best of times. This one looked grumpy—and hungry.

The goblin with the nose ring swatted him. "Careful. Quits tearing of the last of me lichen."

I took advantage of the distraction and retreated to the line of automatons watching over the human relocation.

A pair of pesky goblins I recognized in mercenary leathers were trying to tear an automaton apart, tugging on limbs and head, without much luck. The automaton swatted them off.

"Drats. Good salvage going to waste."

The other goblin smiled with a huge mouth full of needle teeth and said, "Maybe they's like to fight?" He thumped the automaton's chest. "Hey, you. Fights me."

I crossed my arms. "Wasn't losing to a grall enough to teach you both a lesson?"

"It's crazy lady!" The goblin with now-bruised knuckles hugged my legs. "Please make the grall give us a rematch."

"Something even better is on its way for you to fight. Come up to defend the walls with the humans, and you'll see. Werewolves."

"Yes!" the one now trying to hack off automaton limbs with his axe jumped down. He ran after the departing humans, his buddy close behind, their mad war cries hurrying the refugees along.

You could always count on young goblins to run headlong into a fight. Crazy. Although they thought I was crazier, and maybe they were right.

Not all the civilians were as keen as I was to put themselves in harm's way, though. Many parents with younger children tried to stay behind, huddling around campfires, but the influx of goblins, and the troll especially, convinced them to dare the dangers above instead.

The soldiers went aboveground first, followed by refugees and then automatons. Gas and Bell were nowhere to be seen, and I worried, not knowing what Aguragas was up to.

The Southern soldiers numbered in the thousands when gathered together. I'd only seen a score on the raid, but other enclaves had been encamped in abandoned buildings throughout the city. I got the sense there might be even more in reserve, but General Moore was reluctant to reveal too much, which was fine. All that mattered was they'd fight for my town.

I accompanied the general to the Smiths' District, neutral ground where human rebels could meet elven troops face to face.

Captain Uanal wrinkled his nose. "It looks like you succeeded in your mission, Miss Thorne. They have agreed to the truce?"

"As long as I maintain control of my people," General Moore said. "Any new orders from the palace go through me. My men have control of the northern section of the city. You keep your elven troops near the docks and main gate. My people don't feel comfortable with guards around who might stab them in the back when an opportune moment arises."

Uanal didn't blink. "Very sensible of you. All right then, we'll pull back to the market and barricade the northern entrance to the Central City. We don't want your people taking advantage of an opportune moment to overrun Elven Protectorate and assassinate King Fharen or any of our nobles."

"Very sensible of you," General Moore agreed.

They didn't shake, but there was a mutual nod and grunt before they went their separate ways.

I was torn between accompanying the humans and the guardsmen, but my house was in the elven-controlled area, so I stayed with Captain Uanal, Nanny, Vicky and Morgan trailing not far behind.

Uanal looked at me like I was an annoying flea.

"And what about the dwarves?" I asked. I could give him an annoyed look too.

"They have been uncooperative," Uanal admitted. "But they were happy to receive food and freedom. I think it was a miscalculation, as now we have nothing to offer them."

"Let me talk to them. They'll defend their districts I hope, and then Tha ... Fharen's generals will have less to worry about. Follow me."

My status—and the rumors of necromantic control—must have spread far, because none of the guards grumbled at my orders. Although, Uanal did grind his teeth.

My family continued back to the Outskirts while I led elves into the center of dwarven territory. There were glares from those freed from the camps just this morning, but no one was strong enough to stand, let alone fight the newcomers. It took some time to find someone I knew.

Reginald was weary but smiling when he saw me. There was a small army of freed dwarves with him.

They gripped axes and swords, keeping a wary eye on the elves. Looked like I had to play peacemaker again.

I gave him a hug, difficult to manage with an axe between us, but I felt him soften. I wasn't big on displays of affection, so it shocked him.

"How's Bert?" I asked.

"Healin'. Any word on me mum or the others fled to Gernwold?"

I shook my head. "The pardon is for Highcrowne only, but as long as she and anyone else you care about remains in Dwarf Lands and doesn't field against us, they will be safe."

"I cannot say that won't happen. They will obey whoever wears the silver crown, and me mum's clan is good fighters. They's will be called upon."

"I'm sorry. It's probably best then that you and the others don't face off against family. Is this all of you?" There were fewer of them than the Southerners.

"The rest are too weak."

These ones didn't look much stronger than those I'd passed on the way in, barely able to stand, cheeks hollow. Highcrowne had been home to hundreds of thousands of dwarves before their exile, more than any single city outside Gernwold, and to see the once impressive dwarven districts reduced to this….

I clenched my fist, feeling his pain and fury, and I understood the restraint it took to keep from attacking the elves who had done this to his people.

"You're to supply arrows, pitch and other ammunition to the walls and defend against incursions," I told him, revising the dwarves' part in the plan. They were half-starved civilians, not soldiers. "Hopefully, you won't need that axe."

"I'll fights whoever I need to." Reginald clutched the weapon tighter, as though we might take it away from him.

There were bruises under his eyes, and his skinny arms trembled from the weight. Even the 'able-bodied' were not in that great a shape, and he had to know it.

"I believe you," I said. "But let's fight smart."

After opening the guardhouse armories for us, I sent Uanal and his troops away to help with the preparations at the gate near the docks. The Captain hesitated only a moment before happily leaving me behind.

I stayed with Reginald and the other dwarves he'd gathered who had knowledge of the neighborhoods. We worked to set traps in alleys, placed munitions where they were likely to be needed, on roofs, as well as at the base of the walls. There were arrows tipped in Avian goo, bombs and mines, everything we could haul out of the armories.

And I made sure there were plenty of defenses near my house to keep Little Viktor safe.

Just laying out wolf traps was a lot of work. I mopped my brow, muscles aching.

"How did you and Bert get caught to begin with?" I asked Reginald when we took a break. "One werewolf can do a lot of damage, let alone two and however many others interred in those prison camps."

"The elves were ready for us. Seems King Fharen, after he got off *The Mathésis* in his fancy escape balloon, locked up Highcrowne tight.

"The arm'stice that allowed most dwarves to escape to Queen Gypsum's side was short, but it did the job. Them elves realized just how many dwarves there was in the city compared to everybody else, and they knew they didn't stand a chance if we were on the wrong side of their walls.

"Bert and me came back too late. We should have gone straight to Gernwold after Baroness Syla and the rest dug us out of that cave, but Highcrowne is our home, so o' course we came here first. We stupidly walked into silver nets and mage traps. Magic can't stop us, but it seems Avian goo can, and they built their traps with that.

"This, afore the guards set us free, kept us meek while they starved and froze us in the mud." He showed me a silver bracelet, with Avian markings and a green residue in the etchings. Before returning it to a leather pouch around his neck, he added, "I'll keeps it as a reminder of what being stupid feels like."

"The Avians weren't a part of this too, were they?" I wondered aloud.

"I dunno, but it is their magic."

You really couldn't trust anyone.

The day passed too quickly. Thane had his own preparations, so we didn't see each other before darkness swallowed the sun.

Wolf cries echoed from the hills and carried through the river canyon. The ones who had pursued us waited for their brethren and Lili's army to arrive, calling encouragement to them. They must have been aware of our preparations, watching from the hills with their keen eyes, smelling our bombs and other concoctions with preternatural senses.

I hoped we'd all live to see the sun rise again. Lili could come at any time, and all we could do now was wait.

I was aware I'd lost sight of the big picture. What ever happened to my plan to find Ulric and defeat the Dead God before war came to Highcrowne? Things had grown complicated, and I hoped I hadn't made a big mistake.

I went home. Nanny was exhausted from brewing poisons and filling glass jars with dangerous liquids and had left the kettle on while she snored, so I made sure noxious gas didn't fill the place, before covering her with a blanket.

Vikky was playing in his room, so I got him settled, reading a story from his father's bookshop, one of his favorites about slaying dragons. I told him the only dragon I'd met was a good friend of mine and shouldn't be slayed.

I wasn't sure he believed me, until he asked, "Will your dragon friend help us fight tomorrow?"

"I wish, but she's busy."

I wasn't sure where Olyve was. I hadn't seen her since before Sandy told me they would do all they could to keep the Unmentionables from interfering in my confrontation with Harbinger. I'd killed the vampire, but still she hadn't shown. I hoped that didn't mean she'd been hurt, or killed, battling Harbinger's cronies.

"Maybe there won't be a fight," I finally said, wanting Vikky to have good dreams instead of nightmares.

There was always a chance the Avians would show themselves and drive Lili and Gypsum's wolves away. A slim chance. Avians were as distant and unpredictable as dragons.

"And if there is a battle," I said with forced cheerfulness, "it might not be tomorrow. Sometimes armies are slow, or they stop and think for a while, especially before attacking a fortress like Highcrowne."

"It will be tomorrow." He sounded certain.

"Why do you say that?"

"I don't know. Sometimes I know things and sometimes they come true."

"A handy skill to have, foretelling the future. I've never seen anyone accurate at it. Do we win?"

"No. But...I am wrong a lot too."

"I'm glad there's a chance then."

I tucked him into bed and kissed his forehead, but outside his room I shivered.

Clairvoyance or prescience was not uncommon among Solhans, and Vikky could be right. Or not. Still, the certainty of his 'no' gave me a chill, and for all our sakes I hoped he was wrong.

I crashed in my own room for the first time in what felt like forever.

Thane found me there. I woke when he wrapped his arms around me.

"I'm tired." It felt as though I'd closed my eyes seconds before. Not that he didn't feel amazing: his warmth against me, his scent. He held me as I drifted back into darkness.

I was surrounded by the blackness only possible in caves, where tons of stone stood between you and sunlight. I felt the oppressiveness of that weight in the muffled sounds, my stifled breath. I was buried. In a sarcophagus? A mausoleum?

Green light suddenly pushed back the smothering dark, and I realized the cave was vast. It arched higher than the Lightbringer's temple and was wider than Highcrowne's Market district.

The green light pulsed in thin lines across the walls, through grooves cut into the rock, like a heartbeat. Their paths formed an intricate design that stretched the length and breadth of the place. I couldn't make out what the patterns meant, or the rhythm, but I was certain it had purpose.

As my groggy wits coalesced into clear thought, I recognized the green light was Avian goo, the magical creation they sold to power lights and machines, like automatons, across the Three Kingdoms. I had never seen so much of it before. This would be a fortune.

A person was illuminated by the strange glow. He sat cross-legged on the stony ground.

My uncle.

His rich suit was replaced with rags, his immaculate grooming given way to an unkempt beard and dirt-smeared cheeks. I would never have recognized him if not for his eyes. Dead white, fierce and unyielding.

"I found you," we said at the same time.

"You were looking for me?" I asked.

"I am shielded here. To protect me from the First Soul. As long as you held it, I dared not risk its attention," he spoke in clipped sentences, his rich voice now weak, as though crushed beneath the mountain above us.

"But all those weeks when Thane shielded it with glamours, why didn't you answer my dream calls then?"

"It was awake. Thane enchanted you just now. Into a recuperating sleep. Our Lord Death is Lord of Sleep." He said the last like a prayer. He could have been a priest, if he weren't a criminal.

"I know sleep is one of His things. That's how Thane once captured Ilsa and Bell. I hadn't realized he'd enchanted me. That's why I feel so good, why this dream is so clear?"

"Yes. His enchantment has soothed the First Soul too. It cannot hear us. You must know it is waiting. For a chink in your will. For an opportunity. It waits to consume you, Eva. You must be rid of it. Bring it to me."

"No." Could I trust the relic with my uncle if I couldn't even trust it with myself? "At least, not until I use it to send the Dead God away. That's why I'm glad I found you. I need your help. The First Soul must be one of the keys No-Thing told me about. I know Lili used it to summon Death, so how do I use it to undo the ritual?"

He shook his head. "I already told you. She borrowed the Nine's power, but she led the rite. I don't know how she did it. Klaus might. Bring him to me. I can speak to him."

"What are you talking about?" The only Klaus I knew of was the father I never met.

"You have his soul jar. I've scryed your movements. I saw you steal it from Lili. Brazen. Stupid. You were lucky. Thane as an ally is a boon not to be taken lightly."

"I know," I said, distracted. My mind reeled from the revelation that the little blue soul jar in my pack contained my father. No wonder it knew my true name. Why did Lili have it?

I forgot thoughts were spoken as clearly as words in a dream walk, and Ulric answered, "She killed him. To steal the power he would not give freely. Let me speak to him. He has the knowledge you seek."

My mother killed my father?

That was all I heard.

A snake of sickness coiled in my stomach. I knew how evil Lili was, how she'd been trying to kill me since I was born, but 'knowing' was different from 'believing'. She'd already succeeded at murdering someone she should have loved. No 'trying'.

I suddenly understood there was no chance of talking her out of all this, of turning her good—if she ever had been. So many fleeting, childish dreams had crossed my mind at one time or another, and they were crushed in an instant. The horrible depths of what she was capable of were suddenly real to me.

Uncle was talking, and I replayed what he'd said: "Come to me."

"Where are you?" I managed to ask, pushing the twisting serpents of fear and revulsion in my belly deeper, clenching my muscles around them until my toes curled and they couldn't move.

"Not far. But you will never find me without a guide. I will send … It's waking up."

Uncle was gone. Like any dream, the details faded. I couldn't hold onto them no matter how hard I tried. I thought it had been a dream walk, but when I'd done it before, everything had been clear upon waking.

Had I dreamt something about my uncle? And my father? I couldn't remember.

Peculiar, the First Soul whispered.

Indeed.

I thought the orange glow in the room was morning light, but then I smelled wood smoke from the fireplace. Thane held his hands out to the flames.

"Are they here?" I asked.

He turned. "Sorry to wake you. No attack yet. The elvish mages predict the dwarven forces from Gernwold will reach the bridge at the same time Lili's ships land at the docks—around midmorning. Judging by past actions, she will attack immediately."

I rubbed my eyes and swayed. I felt I hadn't slept at all. "I want to check the Southerners' preparations again. Bell has been acting strangely."

"There's hours until sunrise." He touched my shoulder and goosebumps formed, the delicious kind.

The grogginess vanished, and I felt refreshed and ready to take on the world.

"Lord of Sleep?" I smiled.

"Also, Bringer of Gifts." He indicated an odd shaped mass resting on my dresser. It was covered with an embroidered blanket bright enough to pass for wrapping paper.

"It's not my birthday."

"Call it a war gift."

"Is there such a thing?"

"I begin to realize the transience of things. Life is not forever. Each moment of time likewise dies and gives rise to another. The flavor of each resurrected second is different from the last, and therefore precious."

"Have you been reading poetry again?" I hated the stuff, but Thane had a way with words that turned incoherent nonsense on a page into pure sensation.

"The point is, I thought it worthwhile robbing you of some sleep to gift you this." He pulled off the blanket to reveal something that looked like a wooden box with a huge brass horn attached to it.

I smirked. "That looks suspiciously like some gadget. You know I don't like gadgets—"

"—from the South," he finished for me. So, he did know. No excuse then for the poor choice of 'war' gift.

I should be grateful. I kissed him, grateful at least for these stolen, predawn hours, but my mood was not as it had been when we travelled, just the two of us. I missed those days already. Being hunted was better than being trapped.

The city was my home, and it was also my cage—a dingy one, with its oppressive history of refugees and slaves. The things I'd seen in the dwarven camps couldn't be unseen, a stain on the already filthy fabric of Highcrowne that couldn't be washed away. My friends were unrecognizable, turning on each other, like Bell and Duane. It didn't feel like home anymore. For the first time, I longed to escape.

I couldn't conceal my emotions, and Thane knelt before me. He cradled my chin before giving me a deep kiss. The heat of his soul pushed back the chill that had crept into mine.

"Gifts, poetry, and now kisses. The elven seers must predict a pretty bloody battle ahead. Do we lose?" I asked, remembering Viktor's prediction.

"There is a slender chance we can win. Sometimes, it is the action, not the result, that matters. Eva, there is still time to flee."

"No." I shook my head. There would be no one left to save from the Dead God if we didn't fight here and now.

"Do not despair, then. All things, even suffering, are temporary. And why not entertain joy amidst it all?"

He went to the machine and cranked the handle on the side. "This will change your opinion of Southern inventions. I encountered one on my travels many years ago. Listen."

I listened. The amplified scratching sound, as he moved a large needle into position on a spinning disc atop the box, did not impress. Then came the first notes.

I looked around, for it sounded like violins in the room, but there was no musician hiding. I glanced out the window and saw an empty street, dark but for the glow of a distant streetlamp reflected on damp cobbles.

The music was followed by singing, and once more I was confused, for it wasn't Thane singing. It came from the brass horn on the machine. I put my ear against it, but it was too loud to bear, and I stepped back.

"An orchestra in a box?" I raised an eyebrow. "Are they shrunk forever, or can they be returned to full size?"

He laughed. "An entirely different kind of magic. One that requires no power from souls or the Void. Only human cleverness. They are not without their merits, which is why the Dead God chose to watch over both them and Solhans."

"'Watch over' is an interesting turn of phrase."

"Take a turn with me around the room." He held out his hands, and I knew he meant dancing.

"Oh, no."

"I told you, I know what you truly want."

I was protesting to the only person I had no need to lie to.

Like every girl, I loved to dance. In the privacy of my room, when the street performers played outside, that was. Not in public. I always hid it from Nanny, but I suspected even she must dance sometimes.

Thane knew my deepest self, so I let go of the façade. "Alright." I took his hands and sailed across the room in one sweeping turn, before I hit my shin on the bed. "Ow!"

"We need more space." He shoved the bed aside, and I helped.

"Where did you get this machine?" I asked, breathless, as we cleared more furniture away. I felt the vibrations of song dancing along my skin and wanted to get moving again.

"I saw the phonograph in the marketplace when we returned some dwarves to their homes. The man wanted to give it to me in gratitude. I wore this form and not Fharen's kingly face, else he would not have been so overjoyed. I gave him coins enough to buy a shop of phonographs. He should sell them to everyone, so all can know it's beauty."

"Real coins?" I hoped so.

"Of course. From Fharen's treasury."

What better use for such tainted wealth?

He lifted me by the waist, and I laughed. In his half-Solhan guise he was taller than me, despite the elf blood thrown into the mix. My feet didn't touch the floorboards as he swung me about.

I giggled, growing drunk with dizziness. The song ended, and I couldn't stop laughing, my cheeks flushed. I wanted to go again, but before I could ask, another song started on its own, the needle on the phonograph winding its way closer to the heart of the disc it traced.

This music was softer, slower, the singer's voice high and haunting, like a poignant call to the last spark of sunlight on the horizon.

Thane loosened his grip on my waist and held my hand ever so gently. He gazed into my eyes, and I was lost.

I don't know how long we danced, touching each other with gentle reverence. Our souls danced too, joined in a haze, the poetry of his sinking into the staccato mystery of mine, and I was no longer simply Eva.

When we finally noticed the needle scratching at the end of its disc, over and over, he leaned down and kissed me.

If I had been lost in his eyes, I died with his kiss, and we made love for what I feared was the last time.

The sun crept over the horizon, and its orange light burnished the phonograph, turning its bronze horn into rose gold. The music had long ago distorted itself into the hollow scratching of the needle trapped forever in its last groove.

Thane knew what eternity meant, and I longed to share it with him. But Thane had also known life, and he knew duty, as did I.

"Time to fight," he said.

"Time to fight," I echoed, wanting this peace instead. We never get what we want.

He turned off the phonograph. We went to the door, hand in hand, only to find the threshold blocked.

Duane stood there. No fancy suits this time, or even the plain shirt he'd sported every day of our lives growing up—he wore armor. Guard's white, with a silver sword at his waist. It contrasted with his bronze skin and green eyes, making him look even more out of place.

"Eva," he said. "Come with me."

Duane a guardsman? Not possible. He was a career criminal and merely dressed as one of the good guys. My heart ached, remembering Conrad in such armor, but the pain was fading.

Not so the pain on Duane's face. Some agony drew furrows in his brow and made his lips so tight they were white. But he was a tough guy, and he quickly smoothed his features into a blank canvas.

"Come with you?" I echoed. "Are you trying to arrest me or something in that get up?"

"Would that work?"

"Of course not. Besides, Bell says you're the one people are looking to hang. Oh, I get it now. That's why you're in disguise."

A faint smile turned up the corners of his mouth. "I'm not very good at disguises. Hiding was never my thing. Never being seen in the first place is better. It won't be forever."

"Because Bell will catch and kill you?"

He shrugged. "You know what I did?"

"I do."

"No lecture?"

I'd done dark deeds. I was no longer in any position to judge, so it was my turn to shrug.

"I understand why. You saved your family—my family—everyone you care about. You sacrificed strangers and refugees to do it, which makes you a monster. But it's never enough. You can't save everyone."

I'd learned that too, and the lesson was hard and painful. Because I still wanted to try.

Duane looked me in the eyes, and it seemed his green irises were sharp as any blade, dissecting an unknown specimen. We'd never spoken without arguing before, and he was off balance.

"You look like Eva, but you don't sound like her, or Ilsa. And who's this?" He was always nervous around new people.

He'd be more nervous if he knew it was Thane. All I said was, "Long story. I have work to do, so what do you need?"

"I was sent as a guide."

"Guide?" A memory niggled at the back of my mind. My dream.

"Ulric sent me," he added.

"Eva," Thane whispered, "this is what we've come for. Go, speak to him now."

I shook my head. "Where has Uncle been hiding? Why can't he just tell me what I need to know?"

"He says it needs to be face to face. He needs the soul jar you're carrying. And we should hurry."

I cast about the room for my pack. I felt for the jar inside. It was still there. More fuzzy dream memories surfaced, only to be lost again.

The emotion remained, though. Deep sadness. And urgency.

I slung the pack over my shoulder. "Who will keep the humans and dwarves true to their bargain?" I asked Thane

"I'll manage." From our bond, I knew he was considering possessing General Moore or Aguragas.

I'm not sure either was vulnerable, as I'd never spotted the Dead God's mark on them, but even if Thane managed it, Fharen would be unleashed. Thane couldn't be inside two people at once, and there was no one else we could trust to maintain the peace except Fharen.

As much as I liked to credit my persuasiveness and reasoning, the truth was 'Solhan necromancy'—fear of me—was the only thing keeping humans, elves, and dwarves from killing each other again. We probably didn't stand a chance against Lili and Gypsum, but divided I knew we didn't.

I took a breath. "As I've said, there's no use figuring out the relic and defeating the Dead God if everyone I care about is dead. I'm sticking to the plan. Ulric will have to wait."

I set the pack down.

"As you wish." Thane took me by the shoulders. "We will see each other again when the day is done— no matter the outcome."

I knew he meant whether we lived or died.

I gave Thane a farewell kiss. If I found him in the Halls of the Dead, he would not be my Thane anymore. He would rejoin the Dead God and become a faceless power, reigning triumphant. And all of Highcrowne—no, all the world—would be dead and serving in His kingdom.

The kiss lasted no longer than a heartbeat, but we joined in that instant, and it became an eternity. Only the weight of time passing made me pull away. I was left with a hollow ache.

Duane was still blocking the door. I'd forgotten he was there. I had forgotten everything for a moment.

"Tell Ulric he can wait," I said.

"No." Duane crossed his arms.

"No?" I was about to go back to familiar arguing in a moment.

"I won't play messenger to Ulric when others," he indicated Thane, "are fighting for my city. I blame this armor for making me loony, but I'm staying. I'll show you to Ulric later, if I live. If not, he can send another messenger boy."

"Eva, breakfast!" Nanny's voice screeched from down the hall. She was always up at dawn, and soon Little Viktor would be too.

"I'm not hungry!" I yelled back. At least not for Nanny's cooking.

"I've got nicely aged entrails! Wait a minute and I can boil some eyes too!"

See what I mean. A battle was more appealing.

"I'm heading out!"

She knew what that meant and went blessedly quiet.

Duane moved aside to let Thane go first. There was a moment where they were almost chest to chest, assessing one another, but Thane did not make it a contest. He hurried down the stairs, his mind on the real confrontation ahead.

"Come on," I told Duane, "before Nanny raises the protective wards on the house and tries to kill you as an invader. She never liked you much."

"Says who? She always made me breakfast. We should stay for the fresh entrails at least." Duane could eat anything.

"Her feeding you is not a kindness. Nanny cooks in the same pans she brews rat poison."

Duane followed me out into the street. Thane had vanished, but I sensed his presence. He was headed to the Central City where he could command mages and his elvish army from the war table. There were too few of them. I was hoping Moore's army could turn the tide, but I was too worried about them turning against the wrong enemy.

"This street looks good enough as any other to defend," I told Duane. "Good luck."

He clanked down the street behind me.

"Have you turned puppy? You won't be welcome where I'm going," I said.

"A grall might." He whistled, and booming footsteps joined the sound of his clanking armor.

"Jorg!" I gave the giant a hug, which meant wrapping myself around one of his massive arms. "Where have you been?"

"I should ask where you've been these past months, Miss Thorne." His tusks made his words come out strange, with a bit of drool, but he really was a civilized grall. Someone had even sewn him a new suit.

"You know." I shrugged. "Fighting bad guys. I thought I'd ditched Duane in a cave in, but here he is following me everywhere. Reminds me of when we were kids."

The grall chuckled.

More seriously, I asked, "What happened to Karolyne? I saw the café. Is she with you two? Is that why they branded her traitor?"

Jorg shook his head. "She…."

"She took Gypsum's side," Duane finished for him. "She's out there with the dwarves and the wolves and everything else trying to destroy Highcrowne."

"Not Karo." I stopped. Had she known about Gypsum? They'd always been close. Did I have any true friends?

The shock must have shown, because Duane added, "She didn't have any choice except to flee after they burned her out. I did try to help, but I was a worse traitor in her eyes.

"Her doom was speaking up for Gypsum and fighting to keep our dwarf friends out of the camps. Elves and humans both turned on her. She tried to stop Ulric and me from branding refugees too. She told me 'following orders was no excuse', and it was like she was speaking with your voice, Eva." A bit of the pain he'd plastered over showed through the cracks for a moment. "But no one remembers that. Everyone tars her with the same brush as me."

So, Duane had been following orders? Typical. He didn't say why he'd turned against his own people for Ulric, but I knew why. He owed my uncle everything.

"Thanks for the truth about Karo, but I mean it when I say you should stay here. Grall or no, Bell isn't the one calling the shots where I'm going. The

Southerners look like a real fighting force, and Agura-gas is whispering in everyone's ear."

Duane clenched his fist. "I'm done hiding." No one hated Gas more than he did, except maybe me.

It was his funeral—or maybe not.

I caught up with Jorg as we walked to the rendezvous. I was surprised to see him in Duane's company. "I thought you didn't want to be a thug?"

"I'm Mister Rose's accountant."

"That's worse. Duane's accounts are shadier than his back-alley murders. No offense."

Duane didn't take any, because he wasn't paying attention, lost in his own world.

"I mean his legitimate accounts," Jorg said. "I don't want to know what I don't know."

"I thought you loved cooking?"

"When things got bad for humans, they got bad for gralls first. I should say 'the grall'. I had nothing to do while hiding in your basement all day, so Mister Rose gave me a job suitable for candlelight."

Everything had changed, and once again I felt guilty that I wasn't there to prevent it.

"Lucky Duane is taking his accountant along to this meet and greet with highly armed rebels then. I'm sure your math skills are devastatingly impressive."

"My muscles too." Jorg chuckled. "You don't have to protect me, Eva. I know what I'm doing. Mister Rose is a good man. I don't wish to see him come to harm."

I wasn't going to argue, as my judgement of good and evil was all out of whack.

An army of automatons awaited us at the rendezvous. General Moore had agreed to bring the bulk of his fighters to defend the Red Precinct and Bridge Gate. The bridge over the river was a key strategic location, and it needed a real defense. I was impressed by the mechanoids—all facing outward like they expected attack from any direction—but disappointed by the human turn out.

"Where is everyone?" I demanded. "Elven mages predict the main vanguard from Gernwold will come this way. They must be held at the gate. Too much depends on it."

"Elven mages and predictions are a few of the problems," Gas said. He lurked behind the front row of armed automatons, like a demon whispering in their ears. I saw only a glimpse of his face when he spoke. No sign of Bell.

"What our wise ally means," General Moore began more diplomatically, "is that mage predictions are fallible. I know from experience. So, we have varied the strategy somewhat. Have no fear, we will do our part. But...."

"We don't trust elves," Gas finished for him. "They will turn on us once we're done with the invaders. We want more guarantees."

Duane was facing the other way and acting very guardsmen-like, so most assumed he was an elf. Glares bored into his back. He stiffened, but I knew it was Gas's hated voice that grated.

"Negotiating on the eve of battle irks me, Gas, but it shouldn't surprise me. You have pardons, gold," I reminded the white-haired Darrubian, "so, what else is there to give you?"

"Highcrowne." Gas's voice turned my stomach. I sensed he believed ownership of my home was tantamount to ownership of me, which he'd always wanted.

"Not happening," I looked at the general when I spoke, because Aguragas was irritating me. "Dwarves, elves, even goblins, have dwelled here for ten generations. Avians since the beginning of time. We're the interlopers. It's theirs; the South is yours. Let's focus on getting it back."

"That may or may not happen," General Moore said. "It requires we defeat a god. Sanctuary is here, now, and seats in the Assembly is all we seek."

"And a Crown of our own," Gas added.

That I was in favor of. Citizenship had been at the top of my wish list, but the Crowns made the real decisions, and a human ruler would ensure whatever freedoms granted in time of war would be protected later.

"Gas isn't eligible," I said. I knew he had some connection to royalty in Darrub, but Darrub was gone. "Let's get that straight from the start."

"Wouldn't dream of it." I hated the lying smile on his face.

"Elves and dwarves have kings and queens. We're human refugees who know from experience that no ruler with royal blood ever did anything worth anything. We have elections after this is over. We choose our king, representative, whatever we want to call him or her." That was Duane, and I could have kicked him. We might have gotten through this entire meeting with no one knowing he was here. As it was, swords were drawn.

Jorg took a rumbling step between his boss and the crowd.

"Put your weapons away until they're needed. We're fighting what's out there, remember?" I pointed to the city wall, a small orange ball of autumn sunlight creeping over the edge of it. "Negotiations and elections are pointless unless we win."

"First elves and now this traitor. How can you expect us to deal with you, Eva, when you are the least trustworthy of all?" That was Bell's voice. I hadn't spotted her before, because she was inside one of the larger automatons, wearing it like a suit of armor.

"Do we really need to go into this again?" I was tired of arguing.

Frustration must have shown on my face, because the Southerners who had seen me angry in the dwarven camp held tighter to their weapons. Spears and swords shook a bit from the tremble that crept into their limbs.

"You need us, and we need you," General Moore said reasonably. "That has not changed. All of us were pardoned, and so I assume that man was as well."

"Duane didn't commit an official crime to begin with, but yes let's all stay in a forgiving mood. You can fight it out later." *When I'm gone*, I thought.

"Very well," General Moore pronounced. Bell's automaton clenched its fists with a loud whirring of gears, but the Southerner had a commanding tone, and all his guards sheathed their weapons. "We will fight for this city as agreed. After you confirm our demands have been met."

"There's no time for this!" I shouted. Humans were idiots.

"You have the Elf King's ear, so it should be simple," Gas said. He paused, eying the rising sun, "But you might want to hurry."

"There's politics, other considerations...." I knew I sounded like an elf, so I shut up and walked off.

Duane and Jorg's clatter as they followed made it impossible to hear my own boots angrily hitting the flagstones.

I couldn't go quietly, so I turned back and shouted, "I hope you fools are smart enough to defend this bridge and stay alive, even if I'm not back in time. Because, Lightbringer help us, you're all we've got!"

8 CLAIMS AND COUNTERS

"Stupid, idiotic. Those morons don't deserve to live," I ranted all the way back to the Central City.

"The problem is," Duane said, "deep down you expect people to be smart and do the right thing. That always leads to disappointment. The trick is to force them to do what you want or what's 'right', without them knowing they were forced."

"That's called coercion."

"No, it's manipulation. I also like ''molding', 'influencing' or 'maneuvering', but I might as well be clear that the objective is to get what I want."

"How's that working for you?"

"Better than I'd like."

I was surprised to hear so many words from Duane, so it was a relief when he went quiet again. Disturbing to think he'd been thinking so much all these years.

"I can go back and defend the bridge," Jorg volunteered. "No one will get past me."

I remembered him taking on a gang of thieves in the Night Market when I first met him, but an army was another matter. "Not by yourself. I'll get the assurances they want. It's the timing that sucks."

I tried reaching out to Thane with our soul connection again, but he must have been in the map room, which was shielded.

Duane punched Jorg in the arm, the equivalent of a tap on the shoulder for a grall, and indicated he should follow.

"Where are you two going?" I hadn't wanted either along to begin with, but I was getting used to them.

"I might have a way to help 'manage' the situation more quickly," Duane said.

"Go back there alone, with Gas calling the shots, and that armor won't protect you."

"I can take care of myself. Besides, I'm not going backwards."

With that cryptic word choice, he ran off, Jorg keeping pace with slow, giant steps.

Alone again, I could hear my own footfalls and labored breathing as I hurried. Stamina was not my thing. Dealing with elf politics in the little time left before Lili attacked even less so. What Gas and

General Moore had asked for was impossible. It had taken days for Hilja to even explain 'parties' to me.

It was a moment before I realized I wasn't running across cobbles anymore. I was on soft grass dotted with wildflowers, summer sunshine dazzling my eyes. Buzzing insects and a forest had replaced the market district, but this was where it had been. It was ruins. The only structure remaining was a quartz spire, which rose from within the Central City. A mage tower.

"What the?"

"You like it?" Governor Walz asked, suddenly appearing beside me.

"Where are we?"

"In my mind. I find this image most pleasant. A future without all the common mess of Highcrowne. No outsider's wars and impurity. You are all a scourge. But even filth and offal melts into the soil in time. It rots away to feed a glorious elven future."

"Not sure that's the best metaphor. An elven future based on dung?" Then again, elves smelled like it already.

Walz didn't batt an eyelash. I got the sense that to him I was like one of the bees flying about, beneath notice, except for the possibility I might sting a little.

The unbelievable arrogance of elves.

My sting was deadly.

But I'd warn him first.

"Lovely you take time to concoct such an elaborate daydream with an army on our doorstep. It's detailed.

Delusional beyond all belief, but I have to give you points for creativity. You know it's impossible, right? The Dead God is just starting with Solhans and humans. You elves are next."

"The Compact protects us."

"We're talking about Death. All go to Him in the end." I couldn't help my Solhan chants.

"You shall go to him even sooner, necromancer."

"Oh, I'm no necromancer."

At least not a fully schooled one, not like Erick had been or the liches of Solheim, like my mother. I was the more dangerous kind, with little knowledge but a whole lot of power to throw around. I had the First Soul.

We kill the elf? it asked.

At least it was honoring our bargain and asking first. I wanted to kill him, but I wanted to kill lots of people and didn't. Usually.

"Drop the illusion," I said aloud for both the relic and Governor Walz to hear.

The First Soul obeyed. The mage tower and decayed market district vanished, revealing the real market district, which didn't look a whole lot better. It had served as a dwarf concentration camp recently and was covered in filth.

"That's the smell I was expecting." I smiled, pretending to enjoy the deep breath of sour air I sucked in. The elf's glamour had been so powerful, he'd even simulated the cloying aroma of flowers, which usually made me sneeze. My nose hadn't started running, though, and that's how I'd known it was fake before Walz ever said anything.

"How did you do that?" he asked. Like I'd tell him.

"I don't know what hoity toity elven province you come from where you think you're all powerful, but you are an insect to me." I looked at him with one eye closed, framing the image of him between my thumb and forefinger so he appeared about an inch tall. He wasn't the only one who could look down on people. I'd learned from the best. "Don't try to mess with my head again."

I started walking, and he followed. Elite Protectorate soldiers in black berets lurked in nearby doorways, and they moved to shadow us. He'd brought bodyguards and was even smart enough to keep them at a distance, so they didn't overhear anything.

Governor Walz was all about protecting his influence, hoarding leverage and power to tug on the strings of government from afar. I read it in his soul. It was killing him that I could pull Fharen's strings so overtly. He'd swooped into Highcrowne's vacuum of power, expecting to be unopposed, only to find me there, doing lots of opposing.

"What do you want?" He'd asked, but he didn't really care. He just wanted to understand me, so he could manipulate me.

I wouldn't make it easy on him.

I turned on my femme fatale, that slinky Ilsa seduction that had made everyone love her—I'd absorbed some of it when I stole her soul—and drawled, "Why, Governor, you know exactly what I want."

He raised an eyebrow. "You don't mean?"

I batted my eyelashes. "Oh, no, you flatter me. I mean, I want to have everyone be good friends, to end all this fighting, and protect this beautiful city, which I so dearly love, as it has protected me. And I am ever so grateful that, no matter our differences, we can all agree that survival is most important right now. We can sort out where to build mage towers later. Plenty of time for that once the Dead God is defeated and all us humans and Solhans can go back home, to our lands. Doesn't that sound good?"

Something clicked behind his eyes. A chink in his thinking.

Until now, he'd thought human extermination was the obvious way to go. Elves. It hadn't occurred to him that defeating the Dead God, with some human cannon fodder to help, rather than waiting for the god to kill us all first, would make things so much easier for his kind later. With plenty of safe spaces out in the wide world, there would be no more refugees pounding on Highcrowne's gates. Elf Lands could be Elf Lands again, and so could Dwarf Lands and Avian Lands be Elf Lands. The rest could follow in due time.

I was disgusted by what I read in him. Dreams of empire had gotten the world into this state to begin with. No one ever learned. But it made it easier to play him

"Now you understand what I want, and I think I can help you get what you want," I said. "You and Fharen are on the same side. I'm helping him, so there's no reason I can't help you too. We can help each other. When this is all over."

I'd set the price. Would he shy or pay up?

He thought a long while, and it was hard to read the nuances of it, because my soul sense only revealed his unwavering ambition and yearning for elven dominance.

Finally, he said, "You'd best return to our king's side, as the invaders are making their approach. He will be on his way to the docks. I will ensure the elven troops demonstrate their superior abilities as warriors to your human and dwarven comrades—and you shall see why we are naturally the masters here."

"I look forward to it," I lied.

He was still an ass, but at least he would fight for Highcrowne. No undermining things through political maneuverings at the last moment.

From reading him, I knew Walz had no desire to sit the throne himself. He preferred others to be the face while he was the brains. I'd come in and taken over his role as manipulator, which is why we'd gotten off to a bad start.

As soon as he realized I was just another cut out between him and the king and any repercussions of royal actions, he seemed delighted. He even lent a few of his EEP guards to escort me safely to the docks.

I watched them the whole time, my Ashur and green fire at the ready, just in case I'd misread Walz entirely.

When I found Thane, he read my soul far more easily than I'd read the governor's. We were so in tune these days. I could get used to never speaking with words again.

He called for pen, parchment and the royal seal, and sketched out the assurances General Moore had demanded in a hasty hand.

While he blew on the ink to dry it, he said, "This is a lie, you realize? King Fharen—I—cannot promise a Human Crown without approval of the full Assembly. I'm not sure it's possible even then."

"Anything is possible. You're practically a dictator, as long as we keep Walz on your side. His glamours are powerful, maybe even better than yours. I keep pinching myself every once in a while to make sure I'm actually here and not his prisoner somewhere."

"He is only one problem. No matter how convincing you think you are, Eva, the real difficulty is the

Avians. Until they reveal themselves and their intentions, there is a chance they can undo every proclamation I and the Assembly make. Rulership of the Three Kingdoms is not fully equal. They have veto power, not just because of ancient rights as the oldest beings to inhabit these lands, but because of their magic, which is beyond elven or dwarf understanding. A handful of them have managed to hold power for so long because we all fear what they can do."

"What you *think* they can do. I don't just think, I know what Lili and the wolves are capable of, so let's worry about the here and now."

He nodded and rolled up the decree, affixing his seal.

I took it and said, "Is there someone super official and convincing who can deliver this to them? I'm not welcome with Bell and the Southerners, and Gas still lingers like a bad odor."

Good one. I didn't know if that was the First Soul laughing at my jokes now, Thane in my head, or a sign I was going insane.

I needed to simplify my life.

Thane summoned twenty black garbed EEPs, who assumed a pretty formation in the center of the street. Then he took the scroll back from me and said, "I'm the only one they will believe."

I groaned. Walking back across the city again would be killer on my legs. "Then I'm coming with you."

"No. You're the only one I can trust to defend the docks in my absence." Soul to soul, he said, *the elves fear you. Once they see what Lili brings with her, that fear is the only thing that will counteract their desire to run.*

I gulped. *Me? I'm not a general.*

Listen to the advice of the generals, or more aptly their officers, as my generals seem to be most concerned with the defense of the Central City.

I'm a figurehead, then?

No. You must decide whose advice to listen to. Then he said aloud, his voice amplified so all the forces assembled at the dock gate could hear, "Obey Miss Eva Thorne. She is my voice."

He and the EEPs headed towards General Moore's encampment, and a few moments later I stood all alone with a lot of elf eyes on me.

The hundreds of guards-turned-soldiers waiting along the wall or in the streets below made a distinct rattle of chainmail hoods when everyone turned away at once, pretending they hadn't been staring.

With the EEPs gone, Captain Uanal was the most senior officer in sight.

"Am I wrong, or are there supposed to be more ranks between general and captain?" I asked him.

"The colonels and majors, as well as our elite soldiers, are all guarding the wall around the Central City. We are the, ahem, delaying action."

"Fodder, you mean. Well, right away I don't agree. Send a runner to the palace and tell them King Fharen demands another ... cohort?"

"A regiment would be a better number," Uanal suggested.

"Tell them to send that."

"Gladly."

I fully expected my demand to be ignored, but Governor Walz came himself a short time later with more soldiers than I expected, mostly archers. The Central City must have been left with few defenders, which meant he'd exercised considerable influence.

So, we did have an understanding. And he valued his skin enough to make sure wherever he stood was well protected.

We acknowledged each other with a nod. It was grudging. He still wanted my kind exterminated or expelled at the earliest opportunity, and I still wanted him to die for his role in the internment of the dwarves and my family, but we had silently agreed to a temporary truce.

Our war would resume when this one was over.

The governor and Uanal spoke, distributing the new arrivals, and I took a shaky breath, retreating from the spotlight. I positioned myself on the battlements by the Dock Gate, so I could watch the port and keep an eye out for Thane's return.

Long minutes passed as I waited. Where was he? Had Gas's followers killed him? I was an idiot to send the last king of Highcrowne within reach of its most deadly assassin. But Thane was powerful: knowledge of necromancy and most other forms of magic, not to mention glamour, in one immortal package. He'd be okay. Still, where was he?

And where were my mother's ships? She'd been close enough to attack for hours now.

I'd never been in a siege before, but the crazed battle in Faellion had taught me things could get worse. At least death by werewolf would be quick. This interminable waiting shrouded everyone in doom.

As I thought of death shrouds, a white layer of fog rolled across the river, blanketing it like a corpse.

A commotion in the courtyard below drew my attention away from the preternatural change in weather. It was Duane and Jorg.

The earth rumbled as the grall shifted uncomfortably. He was carrying a giant backpack. It looked heavy, and Duane added his own weight when he scrambled up and rummaged through the sack. He tossed something to Jorg, who promptly dropped it with an, "Oops."

Duane's eyes widened. He leapt down and grabbed a nearby soldier's shield, throwing it and his body over the dropped object. The elf seemed dazed by how quickly he'd been disarmed, but he was even more dazed when the ground exploded.

Ears ringing, I rushed down the ladder. A large, smoking crater lay at Jorg's feet. Duane had been thrown back, riding the shield like a sled, and surrounding elves in white Guard armor were fanned out on the ground like fallen snow. Jorg was singed but unhurt.

"What happened?" I asked, coughing and fanning smoke away from my face.

"Boss?" Jorg poked at Duane's inert form.

"He's not having you call him that too?" I expected one of Duane's usual retorts to my teasing, but he didn't stir. "Are you alright? Shake it off, Duane. Get up."

I put my head against his chest. The armor made it impossible to hear a heartbeat. I could reach out with my soul sense to see if he was okay, but … this was Duane. I didn't want that kind of connection again.

Then I heard a snicker.

I slapped him.

"Ow." He rubbed his jaw. "You never hit that hard before."

"When have I slapped you before?"

"Lots of times."

"Oh, that's right, and you always deserve it." I helped him stand. "Better?"

"No thanks to you."

"What happened?"

Jorg shrugged. "I slipped."

"With what? A mage bomb?"

"Avian-made," Duane corrected, pulling out a bandolier containing tubes of glowing goo. Jorg's body had protected the giant sack of weapons from the explosion.

"I have a supplier," Duane continued. "I made sure Bell's people by the bridge are fully outfitted. Jorg hauled over a wagon of these earlier."

I raised an eyebrow. "Bell didn't kill you, I see."

"King Fharen was there with an army of elites. My arrival was a welcome distraction amidst tense negotiations."

"Is he alright?" I began. "I mean, was the king successful? We need the Southerners to fight."

"They'll fight. So, will we." He began handing out more bombs and other Avian-made weaponry from the sack. The elven guardsmen didn't turn up their noses for once, welcoming the improved arsenal.

Duane would never reveal a supplier, but still I asked, "Your 'source' has been hoarding all of this? I didn't even know Avians made weapons. I thought it was elf mages who added the raw goo to their arrows? Come to think of it, these arrowheads you've brought look different from anything I've ever seen."

"Avians make a lot of things." He didn't say more, and I knew not to press, even though curiosity was killing me.

"They're here," Uanal called from above.

Now? My stomach heaved. After all the waiting, I'd hoped Lili's army had changed its mind and decided to go back to Solheim.

This was really happening.

"Get ready," I told Uanal and Duane, but they were ready. It was me who wasn't.

Duane exuded his usual air of calm. Whether masterminding robberies, torturing rivals, or assassinating powerbrokers he'd always stayed cool. So, it was surprising when a crack suddenly appeared in that mask, and he said, "Stay alive, Eva. I know death is easier for both of us, but ... stay alive."

I nodded. "You too. I'd feel a whole lot better if you took some bombs over to my street to defend Nanny and Viktor."

"That's the plan." He set off with Jorg in tow.

I climbed up the steps to the wall, slowly, hoping if I delayed long enough Thane would be back already, and I wouldn't have to do this.

Everyone's attention was on me again, so I stilled my shaking hands and gave the soldiers stationed along the outer wall my best glare. Thane said they needed to be more afraid of me than of the enemy, and a white-eyed Solhan stare always did the trick.

Guards readied bows, and I sensed power rise in the mages, Captain Uanal among them. There were only five with us, positioned a few hundred feet apart, and dressed like mundane soldiers to confuse the enemy. If Lili or the necromancers had anything like my soul sense, though, the mages were obvious.

I studied the empty docks in the ravine below, the Serpent's Ribbon still shrouded in fog. A horn blew, and a chill went up my spine, for accompanying the horn were howls. A few at first, followed by more, until the chorus was deafening. Werewolves.

9 THE FIRST WAVE

They boiled out of the mist, a blur of dark fur and glowing eyes, and then they climbed the switch-backed road from the docks in seconds. It took me a good half hour on foot, a bit less on a miniature locomotive.

We were outmatched. I knew it. We would not win this without too many people I cared about dying.

Werewolves crashed into a barrier of mage-summoned force a stone's throw away from the wall where I stood.

The elves' magic wavered, like a rainbow shifting on the surface of a bubble about to pop. The werewolves' very nature seemed to blunt or even negate spells cast against them. The barrier would not hold, but it gave the guardsmen-turned soldiers a moment for their senses to catch up.

Arrows coated in Avian goo or etched with enchantments began to rain down. A few lobbed Duane's new bombs, but wherever they aimed, the werewolves dodged, gone before the missiles reached them.

Some archers were smart or lucky enough to compensate, but once more, the magic was blunted. Mage or Avian bombs, neither even dazed the creatures. But shrapnel from broken stones flew everywhere and did cause some to yelp and pause, licking at bleeding wounds.

Silver arrowheads worked best. If one penetrated their thick hide, the silver forced them back into dwarf form. A handful collapsed, naked and bleeding.

Then the barrier disintegrated. The first one who got through hooked a paw into the stone wall below me and catapulted over my head. It landed atop a house on the other side of the street.

The soldiers in the courtyard below dealt with it, more silver arrows filling the sky before the wolf could escape. The dwarf he shifted back into skid down the roof tiles and landed on the stone with a disturbing smack.

These were our people. There had to be a better way.

My gaze turned inward, and what had been a dark and frenzied blur of carnage became bright smudges in my soul sight. I had never attempted to affect so many werewolves before, but I had to try.

Their souls were a glowing, amorphous mass. I could barely distinguish one wolf from another. All exuded animal hunger, desiring the hot, salty taste of blood.

Queen Gypsum had given them this. Power flowed from the silver crown she'd stolen and sang to them of glory. They thrilled at their strength and freedom, sensations many had never known as dwarves beholden to clans and matriarchs and civilized society.

There was nothing civilized about war, and a tiny voice inside some of them screamed this was not right.

I was going about this wrong. I didn't need to grapple animal souls and turn them dwarf again. They were already at war with themselves. I focused on that voice of doubt within them.

I reached out to each soul that crossed my path; one by one, I whispered to them of home and their mother's voice, of tea and a biscuit in the morning. As the First Soul tempted me, I tempted them, but not with death and glory and power. I made them remember what peace was like.

It worked with most; a nudge was all they needed to return to themselves. To become someone's son or brother again. They stood bewildered, wondering how they'd come to be standing naked in mud.

Some, however, loved the freedom too much. Hate and resentment built up from years in the mines had burned away any love for the families who had consigned them to servitude. A lot of suffragists were among them, riled up by rhetoric and fierce belief.

Them I forced to cage the beast. I shoved that primal fire in their souls down tighter and tighter until it was a dull coal of extinguished heat, a dwarf caged in his shell again.

I may have drawn on the First Soul a bit to do it. Just a bit. I had no time to worry about the little chuckle it gave, or its dark joy.

I transformed one after another after another. I lost count.

One werewolf made it atop the wall beside me. Soldiers screamed as they died. Then I felt the heat from mage fires. Arrows whipped past my ear, accompanied by the wet *slunck* sound of swords hacking flesh, and the crunch of teeth gnashing bone. I was in the thick of it, but I focused on one soul at a time.

And Thane's hand in mine.

He'd returned.

Thane was covered in wolf blood and wielded a silver sword in his left hand, keeping his right clasped around my cold palm. His warmth shut out the relic's voice, and I was amazed by the relief I felt, like a thorn had been removed.

The first wolf died, but more came for us; they recognized the Elf King. I transformed one after another, until a ring of dazed dwarves surrounded us. Their wolf comrades cut them down to get at us, but they never got past the few surviving EEPs intent on protecting Thane.

"Look. The barrier," Uanal cried, triumphant.

My sight vanished. Gone were the bright lights of souls, and in their place was a magical barrier that blocked my soul sense along with the enemy attack. Wolves howled their frustration, and I felt as though I'd been blinded.

This barrier was different from the one made of light the mages had used earlier: it was a silver net that shimmered with green goo, suspended in front of the wall by hovering, winged Avians.

Avians. No one had seen them since all this started, and I'd given up hope they'd help.

Once they had the enchanted mesh in position, it hung in midair of its own accord, and they flew back to the mountain in the center of Highcrowne.

"Not even a hello." I was disappointed.

"They've given us time. That's what matters," Thane said.

"Time for what? We barely survived their first attack."

And there was no sign of my mother. The real thing I feared. Was she waiting for the wolves to soften us up, or was she somewhere else?

"The bridge!" I gasped.

Thane shook his head. "I've just returned, and the deal I made with the humans will ensure it is well defended. They will destroy the bridge before anyone makes it across."

"Does Lili even need a bridge?"

Thane paused. "I know I need you here in case more werewolves attack."

The Avian barrier might prevent me from sensing the enemies' souls outside, but Thane I could sense clearly. He was trying to protect me.

Captain Uanal trotted over. "A few werewolves got past us. They're in the city doing untold damage. Permission to hunt them down?"

I let go of Thane's hand. "Yes, Captain. Let's hunt them down, and I'm going with you."

"Must you?" Uanal said, reluctant. He looked at Thane, but the king hadn't ordered him not to obey me anymore.

I spoke to Thane soul to soul, so Uanal wouldn't overhear. *You have the Avian's net and Walz's soldiers armed with silver, which is just as effective as my power at stopping wolves. You don't need me here.*

You were relieved when I came back to you, he said. *I felt it. Why are you so intent on separating again?* He had to ask, because it wasn't clear, even to me.

I thought for a moment, looking within, to those dark parts of me I tried to avoid. *Because you want to shelter me, when there is no shelter. I have the First Soul, and power of my own. I want to do something, wield that power, whatever I must before it's too late to protect those I love.*

That is what I feared you would say. The First Soul will consume you if you let it.

I won't. It and I have a temporary truce ... and I'll be careful.

I didn't wait for his okay. I didn't need it.

I climbed down to the courtyard, and when Uanal hesitated, I said, "Let's go, Captain."

"Very well," the guard sighed, resigned.

Minutes later, he had gathered a score of soldiers, and we set off.

I stretched out my soul sense. It worked here within the Avian barrier but couldn't reach outside the city.

I had no idea Avian magic could interfere with necromancy, and I wanted to know what else they could do. Or if they'd come back.

Soon enough, I detected the wild souls of three wolves. Two were near the Central City, but one wandered through the Outskirts. My neighborhood.

"I'll get that one." I pointed towards the one close enough to threaten Nanny and Little Viktor. "Other two are likely headed for the palace. They're yours, Captain. They've split up, but a silver arrow will find them."

"I have fought werewolves before, Miss Thorne, just this morning, and I know what silver does to them." Uanal's tone always made the people around him feel like an idiot, or at least me.

"Then you know this trick?" I pulled the Captain's sword from its sheath before he could blink and balanced the flat of the blade on my palm.

The blade was only coated in silver, while the core, including the handle, was toughest steel. That meant most of the silver was on the blade. It twisted on my palm until the silver tip pointed towards the Central City.

"A professor showed me this. Seems the essence of the silver crown that infects these dwarves is vulnerable to natural silver. They are drawn to one another, at war with each other's nature. Let this guide you to the wolves," I said. "But I recommend you stop by the Smith's district and find more silver weapons before you catch up to them. Drown them in silver if you have to. It's the only thing that will save you without me and the rest of the army to back you up."

Uanal took his sword back. "Very well, Miss Thorne. I will heed your advice. Don't expect your 'detective' agency will receive a consulting fee for this, however."

"I wouldn't dream of it. I do want to see case files when I ask in future, though. When this is all over." It was nice to imagine all of us surviving this. Imagining a future.

He smiled. "I wouldn't dream of it."

Same old Uanal.

I took off running for my house. The wolf was drawing closer, and there was no way I would beat it there. I only hoped Nanny would take some pity on the creature. Not likely.

10 CESURA

The farther I got from Thane, the more uncomfortable I grew, like an itch beneath my skin, burning along my nerves. Instead of whispering to me of power, the First Soul summoned my doubts, fear and hate, tempting me in new ways.

They need me, and I will be too late, I thought. Little Viktor and Nanny will die because I took time to help elves.

I wanted to be angry at the relic. We had a bargain: do this my way first. I knew it was cheating, but I was too afraid, too short on time to stop and fight it.

I used its power to help speed me along. Still, I was breathless when I reached my street.

I sent out my soul sense, hunting for any trace of the wolf. I wanted to kill it for daring to threaten my people, my city, but I couldn't sense it anymore.

"Where did it go?"

"Shhh." A voice in the shadows made me jump. I'd shut off my awareness of Duane so much, he was invisible to my soul sense.

That didn't explain why the wolf was.

I stood beside Duane and looked where he was pointing. I could see my house around the corner, Jorg the grall blocking the doorway in an intimidating way. Standing in the street was a naked dwarf.

I hadn't sensed any of them, and I panicked. What was happening to me?

You need me, the First Soul whispered. *You are weak without me.*

"Shut up."

"I didn't say anything," Duane pointed out.

"Not you." I'd been drawing on the First Soul too much, I realized. Its claws were stuck into me, draining me of hope.

I wouldn't let it win. I took a deep breath and tried to forget about it, just as Thane always made me forget with his glamours. The relic was of no importance right now.

Instead, I eavesdropped on the wolf-turned-dwarf I'd been tracking, trying to focus on what he was saying.

"For the last time, I'm here to speak to Miss Eva Thorne." He was a young dwarf, still beardless. I didn't recognize his voice, and I didn't remember meeting him before.

"She's not here," Jorg grumbled like thunder, windowpanes rattling all the way over to where Duane and I hid. "Please, get some clothes on and some silver shackles." Jorg rattled some cuffs, which looked like toys in his huge hands. "When you're no danger, then she might be obliged to listen when she does show up."

My soul sight flared to life again, and a wave of relief washed over me. I hadn't realized it was something the relic could take away from me. The First Soul was playing nasty games, and I was not pleased. We would have words, later.

The young dwarf's soul was bright, strong, but his voice trembled when he said, "Cannot do that. I won't surrender."

"And I won't let an enemy invader just walk away," Jorg retorted.

"I'm no invader. This is me home, and I'm not the enemy. I know what's at stake. I've seen Solheim. And Queen Gypsum."

As soon as he spoke of my old friend, I knew he had something I wanted.

I strode out, footsteps echoing on the damp cobbles. "I'm Eva."

"Oh, my." The young dwarf covered his nakedness with his hands, and then he shimmered into wolf form.

"Bastard." Jorg cursed.

Duane darted past me and tossed a vial of Avian goo. It exploded, sending up chunks of stone and a cloud of dust. The wolf stepped out of the cloud, shaking his head but unhurt.

I reached out for his soul and tried to shift him back forcibly, but this wasn't one of the fledgling creatures we faced on the battlefield. This one had royal blood, like Gypsum. I couldn't shift him without his consent.

He chose to go from wolf, to gray mist, to dwarf in less than a second. He was good ... and apologetic. "Sorry, Miss. All I's got is my fur to cover me in the presence of a lady."

"I'm no lady and have seen enough naked men not to care. We'll all feel more comfortable with your claws sheathed. Now talk."

As impossible as it was to force his soul to shift form, it was equally hard to read his life history there. Those with royal wolf blood were sturdier creatures, it seemed, more resistant to all magic. I would need to listen to his words, and hope he wasn't another liar. Rather, I assumed he would be, and I'd have to listen to what wasn't said.

"It's hard not to consider you's a lady, milady, but I'll try. Never comfortable hanging out with the boys naked either, but that's besides the point. I've risked me life coming here, so I might as well risk my pride. I want to prefect."

"What?"

"Did I get that wrong? I means de-fect. That's what I think the military types call it. I'm on the wrong side and want to get on the right one."

"A bold approach for a spy," Duane whispered.

"I'm no spy, but I can get you the silver crown. I know where it is."

I thrilled. He did have something I wanted.

Gypsum needed the crown to control the dwarfs, turn them into werewolves and make them attack their allies. Without it, she was nothing. Well, not nothing. She was a werewolf more dangerous than this one, but without that crown her armies would disperse.

I didn't think Lili was powerful enough to topple Highcrowne and the Avians without the dwarves behind her, else she would have done it long ago.

"You're willing to defy your Queen," I asked, "not to mention the liches of Solheim, and an army of your own kind to retrieve it?"

"I have to. Only ... I need help. I saw what you did in Faellion. I was there when you faced King Fharen. I was hiding when you ripped out Darden's ghost like it was prawn meat."

"A friend of yours?"

"No. He deserved it. But you scared me, which means you're scary enough to help me end this war."

I laughed. It was a haunting sound I'm told, and I saw goosebumps cover his exposed skin. Or was it the breeze? Highcrowne autumn was winter everywhere else.

"This is not the war," I explained. "This is a diversion." I knew the Dead God lay ahead, and I shouldn't even be wasting my time here, but I had no choice. This was my home too, and I understood why the young dwarf would risk everything for it.

"More soldiers are coming from Gernwold," the dwarf warned. "I don't see how we can win this unless I get that crown. Will you help me?"

Going right into the heart of the enemy, alone and vulnerable? It was the stupidest thing I could imagine. That's probably what Lili wanted, a quick death for me and a quick victory over the world, although this was an odd ruse to achieve it.

I gave the young dwarf an appraising glare, making him squirm even more. Finally, I said, "Yes. Crazy plans are right up my alley."

I had been looking for something to do, as I was no general. I was no soldier either, but if I could end the attack on Highcrowne with one stupid deed...? Stupid was something I excelled at.

I would have to face Lili sooner or later. Now was as good a time as any.

"I'll go too," Duane said. "I'm supposed to take you to Ulric, and I can't do that it you get yourself killed."

"So, it's loyalty to my uncle?"

"Always."

"I thought it was power and money that made you follow him, but Ulric has neither to offer you now. Someday you'll have to tell me why."

"No, I don't." When Duane went quiet, there was no digging anything out of him.

"Fine. Since we'll be sneaking through an army, a thief will come in handy."

"I've got your back, Boss," Jorg said.

"No," I told the grall. "I don't care if you work for Duane, you can't sneak anywhere. Stay here and watch over our house, my nephew. Please."

Jorg lowered his head. "Okay. But I'll miss all the fun."

"This won't be fun," I said, "and you'll have plenty to keep you busy if we fail."

I kissed his cheek, and it felt like this might be the last time I saw Jorg.

Duane pulled a spare jacket from somewhere— probably filched it from a clothesline when I wasn't looking—and handed it to the dwarf. "What's your name?" he asked.

"Harley."

"Isn't that a girl's name?" Duane pointed out.

He blushed but puffed out his chest. "It's the one me mum gave me, so don't be saying nothin' about it. I've heard it all growin' up."

"Sorry."

Harley spoke like the lowest born dwarf I'd ever met, but I knew he had royal blood. I wondered if he was aware. Dwarven genealogies were impossible for anyone to unravel, so I doubted it.

He was a born leader, though, so I said, "Show us the way."

"Closest approach to where the Queen is stayin', if you can't turn wolf like me and scale canyon walls that is, is across the Red Precinct bridge."

Where Gas and the Southerners were. "Just great."

The relic was influencing me, manipulating my emotions from despair to overconfidence at its whim. I knew I couldn't sneak anywhere without Thane's glamours, and I tried to reach out to him, soul to soul, contrite about pushing him away, but the First Soul intervened.

No. You only need my power.

Was that true? Could I face Lili now and end this?

You will serve me? I asked. Obey me? No more holding back power, no more interfering with my thoughts, I demanded.

Yes. It was an exultation.

I wanted to believe it. I went to reach into my belt pouch to hold the gem, gaze into its facets and see if there was any truth there, but the young dwarf interrupted with a question.

"Back in Faellion, you know, I was mighty curious about somethin'. You had the Elf King dead to rights. Why didn't you kill him?"

"I don't know." I thought back to how Fharen had begged, opening himself to possession by Thane, anything to save his miserable life.

I wasn't ready to beg the First Soul that desperately. Not yet. I kept my hand away from the belt pouch and forced out the relic's intruding thoughts.

To Harley, I added, "I've learned nothing is what it appears. Not your enemies and not your friends. You be careful. Heroes seldom live long."

Conrad had been a hero, my brother too.

"I'm no hero."

"You are. I can tell. It's a good thing. Where would any of us be without them?"

The hike to the Red Precinct took some time as we wended our way past barriers and other defenses. The First Soul tormented me the whole way, trying to twist my thoughts again.

Its promises and bargains were lies. But I'd come too far to retreat, when the opportunity to stop this lay just ahead.

My stomach grew heavy with dread when I reached the gate and saw a horde of automatons but no Southerners. I didn't have faith in gadgets, especially with Bell, the one person who knew how to keep them running, nowhere in sight.

"Hey! Anybody here watching this bridge?"

The automatons turned as one, the clang of metal feet against cobbles loud as they pivoted. They looked at me with glass eyes and my hairs rose. The undead at least had souls trapped in their corpses, or the Dead God animating them, but these things...they'd never had a soul.

I gulped. "I mean real, living people?"

The nearest automaton opened its mouth and a voice came out. No moving lips, just a dark opening with a speaker, and the effect was creepy. "We are watching. Rest assured, we will endanger humans only if necessary."

"Well, we just held them off at the docks, and they'll be testing for weak spots, so rest assured it will be necessary. Get your craven self out here and talk to me face to face."

The door of a dyer's house opened, and General Moore marched up to me. "Craven?"

"Let me revise that to *cautious*." My tone still called him a coward.

General Moore gazed on his mechanoid troops as he spoke. "Me and my men have faced the Dead God's forces—not the watered-down surrogates commanded by His generals here in the Three Kingdoms. For decades, our people had no Avians, no protections except one ford guarded by the Fortress of Mages. My men faced the worst He could throw at them and held.

Oftentimes with no warlock to back them up. We will manage."

I relaxed a bit. I could see now why Thane was so confident in their abilities.

"What did the Elf King promise you in payment?" I asked, curious.

"Everything we could dream of. That is why I know he does not believe we can win. When we do, he had best not renege, else we will take Aguragas's suggested path and destroy the elvish demons."

I raised an eyebrow. "Let's win then."

"Ready?" Harley asked me.

I nodded. "We have to move fast, before they know what we're after."

"Wait a minute," Duane cut in. "Is there a plan?"

My plan had been to call on the power of the First Soul to cut a swath through the army outside the gates, with the young dwarf leading the way to where we could find the crown. Duane could then steal it while I had everyone distracted. Harley must have been thinking something similar, because he hadn't requested specifics.

I opened my mouth to say as much, but Duane cut me off. "I didn't think so. A frontal attack is not a plan."

Did he know me that well? "What do you suggest?"

"There's a way under the bridge. Smugglers use it."

"Like you?"

"Smugglers in my employ. But I know the way. We sneak into camp. Harley here can go wherever he wants, as he's not under suspicion. You, Eva, destroy things to your heart's content, once we're in position. You're the distraction, while Harley and I slip in and grab the crown. Then Harley speeds the crown and you back with his wolf form."

"And you?"

"No one will even see me."

"Gypsum might when you try to steal the crown off her head."

"I have my ways."

"That plan should work," Harley said. "The crown isn't on the queen; else I wouldn't dare this. The liches keep it locked up until they need her to create more werewolves."

"Liches? This gets better and better. You definitely need me for more than a distraction," I insisted. "Harley, can you carry both of us out of there and the crown without getting caught?"

He puffed out his chest again. "Me job is message runner. Fastest there is. Well, maybe two others are good too, but you killed one of 'em, and we can hope the other one isn't nearby."

Hope was something I relied on a lot, so I nodded. "Sounds good to me."

"You will have an army after you when you return," General Moore said.

I'd forgotten he was listening.

"We have no choice but to draw them here," I argued. "It's the closest way back for us."

"You misunderstand," the general said. "That is a good thing. The bridge is rigged. Draw as many as you can onto it before we destroy it."

"But not us, right?" Duane clarified. "You will wait until we're safe."

"Of course."

The General seemed honest, but I didn't trust any-one.

"Who is in control of the detonator?" I asked.

"Miss Bell, the woman who set it up, but she won't act until I tell her to."

"I doubt that. You hold the trigger and you alone."

"Very well."

I waited until he had it, a metal box with goo-filled wires and a brass switch, before we set off.

Bell lurked in the doorway of a nearby building, a frown on her face. She didn't like anyone messing with her gadgets, but I didn't like Gas messing with her head, so this was the way it had to be.

The gate was braced shut with iron bars.

"How do we reach the bridge without being noticed?" I asked Duane.

He stomped on a trapdoor set into the stones near the gate. "Through here."

"Isn't that a major weak point in our defenses?"

He deftly picked the padlock on the trapdoor, unbarred it, and opened the lid to reveal spiked traps and walls etched with protective mage runes. "Nope," he said.

I agreed. Until he disarmed the runes and the traps in seconds.

"If the enemy has someone like you, they could get in here too."

"There's no one like me."

I rolled my eyes. "Another smuggler who's worked for you then and knows about this spot."

"The general's army here can stomp the goffers back in their hole. Let's go."

I let Duane go first, in case not all the traps were disarmed properly. It was a while since he'd been in the sewers, wearing fancy suits and escorting princesses instead, so he was probably rusty.

The traps were too. There were fresh ones by the entrance, but as we made our way through the narrow passage, I saw plenty of old, corroded ones that had accumulated over the years. I kept way back as Duane dealt with each.

I was more impressed by how he neutralized the mage runes.

"You learned magic?"

"No, I stay far away from it, but I also know I need some to keep the rest at bay." He showed me a leather band on one wrist, something he'd had for years, frayed and unremarkable, but I reached out with my soul sense and realized it was more than it seemed. Powerful magic ran through a silver wire woven within the leather braid. It was almost undetectable, and would be to a mage, shielded and compressed tightly within, but something about it was...alive. That's why I could see it with my soul sense.

"Where did you get that and what is it?" I asked.

"It's a long story. We're outside the wall now, so shhh." He held a finger to his lips, expertly cutting off my questions.

Same old Duane.

Harley was quiet, and I watched him closely, just in case he decided to turn wolf on me here. It was the perfect chance. That's why I also had one hand on the relic in my belt pouch.

You don't have to worry. I will destroy all who would take you from me, it said.

Because you want me for yourself?

Yes.

I removed my hand from the gem and wiped fingers on my dress. The relic had felt oily, the black miasma it exuded thicker than ever. Not for the first time, I began to worry if I was afraid of the wrong monsters.

The tunnel widened, and the walls turned from stone to wood and metal. A few dim rays of light made their way through gaps in the floorboards and walls, along with fresher air. We were underneath the bridge now.

Duane stopped, examining a whole new kind of trap.

It was Avian, green goo glowing within a glass flask, wires and tubes coiled through its rubber stopper. Several of the devices were tied to metal struts.

"Bell's work," Duane pronounced. "I'd know it anywhere."

"This is how they'll blow the bridge. There must be more," I said. I wanted to add he should be careful, but he already knew that. Still I warned Harley, "Don't even breathe on them."

He nodded, eyes wide with fright. Bell's gadgets scared me too and with good reason.

The bridge that spanned the Serpents Ribbon was huge, about five hundred yards wide. We were halfway across when I saw something move through a shaft of sunlight, deflecting and bending the dust-filled rays. A large section of wooden boards was missing from the side wall, big enough for a werewolf to have climbed inside.

My hand hovered over the relic, but I drew my Ashur instead.

Duane already had a dagger in hand before he stepped into the shadows.

Harley sniffed the air, and I sensed his nervous desire to shift, which made me even more uneasy. Then he relaxed and said, "Goblin."

I didn't put my sword away, because goblin mercenaries could be working for either side. They were unpredictable. And crazy.

This one had a bag of Bell's explosives like we'd seen elsewhere on the bridge. The bag hung loosely over one shoulder, the bombs visible because they were on the verge of falling out.

He or she, always hard to tell with goblins, was humming softly while fiddling with wires on yet another bomb.

"Stop what you're doing," Duane said, appearing as if from nowhere and putting a knife to the goblin's throat.

The goblin stopped humming and smiled hugely, rows of needle teeth glinting in the light from the opening.

"Human," it said. "Good to see humans. You pay now?"

"For what?" Duane asked.

"I plant bombs. Bridge will go big boom! Yes? Just likes blonde girl asks?"

"Bell hired you." I guessed. "Strange she'd delegate such a dangerous task to a goblin. Then again, maybe she's smart."

Goblins weren't the most reliable, but they were expendable. Most were crazed, bloodthirsty fighters who were lucky to survive past their twenties. Those who did grew wiser and more studious, at least from my experience, but they were rare.

Bell must have figured that, worst case scenario, the goblin screwed up and blew the bridge before anyone attacked, but that would just make this section of the city easier to defend. No dwarven regulars would reach the gate at least, only wolves who were a threat no matter what. Smart of her.

"Miss Thorne?" The goblin said in a very different voice. He even hunched a bit more, trying to appear more decrepit, and squinted as though in need of better eyesight.

"Doctor Ghunnan?"

Duane removed the blade. He hadn't recognized the doctor either.

"So good to see you, my dear, although I am in need of my spectacles to see you more clearly." He fished around in a pocket and donned them.

"You old faker," I said, disgusted. "You don't need them, do you? Why are you undercover now?"

"As I said, I am on a mission for Miss Bell. I volunteered, actually. Rather, I took the satchel of explosives and set out on my own before she could stop me. Nevertheless, we are in contact, and I have satisfied her that not coming to kill me for interfering was the right choice. You see, I do know even more about bombs than she does, but she would never admit it."

I pinched the bridge of my nose, feeling a headache coming on. "Whatever. I've no time for details. Just hurry and get out of here, because when our job is done, we'll need to blow this thing."

"Your job?"

Like I'd tell him. He was a spy for the goblin emperor, working for whichever side best served goblin interests, or his own side. I never knew. He was a friend, but I couldn't trust him as far as I could throw him, despite him being the size of a child which I could throw quite far.

"See you later, Doctor." I touched Duane's shoulder to get him moving.

The rest of the path was easier, no more bombs to avoid, so we made good time. I did wince, though, hearing Doctor Ghunnan clanking along behind us, hastily setting up explosives as fast as he could. I knew he wouldn't let us get away before discovering what we were up to.

"Hurry," I told Duane. "I don't see any more traps, so let's hitch a ride on Harley."

It wasn't just to get away from the doctor. I sensed something drawing nearer.

I would have called it a 'someone', except their soul was frayed and ancient, like no living thing's. Most people's souls felt fresh and bright as warm balls of sunshine, but this one was a patchwork of broken souls stitched together. It was powerful, don't get me wrong, but far from normal.

Like a blind person, it reached out groping fingers of magic, searching for other souls to steal pieces from. It thrilled when it found mine. And then the First Soul slapped those skeletal fingers of sense away, and the creature's curiosity burned.

The young dwarf transformed in a blur of white mist, werewolf hackles rising as he growled, "Lich."

"Time for that distraction," Duane told me.

"Get out of here first," I warned. "And be quick, as I'm not sure how long this bridge will stay in one piece."

Harley, who in wolf form was twice the size of any human, clutched Duane to his chest with a clawed hand, like an oversized doll. Then the wolf bounded the last stretch of the bridge, a blur of speed, vanishing into the gloom.

"Hallucinogens," the goblin muttered beside me.

"Get out of here!" I told him, but it was too late. It was distraction time.

I wrapped my hand around the relic in my pouch and called on power. It gave me more than enough to tear through the ceiling with green claws of fire.

Debris rained down, the goblin dodging faster than someone of his years should. I summoned a shield of energy to protect him, before I rose up to meet the lich on the surface of the bridge road above.

I knew this creature wasn't my mother before I set eyes on her—their souls were different—but I did recognize this one. I'd seen her along with two more of Lili's flunkies in Faellion, when they tried to imprison Fharen and steal the First Soul. Lili had teleported them all away, so I knew my mother could be any-where. It was the army's slow pace that had delayed her approach to Highcrowne.

"You remember me?" she asked.

"Of course."

It would have been hard to forget the walking corpse, her sexily cut outfit revealing spine and hollow ribcage, leathery breasts like sacks of oranges, and shriveled lips smeared with red makeup. She was the stuff of nightmares. The really disturbing kind.

"You remind me of Karo's mum, the sort who doesn't realize she's really too old to dress like that."

"I am younger than any Asheen before me, but the power one wields marks flesh as well as soul. I tore power from ancient hands, and I was rewarded with this glorious, if wrinkled, immortality. But come, let me show you how sweet my kiss remains." She took a step forward, still on the other side of the bridge, but I didn't want her any closer.

"Where is your mistress?" I asked, feeling goosebumps run down my back. I itched to look behind me, in case Lili was sneaking up.

She laughed, and that gave my goosebumps goosebumps.

"Lili of Solheim is not my mistress. No one is. We have common purpose is all. How hospitable of you to come out and play, for it will make this excursion so much simpler." She blew me a kiss, her shriveled lips painted red, protruding yellow teeth ruining the effect I think she was going for.

"So, she sent you to kill me rather than doing it herself?" I poked. "Sounds like she's made you her slave, whether you admit it or not."

"Lili understands you have the real First Soul, not the illusion Fharen foisted on her. She just wants to be sure."

"You're the guinea pig then? That's worse than slave."

"No, I am the distraction."

Wait a minute. That was my job.

I saw it then, activity over by the docks. Wolves tried to scale or jump the Avian mesh suspended across that side of the city, but one distant black form after another went up and came right back down again. Everything stopped at that barrier.

A chill wind howled through the river valley below, and I drew my cloak tighter. I looked over the side of the bridge—not my favorite thing to do, as I was afraid of heights—and I saw furry black shapes that weren't so distant. It looked like they had come off the boats to scale the steep bank. Werewolf claws cut into the stone like butter, and they climbed the massive cliff near the Red Precinct like I would a ladder. If I was inhumanly fast that was.

They were going right for General Moore's army. The Avians had placed no barrier on this side, and there was no sign they would swoop in to correct the situation before it was too late.

"No." I focused my soul sense on the nearest attacker and forced him back into dwarf form with a pang of regret. He fell hundreds of feet to his death.

More were coming.

The next wave was not wolves but regular dwarves following their queen's command, armed and armored, marching in practiced lines across the bridge. They bristled with spears and axes. The front ranks sat astride armored horses, and one rider sounded a war horn before the mass of them charged.

I started with the best intentions, trying to subdue their souls into a deep sleep, as Thane could do. But the First Soul's power surged through me, and my control was already lacking, so I ended up ripping out the soul of the one with the war horn just to shut him up. Then I ripped out the souls of those galloping inexorably toward me, and even the horses when they wouldn't stop.

I knew their lives as I extinguished them. One grumbler I'd seen at that Suffragist meeting. One who'd spent his life selling flowers on the street, although I'd never bought any. I'd always passed him by. Until now. I killed one after another until their lives blurred into a sound like a giant ocean wave crashing over me. What choice did I have?

Better they not suffer.

I ripped out five souls at once, hoping their individual voices would be lost in the din. They hovered over their bodies, and I fought the desire to pull them into me. The Dead God consumed to cleanse and free them from this life, but I couldn't do it, even though I had the same power. That would be utterly giving in, so I let their souls go, like dandelion seeds on the wind. I hoped they found their way to the Lands of the Dead, but I wouldn't escort them there.

The lich in front of me laughed again, and as she'd promised, it was a distraction—especially when she rose the fallen soldiers I'd killed.

This must have been what it was like when Solheim ruled ages ago. They'd send armies of innocents enslaved to them to die at the base of castle walls, then raise their abused corpses, so they could fight over and over until nothing remained.

I wished I'd gone with Duane and Harley. At least then I wouldn't be a part of all this.

The risen corpses were on their feet. They didn't speak to me with the Dead God's voice, and they were not so fast and strong as His creations, but in a way they were worse. The lich had summoned their souls and lashed them to their bodies. Each one I had torn free was called back and found no peace.

I didn't even know how to fight these creatures. As I thought about what to do, more living soldiers rushed me, side by side with the newly risen, whose stumbling gait and blank stares was the only thing to set them apart from the fresh wave of dwarven troops. I drew my Ashur and fought for my life, as worthless as it felt at that moment.

I parried a spear thrust, dodged a swung axe.

There was something about the smell of oiled steel, the creaking of leather, and labored breathing of dwarves as frightened as I was that made each moment stretch into an eternity.

I could die here as easily as they.

After that, I forgot about steel and reached for power. I paid less attention to each life I snuffed out. I tore through them like a field of wildflowers—better them than me—and soon the sky was filled with their floating seeds, their souls adrift on the aether.

Dead surrounded me then, but their souls were not mine to play with anymore.

In my mind's eye, I saw a Solhan rune branded into their light. It was the necromancer's name, Organa, and it didn't matter how much power the First Soul lent me, for this was a knot that required skill and not force to untangle.

I can give you fire, the relic tempted. *Burn them to ash. Send a hurricane of fire to burn them all.*

No. I would not risk incinerating Highcrowne along with them. *My way first*, I reminded it.

I realized this was a battle of wills. Organa and me.

Her red painted lips turned up into a shriveled smile as our gazes locked.

Dwarves and werewolves poured around me from all sides, keeping a safe distance. I was distracted, but I could still reap a score of them when they drew near enough to threaten me.

A torrent made it past me and past the automatons too.

Wolves shredded the gate with preternatural claws and cut footholds into the stone for the ordinary soldiers in their wake to climb. The mechanoids were strong, impervious to most weapons, but not to wolves who tore through metal as easily as mud. Automatons collapsed in twisted heaps, axes or swords swinging uselessly. Those with crossbows fared better, as they used elf bolts, silver-tipped, and the metal forced the wolves to shift.

And then General Moore and his Southern soldiers stepped forward with silver weapons, cutting down the dwarf and wolf alike with practiced ease, stopping the attack before it ever reached the civilians who clutched kitchen knives instead of daggers, ready to defend themselves and their children if need be.

The dead were more work for the Southerners, but they had a system like the city guard's, where they raised shields and surrounded a risen soldier, hacking it from all sides until the creature was destroyed. The Southerners were more skilled, though, and managed to trap groups of three at a time.

Still, Organa continued to create more. She would go on doing it until we were all dead—unless I found a way to unweave her spells.

She was raising them in batches of nine, like the Solhan Nine, and I wondered if that number was significant? All I knew was I could spend forever trying to erase her name from the risen souls around me, one by one, and never beat her. There had to be a better way. The key was in her somewhere.

I focused again, ignoring her leer, and looked into her soul.

Never thought I'd say it, but I wished I'd learned more necromancy when I'd had the chance. Now, I had to teach myself.

I watched the shifts of power within her as she turned a slain dwarf into her servant. I watched the twist and warp of the soul's light as she knotted it around a slender thread from her own soul. She was like a puppet master, controlling scores upon scores of strings. They stretched out from her in all directions. Each one was like the connection I had forged with Conrad before the Dead God took control of him from me.

I thought back to how I'd forged that connection, feeding Conrad's soul back into his body in an effort to undo what I'd done. Some of me had gone inside along with him.

That's how it worked.

It meant she could only control so many before her own soul was stretched too thin … before she was vulnerable. That's why there were necromancers, plural, here. Without the Dead God lending his power, it took several liches to wield so many risen.

I sent my soul sense searching for the others. The tattooed dwarf I'd seen in Faellion was near the main gate by the docks. His soldiers were battering at the Avian barrier, hoping to wear it thin.

Only two. The others I'd seen, and Lili herself, were elsewhere, doing who knew what. I'm sure it would be terrible for us, but all I could do was focus on the terrible right in front of me.

The Southerners and I—just in self-defense against the ones charging me every few seconds—were creating plenty of dead for Organa to wield, and she might reach her limit soon. Might. I didn't know what her limits were. Even more important, killing dwarves to overwhelm her capacity was a crappy strategy. In my heart, I knew these were all our people. There were only two true enemies on the field.

Time to take one of them down.

"Organa," I shouted to get her attention. She'd never taken her creepy glowing eyes off me, but I knew the bodies she controlled required focus. When she did give me her full consideration, her ability to create new risen slowed. I had a better tactic already.

"Yes, my sweet? Don't tell me you're not having fun?" she asked.

"Loads. It just occurred to me, however, that I know so little about you. They say the best way to truly know someone is to—"

"—kiss them?" she interrupted, blowing me another of her hideous kisses.

"Fight them."

I summoned green claws of energy and strode forward, severing the soul threads connecting her and her risen as I went along. Dwarves fell like sacks of grain, sometimes in the same spots they'd first died. It would take too long to release each soul, and Organa could easily reestablish her control over them, but doing so slowed her down. Time to slow her down even more.

I strode past the halfway point of the bridge and stretched green claws of magic as long as I could make them, until they were whip like, and struck her.

She had a protective shield, the magical barrier briefly visible as a pink bubble of electricity. I felt its effects too, the shockwave travelling back into my fingers and arms. My nerves tingled, numbed. What was I doing fighting an Asheen necromancer when I didn't know anything?

Because you have me, the First Soul whispered knowingly.

"That's exactly right," I said aloud, eliciting a quizzical expression from Organa.

"Who are you speaking to?"

"This." I pulled the First Soul from the pouch at my waist and held it high above my head.

Organa's adoring gaze locked onto the relic. She licked her lips. "Give it to me."

"Be careful what you wish for."

11 THE FACE OF THE ENEMY

I couldn't remove Thane's glamour over the gem, but I didn't need to. The First Soul tore free of its bindings all by itself and its darkness spread across the battlefield.

Organa smiled wider and reached out to the black miasma, expecting a kindred power, something steeped in death and decay like her. The First Soul was worse than Death. It was a void that wanted to absorb you, gobble you up until there was nothing left. Only love soothed it. Unconditional love for the un-loveable was the only way I could make it content for a time, but Organa had no love of any kind inside her.

The First Soul swallowed her. I don't mean like a fog of inky blackness, for it did that too. I mean the million souls stitched inside her were torn apart at their seams. It stole all that sustained her and left her a husk, the dimmest spark of her own soul left, and she crumpled like a rag doll. That faint spark of soul left in her was eerily similar to what I had left inside my sister after I drained her.

I shuddered at the memory of Ilsa, and the First Soul paused. Its black miasma shrunk in on itself, like a spider shriveling in the heat, and it was once again a colorless gem resting in the palm of my hand.

Why was I holding it? I put it back in its pouch and felt relief at having it out of my sight.

I felt tired too. Ready to lay down and sleep like the lich the relic had laid low in less than a heartbeat.

Organa did not rise, her desiccated form splayed across the planks of the bridge, tufts of cloth swaying in the wind that blew across the river and dispersed the unnatural fog.

The risen she had controlled fell when she fell. They were scattered around the walls and courtyard or slumped at the feet of human fighters who continued to hack and cleave, not knowing if they would rise again.

A surge of power bloomed in my soul sight. Had Organa recovered? I didn't think I could go through that again, especially if it hadn't worked the first time. I was so tired.

No, it wasn't her. Another lich appeared, climbing the ridge on the opposite side of the river valley. Not just any lich—Lili.

A war horn blew, echoing through the mountains. A fresh mass of dwarves marched into view on the other side of the bridge, a few wolves running excited circles on the flanks, yearning to be unleashed. Reinforcements from Gernwold.

At their fore stood a skeletal figure. My mother's eyes glowed green in her shrunken face, and her dead smile was chilling.

Then the First Soul dug into me. Even though I had not summoned its power, it reached out and wrapped its black tendrils around my throat. Needle tips of power dug into my veins. I could feel it reaching inward, toward my heart.

"Retreat," I croaked. I was the only one outside the walls, exposed, but I didn't know if the goblin still lurked stupidly nearby, so I drew another breath. It was a struggle with the Soul feeling its way into my lungs, and I cried, "Run!"

I staggered back toward the gate. The First Soul was a weight, dragging me down. It wanted me to stand and face them all, destroy them all, but its price was too high. It wanted to hollow me out and crawl inside. It wanted ... I was sick.

I threw up before reaching the broken gate.

The air was thick with the stench of rot. The corpses around me were only minutes old but decomposing before my eyes. They liquified into yellow and black ichor, becoming a quivering pile of sludge. I shivered to see souls trapped within putrid flesh. And then the liquid dried and exploded in a cloud of noxious gas.

The First Soul shielded me, sapping my veins even more. Others were not so lucky. Lili's blight decimated most of the Southern soldiers. When the putrid gas struck them, their skin burned and blistered as if touched by alchemist's acid. Those lucky enough to avoid the putrid explosion linked their shields and ducked behind them, the gas billowing around and burning a few on the edges before it dissipated. At least those in the center were protected.

A figure ran out the gate, waving wildly for me to get across. It was Bell.

I knew it was time to blow the bridge, but they were waiting on me. Bell didn't want me dead after all? That was a good sign. We could be friends again, if we all didn't die here.

Soothing, whispering promises, nothing I tried could lull the Soul back to sleep. All I could do was focus on my feet, making them take one step after another.

Lili drew closer. The corpses within Highcrowne's walls had been destroyed, but a fresh wave of dwarven troops were right behind her. Their marching rattled the bridge so much I had to hold on to the side. I used my arms to drag myself forward.

A wall of air hit me from behind and slammed me down to hands and knees. The explosion was accompanied by a rush of sound, like the largest waterfall I'd ever heard, but then it was all muffled. I could barely hear anything, my ears ringing. Dazed, I turned and saw the bridge shear into four sections, tumbling apart like a flower opening. The stones crashed into the Serpent's Ribbon below, crushing some of Lili's sailing ships and blockading the harbor and docks.

Before the dust settled, wolves leapt across the rubble, jumping section to section.

I reached for power and couldn't find my own, but the First Soul lent me tendrils of inky darkness, which encircled the approaching wolves. They transformed instantly at the icy touch, and their howls of pain made me shiver.

The First Soul's insistent whispers were impossible to ignore now. *See how easy that was. We have no need to run. We are invincible—as one.*

I struggled to sit. I sensed its wordless offer to help me stand, and I needed the help, desperately, but I knew it lied. Nothing was easy now.

I felt hollow. It fed me power only to take it away again, stealing a bit of me each time. I was not stronger than before. I was weaker.

I looked up to the sky and everything spun. I threw up again before laying on my back, wishing the sky were blue instead of lead gray. Stone gray. Like the lid of a sarcophagus.

Something floated across my vision, like dandelion fluffs but larger. White parachutes. Unable to move, I watched the sky like it was a stage play.

Dirigibles passed overhead next, cylindrical clouds of elegant elvish design, but others soon crowded in among them like nothing I'd seen before: armored and dotted with catapults. They were built for war and manned by wild-eyed goblins. As I recalled, the air in a dirigibles' balloon was flammable, yet the goblins had campfires on their decks, which they used to ignite the flaming arrows they shot down at the dwarvish forces. Crazy.

The elvish airships carried mages. They bombarded the enemy around the broken bridge with magic vines, entangling them like flies in a web. It seemed more humane at first, until they followed up with mage fire to incinerate the helpless soldiers.

I was helpless too. Too weak to shout at them for this stupidity. We were all fighting the wrong enemy.

A parachute shrouded me, and I couldn't breathe. The crowning piece of my tomb.

But the goblin the chute had been carrying dug me out, wrestling piles of silk aside and almost suffocating himself. When we were both free, he lifted his goggles to reveal the familiar face of Doctor Ghunnan.

He squinted and quickly replaced the goggles with spectacles. "At your service, Miss Thorne."

"Have you seen Duane?" I asked. "And the were-wolf he was with?" Their side of the river was being mercilessly bombarded, and I couldn't imagine either escaping.

"Afraid not." The goblin helped me sit, and we were the same height for once. "After I fled your side, which was some time ago, although I doubt you noticed, I took a short jaunt through a nearby 'doorway' and joined my people waiting on the other side of the Avian's mountain. Coordinating elves and goblins into a unified fighting force seemed to be a never-ending point of debate, which I had retreated from to aid Bell's bomb-setting efforts. Seems they either figured it out on their own or decided they'd run out of time."

"Sorry to interrupt, Doctor, but there's another werewolf coming our way." I didn't want to call on the First Soul, and I couldn't find my own strength. I searched for it, for even that spark of soul I'd stolen from Ilsa, but I felt washed out.

"Werewolves? Again?" The goblin frowned. "All I see are huge war dogs and naked lunatics suffering a dwarven variation of the human plague. Fortunately, I've devised an antidote." He loaded his crossbow with a hollow bolt housing a glass vial of gray liquid. "Colloidal silver to burn out the infection permanent-ly."

He shot the wolf, which had gotten a little too close for my liking. Not only did the creature transform back into dwarf form, the cloud of silver created on impact billowed out in all directions, catching more wolves at the edges of Lili's newly arrived forces. They collapsed, squirming as the element infused their blood. Would it work as the doctor believed? I didn't think it so, but it would certainly last longer than a wound from a silver blade.

I smiled weakly. "Glad to have you on our side. You are on our side?"

"Of course. And on the side of the Emperor's new ally, Queen Hilja."

"Queen Hilja? She finally stopped propping up that idiot, Prince Gallan, and took charge herself?"

"Indeed. Although a goblin army behind her did help. I am glad I was able to complete those negotiations, despite our thrilling side excursion to defeat Harbinger."

That's what he'd really been doing in Faellion. Always schemes within schemes when it came to the doctor.

I recognized the seal of the Elf King on the lead dirigible now. It was a massive, gaudy thing, not as impressive as *The Mathésis*—the largest ever built before Bell and I crashed it—but designed more to elven tastes. Magical construction made it seem like wings of white silk kept it aloft, not to mention the glowing sparkles emitted by chained pixies. I'd have to have another discussion with Hilja about how slavery was not a nice thing.

I'd also have to explain Thane. Later. If we survived. She couldn't know what he truly was, no one could. She would be surprised to see her father still alive, and with me, so I'd have to think of some explanation besides the real one.

The werewolf advance was slowed by the doctor's silver gas weapons, and the remaining dwarf soldiers were soon occupied fighting the goblins who dropped from the sky on top of them. Goblin mercenaries were known for their ferocity and taste for blood, but among that wild horde were also groups of trained commandoes: Elite goblin soldiers with crossbows, bombs and cunning to make them even more dangerous.

But the enemy had a bigger weapon on its side than teeth, claws and force of arms—they had Lili of Solheim.

She watched me calmly from across the broken bridge, her expression curious, as I imagined she would observe an animal in a trap. Had she known the First Soul would do this to me?

"Come, Eva." Her voice was inside my mind. The distance didn't matter. It sounded like she was standing beside me, and I stopped listening to whatever else the goblin was saying.

Lili reached out her hand, and with my soul sight I saw long fingers of green energy tear into my chest and clutch my heart. I knew she was after my soul, and I couldn't fight her.

She's mine, the First Soul whispered. That whisper carried along those reaching fingers of power and vibrated them, shook them so hard Lili's grasp on me broke. She staggered back.

"I thought I was yours? Why did you flee from me and let Ulric steal you, when you had promised me so much?"

Lili had been betrayed by the relic. It must have whispered its sweet nothings of power to her as well. She had succumbed and was left a deathless shell. And now, despite all the Dead God had given her, she hungered for more.

And now that I'd given into the Soul, would it use me up and discard me too?

Shh, the First Soul soothed. *You are special in a way she never was. The last living child of the last Keeper.*

Lili reached out again, but this time with no subtle spell. She sent the icy shadow of death, the one that had frozen my wrist and left it a gray husk that required my will to keep animated. All with one touch. I did not think I could survive another.

The shadow crept across the broken bridge, stretching longer and longer, as shadows do at sunset, but it was almost midday. Anyone in the conjuration's way, whether goblins, dwarves, or werewolves ... they screamed when it touched them, their voices turning into a pathetic mewl like an animal that knew it was doomed. They died. The life—not souls for I saw them flee—the warmth, the spark of life within each cell of their body was drawn from them to feed the shadow. The darkness grew denser, larger, its reaching fingers longer and longer.

The instinct to flee fluttered in my stomach, but thoughts and action froze at the memory of its agonizing touch.

The First Soul laughed at my terror and at Lili. *This was my gift to you, it said. You cannot turn it against me and my chosen one if I do not allow it. Go and leave us be. I fled from you and hid beneath the deep ocean until my beloved came for me. You are the one who should hide now.*

The First Soul's 'light', which was the opposite of a true souls' light, touched Lili's creeping shadow and pushed it back. The shadow fled back to her, merging with the feeble shade her half-dead body cast in the noonday glare.

The First Soul's aura stretched farther, chilling those around Lili until they fell to the ground, huddling for warmth. More and more of her forces screamed from the cold shadow that was turned fully on them now.

"Stop," I ordered the Soul. "Stop it. They don't deserve to die like that."

Howls filled the air, and I thought the First Soul had disobeyed me. But it hadn't. Its aura withdrew and curled up into a sleeping beast, safely stowed in my belt pouch. I felt its purr, or its equivalent of that contentment. It obeyed me—for now.

Lili retreated. Her decayed gown blowing in the wind as she climbed astride a white horse and rode off.

The howls continued, and I realized they were not pained but joyous.

Dwarf after dwarf threw down their weapons. Wolves transformed into naked soldiers and cheered. Was this because of Lili's retreat? Then I saw the young dwarf from the Outskirts carried aloft on burly shoulders. It was Harley—wearing the silver crown.

I spotted Duane then, or he allowed himself to be spotted. Gypsum was shackled with silver, and he dragged her behind him.

He smiled and shouted across the canyon. "You just had to destroy the bridge?"

The liches were gone, and the dwarves had given up the fight.

Victory. For everyone but me.

12 THE HEIGHTS OF IDIOCY

I couldn't stand. I didn't have full control of my limbs. Something else did, and *it* struggled with the unfamiliar. Like an infant learning to lift its head or crawl. I saw it with my soul sense, some of the relic's black tendrils were inside me, taking me over.

I was the puppet now.

"No." I fought to push it out, heaving and retching until I threw up what remained in my stomach. It was too strong.

Everything went black. I don't know how long I was out, but it was long enough for Duane to have found a way across the gorge. He was next to me, shouting, "Wake up," over and over in my ear and slapping my cheeks.

It didn't hurt. Pain and sound were both distant. My body felt distant. Not my own.

"Eva." Thane was there too. He held me, and soul to soul he whispered, *What have you done?*

Was he speaking to me or to the First Soul?

"Nothing I didn't have to," I said. Or was that the First Soul using my lips? I was confused. At least the words, whoever's they were, shut Duane up. But only for a moment.

"I need to take her to Ulric, now," he said. "It may already be too late."

Thane stiffened. "Why now?"

I opened my eyes, trying to focus on their exchange, blurred faces hovering over me, tight jaws. I saw Duane swallow, but his expression was neutral. I felt the turmoil in Thane, the fear for me.

"I'm not dying," I tried to say, but the words came out, "They will all die." I didn't think I had control of my tongue. Or my mind.

"Ulric can heal her," Duane said. "He didn't explain why, but he warned me something like this could happen. I've already delayed too long."

I don't know how to help you, Thane admitted to me. *I'm sorry.*

Good, the Soul in my body replied.

"Alright," Thane said, "but I'm coming as well."

"The Elf King is not welcome where we're going. If that's who you are." Duane knew Fharen. As good as Thane was at mimicking those whose bodies he took

WAR OF THORNES

over, he had slipped up. Fharen had never shown such tenderness or concern toward Ilsa or anyone.

Thane turned his gaze to the onlookers. The Southerners were there, Bell, goblins and surrendered dwarves. It was too public a place and too delicate a time for him not to be Fharen.

"She carries something of value to me," Thane said in Fharen's best snooty tone. "You would be unwise to lay a finger on it, thief. When she is well again, bring her to me immediately."

"Of course, My King," Duane said, but I knew him well enough to know he was not fooled.

Duane found a small wagon and loaded me in the back. I couldn't help but recall a similar hand-drawn cart, the one Erick had used to bring me to the ritual that changed my world. He had opened my eyes to real darkness. I'd been helpless like this then too. The memory sent my heart racing, and I managed to get one hand under my own control.

I used it to swat at Duane when he put a rolled-up blanket under my head.

"Ow. I'm trying to help you, Eva."

"I don't want help." That was definitely the First Soul talking, because I did want help. I just wasn't very graceful about accepting it.

He retreated to the other side of the wagon, took up its long handles and pulled, getting his revenge by hitting every bumpy cobblestone in his path. At least that's how it felt.

I saw Doctor Ghunnan's face at one point, Bell's too. They peered in at me and seemed to be arguing about whether I needed a rescue or not. When no rescue came, and we made our way deeper into Highcrowne, I saw other faces, grasping climbers from the palace thrilled at seeing me laid low, as well as people I didn't know, taking in the spectacle of a prone Solhan necromancer. That's what I was. A bump in the road from becoming a lich.

Your fate will not be Lili's, the First Soul reassured me. *Surrender fully, lend me your arms and legs willingly. Let me speak through your mouth when the time calls for it. Give me something akin to the life I was never granted, and I will ensure that your life lasts forever. Exactly as you are. You will never know age or disease or death. You can leave Death behind, destroy Him. With my help.*

"No." My voice was mine and I shouted the word with such force, Duane paused and came back to check on me.

"Eva? What's happening to you?"

"Leave me alone." My words were meant for the invader inside me, but Duane reluctantly nodded and went back to the task Ulric had set him.

I gained a little more control as my internal battle against the First Soul waged on. I could move my head now, and I watched the people watching me from upper stories of buildings, the occasional bird gliding through gray sky. Where was a dragon's shape when you needed a godmother? Where was Olyve? She had set me the task of retrieving the First Soul before Harbinger could. She had watched what became of Lili. Had she known this would happen? Had she even cared?

I was sitting up by the time we reached our destination.

In the heart of the Central City, the Avian mountain rose above the palaces, its snow-capped peak serving as the final ornament atop the frilly layer cake that was Highcrowne. The peak had looked down on me all my life, so close yet unreachable.

Duane helped me into an outfit that seemed built for an excursion to the end of the world. The jacket was thicker than anything I used in the middle of Highcrowne winter, the boots and gloves so puffy I doubted I could move with them—even if I'd been able to move.

"It is the end of the world," he said after I commented.

"*Edge* of the world is what I meant to say." My mouth still isn't working.

I knew my battle with the First Soul wasn't over. It's dark tendrils still lingered inside me, searching for a place to take hold. I had sent it into a tactical retreat. It knew I would have no choice but to willingly call on it if—or when—I faced Lili again. Let alone the Dead God. I was cornered, while it could afford to wait.

"What happened to you?" he asked again.

"I'll tell you when you tell me what my Uncle wants, where we're going, and what this is all about."

Silence. Typical Duane.

I was dying of curiosity, especially as Duane hadn't needed Fharen's help to get us this far. He'd flashed some amulet when wheeling me through the central gates and whenever troops came to investigate. Anything that kept elves from harassing humans had to be powerful magic—or backed by political power that even my uncle had never wielded before. What was going on?

We were beside what royals might call 'a shack' at the base of the peak. Everyone else would call it a mansion. Probably had six bedrooms, several living rooms. The grounds were terraced and manicured, crowded with noxious gardens, typical elven ostentation. Its main point of uniqueness was its proximity to the base of the mountain, which was only a few strides away.

No structure was allowed to touch the sheer, gray stone of the Avian's sanctum. Not trees or grass even, and certainly not stairs. The only thing marring the perfect surface was a copper tube that descended from the cloud-shrouded apex in a straight line, before it bent at the ground and followed the surface, disappearing into a squat mage tower nearby.

"Avian goo is supplied through the pipe," Duane explained, "so don't touch it. It's volatile."

"I hadn't planned on touching anything. There's nothing to touch. I'm all geared up, sweltering in this coat, but there's nowhere to go, and I can barely stand." I could put weight on one leg but not the other. It was like the First Soul wanted to remind me it still had a claim to some part of me.

All of you, it argued.

I shuddered, and Duane grabbed my shoulder to steady me.

"We're going up," he said.

"Climb? I can't climb. Didn't you hear me about the not standing part? My arms are even less reliable."

He smiled. "It's safe, don't worry."

He showed me how to pound in a spike and secure a rope we could share between us. There was a whole lot of detail about spacing, where to put your feet and hands. He was going first and doing all the work, but I needed to know what to do if he fell.

I couldn't hear any of it because my heartbeat was loud in my ears. I couldn't do this on one of my best days.

"No." I shook my head so much I thought it would fly off. "Tell Ulric to get his ass down here, dream walk again, anything."

Duane looked seriously at me for a moment, before he said, "Oh, you thought I meant we have to climb? I was keeping you entertained. We don't need this. Avians are magical, and they can fly."

He dropped his pack and other gear and even kicked off his spiked boots. "They can't carry much weight, though. Seriously. You need to take it all off. Except the coat. It is cold up there."

I almost shoved my spiked boot in his smiling face. "You bastard. I'm never trusting you again."

"Nothing new then."

"You're wrong. I always thought you trustworthy and reliable—I can trust you to reliably look out for your own interests. Practical jokes don't suit you."

"I've told you often enough, you don't know me."

I could read souls, but I shied from reading his. He was right. I didn't know him, and I didn't want to. I was tired.

"Can we go? It's a long way to Solheim, and this is only the start for me."

His rakish smile faded. "I'm sorry. I thought you could use a laugh."

"I'm not laughing."

"But you do feel relieved you don't have to climb?"

A tiny smile turned up the corners of my mouth. "Yeah. I do."

An even bigger smile spread across my face when the first Avian descended through the clouds.

The Avian glided down, circling to a gentle landing beside me. He was brown and slim, taller even than me, not counting the cream-colored plumes on his head. Black bird eyes were set close together, centered above his hooked, orange beak. Standing, his wings hung like a cloak, and a pair of talon-like hands reached out to shake mine.

"Truthspeaker," he said. "It is an honor to meet you."

"Me? I mean. Likewise." No one spoke to Avians, and I'd already met three in the last year. I was lucky. Or unlucky, depending on how you looked at it. It was a curse to live in interesting times but even worse to be the source of interest.

Another Avian flew down beside us, this one's cream-colored feathers speckled with gray, and he had a black ruff around his neck. I knew him. Sort of.

"I never got your name before you dived out the door of that dirigible. You knew there were werewolves onboard." My tone was less honored with this one. He'd abandoned me, and I was still kinda annoyed.

"My name is Roosal, while my friend here is Naren," he said, indicating the brown one. "And when are there not wolves about when they number among our citizens? I do apologize for leaving, but I prefer to observe, much like our Voidwalker friend. You were more than capable."

"I crashed the ship and was almost sacrificed to the Dead God. I almost ended the world."

"*Almost* is far from truth. Almost never happened—it is a lie based on worry and supposition. Speak truth among us, and you will always be welcome. By 'always' I do mean eternally, alive or dead. You have brought the soul jar you stole from Lili?"

"What?" My brain had whiplash from his strange shifts in subject matter. And how did he know about that jar?

"Yes." Duane dug it out of a small sack I hadn't noticed wedged into a corner of the wagon. When had he stolen it from my house? Or put it in there? Damn, he was sneaky.

"Tell me what in all the hells is going on and why you want what's mine." I reached out to take the jar from Roosal, but the Avian tucked it under one wing and stepped back. I stumbled just trying to reach him and had to grab hold of the cart again.

"All will be revealed when you are our guest. It was not safe for your uncle down here, which is why he is our guest as well. It is unsafe for all of us, so we should not tarry."

Roosal removed a rope bracelet from around his wrist, like the one Duane had used to circumvent mage wards. Between each braid writhed lines of glowing Avian goo. He stretched the loop between his scaly fingers and it suddenly expanded. He tossed it over my head, and it dropped down to encircle my waist. I rose slightly, my toes barely touching the ground.

"It displaces mass into the Void. I understand you have been learning of these things from Olyvandra," Roosal said.

"You know about her?"

"It would be simpler to specify the things we do not know. Otherwise you will endlessly be sharing your dismay, and the awe of the young can grow quite tiresome when the wise have experienced marvel after marvel many times over. It is important, however, that you be aware Olyvandra cannot and will not help you."

"Stupid Unmentionable neutrality." I frowned. I'd been hoping she'd put in an appearance at some point, even if just to help me understand the Soul better.

"You misunderstand," Roosal said. "She has been captured."

"What?"

"Kerrik waits above, and he can tell you more. Come." The Avian spread his wings and launched himself into the air.

I wasn't sure what I was supposed to do, and I didn't know who Kerrik was, but the answer to the first question turned out to be 'scream'.

Roosal circled around and grabbed my shoulders with clawed feet, which were as agile as his hands, and I was suddenly flying, gaining altitude rapidly. My scream cut short when the soul jar slipped from the Avian's feathery pocket or wherever he'd put it. I caught the jar and held it tight, as the sheer rock face of the mountain blurred past.

The only thing in focus was the other Avian, who carried Duane beside me at the same incredible speed. Duane looked as comfortable and relaxed as if he were leaning against a wall in the old neighborhood.

"How many times have you done this?" I shouted over the wind whistling past my ears.

"A few," he shouted back.

I ground my teeth. He was piquing my curiosity. What were Duane and Ulric doing with Avians? Phrased another way, why were our revered rulers harboring hated murderers, thieves, and necromancers?

This Truthspeaker wanted to start hearing some truth. Right now.

I was glad for the coat, which was drenched after we passed through the cloud layer. It was hard to breathe; the icy air made my lungs ache and my head light from lack of oxygen.

I almost spent my last breaths screaming for help, but as soon as we reached the peak, I was fine. Sunlight warmed my damp clothes and glinted brightly off snow. Cave openings and standing stones dotted the white surface below.

My magic sense told me the standing stones positioned in concentric patterns were what made it possible to breathe. The stones had etchings filled with glowing goo. I could read the language and recognized spells for life, air, food, water, warmth—home and hearth. I couldn't say how I recognized them ... until I read the spells for knowledge and wisdom.

Just being in the Avian's home made you comfortable, as well as smarter, wiser and kinder.

Roosal set me down, and the snow made a soft sound, not the crunch of ice I expected, because the ring around my waist made me as light as air. Roosal removed it, and my feet sunk deep into the pristine white surface.

Our guides led Duane and me to the largest cave entrance. There were dozens of smaller caves, and I wondered if each was a different home or workplace? I had no idea how Avians lived.

I had imagined, however, something grander than the elven palace once inside the main cave—these were the original rulers of Highcrowne, after all, the oldest race outside the gods themselves as far as I knew—but the wide cave mouth framed a small chamber no larger than my living room. The only furniture was a throne made of copper and colored glass, the floor before it covered in sticks and shiny trinkets, like a magpie's nest.

The Avian on the throne looked like a Magpie too. She was black, except for white feathers circling her neck and outlining her wings, which were so long they hung like a gown. When she stood, she revealed scaly ankles adorned with gem-encrusted bracelets.

"Queen Calka." Duane bowed, nudging me to do the same.

I curtsied, barely remembering how to do it. I avoided curtsies as a rule, but for the Avian Queen I'd make an exception. "Your Majesty."

"Rise, Truthspeaker. You carry my feather." She raised a wing, and I saw where a white one had been clipped off. "It pleases me we can finally meet."

I was stunned when she hugged me, wrapping me in wings and pushing my face into her warm chest. I tried not to swallow downy fluff. Her heart beat faster than mine did when terrified, yet she exuded only calm. I'd never had a mother—at least one that wasn't trying to kill me—but this was what I would have wanted. Other than her being a bird of course.

It felt cold when she pulled away. "Pleased? By me?" That was a first. Usually people found me a pain in the ass.

"Yes. Of all the denizens of Highcrowne, only you stood up to King Fharen."

"A whole bunch of rebels, like Bell, have done that. I just tried to have him arrested."

"Exactly. You chose law over violence, peace over conflict. You spoke truth even when none would listen. They listen now."

"Because Fharen told them to."

"Because you told Thane to tell them to. You must always speak truth to me."

"Roosal said the same. Okay, here's the truth—I'm no hero. I'm scared as hell I'm the bad guy, especially as I tend to fall in love with them. What the hell am I doing? Please. I need someone to tell me."

Maybe it was the motherly hug or the standing stones with their enchantments, but I had let it pour out, and it felt good. I didn't even care Duane was listening. I was too frightened to be guarded.

"And the First Soul," I began, but I felt it twitch its tendrils inside me, and the leg it controlled weakened. I fell to the floor.

Calka helped me stand and opened her beak in what I interpreted as a smile. "I cannot tell you your truth. It is not as absolute as you might think. A lie to one person may be another's truth, if they believe it. You say slavery is an evil and you speak that truth. You say law should be the first resort and murder the last, and you speak that truth. That is why I have honored you in the past and seek to help you now."

"You can help me?" All my limbs weakened, and the queen was not strong enough to support me this time. Duane helped me into a litter that Roosal fetched from a corner of the room.

The First Soul not only sucked away my strength, it drained the warm glow of joy Calka and the Avian home had infused me with. Into that hollow in my gut, it whispered, *You are mine. No one can help you. Accept it.*

"You can't help me," I repeated to Calka. "I'm a hypocrite. I killed Jhenna. I killed Erick, and a troll, Yal his name was. I knew his whole life as I drank him into me. Same for a dwarf-turned werewolf-named Darden—and I killed Conrad. Thane wanted me to believe I hadn't, but I did. Not to mention all the foot soldiers I just slaughtered protecting Highcrowne. I am as much a murderer as Duane here. In fact, I think I may be much, much better at it."

"You have stopped lying to yourself," Calka said. "Now I must do the same. My people are dead, Eva. Only we remain. That is why we need you."

The Avian I'd once met among the Unmentionables stepped forward. He put a hand on her shoulder. Roosal and Naren drew closer, and it turned into a group hug. Who knew Avians were so cuddly?

"Wait a minute," I said as it dawned on me. "Four of you? That's all?"

Calka nodded, and thick mucus formed in the corners of her eyes. Their equivalent of tears.

"What about the one I read about in textbooks, the beautiful golden one? Your mate?"

"Saral. He chose to be my representative on the Crown Council when it became unsafe for me as the one remaining female of our kind. He was killed by an assassin who was after me."

A lump formed in my chest, and I remembered the coin Aguragas gave me, the death mark that bore Calka's image. He had wanted me to give it to Duane.

I glared at him.

Duane raised his hands. "It wasn't me. Gas came to me, but I refused. I don't know who it was, but he was good."

"All the people you killed for him, for yourself, why did you refuse?" I couldn't keep the accusation and disbelief out of my voice. I knew I was as bad as he was, and I shouldn't judge, but Avians ... they were the magic in my world.

Mages, necromancers, warlocks and whatnot, none of them were as impressive as the mysterious Avians protecting the Kingdoms from the hell of this war. I had always believed in and revered them more than I did the gods, because they were right here with us. To think that one of their kind was murdered? I felt sick.

"I have served Calka since the day she spared my life," Duane said.

I sensed a story there, but Duane went quiet again, and Calka changed the subject.

"The point is, we cannot protect the Kingdoms anymore." She sat on the cave floor, the raw ground dirtying her feathers. "All depends on you, Eva. You are the one thing that can save our world—or end it."

Compared to my previous experience with Avians, this conversation had been fairly cogent until now.

"What do you mean? You want me to defeat the Dead God? I'm working on it, but I don't know how. I could use your help."

"Even if you gathered all those who follow you and believe in you, and all those who hate and fear you, and all those you fear or revere, Avians, Unmentiona-bles ... even if you took us all to war, we could not defeat a Primal God. That is why the Compact was made. Why you must not try to defeat Him. You must leave things as they are, an eternal stalemate."

"Stalemate?" I hissed. "An assassin killed one of you, while the rest of you huddle in fear. The Kingdoms are being divided between elves, dwarves and human refugees with, literally, no place left to go. Lili's army almost kicked our asses just now—with no hordes of the dead at her back, just our own weakness to blame. We are well past stalemate and on our way to extinction."

"There are worse things than the Dead God," she said.

I knew what she meant. The First Soul.

That's why I needed it.

You see, the relic whispered in my mind. *There is no fight left in any of them. Surrender to me, and where there is defeat, I will give you victory. Where there is despair, I will give you power.*

"What choice is there?" I asked aloud.

Didn't the Avians, with all their magic and ancient knowledge, have some wisdom, anything they could offer as an alternative? Because, if this was the key to unlocking the First Soul and sending the Dead God away, if losing my soul and my life was the price demanded ... there might be no choice but to pay it.

"The Fates rule all," Calka said, studying my eyes. She must have seen something desperate there, because she added, "But, while even Time and gods, Primal or Elder, bow to Their impenetrable desires, there is a paradox: Fate is immutable, but souls choose their own fate from the straws on offer. Long or short, soft or sharp, bright or dull, we each choose the makings of our nest. But your straw, Eva, has entangled its sharp thorns throughout so many nests. We all live or die by your fate. What fate has your soul chosen?"

"I don't know." I didn't peer into my own soul. Ever. I didn't want to see the darkness within, barely kept in check. I certainly didn't want to see some unavoidable fate written there.

Avians were wise and immortal—but not necessarily right.

"I don't know anything. But when I decide to do something, I do it, and I've come here to speak with my uncle. Take me to him."

She inclined her head. "As you wish."

Calka spoke in Avian, with a rattle in her throat that reminded me of a crow's laugh. At her command, the Unmentionable stepped forward and gestured for Duane and me to proceed him onto the mountaintop.

"My name is Kerrik," he said when I asked.

"Ah, the Kerrik who Roosal mentioned earlier. You know what's happened to my godmother, Olyve?"

My legs were weak, and I tired a few steps outside of the main cave. I hadn't given into the First Soul yet, but it sensed my weakening resolve and was hunting for a way to dig its dark tendrils deeper into me.

I stood panting for a while, and Duane held out an arm to steady me. I let him. I even leaned on his shoulder as we caught up to Kerrik. The Avian had kept plodding ahead through the snow, leaving V-shaped tracks for us to follow.

And he hadn't answered my question, so I persisted. "Olyvandra? Where is she?"

"Captured."

"By who?"

"The enemy."

I was beginning to suspect Avians were not cryptic and wise, but mad. They'd lived too long, and the end of the world had broken them first.

The huge, copper pipe that ran all the way down the mountain originated in a small cave nearby. I stared, curious to learn where their miraculous goo came from.

"Do not go into that place," Kerrik insisted. "It is not safe."

I knew when someone was hiding something, but it wasn't important in the grand scheme. I had bigger problems than Avian mysteries. It's not like I cared to steal their invention. If the goblin had been here, then they'd have to worry.

We entered another cave, this one wide and shallow. It gave way to a narrow tunnel, which was blocked by a silver gate. It reminded me of the gates to the Central City, ornately carved bars that looked like flowers and vines—but which were still bars. There was even a lock, which Kerrik opened using a goo-etched key.

"So, Ulric is a prisoner?"

"No. This is for his protection. An assassin reached Calka's private chambers, but Ulric is far too precious to risk."

"Ulric? Really?" I looked a question at Duane. He seemed to come and go as he pleased, so maybe he could explain the strange world I found myself in.

"Go ahead, Eva," he said. "It's for Ulric's protection as Kerrik says. I swear."

Duane had never lied to me. Not once. I called him a lying thief because he bent situations into opportunities for himself and did plenty of things that were downright despicable.... But he never told me something he didn't believe was truth. Even the annoying prank he'd pulled earlier hadn't required a single lie. He must have spent a lot of time among Avians to respect truth so much. It's probably why he hardly spoke. No lies were required if you didn't open your mouth.

"Fine," I said. "But you go first, Kerrik. And let me hold the key."

He did not hesitate before handing it over, which surprised me. "You are already the key to life or death, so you may as well hold this key too," he said.

I felt a lot more confident after that. And a bit sick to my stomach. If they told me one more time how important I was or how easy it would be for me to goof up and kill everybody…. I could see why ignorance was bliss.

Or was it 'stupidity is sublime'? I was terrible at sayings. I also couldn't read the Avian script on the walls anymore. I think the spells for smarts didn't apply down here. Probably another safety precaution.

The tunnel opened into a massive cave etched with Avian symbols glowing with green goo.

It was the scene from a half-remembered dream.

Uncle Ulric looked small and destitute, a supplicant who bowed to nothing but the room itself, for there were no statues, no gods, no shrine. No sign of the gods he had revered and adorned the house with my entire life.

His back was to me, clothed in threadbare linen, feet naked and dirty. He should be freezing this high up the mountain, but the chamber was volcanic hot, and I suddenly wondered if Highcrowne's peak was a volcano all along and no one noticed, because it hadn't yet woken and killed everyone at its feet?

Ulric had the same feel about him. A dirty heap, easily overlooked, but a volcano of untapped power, a maelstrom of destruction waited inside, poised to be unleashed by some unknown and unexpected provocation.

"Uncle?" My voice echoed through the huge chamber, and I cringed at the reflected sound of it.

There was no response.

I stepped tentatively into the room, and the First Soul jerked inside my belt pouch. This was more than a startled thought, an unexpected dread whisper it inserted into my mind from time to time: this was a physical movement, like it wanted to recoil from the room. But it was too late for it to run or sense the trap, and I was inside.

And it was quiet.

The First Soul, whose presence I'd felt no matter how far away, ever since I claimed it from beneath the ocean of Ismerkel, who whispered endlessly to me between cinnamon dreams ... the First Soul was just a stone in my pack now. I felt nothing from it. Nothing.

"By the gods," I said. "What is this place? You've freed me from it. How?"

"Do not grow too jubilant, niece." Ulric's voice boomed like thunder in the chamber, and I had to cover my ears. "The Soul only sleeps here. And as tempting as it may be for you to let it sleep an eternity, that option no longer exists. The damage has already been done."

LOREL CLAYTON

13 THREADS AND TEARS

When Ulric's voice faded, I said, "Have you grown as cryptic as Avians too? Speak plainly, or I walk out of here and deal with the Soul my way."

"No." He was on his feet and looming over me, fury contorting his features.

Duane stepped between us. "It's the strain, Ulric. Listen to yourself."

"Calm," Kerrik said, interposing his body between us as well.

I wasn't afraid of my uncle anymore. I didn't need defenders, but their words did calm him. I bit my tongue on what I wanted to say, which would most certainly have had the opposite effect.

"Yes," Ulric whispered. "You're right. The strain is far worse than I expected. I fear we are running out of time. I cannot mask so many souls for much longer. Eva..."

I held up my hand. "Truthspeaker here. And I want truth. The complete truth. What is going on?"

"It is a trap for the First Soul," Ulric said, sitting and folding his legs. He even closed his eyes, as though every word required concentration. "Kerrik, can you...?"

"Of course." The Avian turned to me. "Let me explain all I can, in order to preserve your uncle's strength until it is needed."

"Needed for what?"

"Unlocking the riddle of your father's soul jar. When we learned you had it, it seeded hope in all of us."

"Hope sounds good." I crossed my arms and listened for once. Kerrik had already spoken more in the last minute than I'd imagined was possible. I wouldn't interrupt.

"But first," Kerrik continued, "understanding requires context. As Ulric told you, this chamber is a trap for the First Soul. It was built millennia ago, soon after we learned The Trickster brought that vile artifact to our world.

"We sought in vain to steal it from him. Many ways we tried over the centuries. And then he gave it to a Solhan, the first of the line of Keepers. The Solhans were already powerful and dangerous, but Trickster is mad, and there is no discerning his reasons. We hoped to seal the relic away as we have just accomplished here, for surely even a Solhan must see the need? That was when we saw firsthand the effects the Soul has on mortals. We had heard stories on other worlds ... but to see its corrupting influence was a shock. The Solhan Keeper and the First Soul had bound together so tightly there was no extracting it.

"We tried taking it by force, Keeper and relic both, to no avail. Its vast power was turned against whoever we sent. We lost many Avians in the attempts. Then mercenaries, assassins, generals ... wars were fought, and in the end, we had no hope. By the time a Keeper was born strong enough to resist its whispers, your father, the damage was already done."

"Ulric said the same. What damage?"

"The Devourer."

The Devourer was the greatest god in the Solhan pantheon—'greatest' as in most feared. He destroyed worlds, universes ... to make way for the new.

"What are you saying?" I laughed, preferring a cruel joke to even contemplating the alternative. "It's absurd. The Devourer destroyed the old universe to make way for this one. It's creation myth. It can't happen again."

Kerrik puffed up his feathers. "It has happened many times, to many worlds and many universes."

I sat down, like Ulric. The cold stone of the cave floor seeping its chill into me, numbing me, and I embraced the feeling. The discomfort of my body distracted me from discomforting thoughts.

I knew the gods were all too real, despite what the goblin doctor liked to believe. So why not the Devourer too?

"He is coming," Ulric said, opening his eyes and looking at me with those deathly pale irises. "The Devourer has been summoned."

"My mother?" Was this her fault, along with orchestrating the arrival of the Dead God?

Ulric shook his head, but perspiration coated his brow, and Kerrik finished the explanation.

"The Devourer chases the First Soul from world to world, trying to extinguish the abomination. It is a beacon to Him. Like a fish ever trying to swallow a firefly out of reach. He swallows all things around it in His vain attempts. Even if the Dead God is defeated, our world is lost. The Devourer knows the Soul is here, and He is coming for it."

My brain kicked into high gear, searching for a solution. "Then we send it away through one of the goblins' doorways. Or we hide it. You say you built this room for that purpose, and it's working. I can't sense the Soul at all anymore."

Kerrik sat down on the floor too. "If we could bring ourselves to send the Soul away to doom another world—and that is not an option—or be certain of this untested trap in which we stand.... It does not matter. The Devourer is already on His way. Days, perhaps weeks are all we have. He cannot be turned aside, for He is like an ocean wave, set on its course until it smashes the land." Kerrik drooped and buried his beak beneath a wing. Goopy tears formed in the corners of his black eyes.

I couldn't accept what the Avian said, could not fully comprehend it even.

"Klaus said he had a plan. To stop it. Before he died." Ulric panted as he spoke, as though he were in the middle of a marathon.

"Then ask Klaus now. How do we fix this?" I handed over the soul jar I'd been holding ever since I got it back from Roosal. My hands shook so badly I feared I'd drop it at the last second, so I laid it on the stone floor in front of me.

Duane brought the jar to Ulric, who clutched it against him like an infant.

"What's wrong with my uncle," I asked the Avian. Kerrik had known about the Devourer for centuries, so he could get over his grief enough to help me through my shock. And do something. Anything.

"We have asked many difficult things of Ulric, and they weigh on him like a burden, sapping his power. Release their concealment for a time, Ulric," he said. "Our nest eggs are of no benefit if the Devourer comes. Focus on finding the answer we all seek."

Ulric nodded. It seemed a difficult thing to let go of whatever spell he was maintaining. It took a few minutes, but gradually his tense muscles relaxed, the lines on his face smoothed into a more familiar expression, and he took a relieved breath.

"Eva," he said. "I am glad to see you survived. I had no idea before I came to this place just how crucial my guardianship of you was. I had no idea ... I was often harsh with you, as a Solhan father should be. But... Forgive me."

He was really creeping me out now. My uncle, showing kindness?

"The soul jar," I reminded him. I didn't care about the past, blame or forgiveness were irrelevant when so much was at stake. "Focus."

"Too right." He took the cradled jar and raised it overhead. "Blow on it," he instructed. "Let your father feel the breath of life."

I obeyed. I knew enough about Solhan rituals not to question the tiniest step. And this was perhaps the most important ritual I'd ever witnessed.

My father's ghost might well know how to stop this. He had been bonded with the First Soul longer than me, and he must have learned some of its secrets. He had resisted it enough to send it away with Ulric, so perhaps he could help me in my internal struggle against the Soul as well.

"Open the lid and let him taste your shared blood," Ulric said.

I pulled my silver dagger rather than my Ashur, sensing my mother's blade might not be the best instrument to use, and sliced the tip of my finger. It bled quick, a deep red the same color as my lips. I lifted the jar's lid and let my blood trickle inside, a rivulet that made the gray ashes turn to black clumps.

"Lastly, touch your soul to his and speak your questions. You do know how to reach out with your soul?"

"Yes." I'd learned that and more as the power I'd been given by the Dead God allowed me to play with souls as deftly as a skilled puppeteer commanded his toys to do whatever he desired.

Father, I whispered. I'd felt the presence in the soul jar off and on from the moment I stole it, but now it felt like a full soul, a person standing before me, rather than an echo. I could even see him in my mind's eye. Pale and dark-haired, but with Viktor's kindness in his eyes. His brow was wrinkled, lines deeply etched around his mouth, which could have been laugh lines if not for the frown that marred them. My father.

Eva, my darling girl. My Eva.

How do we save everyone? Tell me, I commanded. I didn't waste time asking how to save myself when so much more was at stake. Save the world first, before the opportunity could be lost forever. It seemed my father had other ideas, though, and his soul was not my plaything. I could not command it. Why?

Because I am a Keeper, and because I know your true name, for I gave it to you. That is why you have no power over me, Eva. You must know why I allowed Lili to prepare you for sacrifice.

It's not important.

It is. You and Ilsa were my girls, and you—

I was talking to my dead father. I'd spoken to ghosts before, but never had it mattered so much. I didn't want him to reveal that he was Solhan after all, evil at heart. I wanted him to be better, and so I wouldn't let him finish. I didn't want to know why he allowed me to be married and left as a sacrifice to the Dead God. If Morgan hadn't come back for me....

"Just tell us how we stop the Devourer from coming," I said aloud. "That's all any of us want to know." I wanted to hold the vision of him in my mind, the soul I could see. I wanted to melt into him and smell him, have him hold me, but I kept my tone cold. I'd learned from the best of Thornes.

I sensed his ache as though it were my own. My soul sense was a curse that way, when I was the cause of the pain I experienced in others. But my pain was far worse—it stabbed when I rebuked him and burned when I thought about entertaining his excuses. This was agony, so I needed to get it over with. "Tell us."

If I could have ripped his secrets from him, I would have.

His soul gave a tiny shudder of surrender, as though he almost wished I would tear it to shreds, swallow it as the Dead God did—as I had almost done to Conrad—and release him from memory and regret and shame. I couldn't give him that solace.

You were the lure for both the Dead God and the First Soul, he said. *I knew you would be stronger than me. I knew you could resist both. Now you must convince both. Convince the First Soul to trust you, then convince the Dead God to take the Soul and become its Keeper. Only He is powerful enough to draw The Devourer away from here. The Dead God is our only hope. And you are the only one He might listen to.*

Because He loved me.

I suddenly saw how inexorable fate was, how it had thrown Thane and I together. Had I ever had a choice? Had he? It made it tawdry and cheap for some reason. Knowing it might never have been my choice.

Fates or no, I felt what I felt. Maybe that was how they worked, those three dark sisters who wove the threads of lives together, entangling them, cutting them short or stretching them long through a fabric made up of thousands, millions, whole worlds whose existence depended on one thread doing what it must, not unraveling, no matter how much she wanted to. They depended on us feeling love, duty, fear. They knew we would accept our fate, because we had no choice, driven inexorably to it because of who we were.

One simple thread like me could not spit in the faces of Fate, because They governed our lives for a reason. Sometimes They were right. Or maybe They always were, and sometimes we agreed. It didn't matter, really. Not even gods could escape the will of the Fates. What mattered was how much you suffered by struggling.

I sighed and sat on the stone floor opposite my uncle, cross-legged and cradling my father's ghost. The soul jar went quiet without Ulric's power lent to it.

I didn't tell my father goodbye. What was the point? I would see him soon.

As the fight went out of me, I hung my head, letting my dark hair shroud my face, concealing the warring anger and fear and sadness that transformed it like the shadows of passing clouds.

Ulric's guard went back up again, his working with the soul jar complete. I sensed his focus, his powerful soul stretched thin, weaving its way through the cage of the room, through cracks and crevices only he knew about to work in the outside world. The First Soul had been lulled and trapped, but my Uncle understood the secrets of the chamber. I suddenly realized the Soul would discover them too. There was no hiding here forever. I'd have to step out again, face the Dead God and my destiny.

"You learned what is needed?" Kerrik asked. "You know what we must do?"

"I know." I didn't like it, for it meant betraying the only man I'd ever loved, betraying my own dreams and wants. But that didn't matter. All along, I'd been fighting what was inevitable. I would go to Him.

But I preferred to do it alive.

"What is the answer?" Kerrik pressed.

"I'm the answer. It's been me all along. I have to face the Dead God."

"That's impossible." The Avian chirped, and I saw a shimmer of magical force surround him.

The hairs along my neck stood up. "What are you doing?"

"Ulric?" Kerrik asked, ignoring my question.

"It is done," my uncle told him with an exhausted gasp.

He closed his eyes, and I sensed he'd completed his spell in the outside world. His power now filled the chamber, and runes in the very walls shifted, closing off those tiny cracks in the cage he'd been using. The chamber was sealed.

"What's done?" Duane asked, beating me to the crucial question. At least he wasn't a part of Kerrik and Ulric's little plot, whatever it was. Unwitting dupe, just like me.

I began to guess what Kerrik would say before he said it.

"You can't leave this chamber." The Avian had his Unmentionable demeanor on, and I wondered if he was that first and an Avian second, or the other way around? The answer could decide what would happen next.

"Why not?" I asked, a dangerous note creeping into my voice.

"Because the First Soul has dug into you, hollowed out a spot for itself," Ulric said, his eyes still closed. Either he was afraid to look at me, or he was so exhausted he intended to sleep sitting up. "Only a portion of the relic remains in that gem you carry. You can't leave, Eva. You can never leave. I had hoped my brother's shade would offer a viable alternative, but he is gone, fragmented as well. This is the only way to stop the First Soul and keep the Dead God trapped. We let the Devourer come for them both and pray He spares this world. I will pray every moment that remains to us."

"Are you praying for everyone, or only Solhans? Maybe only yourself?" I scoffed and circled him. He remained seated, head bowed, and I noted the carvings etched into the floor. His protective circle wasn't made of ash or blood, anything easy to erase. It had been cut into the mountain, drawn from the planet's core. He was confident in its protection. From me.

"I am here with you and the Soul," Uric said, calm. "We will not be spared, none of us here in Highcrowne will be. That is why we have survivors secreted elsewhere. It is time to embrace the Devourer's coming."

"I've never shared your piety, Uncle. But this is worse than usual. It's insane. We have to at least try."

Ulric went on, ignoring me and saying what was on his mind, like he was off in another world already.

"Duane showed me the ritual chamber you discovered, the one that Viktor had built before he died. Even your brother surrendered to the Devourer in the end. Heed his wisdom."

Duane clenched his fists. "I'm trapped here too? We're going to starve, waiting for a faceless god to gobble up our corpses?" He shook his head. "I've owed you so much, Ulric, and listened to your wisdom, but I'm with Eva on this one. It's just crazy. You're exhausted. Take a moment to get your mind straight and you'll see how senseless it is."

"We have Celon here, and it will sustain us until the end," Kerrik said. He demonstrated by going to a well in the corner of the room, pulling out a goblet from some hidden pouch in his feathers, and filling up the cup with glowing Avian goo. Celon must be their name for it. He drank it straight. "Now, I will have no need to eat or drink for weeks. The Devourer will come before then."

He handed the empty goblet to me.

Wasn't Avian goo explosive? I shuddered at the thought of drinking it, but then I warmed to the idea. I filled it to the brim.

"No, thank you. I'm not that desperate yet," Duane said. "Ulric, please. Listen to reason."

"He's a fanatic," I said, returning to stand over my uncle and sniffing at the goo in the brass cup. The goblet was plain and tarnished up close. Like the Avians themselves. "Logic doesn't work on fanatics.

"I am listening, Eva," Ulric said, "but as always, you do not see the greater view. If you face the Dead God, even with First Soul in hand, you will not survive. Either He—or Lili and her armies—kill you, completing the summoning and releasing Him fully into this world to destroy what few living humans remain, erasing any hope of survival. Or, you win, but at the cost of your soul. The First Soul will control you utterly, it will have a better vessel than an inert gem, and it will destroy this world. The Devourer wants one thing. If we give it to Him, there is a small chance He will take it and go. It is a chance."

"Regardless, we stop this endless chase," Kerrik added. "Let the Devourer take the Soul, and no more worlds need fall. We Avians have travelled to many, seen too much, and we are willing to sacrifice ourselves here, ensuring the First Soul does not escape this time."

"Very noble, all of you," I said, lifting the goblet in a mock toast. "But I have a better plan. Winning."

I poured the Avian goo across the flagstones etched with Ulric's protective circle. At the same time, I pulled my trusty striker from my belt pouch and ignited the liquid as it fell.

It burned a brilliant yellow, like molten gold, before the light grew blinding.

I tried to throw myself out of the way, but that was too much coordination for me, and I careened into

Duane. We both lost our feet but didn't hit the ground before the explosion hurtled us across the room.

I was glad my magical instincts kicked in on their own and surrounded us with a spherical shield of force, because I couldn't think clearly after the wind got knocked out of me.

Duane and I crashed against the wall, the shield softening the impact. I grazed my elbow on Duane's teeth, but other than that we didn't even get bruised.

Duane had a fat lip of course. He scowled and licked blood away. "Blowing us all up was your plan? You're as stubborn as Ulric."

"This is step one, ye of little imagination," I said. But I didn't waste more than a moment trading words with Duane. My real sparring partner was now on his feet.

Ulric had shielded himself and Kerrik too, but he hadn't protected his circle. His mouth hung open at sight of shattered stone, cracks running across the chamber floor and up the walls, disturbing not only his personal ward but the structure of the trap the Avians had built for the First Soul millennia ago.

"What have you done?" Ulric asked, dismayed.

"What I had to," I said.

What I wanted you to, the First Soul added in my mind.

I didn't answer it. The Avians' trap had managed to do one thing useful—dislodge the relic's grip on me. Its tendrils were still curled up inside my belly somewhere, but it no longer reached into my mind and could no longer control my voice or my limbs.

I would not let it in again. I was my father's daughter, a Keeper born, and if he had not succumbed, neither would I, no matter the temptation.

I had a plan, but I dared not even think it let alone speak the details with the First Soul listening again. Instead, I let my uncle see the certainty behind my eyes, even as I erected that magical barrier I'd only managed to create on instinct before.

I had power of my own. I could do a lot of damage without calling on anything else.

"Do you really want to fight me on this?" I asked Ulric. "Your cage is destroyed, and you won't win. We do things my way from now on."

Ulric and I were more alike than was comfortable to admit. I saw the twitch in his fingers, sensed a voiceless spell being woven, the strength of his soul unbowed despite circumstances turning against him.

But he saw into my soul as well. I let him. And whatever he saw there made him clench his fists until they relaxed, the energy he'd summoned dissipating, and he sighed.

"I suppose you're all grown up now, Niece. So, what do we do?"

14 KNOWLEDGE IS POWER

I knew we needed more than me or Ulric. We needed dwarves and humans and elves, even goblins. And especially Thane. Winning would require all of us.

First, I had to convince Calka.

"All hope is lost," she said, when the First Soul and I stood before her magpie throne again.

Kerrik had hardly spoken since the explosion. He drooped like a wet branch, head bowed before his queen and gummy tears filling his eyes.

Ulric had stayed behind in the chamber, sketching new wards in blood and charcoal across the floor and murmuring to my father's urn. I didn't know what new magic he was conjuring, but I sensed it wasn't aimed against me. He knew he couldn't face me with the First Soul at my command, so I hoped he was doing something useful to help us survive. To win.

"It's not," I told her, part of me wishing for another of her warm hugs. "I have great hope—and you have nothing to lose by sharing it. My destiny has always been to face the Dead God." My father had revealed that much to me, and I understood so much more than what his ghost had said, "I'm ready. But I need your help. You are one of the Three Crowns. If you speak, everyone will listen."

"What have I left to say? We screamed into the hurricane for so many long millennia, unheeded, until we lost our voice and our will."

"You were willing to die by the Devourer's whim, why not summon the will to fight and live instead?"

"We are tired of fighting," she said. "We grew tired long ago."

"And that's why you've been slowly dying. You asked me for truth, so face your own. Life belongs to those who cling to it the fiercest. Why ever did you care for this world to begin with? What in life brought you joy?"

"Knowledge," Kerrik said bitterly. "Watching the shifting of mountains, comings and goings of deserts and those living creatures that rose and fell upon that stage, patiently entertained by it all, yet safe in the knowledge some things endured eternal. We were eternal."

"But you're not," I said stating what he'd left unsaid. "Your knowledge was flawed then and your solution to the Devourer is flawed now. Whether you like it or not, you are just like us transient beings. If you want to really live, embrace the fact it was never going to be forever. An assassin taught you that not long ago. Sacrificing yourselves, all of us, to the Devourer is not something noble and tragic but stupid and weak. Fight with us, and you will find the will to live again."

"Who is *us*?" Calka asked, cocking her head. "Does the relic speak with your lips?"

"No. I mean Highcrowne. All those who seek refuge within its walls. They look up to you, literally. Lead them."

"You lead them," Calka said.

I blanched and took a step back. That's not what I was looking for. Power should never have been given to me, and I already had more of it than I cared for—or was safe.

Duane raised his hand. "I'll take a crown if you're giving them away." He sounded like he was joking, but I knew he was serious.

I laughed, not just because a crime lord was the worst idea for a leader of humanity, but because he'd broken the tension, and I could relax.

"That's not part of my plan," I said. "If you really want to give humans the Crown they've demanded, save it for after the war, because they will squabble over it and start a whole new one. All I ask of you, Calka, is to set aside fear of assassins and take your throne below. Lead where Fharen and Matriarchs failed. Give them the courage to fight Solheim."

"For what purpose?" Roosal asked. "Lili of Solheim and her pet liches have retreated. The Dwarven Usurper, Gypsum, was captured and the Dwarf Crown recovered. Highcrowne is secure and stalemate has returned—only it is a pointless victory. The Devourer comes, and there is no fighting a Primal."

"But that's what I was born to do," I said.

Calka and the others listened to what little I dared tell them. Hope can be infectious. It tastes so much better than nihilism, and in the end—in their regal postures and the way Calka polished a few of her shiny baubles with a wing feather—I knew they wanted to live. They would fight.

A few minutes later, I was trudging through the snow, on my way back to Highcrowne. The Avian mountain was within the city, but this place far above the world could never be my home. I could not escape the muck and the grime and the struggle below.

"What are you thinking about?" Duane asked, pulling be out of my reverie.

We'd left the Avian caves behind, and he used a hand to shield his eyes from the blinding snowfield.

"I know that look," he pressed. "It's something like terror mixed with anticipation. You wore it every time we freed pixies from the food market."

I smiled, remembering childhood dangers and how monumental they seemed at the time. "Something that will certainly get me killed. Everyone else too," I said.

"So, no worse than now?"

"It would be hard to mess things up more. Why didn't the Avians stop all of this from happening in the first place? Why didn't the Unmentionables? Or the gods? I guess it doesn't matter. It falls to me now, so I'm doing this my way."

"What is your way?" Duane tried to be nonchalant, but I wasn't fooled.

"You're dying of curiosity. I know your expressions too. Patience."

"Always."

Roosal and Kerrik were ahead of us, walking lightly over the top of the snow, so I picked up the pace. Duane matched me.

Breathing heavily, I said, "By the way, I'm glad you didn't die in that cave in."

"I'm glad you got away from that dragon."

Seemed a lifetime since then. "We do forget to say hello."

"We do."

"And goodbye." I didn't intend to say it this time either.

I went to Kerrik, who was my ride down the mountain. He wrapped that magical loop around my waist then also clasped his scaly arms around me. I tried to stay true to form and ignore Duane, but things were about to get a lot scarier, and I didn't simply mean diving off a mountain with only a hollow-boned bird man to keep me from getting flattened.

The whole world was going to take a frightening shift.

So, I said, "Take care, Duane."

"You too."

I was about to say that was impossible, when case in point, I was plummeting, with freezing wind rushing past my ears.

Going down was even worse than going up. I thought Avians flew?

I screamed. I couldn't help it, and I regretted it a moment later when Kerrik suddenly stretched out his wings.

Our descent slowed, and we drifted gently in circles down to earth.

I had time to take in my home then. The impassable Central City with its rarified gardens and snobby elite. I could walk those halls of power now, simply because no one could stop me.

But what made my heart ache was the Outskirts: fragile and ramshackle, huddled against the sturdy base of the craftsmen and artisan districts, the smiths and factories that kept everything running. Only they were quiet now too, the frazzled dwarves who ran them too shocked from the short war that put them on the other side. They would need to be embraced by The Kingdoms again, forgiven for what was not even their choice.

But there was no time for healing.

All of us fragile few were needed to end this. For we'd be ended if we didn't work together.

As soon as my feet touched the ground, I hurried to the palace to do what I did best—pester everyone into doing what needed to be done.

Instead of drunken victory celebrations or exhausted soldiers sleeping on garden benches as I'd expected to see after a battle, Highcrowne elves were yelling at Faellion elves on the footpaths. Fharen supporters had swords drawn against Hilja supporters. The elvish civil war had spread to the Central City.

No blood had been shed yet, but they seemed to be arguing about everything.

Take the goblins. They were foreign spies according to some, invaders taking advantage of the turmoil according to others. And to make matters worse, they had apparently set up a camp on the other side of the broken bridge and were questioning and examining werewolves with all manner of scientific instruments without a by your leave from anyone. Not that anyone knew who was in charge.

Then there were the dwarves. They'd returned to their homes as if nothing happened, except Harley and the King's Guard, who were trying to make the Dwarven Palace (aka Rutgard's mausoleum) livable. Seemed that silver crown meant shut up and obey, whether frozen king, living queen, or an upstart young wolf not even out of his apprenticeship. There was no argument among the dwarves that Harley was now their ruler, but the elves seemed put off they no longer had a dictatorship.

If the elves were inconvenienced by the dwarves' return, the humans, who were suddenly kicked out of the underground spaces and back up to the daylight, were ready to start fighting again. If not for the knowledge of those wolf forms lurking beneath tiny dwarven frames, they might have fought for the security of the catacombs, which were also drier and cleaner than the Outskirts. Only the Southerners and Bell's enclave were left alone. Not even a werewolf who saw their steely, battle-worn looks and automaton guards dared tell them to move.

The dwarves who'd been imprisoned in Highcrowne were another steely-eyed and angry bunch. Their reunions with family were tinged with fury when those freshly returned from Gernwold saw how those trapped in Highcrowne had been treated. The rumblings against the elven elite were loud again.

I plucked all these memories and thoughts from soldiers and courtiers using my soul sight as I hurried past, taking advantage of everyone's distraction to make my way unimpeded.

Dwarf against elf against human in an endless circle of shouting, fist waving, and muck throwing. Literally. There was enough ammunition lying around that any-one could pick up a handful and throw it in someone's face to end an argument. And there was no sign the filth would be cleaned up any time soon. The goblin muck-rakers had joined the ranks of the goblin new-comers, who were not the muck-raking type. They were hardened commandos and crazed berserkers wait-ing eagerly for a new fight to begin.

Seemed peace was more difficult than war, but that was fine. I'd soon give them what they craved.

When I reached the throne room, Thane read my soul and barked commands to his advisors and generals. It was a relief not to explain myself. It was an even bigger relief not to have to lie to him.

He knew I was hiding things, even from myself, but he didn't pry, because he also knew how fragile my control over the Fist Soul was, how it almost had me. He could see clearer than anyone that part of me was hollow and missing and might never be returned.

I studied the war table as I waited, letting fear of war replace the worse fear lurking inside me.

Hilja arrived first, the swish of her gowns loud to my ears, and I knew there would be a battle of wills. She had her supporters along, and they were not Fharen's. Harley joined next, timid and too self-conscious to wear the silver circlet. He had it on a chain around his neck, like a giant pendant. After him came General Moore, de facto leader of the human insurrection.

Gas hadn't shown up, but I knew he still lurked somewhere, devising murky plans. If only he hadn't pulled Bell in with him. I thought her smarter than that, but hate and fear can turn anyone towards dark deeds. I knew that all too well.

Finally, the hangers-on joined us. I saw bodyguards and councilors, Captain Uanal, Hilja's Seneschal, Ernest, who sought freedom for his class. I smiled broadly, and he gave me a serious nod. Ernest seemed more than Seneschal now, wearing some badge of office I didn't recognize.

An old man among the elven retinue watched me with a keen gaze. To look that old for an elf, he must be ancient and unable, or unwilling, to cast glamours.

Duane leaned in a corner, somewhere between Moore's human mercenaries and Hilja's servants, easily overlooked if you didn't meet his sharp, jade eyes.

As soon as Thane opened his mouth, Hilja cut him off, and the shouting began.

"Who else's head can we put on a pike?" Hilja asked, heated. "You can't have a victory without a blood sacrifice. I daresay it's poor form to execute royalty, but Madam Gypsum's claim is weak. I think we'd be safe, as long as we called her a Pretender. If it were her sister, Syla, a genuine Matriarch, I would argue differently. As it is, elves demand blood."

"And what about us dwarves?" Harley asked, his nervous demeanor lost beneath the passion of his argument. "Our poor old ones, and those too slow to evacuate, like my old master. They is dead. Dead. We are victims too." Harley may only have been king for a day, but he was not about to back down.

"Victims?" General Moore shook his head, his air of long command and quiet wisdom made both Hilja and Harley listen. "None have been more victimized than humans. Enslaved, kept in camps—even before the battle today. Elves are to blame for that, so why not an elven blood sacrifice? Where do we begin and where do we stop?"

"We stop at the line between life and death," Thane said. He was still Fharen to everyone present, but he did not bother to adopt the King's manner. He was all Thane at that moment, for who had more knowledge of Death?

"Blood sacrifice, reparations, squabbles over crowns and who rules the Kingdoms," he said. "You are mad to think of these things now."

After what I'd learned, I knew their bickering was pointless, but I let them go on, expelling their pain and rage, and I was envious of their naivete. What I had to tell them would bring nothing but more pain.

The council doors shuddered, and everyone jumped. I could see the fear in their eyes—was it another bomb, another enemy? An Elven Elite Protectorate soldier was the first to risk a look outside. He suddenly bowed his head and backed away, flinging the doors wide.

Queen Calka strode in, her black and white feathers like the finest gown, adorned with bibs and bobs of gems and sparkling treasures. Behind her was Kerrik and Roosal. Only the orange-beaked one had remained on the mountain along with my uncle and his secret work.

"Queen Calka." Hilja curtsied.

Everyone showed deference in their own way. The humans were a bit befuddled, some rudely locking gazes with the monarch, while others fell to their knees, heads bowed. I'd heard Avians were seen as demons or gods in some lands, depending on whether you thought them cruel or kind.

Calka paid no attention to either supplication or disrespect. She took Hilja's hands. "Queen to Queen I welcome you my child."

A gasp rose among the elven courtiers in attendance. I saw those around Thane, who still thought him Fharen, put hands on ornamental daggers. Their king shook his head, so weapons remained sheathed for now.

Calka went to Thane next. "And King Fharen. How good of you to maintain order while we were occupied. You hold our every confidence. We are also glad to see you have a suitable heir in training."

Thane sent me a silent query. I told him, *Politics. Play along.*

"Thank you, Calka. I look forward to handing my burdens to Hilja. When the time is right," he said aloud.

"We shall see if such time comes soon enough. Eva..." Calka turned to me and hugged me as tightly as she had on the mountain.

The murmurings grew even more frenzied and confused.

"We depend on you," she said loud enough for all to hear.

Next, she greeted the young dwarf kindly, and General Moore formally. Not until she took station around the war table and looked expectantly at me did silence return.

I could hear people breathing. I felt eyes on me.

Before heat could rise in my cheeks, and I looked like an idiot schoolgirl, I told them what we had to do.

"The Dead God is still out there," I said, "and His servants will continue to eat away at us until we are all among His Risen ranks.

"First thing you must know about the Dead God is—He is mine to face. You will leave Him to me. But others stand between us. Lili of Solheim, her Asheen necromancers, and hordes of Risen. All the living lands that live no more stand between me and Him. And while I am Solhan and wield power beyond your comprehension..." I felt the First Soul stir in its pack. "...even so, I hold no power over those creatures. The god's essence infuses them, and I dare not battle Him or let Him know my true whereabouts until it is too late. I cannot do what must be done unless all of you distract Him and His forces, especially Lili of Solheim."

I didn't tell them about the Devourer, or how we had no time to hide behind walls and wait to be killed slowly. What would have been the point? Not even the Avians or my uncle in their wisdom could do anything but cower in fear at the thought of what was coming.

"Are you saying we attack Solheim?" Harley asked.

"Yes."

"Someday, perhaps, but not now, surely?" Hilja said. "We need time to regroup, provision and plan."

"Why?" I asked. "All your armies are here now, brought together to save Highcrowne, but the city is already starving. There are no provisions to be had but what we can recover from the wall and the outposts in between. We might seem safe but.... You saw the

Asheen necromancers raise elves and dwarves as easily as humans to serve them. Lili will be back. And each of us that die as 'blood sacrifices' or 'examples', each head on a pike or starved old peasant will become one more of them, an ocean of undead to sweep away the living. They will keep whittling away at us until nothing is left."

Hilja's brain was calculating possibilities at a frightening speed. At least they'd all shut up.

Thane was the first to break the silence. "We are all on the same side. A losing one if we do not act now."

"How?" Hilja asked.

"I know a way to reach the Dead God," I said. "All you have to do is keep His armies looking another way."

"For how long?"

"Until we win."

I thought it best to end on that hopeful note. Trust General Moore to see the tactical issues.

"In order to strike at Solheim, we will need to get armies across the wall, and it has no gates. Once we do cross, scale our way over or blast a hole, we must strike at them. We will be bottlenecked and won't last long against their superior numbers."

"There are more troops we can draw on." Thane was thinking of the plant soldiers incubating near the wall. They might well be enough to cut a path ... if we were willing to be bastards enough to use them. They were human. Or had been.

"Wolves," Harley cut in, "wolves could do a lot of damage, even if you snuck in only a few. Of course, we could climb the wall and go straight down the middle of the plain. I know the way."

"Good options, and we should consider how best to use your forces King Harley," I said. "However, what Tha ... King Fharen refers to is an enchanted army that is almost unstoppable when mature."

"Those plant things?" the dwarf shuddered. "I saw them in Faellion. But we beat them."

"Those were hatched too soon. A new crop awaits, planted near the wall for just this purpose," Thane said.

I didn't like thinking about how that 'crop' came to be. All the people sacrificed. Were we really going to use them? The wolves sounded like the better option, but the Dead God's army was massive. More people might survive if we made use of the abominations. I didn't want to make such decisions. Every direction I looked I saw only pain. That's why I'd called this council.

Duane cleared his throat. "I wouldn't rely on those plant creatures. No telling if they'll wake up."

Thane pursed his lips. "If?"

"An alliance with the goblins," Hilja said, perkily. "That's our answer. I've worked with them to secure the Elf crown, no offense Father, and I'm sure I can extend the alliance further."

"They're not suicidal." I meant the leaders, not the grunts. Goblin mercenaries were known for their ferocity—point them at an enemy and get out of the way. "But it could work, if you can convince their Emperor that this is worth his while. Maybe cede some lands near their swamp?"

"Not Elf lands!" Hilja protested.

"Enough problems with goblins stealin' from dwarves as it is," Harley said at the same time.

"They'll want something," I insisted.

"What about the common enemy? Don't they see it's in their best interests to join us?" General Moore was wonderfully naïve for someone so experienced.

"Easier to let us deal with the god's army, then they can come in later to glory and victory." Duane must know them too, maybe from his dealings in the shadier sides of Highcrowne.

Hilja said, "Perhaps the dwarves should show contrition and prove their obedience by attacking first?"

"Suicide." Harley cut in, not shy for once.

"Humans say the first to sacrifice themselves should be the elves under my father's command," she continued, "the Elite Protectorate and loyalists are the true villains." More dagger clasping and angry whispers at her words. "While others say this is a human god and punishment for human sins, so let us leave them to it. None expected the Avians to reappear, so we know not what solutions you offer?"

"Not what you'd hope," Calka said.

"Then what do you advise, Mistress Eva?" Hilja sounded uncertain of my title.

"I say we send the goblins first. I can convince them to do it." There were no representatives to grumble on their behalf, and this triggered a wave of nods. I plunged on while they were in a good mood. "They can use their bombs and devices from the air, suffering no casualties. But they will run out of contraptions and gadgets. The tide of the enemy is too massive to turn aside easily. So, after that, you must all attack. At once. Together."

I got some angry looks then.

"We all live or perish together," I said. "So, find a way. I am no tactician, but I know wolves are quick and unstoppable if protected from silver. Humans are cunning and brave, able to hold wherever something must be held. Elven glamours can charm a viper or necromancer in equal measure. And now I give you Avians, for their legendary magic and wisdom.

"Start your plans again. Whatever stratagems you devise, and whether you reach the wall by dirigible, train or magic, you must attack at the right time, when the smallest moon is full, and I am where I need to be. I'm relying on you to distract Lili and her servants long enough for me to reach the Dead God and stop Him."

At least I hoped an army would be enough of a distraction. I could sneak past the hordes of undead beyond the walls, and I might even be able to avoid Lili's generals, her tame Asheens—but my mother? The Dead God was her source of power, and she couldn't let me use the First Soul to send Him back. It would be her undoing. If she killed me, she'd nip that problem in the bud and finally have her sacrifice as well. Giving my soul to the Dead God would complete the bargain she'd made with Him, and her command over this world would be assured. She cared only about killing me, but if Hilja and the others got in her way it would slow her down. At least, that was the plan.

I strode away, leaving them to work out the details and make the decisions I couldn't. I'd already made the toughest one I was capable of. I would face the Dead God and end this, even if it meant my end.

General Moore called out to me to return and explain more, but Thane told him, "She is giving all she can. All that is possible to give. Ask nothing more of her."

I suspected they were mainly curious to hear how I would defeat the Dead God. I couldn't even think of my true goal with the First Soul awake again. It was unable to read my unformed thoughts, but it sensed my emotions.

What frightens you? I shall destroy whoever or whatever it is.

The Dead God, I lied. But it was close enough to the truth to be believed. *You will help me face Him?*

I will never leave you. You are mine.

I was tired of being 'owned'. By Uncle, by the Dead God, Trickster, Fates, the First Soul .... One way or another, all that would end when I was done.

Good, I told it. *Good.*

But I needed something the Soul's power couldn't give me right now. I needed a way to bypass armies and battles, to cut to the heart of the matter.

I went in search of Doctor Ghunnan. He and Miss Kissel were crucial to my plan.

As an orange sun hovered above the jagged horizon, I realized we had survived the day, which was more than I had dreamed possible at dawn. We'd even had a gasp of peace, but this war was far from over. It was just beginning.

15 A Farewell to Peace

"An offensive?" Doctor Ghunnan exclaimed after I told him what was happening. "Are you mad? I should say, madder than usual? Why on earth would we leave the protections of the Kingdoms behind, cross the wall, and face the enemy on his own ground? If you want to visit Solheim, I have other ways of getting there."

"I'm counting on it. I need you to take me back to that doorway in the old temple. Help me reach the Dead God, so I can deal with Him."

"Return to the ruins and the cave in which Baroness Syla barely managed to excavate in time to save us from asphyxiation, all so you can fight a fictitious god?"

He acted like I should remember the cave in, but I'd been kidnapped and taken through the portal while they were being rescued. For someone so smart, he managed to forget a lot of things.

"Yes," I said. "That's the gist of it. And we leave tomorrow."

I knew I sounded more confident than I was.

"But Lili of Solheim," I continued, "the real madwoman behind all of this, will not die easily. And I mean that literally. We need to distract her if nothing else. That's why I need Miss Kissel too."

"I don't see why our Emperor should help when we've received no aid on the Southern front," Miss Kissel said. "Our lands have been invaded, and we are fighting a guerilla action, when not preferring simply to hide. We don't have the mercenaries or resources to spare on a suicide mission."

The female goblin had been resting, lounged on a stack of wooden boxes at the air dock where the zeppelin she and her commandos had arrived in was re-provisioning. Most of the provisioning was in reverse: she had brought arms, which had been effectively demonstrated during the recent battle, and were commanding a high price from elven merchants and nobles interested in personal protection.

I thought Captain Uanal and the Guard might have something to say about too many mundane bombs in careless civilian hands. That's why I'd asked him to join me. I expected him any moment, so I needed to hurry to get the timing right.

"I don't need your mercenaries, just your ships and bombs," I said. "There's no reason the goblin Emperor need know..." I paused, waiting for the sound of boots and clanking armor "...for you won't be telling him."

"Seize this ship," Captain Uanal ordered.

Merchandise was seized too. Bombs and mechanical contraptions resembling bear traps etched with Avian goo were taken from browsing shoppers and handled with two fingers, like diseased insects, by the guardsmen who placed the confiscated items on a padded wagon.

"I am an ambassador. We have diplomatic immunity!" Miss Kissel insisted.

"Not the moment you stepped off your ship and onto Highcrowne soil. You look like refugees to me, and you cannot be allowed to run about armed until you've been processed."

Soldiers moved to shackle the mercenary commandos, which is when it got really tense. The goblins were not push overs. They bared needle-sharp teeth and reached for weapons.

I raised a placating hand. "There's a simple solution. I'm willing to vouch for all of you, ensure you and any goblins seeking asylum are taken in ... if you do your civic duty. Nothing suicidal. Simply fly your airships and send your people aboard the elven ships, and once over the Dead God's army, you drop some of these pretty little bombs where directed. We'll even pay. You are mercenaries, are you not?"

I knew Miss Kissel was a spy, but her soldiers' eyes brightened when I waved several EEP guards forward. They carried a bag of gold and gems worth at least ten times the value of the goblin's airship and its cargo.

"Miss Kissel, I do say..." Doctor Ghunnan began in a reasonable tone.

She held up a hand before he could finish and smiled at me. "Admittance to the protection of the Kingdoms for all goblins?"

"Certainly. I'm sure I can speak for King Fharen and Queen Calka on this matter, and from what I hear, King Harley is a reasonable chap."

Miss Kissel nodded appreciatively at the impressive nature of my connections. She spat in her hand and held it out to shake. "I can find you if you fail to deliver on your promises."

"You're welcome to." I smiled, shaking then wiping my hand on a burlap bag. "You're likely to find me in Solheim. By the way, you should know that if this distraction fails and I fall to the Dead God, you get nothing. In fact, everyone is likely to die soon after I do. So, why not give it your all, call in a few more goblin commandos, whatever it takes. Understood?"

She growled. "Understood."

I clasped the doctor's shoulder. "Looking forward to travelling with you again, old friend. We leave at day-break."

"This is a stupendous opportunity," he said. "I can finally unravel the trickeries of this 'god' and dispel our people's fear of this vile conqueror. Plus, there's something else in Solheim I've wanted for some time."

"Don't tell me you now need the blood of a banshee or some such?"

"I won't."

"What?"

"Tell you."

The goblin doctor using monosyllabic words was creepy enough, and I needed him more than I needed my curiosity, so I nodded and said, "Be ready for anything."

Armies couldn't be organized as quickly as goblin explorers, and dawn was an impossible deadline for the Crowns, but we had to do impossible things, and they needed to get used to the concept. I had to at least know they were committed before I set off—because I wasn't coming back.

My preparations involved going home to pack a bag and say my goodbyes.

I watched Little Viktor playing in the street as if nothing had happened, as if his time hiding in catacombs from elvish slavers or werewolves and lich-led armies was nothing but a game.

He and his friends were rolling barrel hoops and warped wagon wheels, hands covered in muck but laughing so hard I couldn't interrupt. I soaked up the sound, wanting to carry it with me to Solheim. I set Little Viktor's smile in my memory too, firmly fixing it alongside my brother's face. They were so alike.

All nostalgic and melancholy, I wasn't paying attention when I reached the front door. Big mistake. I touched the handle, and a hex smacked me so hard I went flying and rolled down the steps. I lay there hurting and groaning, dazed, for who knows how long, until Nanny slapped my face with cold, wizened hands.

All I saw was hands, until my eyes focused on her scowl. Her wrinkles looked like they had wrinkles, thin red capillaries and broad blue veins showing through her transparently pale skin.

"Trying to get yourself killed?" she screeched. "You might as well have let Ilsa finish you off when you were ten, not that you're any wiser these days. You should know better than to cross a threshold before checking for runes."

"It could have been Viktor or one of his friends! What were you thinking?"

"The boy knows better, and those little lice on rats he plays with know better than to come near me. What's your excuse?"

"Stupidity," I admitted. This was Nanny's house too, and we had just fended off a werewolf invasion, so

I should have been more careful. "We did win the battle, you know."

"Win?" Nanny's scowl deepened further, something I hadn't thought possible. "I can't go to a dwarven smith or baker for fear he'll eat me."

No wonder Nanny hadn't removed her protections.

"Don't worry. I think even werewolves would find you too prickly, not to mention a bit old and chewy."

"Old?"

That's what she focused on? "You're over a hundred, Nanny, so if you're comparing yourself to elves, no you're not old. And you should be able to learn new tricks. There have always been wolves. Some of them. We just need to get used to it."

"I'm not wasting time getting used to anything, because the world is ending. I've read the signs. The Devourer..." she seemed reluctant to say the rest.

"The Devourer is coming. I know."

She made so many signs to ward off evil I thought she was having a fit. "You brought this on, didn't you?"

"Of course not." The damage had been done long before I was born.

"Must be Lili then. I knew that woman was trouble the day she came a courting your father. Viktor's mother wasn't cold in her grave before that she-lich moved in. I don't doubt she killed poor Margrit. Then she had her ulterior motives for begetting you and Ilsa, didn't she? The cow. The vile, horrible...."

"Viktor had a different mother? And Lili was a lich already?"

Nanny had never told me any of this before. The world must be ending.

"No, she was no lich then. How was she to have babes if she was half dead? That came later, with her rituals and machinations. She drew Klaus in and doomed him. Nearly doomed my Ulric too, but your uncle is smart. He listened to my counsel. We got going while we could, we did."

"For my sake, I'm glad he listened." I touched her shoulder, and she looked at my hand like it was a tarantula.

"What do you want now?" Nanny would forever distrust the part of me that came from Lili. That taint is what made her dislike Ilsa and me. I finally understood.

"I want to say goodbye. I'm going to stop the Devourer. If I can."

She looked into my eyes then, really looked, like she was trying to read my soul. I could read hers, and I knew she didn't have the same power as me. But she was appraising, and she finally nodded. "Good. You might just be the one. Now aren't you glad I raised you good?"

I remembered her screeching at me more than anything, but I smiled. "Yes, I am."

I gave her a hug and turned to leave before I started crying, but then I thought of leaving her and

Viktor behind forever. Ulric wasn't around to watch over them now either. I wanted them to have powerful protection, more than her runes offered. I wouldn't try crossing the threshold again, though.

"One more thing, Nanny. Can I have a bottle of cream and a dish?"

She raised an eyebrow and screwed up her features. "Crazy as her mother though," she muttered, trailing off into a string of unintelligible remarks I was glad I couldn't make out, but she went into the house and emerged with the requested items.

The milk was warm, the ice box probably not having been stocked with ice for months during the summer. At least the dish was clean, glazed in my favorite sky-blue color, and had enough depth to work perfectly. I went around to the alley in back and set the dish down there. Nanny followed, her curiosity un-quenchable.

I poured out the milk and called, "Sandy, if you're listening, look out for Nanny and Little Viktor while I'm gone. Don't pop them into bubbles or anything, but keep them safe."

After I stood, Nanny said, "Who in the hells is Sandy? And why are you leaving out good cream? Not more of your fairy and Unmentionable superstitions?"

Nanny believed in the gods but not the other stuff, and she'd always chided me for it.

"First of all, it's not good cream. It smells sour, so I hope it doesn't piss Sandy off. Second, fairies and

Unmentionables turn out to be the same thing in this instance. And it's not a superstition."

Nanny rolled her eyes and bent down to retrieve the dish, but a delicate hand appeared out of thin air and slapped hers away.

Nanny gasped and took a step back. She was against the opposite wall of the alley by the time the sparkling fairy with her butterfly wings emerged fully.

Sandy dipped a finger in the cream and licked, considering. Instead of spitting it out as I'd thought she would, she put the dish to her mouth and slurped all of it down.

"Fermented, just as I like it," she said. Only then did she seem to notice me. "Oh, it's you. Do you have to stand so close?"

I backed up to where Nanny stood rigid.

"You drank the cream, so you agree to my conditions?" I said. "You'll look out for my family? Protect Nanny and Little Viktor?"

She sagged. "Oh no, there were conditions? I really need to pay more attention. But, okay, fine. I'll do it. What, a century or so? Descendants too?"

"If it's included in the deal."

"Fairy godmothers have far more experience than dragon ones, Eva. Believe me, I'll do a bang-up job. If I can remember where I put my wand...?"

"Speaking of dragon godmothers, what happened to Olyve?" I asked. "I heard she'd been captured. Are the Unmentionables doing anything?"

"Well, about that." Sandy looked sheepish. "Most of the others have, well.... They've decided to help the Dead God. In exchange for certain immunities, concessions, and so forth. Not me, though! Oh no, I'm staying in my lands, just popping in every once in a while to watch the show. And take some photographs. You know, before it's all gone. Sad really. I'll miss this world."

"What?"

"I know, so many annoying, ugly people, animals, insects ... you'd think I wouldn't care! But the plants too will die. I've seen what's happened other places. Barren wasteland when they get done, the Dead God and the Devourer in their unending dance. Sometimes there's even lava. I'm not a fan of lavascapes."

"I meant the Unmentionables. They've betrayed us all? I thought it was their duty to protect this world. The one thing they could all agree on?"

"Seems they can agree on protecting their own behinds even more." Sandy shook her head. "Especially after you killed Harbinger. He was our glue. A dark, menacing, blood-hungry glue, but effective."

"Why didn't Olyve step in? She's pretty dark and menacing too." All the Unmentionables were, really. I shuddered, remembering the spider.

"She did. Why do you think Harbinger's friends didn't come to his aid when you...?" She made a throat-slitting gesture. "They're dragon lunch, that's why. Except Shevic and ravager and a few of the minor ones good at hiding, and good at cunning revenges.

"Olyvandra killed Unmentionables. The one law we cannot break. That is why those who escaped rallied the neutrals and imprisoned her. It took all of them, but they managed it. If No-Thing had been with us, it might have gone differently. As it was, Olyve told me to flee, and you don't need to tell me twice."

I kicked the empty cream dish. It bounced across the flagstones but didn't break. "Why did Olyve do it? She was a stickler for the rules and told me 'no' plenty of times. Why did she risk it?"

Sandy shrugged. "Maybe she thought Harbinger alone was too much for you to bear. Maybe she was going to kill him too, if you hadn't finished the job, and his flunkies got in the way. All I know is that when she was called to judgement, she fought and lost."

"Do you know where the Unmentionables are who joined Lili? Are they guarding Solheim?"

Sandy shrugged again. "Who knows? For some more cream, I could scout out the place for you."

"Deal."

I looked at Nanny who rolled her eyes and went back in for more clotted cream. After Sandy finished it, and the second bargain struck, she vanished, leaving Nanny clutching her chest.

"Those fairies with their sparkles and popping here and there. Frightful beasts."

Nanny thought necromancy was perfectly normal in comparison.

Sandy didn't return, and Nanny added "unreliable" to her list of complaints about them.

I couldn't wait any longer. Time for me to go.

I gave Nanny one last hug, and she didn't pull away like I expected her to. She'd been reading the signs.

Little Viktor was hardest. I wanted to wrap my arms around him and never let go, but I didn't want his last memory of me to be tinged with sadness. I caught his eye when he paused a moment between chases and waved. He waved back with a big smile then launched into some rough and tumble with his friends.

I walked away, pack over one shoulder and Ashur across the other.

Almost all my goodbyes had been said, and the ache of leaving was like a ball of dough in my chest, sticking to every thought and emotion and gumming things up.

As bad as that feeling of loss was, I dreaded my next visit the most.

Northcliffe Prison was not open to visitors. You didn't just walk up to the front gates, brimming with spikes and protective spells, and knock. Usually people avoided the place. You came by appointment only—an appointment with the executioner or the Warden, who told you how you'd be spending the next one hundred years of your sentence.

That's the stories Duane always told, anyway. He'd spoken to friends of friends. Never been there himself, and neither had a Thorne, despite clinging to necromantic traditions and Ulric's less traditional crimes. Truly evil people knew how to avoid the law, because they often were the law. Only the criminally stupid could be found here.

So, I naively went up to the gates and knocked. More like rattled them, as there was no knocker.

"What's that down there?" a gruff dwarf shouted from the battlement. His face was framed by a chain-mail hood, his black mustache matching the black soot smeared across his cheeks and brow.

"I'm..." I didn't have a title. Everyone in the Central City considered me the sorceress pulling King Fharen's strings, but 'what everyone knew' in the royal court didn't matter a lick once you were in Highcrowne proper. "...Eva Thorne," I finished lamely.

"Here to bed your 'innocent' husband who is suffering poorly and needs the comforts of home?"

"No." Did prisons allow that?

"A new doxy then," he nodded knowingly. "Another fool refugee wandered in with no sense, huh? We don't allow the prisoners money, so you won't be getting paid here, missy. It's not right, a lady demeaning herself so. You should think more highly of yerself."

"I'm..." I tried again "...a representative of the Crowns." I wore a nice gown, they were everywhere you turned in the Central City, and I'd grabbed this one before the battle, so it was a bit dirty and torn in a few places. The fabric was expensive, though, so I swooshed to show it off and stood regal. "I'm here to question Gypsum, the Traitor Queen."

"Traitor Queen? What's this?"

"The Dwarf Queen. Don't you know anything?"

He bristled, his pike tilting over the wall and down toward me. "I know there's no such thing as a Queen of the Dwarfs. We have King Rutgard."

I thought for a moment. "When was the last time they let you out of here?"

"Out? I have all I need. A sturdy, straw bed, good food, clothes, company of other guards for dicing and theatre. Quite a few theatre aficionados among us and right good actors and playwrights, if I do say so myself. No reason to go out, not when you're unmarried and unlikely to ever attract a wife. I have a club foot," he explained, showing it to me with a ballerina like stretch.

So, he'd missed the last six months at least.

"I'm sorry. Or, I mean, how great to have such a rich arts community so close at hand and a good employer. You have missed quite a bit, however. King Rutgard was ... killed." I didn't add that it was technically at my hand. "Then the dwarves, I mean your people, rebelled against the Matriarchy at the command of Queen Gypsum, who claimed the silver crown. They made war against the elves, besieged Faellion, and then Highcrowne. But we defeated them here with the help of a young apprentice, Harley, who is now the Dwarf King. He brought the dwarven were-wolves to heel and had Gypsum imprisoned here rather than executed, I'm told. The dwarfs have been pardoned and all is back to normal, relatively. We march against Solheim tomorrow or as soon as every-one can be organized."

"Really? ...Werewolves?"

I put a hand over my eyes and rubbed my temples with forefinger and thumb. This could take hours. "Let me speak to the Warden please."

"Why didn't you say so?" A side gate swung open, and the dwarf, along with two other guards, came down a narrow set of steps from the wall to escort me. "The Warden's office is this way. He decides whether you is allowed to visit a prisoner or not."

I had to go through the explanation of who I was all over again with the Warden. Fortunately, he had a wife and a life outside the walls. He even read the Dwarven Times and had opinions on all matters.

"We can't be hanging a mother, Traitor Queen or not," he said, showing me the headline from the evening edition. "I've made sure she's got the best rooms. My co-husbands cooked a fine meal for her already. They plan to bring her something every day. She's well cared for; you can tell the Crowns that. And tell them I'll have nothing to do with a hanging."

"The paper is spewing gossip with no substance," I reassured him. "The Crowns haven't decided anything. Too disorganized." I mumbled that last part. More loudly, I said, "Can I speak with Gypsum?"

"What for?"

"She's my friend."

"That complicates matters. How do I know you don't want to break her out? Coups and all those royal maneuverings could be a brewing. I'd need a writ from a King."

"How about a Queen?" a familiar voice said behind me. It was Hilja.

The prison guards who had shown her in were trembling. She had five EEPs with her, all dressed in black and menacing with their silver swords. The strange, old elf man I'd spotted with her earlier was along as well. An advisor?

"Were you following me?" I asked, knowing full well Hilja was shrewder than the flighty princess, now queen, she pretended to be.

"Had you followed, Eva. Too tedious to do such work myself. As soon as I was informed you were on your way here, I came. No one can agree on what to do with Queen Gypsum, but I know you can get answers—and I have questions. Shall we discuss things in private? Warden, leave please. We have need of your office."

The Warden looked momentarily befuddled, but dwarves were used to obeying women, so he quickly ushered his guards out to the hallway and shut the door.

"Gypsum won't talk if you're here," I said.

"I know. But I want to make sure you understand how important it is to learn all she knows about enemy plans, positions, modes of supply and transport, strength of arms ... all that tedious tactical stuff," she finished, blowing on her polished nails and yawning as though suddenly bored.

"I doubt she will tell me all that. She still thinks the Dead God will spare her. Her loyalty to Him is the only thing ensuring her survival. We have nothing to offer her but uncertainty and likely destruction."

"Then how do you hope to glean anything from being here?"

"I don't. I hope to talk to my ex-friend and say goodbye."

"I see." Hilja stood straighter, trying to look down her nose at me, which was impossible, as I was a head taller. "The rest of you, give us ladies a moment."

The EEPs hesitated—I was a dangerous Solhan necromancer in their eyes—but a glance from Hilja sent them out of the room to join the Warden. Only the old man remained. So, he was more important than bodyguards?

"We haven't been properly introduced," I said, holding out my hand.

He took it. I noticed right away how dry his skin was, like he sanded wood with his palms. His clothes were impeccably tailored and well cared for, as was his grooming, not a hair out of place. I would have taken him for royalty or a wealthy merchant, at least, if not for those hands. They were as rough as a slave's.

"I know who you are and am pleased to finally meet you, Eva Thorne. You may call me Mister Gardens."

My eyes widened to the point I felt air creeping around the edges of my eyeballs and spurring me into full alertness. "As in the detective, Mister Gardens?"

"Indeed."

My favorite mysteries were a series featuring this man, The Elf Butler. That explained the discrepancy between the evidence of his servitude and his gentlemanly demeanor.

"But..." I stammered. "You're real? I assumed the author made you up."

"I am the author, and I'm afraid I'm not that imaginative. I consider myself an autobiographer, simply retelling some of the intriguing experiences I have almost every day. With the names changed, of course."

"So, Duchess Celia is really...?"

"Me," Hilja said. "Mister Gardens has been the family butler for centuries, and I've respected his council since I was old enough to hear it. You can speak freely in front of him, as you would me."

I didn't feel like speaking freely in front of anyone, but Hilja liked to assume these sisterly intimacies. Seemed she had no peers or siblings growing up and hungered for them, while my sister had taught me to be distrustful and suspicious. I didn't say that aloud.

I took her hands and smiled, as I had to elicit her help when escaping Faellion, and said, "I'm dying to know what all the secrecy is about. You start, and I will fill in all I can."

"The secrecy is for your sake, my dear friend. I know you have be-spelled my father, for he is clearly not my father these days. I wonder at the method. Is there any chance of doing the same with Queen Gypsum to obtain the answers we seek?"

I shook my head. "Unfortunately, the method requires ... intimacy, and I'm not Gypsum's type."

"Sugar." Hilja pouted. "Perhaps one of my guards could perform that part of the spell?"

"No substitutes are possible, I'm afraid."

"I thank you for being truthful at least. So many theories abound about the change in my father's demeanor and your rise to power. I am glad you did not try to deny your influence, even if it means I have every right to imprison you for crimes against the Crown—if I so wished it."

Shrewd Hilja was demonstrating her power and leniency: she couldn't get what she needed with sweetness and honey, so she was showing me the tip of the dagger. I knew it was always there, hidden by petticoats. Court politics. But I'd learned more than I liked, or more accurately, I recognized politics was nothing more than a dinner conversation in the Thorne household, with barbs from Nanny, subtle nuance from Morgan, bloodcurdling threats from Ilsa, and imposing authority from Ulric. I'd grown up with such verbal sparring and never realized how useful it could be to me now.

"Fharen has not yet abdicated to you," I said, "so there might be some ... confusion if I'm not there to explain to him the benefits of a bloodless change of reign. And I do think Queen Calka would be most saddened if I do not do as I've promised her and face the Dead God. So much is at stake, you know. I dare not pause and be distracted by petty matters."

Hilja's eyes narrowed, but she nodded. "Too true. I'd best not distract you further. Nevertheless, Eva," she said earnestly, "I must know what I'm sending our armies into, if they're to have any chance."

"You're sending them into hell, and there is no chance—unless I succeed in my mission. But I agree that no life should be wasted. I promise I will learn all I can." I didn't promise often, and I meant what I said. I just had no idea how to achieve it.

I glanced at the old elf. "With such great minds as Mister Gardens by your side, perhaps many soldiers can be saved with cleverness alone? It may be all we have. Good day. And good to meet you."

The Elf Butler shook my hand again. It was thrilling, knowing he was real and right here. I hesitated, wondering if I could ask his advice about the First Soul and all the madness pressing in on me, but the truth about the Soul and the Devourer, what I had to do, it was too much to share with a stranger, no matter how much I felt I knew him.

"A pleasure, my dear. I do hope we meet again. You can always find me in Faellion." He squeezed my hand kindly.

He'd given me just what I needed, anyway, the thought of something to do and someplace to go after this was all over. Imagining there might be an 'after'. It gave me a jolt of confidence.

But then he said something that turned that jolt into sharp, icy arcs of electricity along my nerves. He said, "It is the role of heroes to die for the greater good. But you're no hero, are you, Eva?"

I didn't answer. I stepped out into the hall and told the Warden, "Take me to her."

They let me go in alone. I was worried the Warden would insist on accompanying me, but Hilja appearing to vouch for me seemed to be enough. He did make me leave my pack and sword behind, and searched me for hidden weapons, of which there were a few. I didn't bother to tell him I didn't need weapons or that the First Soul, which looked like a giant gem worth salivating over, was far more than the mind-boggling sign of wealth he took it for.

"Isn't it dangerous carrying something like that around, milady?"

"Very. Nevertheless, it stays in my belt pouch at all times."

He seemed to be waiting for more, but when I didn't elaborate, he shook his head and pointed down the corridor. "As you wish. It's the door at the end. Shout when you're ready to leave." He closed and locked the gate behind him.

I cautiously approached the first cell, wondering what I'd find inside. It was empty. They all were. All but the one at the end. A private wing for a special prisoner.

The warm orange glow of firelight stretched through the bars of Gypsum's cage. She had a brazier to keep her warm, a shelf of books, cozy blankets and pillows, not to mention a dining table the perfect size for one, complete with cutlery and brass candlesticks. Plenty of weapons there for someone determined to overpower a guard. Not to mention she was a werewolf. I wondered how they'd handled that, and I spotted the silver bracelets, shackles really, around her wrists and the matching collar necklace. That must chafe.

She reclined on her mattress, reading, and she didn't look up when she said, "Eva. What brings you?"

"Smelled me coming?"

"Of course, but I heard you long before that. Wolf ears are keen. I heard Hilja's demands, as well. She's as naïve as that young pup, Harley."

"Bitter because he stole your crown?"

"He won't be king long enough to learn better."

"You weren't queen long enough either."

I must have pricked a nerve, because she went silent. I chose a different subject.

"So ... you can hear all the way to the Warden's office? You must know everything that happens here then," I prompted.

"It's only been a day, but I can tell you not much happens. Boredom is already starting to set in, so I'm glad to see you."

"All these books and centuries to read them. Sounds like heaven."

She raised her eyebrows and looked at me over the edge of the tome she was reading, something called 'The Isolation of Command' whatever that meant. "You can't be serious? Then again, you did spend every free moment in the school library, I recall."

"When not fencing."

"I was impressed with how you fenced words with the new Elf Queen. You know me well. I won't tell her, or you, anything."

"All your husbands and children were evacuated to Gernwold, correct?"

"Yes," she said warily.

"And you do know that Harley has command of the wolves, and thus that city now. Lili and her necromancer ilk have fled to the plains of Solheim."

"Doesn't matter where I—or my family—reside, my bargain with the Dead God means we all get spared."

"Spared death at His or His army's hands. What would happen if someone killed them the old-fashioned way? You wouldn't see your family again until you joined them in the Lands of the Dead, which, if we win, could be a very long, and boring, time coming."

"My husbands, maybe, you'd threaten. But children? I know you, Eva, and I call your bluff."

"You know me, but do you know Hilja? She is an elf of many resources. I know at least one amoral assassin myself who could do it, but she knows dozens I bet."

Gypsum paled. "I can't, Eva. If I forsake Him…"

"Your family dies if you don't. I won't plant the idea in Hilja's head, because it's already there. I read it in her soul. I read lots of things in souls these days. She sent people to seize your family as soon as Lili's army fled. King Harley won't have been told, and they'll be in her clutches long before he can do anything to stop it. As soon as I walk out of here empty handed, she'll give the order to have them carried here by dirigible. She'll kill them one by one in front of you until you answer her questions. She'll delay moving her army until she has your intelligence. I won't be surprised if she convinces all the Crowns to delay until we know more—and I can't have that. We have no time. Something truly terrible is coming."

"You mean more terrible than the Dead God?" She gave me the dismissive look she used whenever I shared a wild theory.

"I can see you don't believe me, but that's fine. You just have to believe what Hilja will do if you don't tell me everything she wants to know. I came here to ask 'why?', to say 'goodbye', because I fear I won't be back after I face the Dead God. But my original intentions don't matter anymore. The moment Hilja showed, I realized I can't leave here without the information she wants. I can't risk any delays in my plans. Will you make it easy, or will you put your life above that of your family's?"

"I thought you read souls?"

"Werewolf Matriarchs are harder, all shifting and unpredictable. Good for lying and betraying."

"You're angry, I know." She set the book down and came to stand nearer. Still the Gypsum I knew, but the relaxed air she'd always shown me was gone. She was stiff now. "Our relationship allowed me to keep watch on you and take you to Him when the time was right. It doesn't mean I didn't like you."

"I don't care if you like me. I care about what you're going to do next."

"Surely, you must know I won't let my children be assassinated? Only ... I've sworn to the Dead God and our souls will go to Him in the end. How will it be for me and my kin after I've betrayed Him too?"

"You don't have to worry about that. I told you: I'll deal with Him." There must have been a dangerous note in my voice, because she paused halfway through giving me her disbelieving look again.

She thought about it, but then she exhaled and shook her head. "I took an oath and bound my soul."

"Enough already." If Hilja's plans couldn't convince her, nothing would. Powerful werewolves like her were immune to my control, and she'd be immune to Thane's glamours. There was only one way to compel her.

"First Soul," I said aloud, feeling strange speaking to it so openly, rather than in the hidden compartments of my mind. For some reason I chose Solhan, the language of ritual, for my next words and said, "I call to thee. Lend me your power. Compel this liar to answer truthfully. Turn her oath breaker if need be."

"What...?" Gypsum began.

The First Soul flared to life, humming happily as it stretched black tendrils from its hiding place in my belt pouch. Those tendrils reached out and encircled

Gypsum. She tried to wriggle free, even called out to the Warden, but the Soul smothered her cry into a muted yelp.

I asked Hilja's questions again, with the Soul compelling Gypsum to take up pen and paper and write out everything. She knew about Lili's armies, about Solheim and the necromancers who guarded it. She even drew a map of the Solhan plain and where the Dead God's generals each had responsibility for command, where his risen hordes patrolled. She knew far more than I'd expected. Those curious wolf ears had picked up much.

I read all twenty pages, blowing on each to dry the ink as she passed them through the bars to me. The First Soul helped me commit the details to memory. It was so overjoyed to be called on again and whispered, *What a sweet start to things we have made. I can kill her for you.*

"No," I ordered, and it obeyed for now.

Gypsum ran out of parchment and used half blank pages torn from her books as well, so the sizes varied. I tied off the irregular roll with a ribbon from the sleeve of my gown and held it in my fist.

Only then did I free Gypsum from the Soul's influence, coaxing the black cloud of power back into its burrow against my womb.

"Eva." Tears poured down Gypsum's cheeks when she was free. Her hands shook. They were clawed and cramped from writing so much so quickly, her fingers stained with ink. "What was that thing? What have you become?"

"What have we all become? Enjoy the comforts of your prison, old friend, and the knowledge your family is safe. I will stop the Dead God and spare you His punishment, the punishment you deserve. I will save everyone, whether they merit it or not."

I turned my back on her. I walked using my Ashur as a cane, so the tap of its silver tip echoed in the empty corridor. It made a satisfying bang on the metal door too, and I called, "Warden. I'm done here."

Hilja was appreciative but not as surprised as I expected her to be.

Mister Gardens raised an eyebrow, assessing me. He knew when something should have been impossible, but Hilja's reaction to having so much military intelligence gifted to her with a bow was one of royal privilege: Of course, Eva, soon to be Queen of the Dead, would obtain and give her, Queen of the Elves, all she desired. It was the natural order in her mind. Her soul I could read easily, and it disturbed me less than some. Her world was simple, with right and wrong, even if others might disagree with the subtleties of her definitions.

"Happy?" I said.

"Indeed. The other Crowns and I will take this into account, adjust our tactics as need be. We may yet set off on schedule."

"Ensure you do."

16 WAR AT DAWN

What I'd done to Gypsum made me feel dirty. I was done fencing with words and saying my goodbyes.

I knew there was Karo still. Thane told me she'd been freed from Gypsum's encampment, and no one thought her a traitor after they saw the scars on her wrists and ankles from the manacles. She'd been kept as a hostage, another potential weapon against me. I wanted to visit her in the hospital and apologize for everything she'd been through, for everything really. But I couldn't do it. Using the First Soul again had left me brittle as eggshell.

And Bell. There was so much she needed to know about Aguragas, about the path she was on, if she'd listen. I couldn't face her now either.

I sought absolution in Thane. The First Soul's residue had infused me, and I needed to wash some of it away.

I went to him in the palace, and when we were secreted away in the most private of his personal chambers, he held me.

He listened without me needing to speak. I couldn't speak. I cried.

"You don't have to say any more goodbyes," he insisted, knowing the reason for my tears.

"Thane. The Dead God wants me, and I will do anything that is necessary to get Him to stop all of this. Anything."

"You still don't get to say goodbye. I'm coming with you, wherever that is, no matter which side of life or death."

"Who will keep the Crowns on task? I need them as a distraction."

"Hilja will lead the elves now, Harley the dwarves, Moore the humans, Miss Kissel the goblins, and Calka will ensure all follow the plan. You need me to shroud the First Soul."

"It's ... it's inside me now, Thane. There's no hiding from it anymore."

His warm arms tightened, until I slowly softened, tense muscles growing slack.

He whispered into my hair, "If anyone can fight that thing—whether living, dead, or god—it's you, Eva Thorne. Not even the First Soul tells you what to do."

I smiled. "I'm that stubborn?"

"Unimaginably."

He pulled back and put his hand over my heart to feel its wild flutter.

His fingers brushed the hollow of my neck, his thumb summoning a warm tingle where it innocently pressed into my breast.

"The fear won't let go of you. That's because you focus on all that is imperfect in this world, in others, and in yourself, Eva. Judgement creates absence. Like picking up a stone from the beach and casting it aside because it displeases you for one reason or another. Eventually, there is no beach left. Think instead of what you want."

"I'd have to be pretty picky to toss aside a whole beach. But I get it. Think positive. I want Highcrowne left in peace. I want peace. Period. Because that means what I care about is safe. Is that positive enough?"

"Why do you want those you care about to be safe?"

"So, they're happy. So, I selfishly get to have them around to make me happy. I thought that was obvious."

"You know what causes pain. But what creates happiness?"

"I don't know. It's been a while."

"What brings Little Viktor joy?"

"Lately, playing with his friends. I'm a bit jealous, as he hardly notices me. Not that he ever did when Duane was around, but I suppose Duane's juvenile enough to be just another kid to Vikky, so that explains that."

Thane smiled, a sparkle in his diamond-colored eyes. "I see. And what makes me happy?"

"Making up for not having a body by exploring the pleasures of the flesh until I'm exhausted?" I grinned then. "Not that I'm complaining about your hedonism."

I shifted the hand he still held over my heart a little more to the left, so his fingers slipped beneath the cloth of my gown. The movement revealed quite a bit more cleavage, but no one was watching ... except, perhaps, for spies and servants in the walls, if this palace was anything like the one in Faellion. I didn't care.

"Being with you is what makes me happy," he said. "Wherever we are."

He was going too slow, so I kissed him, remembering when he'd been Erick, then Conrad. I was always taking the lead, and he didn't mind, whoever he was.

I nibbled at his lower lip, his muscled shoulders, and he nibbled back, which tickled, and I ran around to the other side of the massive bed.

The room was huge, and the canopied bed draped in velvet took up a sizable portion of it. He feinted right, expecting me to run, but I rolled across the mattress and wound up beside him. I was the one hunting him.

I threw him down, and he let me tear off his shirt as I'd dreamed of doing ever since I read a similar scene in a copper-priced novel.

I hadn't expected buttons to go flying and hit me in the face. I cupped my right eye, which was suddenly sore and watery. He kissed my cheek and soothed me with more kisses. All the way down my body.

Things got serious then. What began playful turned needy. I needed him to fill me up, every hollow space. I wanted him to push out the First Soul's inky residue and wash away my fear of what lay ahead. And he did. For a time.

When we'd finished, we lay, blanketed by the orange glow of candlelight, enjoying a peace that could not last.

I wanted more than anything for this moment to stretch forever. I wanted it too much, and the contentment was replaced by a wave of sorrow. I sobbed, and he turned over, taking me in his arms.

"These tears don't match what I know is in your soul."

I wiped my cheeks, and they were wet again before I said, "Because ... maybe I've never truly loved someone before. Not like this. The moment I feel desire, or recall a memory of us, good or bad ... whenever any thought of you swells in me, it's like a pretty shell on that beach you were using to talk about happiness. It's the most beautiful thing I can imagine, but it is swallowed by a wave of fear as big as an ocean.

"It's like I'm looking back on this moment from a time in the future, when this is a distant memory I long for. Wherever I am then, this is no more. It will not last. It is gone already. My tears and me telling you all this have already washed away that one sweet moment."

"We can create more, Eva. What I have learned of love is that it endures all things."

He took my hands, and I gazed into his eyes through a blurry lens of tears.

"In the Lands of the Dead," he said, "this place seems distant. All the struggles of mortals are like a dream. The fear, the pain, even the joy becomes faded. Few experiences are powerful enough to etch themselves into your soul. Love is the most powerful of all. Hold onto it for a heartbeat or a lifetime. No matter how long, your soul will be the greater for it."

The last of my tears trickled down my cheeks, washing away the emotions with them. I kissed him then. Really kissed him. We had joined souls and bodies before, but this was different. This was about me burning the memory of him into me, into my very being, so I would never forget him no matter what happened.

Once again, morning came too soon.

My practical boots and riding pants were clean, and I almost donned them without thinking. But I fingered the gowns hanging in Fharen's closet. Did he have so many ladies coming and going in need of a fresh change of clothes? Some of these might even have been worn by Ilsa. I recoiled at that thought, but the reaction softened to sadness.

My sister was gone, turned into a vampire, trapped in her own corpse as surely as any Risen. Her last shred of humanity had been ripped away and replaced by the amoral hunger of a predator. I'd left her entombed, with no way to escape. Even if she managed to claw her way out, one way or another, she was no more. My hatred of her had died along with her body, or maybe it had vanished the day I stole her soul? I'd had my part to play in her demise.

I found a gown that would have fit her, and thus me, a lovely blue that suited me like midnight. It had been cleaned, so there was no strand of black hair to guess if had been hers, but I imagined it had been. I stepped into the waist and petticoats, pulled up the bodice and stretched my arms through the sheer, silken sleeves. Without bothering to do up the back, for I couldn't without help, I stepped out on the balcony.

Wind tore at my hair and sleeves, and I looked first up at the Avian peak and then across Highcrowne to the golden sparkle of the Serpent's Ribbon in the rising sun.

"You are lovelier than all of it," Thane said, coming up behind me.

"Remember me like this. Soon, I'll be covered in grime from the road."

"I've etched this vision of you into my soul."

"Good." I smiled and kissed him.

I finished getting dressed, leaving the gown on the floor and donning my riding pants instead.

Thane knew the palace's secret passages, and we managed to exit the Central City without being stopped by anyone but the EEPs at the gates. They let Fharen pass, nervous at his refusal of an escort, but by the time we found the goblin encampment in the Red Precinct he didn't look like Fharen anymore. He was my dark-haired Thane.

"Tell me again, Miss Thorne," Doctor Ghunnan said, "why we must set out so early? I had hoped to languidly consume a breakfast of blood sausage and sautéed mushrooms this morning but was forced to gobble it like one of your 'werewolves'."

"We are setting out at sunrise, Doctor, because I don't want to waste another day. We have few to spare."

"If you say so."

How could the doctor always make me feel like a deluded hysteric? We could be in the middle of battling vampires, and if I shouted for him to hurry, his reasoned tone managed to imply I was overreacting. That wasn't a hypothetical example. It had happened.

"And tell me," I asked, "why donkeys? I dislike horses, but at least they keep my toes from dragging on the ground."

I'd tried the stirrups when I mounted the smelly, unkempt creature, but using them put my knees in my face. Either way, feet up or down, the animal was indifferent to the suffering he'd soon be inflicting on me, munching alfalfa with a heavy-lidded, bored gaze.

"Where we were going," the goblin had explained, "there will be narrow trails affording no room for horses to pass. We will have to set even these nimble-footed beasts free before the journey is over."

"I prefer to walk," Duane said, striding up to us with a travel pack slung over one shoulder.

Grim and Gormless silently drifted behind him, one thin and grouchy, the other massive and happy as a child—his mismatched shadows instead of mine for once.

Gormless said, "I wouldn't mind a donkey, Boss. They're cute." He ruffled the nearest one's ears, which flopped about like a bunny's.

Jorg's earth-shaking footsteps preceded his voice. "Wait for me."

"Walking will be fast enough if the grall is to keep up," Duane explained.

I put hands on my hips and scowled. "The grall doesn't need to keep up. None of you do. This is my task. Mine alone. How did you even know to find us here? Never mind. You followed the doctor. I figured it out."

Duane raised an eyebrow. "Well done. You've already got a goblin with you, and..." he appraised Thane, who continued preparing his mount, gently talking to the donkey in elvish, unaffected by the new arrivals, "...the Elf King in disguise. Don't be surprised I know more than you think. Why not King of the Gutter and his court?"

"Styling yourself a king now?" I almost said something cutting—a habit of mine—but I stopped. I didn't feel like insulting him. He was only here to help. Or watch me for my uncle. Either way, he didn't deserve it. So, I said, "Fine. As long as none of you slow us down, the more the merrier."

"Glad you said that, because we're waiting on one..." Duane pointed at the sky, and Roosal descended, "...more. Who's right on time."

It got really crowded when Captain Uanal and Hilja marched down the street surrounded by EEPs. "For the love of..." I began. When they reached me, I said, "Don't tell me you're coming too? This is a secret mission, people."

"We are not accompanying you," Hilja said. "I've only come to wish you good fortune."

"And me as well," Harley said. I hadn't seen him, but then I spotted the young Dwarf King wearing standard issue armor. He'd blended in with his guards. "Our hopes are with you, Madam."

"It's Miss." I wasn't that old. "And thank you. Thank you all. You can go now."

Captain Uanal said, "I'm only here to shut the gate behind you."

"But I'll miss you the most," I said with a smile.

"Humans." He huffed.

"Solhans," I corrected. There was a big difference, especially now.

"Let's go," Thane said. He'd finished readying the donkeys. He'd even said a few words to mine, and the beast seemed to be standing as tall as it could to help me out.

Thane didn't even look back at Hilja or the others before setting off. I liked his focus.

"Don't forget where you need to be," I said as I waved to our farewell party.

Doctor Ghunnan hurried to catch up.

When we were out the gate and across the bridge, Thane ordered, "You two, Grim and Gormless I believe are your names, range out ahead looking for any spies Lili of Solheim may have left behind. Avian, you scout from above. Jorg the grall, guard our backs, and Duane is it? You can take point."

Grim said, "Wander the forest? Looking for spies? I've never left the city afore today."

"Scouting is not why I came," Roosal argued. "I must confer with the goblin about the planned use of portals, for I have knowledge that will prove useful."

"Does being at the back mean I can't talk?" Jorg asked.

"And no one but Ulric orders me around," Duane said, arms crossed. "And not often"

"For crying out loud." I rubbed my temples, a new habit of mine. "Listen to me then. Thane and Jorg can scout—they've both travelled these forests before. I'll guard Roosal and the doctor, as they are certain to get lost in thought, while Grim and Gormless guard the rear. They can follow all our footprints if they get lost."

"And me?" Duane asked.

"You said you don't take orders, so I don't care what you do."

"I'll range ahead too and scout for any surprises Lili's army might have left."

I nodded. I wasn't looking forward to listening to Roosal's and the doctor's arcane discussions, but I knew I should know what they were talking about. I'd let everyone else have all the fun.

"Alright, you know what you're doing. Go." I copied Captain Uanal's command voice, and it got them moving, although Thane did pause to give me a backwards smile.

I smiled, but it faded as they got farther away. I was leaving all but Thane behind before I reached

Solheim. No way was this supposed to be a group mission. If I didn't need the doctor's mode of transport, I would have gone alone last night, vanished before anyone knew where I was.

Roosal and the goblin spoke so quietly I had to shove my head between them to hear their whispers. "What don't you want me to know?"

Roosal looked up, as if the clouds had ears, and then he took out a palm-sized crystal ball etched with glowing Avian goo. He set it on the ground between us, and suddenly we were trapped inside the orb.

I hammered at the glass with my fist, and the green lines brightened, sparking with gold and moving faster in a dizzying pattern across the glass.

"Please, don't," Roosal warned. "I will be unable to reverse our condition if you break the device."

The goblin lowered his spectacles, blinked, donned them again and kept blinking. Once the lights playing across the surface of the orb settled down, it was transparent again. A giant blade of grass pressed against the glass, and an insect the size of a wolf perched there, eying us with twitching pincers.

"Impossible," the goblin muttered. Then understanding dawned. "However, I am with Miss Thorne again. That explains much." This must be another 'hallucinogenic' episode to him.

"Did you shrink us?" I asked the Avian.

"In a way."

This was magic beyond anything I'd ever heard of. I prayed Jorg didn't start stomping about looking for us.

"I'm sorry I was eavesdropping," I said. "Let me out and I'll control my curiosity. I'll try anyway."

"This is not a punishment but a means to satisfy aforesaid curiosity," Roosal, corrected. "My queen would be displeased if she learned I was sharing this information with you and your scientist friend."

"I'm more worried about heavy grall feet."

"Do not fear. The orb is impervious from without. Invisible as well. We use it for observing, especially in worlds inhospitable to life."

The goblin perked up. "Truly? How does it work?"

"We are displaced, most of our matter shifted into a pocket of the world, and our consciousness alone left behind, contained within this orb. We are not really this small or this limited. Once one learns to observe with mind instead of eyes, our perspective can grow and range far beyond these glass walls. However, for my purpose, it provides a secure means of communication."

"I prefer mind reading, soul to soul. This is weird." I had no idea what had been done to me. I didn't like it one bit.

"Such soul magic is not mine," Roosal said, bowing his head apologetically. "But an understanding of the goblin's doorways is, which is why I wanted to confer with him before proceeding. For, you see, I helped to create them."

"Nonsense." The goblin shook his head. "The power required is astronomical. They must be natural phenomena, residues from the Big Boom that created the universe."

I raised an eyebrow. "Big Boom?"

"Catchy, isn't it."

"The power required was, indeed, immense," Roosal said, "but not on the order of that involved in the formation of universes. Nevertheless, it is difficult to create new portals to travel through, which is why I do not suggest it. Those that exist were made to save first the elves and then the humans from annihilation when the Devourer came for their worlds. Now that being is coming here, and what Queen Calka did not say is that we are no longer able to open these faded gateways wide enough again, nor redirect people to fairer lands. We are all trapped on this world."

"So, the whole thing about sacrificing yourselves here to stop the Devourer once and for all wasn't so much your choice as your only option?" I grumbled 'truth, hah' under my breath.

"The Dead God is trapped in the doorway used to summon Him here," Roosal explained. "All portals on this world are connected through the Void, and a being as immense as a god cannot be sidestepped. I fear whatever doorways we use to reach Him will alert Him to our presence, for He is close by whenever we cross through the Void in this region."

"I think I know what you're saying." I tried not to touch the First Soul in my belt pouch. "Olyve and I tore a hole into the Void to deal with Leviathan, and before I sealed it up again, I saw the Dead God. Same when Ilsa and I were taken to the portal in the mountains. I saw and spoke to the god, even if He couldn't step through."

Roosal looked from me to the pouch where he too knew the First Soul resided. "Dangerous that tear you created, and I was on my way to assist in its repair, but you did manage on your own. So, to speak. We dare not use ... that tool of yours again."

"I know."

"What are you two gibbering about now?" the goblin asked. "You tease me with scientific notions, making me almost think something is possible, and then deteriorate into superstition again. It is pseudo-science."

"That is certainly one perspective," Roosal nodded. "Regardless of the words we use to explain these things, the Dead God will detect our use of the doorways."

"I thought of that," I said. "That's why I need the Kingdoms to attack. When the army has Lili distracted, I can sneak past to Solheim."

"It will not be enough. A god's attention can be many places at once. We must cloak ourselves when we cross into the Void, and that is where I can help."

"We don't have to travel in this crystal ball, do we?" I grumbled.

"This device would not work in the Void—as it creates a hidden pocket within this world, as I mentioned—but I do have other means. I could use the doctor's help deploying it once we enter the doorway he is directing us to." Roosal held up a net made of woven feathers, string and beads. It looked quite a bit like the gaudy junk Calka collected in her throne room. Maybe her junk wasn't junk after all?

Doctor Ghunnan sighed. "And what is that supposed to do?"

"You wouldn't understand."

"Not if you explain with gobbly-gook and mumbo jumbo. I do not see the purpose, as I intend to spend as little time as possible in the Void between one doorway and the next. I once wore an undersea suit and air hose through, but I found it made no difference to one's comfort in that place. There is no need for air or warmth, but there is a current of sorts that seeks to expel those crossing that boundless void. I have learned to use those currents to navigate between doorways in an efficient manner."

"Impressive." Roosal flexed his wings. "And you are correct about the currents. In order for my net to protect us, we must keep it spread wide before us, like a parasol, and so someone familiar in those currents, such as yourself, will be a great boon to my efforts."

The doctor sighed again. "Very well. Perhaps I can make this a useful experiment into the behavior of inanimate objects traversing the void at similar angles and velocities. Then the effort will not seem so ridiculous. Can I wake up now?"

The doctor obviously believed the crystal ball and the whole conversation some figment, so I hoped he would remember to do as he promised when the time came.

"How many people can your net protect?" I asked the Avian.

"Alas, it is not large. Three or four perhaps?"

"Perfect." One more reason to leave everyone I could behind. Where they'd be safe.

"Do not reveal to Calka I have told you about our role in the creation of the Void Portals," Roosal said, "It was not my truth to tell."

"How can Calka value truth, yet conceal so much?" I said, shaking my head.

"Truth is not transparency. There is a subtle difference, one tinged with perception."

"I'd like to know the truth about that green, multi-purpose lubricant you Avians produce," Doctor Ghunnan said. "Is it a variant of radium? Another isotope perhaps that emits different radiation? A chemiluminescent substance? I've been unable to puzzle out its full range of properties—or source."

Roosal clucked, a laugh I presumed, and reached out to trace his finger over a pattern etched in crystal surrounding us. "Those are truths I definitely cannot reveal, and which you do not need to know, for they are of no importance where we are going."

The crystal ball was suddenly a tiny orb in the Avian's clawed hand, and we were all standing in the grass at the edge of the forest once more.

"Blimey," Jorg said, jogging up to us, the ground rumbling. "There you are. I thought I'd lost you."

"Don't worry." I patted his arm. "Magic stuff. Or science. Depends on your vocabulary."

"Maybe I need to guard the rear instead." For a giant, he was skittish as a cat in a goblin restaurant. I was the city dweller, and I'd once looked the same, before spending weeks roaming the wilds.

"Didn't you grow up in the mountains? This should be second nature."

"Where I grew up, there were scary things about. You didn't take a leisurely stroll through the country-side. Ever."

That made sense. "Well, this is no stroll. And where we're going, I doubt even you should tread, Jorg. Why don't you turn back now?"

He shook his head. "I owe you, Eva, and I owe Boss."

"Keep yourself safe for me, then."

"This way." Doctor Ghunnan had one of his devices beeping and blinking to indicate the direction we should take.

I let the goblin lead, but I eyed Roosal the entire time. The Avian could have been our guide, for he knew the portals as well or better than the goblin did, but something made him as skittish as Jorg. He kept looking to the skies, and I wondered if he'd gone rogue from his people. The question was whether he was doing something he shouldn't to help us, or the opposite? I was suspicious by nature and experience, so I knew Roosal was up to no good. The question was whether it was a problem or not. I had enough problems.

Duane came running, tripping his way through the undergrowth. "Find high ground!" he shouted.

I really had been expecting a stroll, despite what I'd told Jorg—we were still within sight of Highcrowne—so it was a surprise when a lich came riding out of the forest, a swarm of dead soldiers around him. Thane scrambled to stay ahead of them. He wouldn't make it to us before they caught him, so he dashed into a clump of trees and out of sight.

"Surprise," Duane said between gasps when he reached us.

The only high ground we'd found in the few moments warning we had was a hillock covered in weeds and wild grasses going to seed. The donkeys stamped everything, including my foot, their frightened, eyes showing lots of white.

I hopped on one leg, cursing. It was hard to think about fighting our attackers when all I wanted at the moment was vengeance on my donkey. At least he and the other beasts acted as a shield. They weren't on par with city walls and armored soldiers for protection, though, so I felt the First Soul through my pouch with my fingers. It thrilled at the touch.

I let the relic go. It had nearly consumed me last time I used its power to defeat a lich, and I couldn't risk it again. At least not for this lich.

"This is necromancy," I told myself. "I can do necromancy."

As the lich astride his skeletal horse circled left, Roosal took flight, and the goblin hid behind Jorg. Gormless and Grim came running from the rear. They were behind the dead soldiers.

Duane drew a knife as long as his forearm. With his other hand, he untied the bola at his belt and sent it flying. Leather thongs wrapped around an undead soldier's legs, and it toppled.

These were freshly dead, fallen dwarves from the day before by the look of them. No werewolves, but there were five times as many of them as us.

The tattooed lich galloped in a circle, his risen soldiers following him. They weren't attacking, but his movement kept me turning to watch until I was dizzy.

I felt Thane's presence draw nearer. He lurked in the shadows of the trees, waiting for my lead.

"Why don't you come closer, Asheen?" I asked. "Stop making me nauseated, on many levels, and let's talk."

"You don't want to talk," the lich said. "You want to discover and play on my weakness, suggest I overthrow Lili. You seek to sow turmoil in our ranks ... or buy time for Our Lord's lap dog to build the courage to bite at my ankles with his milk teeth. Come out, come out, Thane. Join us."

I swallowed. "How do you know all this?" How did he know who Thane was?

The lich smiled, and while his mustache hid lips and rotted teeth better than Organa's lipstick had concealed her hideousness, it was not a pretty sight.

"I have a soul sense as well, girlie. Lili exceeds me only in ambition, not power. I sense your soul, little Eva, the flutters of fear and confusion, and I read it as easily as if you had spoken. I recognize Thane through the cracks in his elvish glamour. There are always cracks. Like those in the glamour he has placed over the First Soul at your belt.

"You cannot tempt me to trade places with Lili, for I care not to pay the price of the bargains she has made with the Dead God. But you could buy me with that. The relic is all those who crave true power would ever want. Gift it to me, Child of the Keeper, and I will be your friend."

I clutched my belt pouch tighter. "I have enough friends already."

The others took my words as a signal. Gormless strode forward and wrested a club out of a risen dwarf's hand before crushing the corpse's leg bones with it and hobbling the creature. Jorg didn't need a weapon to smash soldiers; he bent and broke them like twigs in his massive hands.

Grim and Duane moved swiftly but had the most difficult time of it, their blades unnoticed by dead flesh, not until they cut deep enough to separate sinew from bone. Risen could not be destroyed without fire, but they could be incapacitated.

These were not true Risen, however. They were weaker, not as fast or strong. And just like Organa's creations, these ones were animated by green lines of force stretching from the lich's soul and into them. Sever the threads, and it was seven to one, with the odds in my favor.

"Don't try it," the lich said, shaking his head in warning. "Don't challenge me."

I didn't like him reading my unvoiced thoughts, but I was skilled at hiding things from those with soul sight. And two could play this game.

"You stole your power from another Asheen?" I asked, looking into the lich's sunken, black eyes and reading his soul.

He was a dwarf of low birth, but unlike the suffragists seeking equality, he'd sought power instead. Power beyond any Matriarch's dream, and he'd found it in ancient ruins, in history long forgotten. His power grew in isolation, until one day he happened upon an Asheen who had fled Lili's wrath in Solheim. Kershayne—that was the lich dwarf's name—

Kershayne bested the Asheen and stole his soul, offering it to Lili. She made him one of her generals and let him keep the stolen soul along with many others since.

"Souls are the greatest source of power," Kershayne said.

"What makes an Asheen's soul different from that of a run of the mill necromancer, like Nanny?"

"I think you underestimate Solhan power, little one, for no necromancer is minor. That said, an Asheen has mastered all the nine plains of death."

Why had I never asked Uncle any of this?

Grim and Gormless were killing risen to my right, Jorg behind, Duane guarding my left flank while dodging donkey hooves. The goblin crouched near my feet, fiddling with some device, and the Avian hovered somewhere far above in the clouds. It felt like they all existed in another world, and it was just me and Kershayne talking. Student and teacher. He had such wisdom to share, and we could work together to overthrow Lili and save this world.

I realized then I was entranced by some spell. His soul was manipulating mine, like I did that of the wolves when I wanted to control them. I fought against him, but it was like fighting soft pillows that offered sweet sleep when you were beyond tired. I couldn't even summon the will to ask the First Soul for help, because I didn't really want it. I wanted to know more.

"Give it to me," Kershayne said, his tone reasonable. "The ancient one whose power I stole knew much, but not all. We can learn how to use the relic, together."

He beckoned with one bony finger, and I took a step forward.

Duane grabbed my wrist, but I pulled free. He hissed as if my skin burned. I saw he'd touched the dead gray flesh of my left wrist, but it wasn't gray anymore. Green writing burned on its surface. The language was Solhan, but an archaic script I could barely make out. Something about 'flesh of my flesh'.

That's how Kershayne had reached me. The dead arm I'd animated with my own necromancy was a chink in my armor, a piece of me another necromancer could reach into and use to infiltrate deeper into my mind, into my will.

Thane broke the spell.

His glamour was turned up to high, to the point of near invisibility. My gaze slid right off him, not seeing him until he struck Kershayne with a silver sword. He cleaved through a tattooed shoulder, but fell short of his neck, for the horse the dwarf rode sidestepped out of reach.

The lich looked annoyed at the damaged limb. It cracked and broke free, like a dead tree branch. He caught it before it fell away and set it across his saddle, the hand twitching and reaching.

This would not be an easy fight.

Part of me wanted to give Kershayne the Soul, and not because of his necromantic control. Part of me wanted to be rid of it, be done. To have soul sight and know the deepest darkness of the thing you carried. To know it and still try to accept it was too much sometimes. Being a Keeper was hard work, and if he wanted it....

I had an idea. I didn't need to give Kershayne the First Soul—all I had to do was give him the experience of it. See if he liked it then.

Thane, I said mind to mind. *Remember the perfect replica you created in Faellion?*

Yes.

Draw from my thoughts, I told him, *and act quickly when I hand this to you.*

I'd imagined a perfect replica of the First Soul to fool my mother and her searchers, but this version was not as realistic. I emphasized its despair and added in the very real experience I'd had of it hollowing me out, of burrowing in and chewing on my soul like some parasite gouging its way into my core.

Let Kershayne have that.

I let the dwarven lich read the relaxation in my soul, the letting go of tension. Giving up.

"I can't control it," I admitted. "And I'm tired of the evil it brings. If you are fool enough to take it...."

I reached into my pouch and brought out a coin. I felt the edges of Fharen's profile raised on its surface and passed it to Thane.

"Give it to him."

Thane was prepared, his glamour primed, and he put it in place the moment the coin touched his skin. When he opened his palm, a priceless gem had replaced the copper coin.

"What are you playing at?" Kershayne asked, disbelieving.

Was he immune to glamour?

No. The longer Thane held the fake relic out to him, the more time Kershayne had to 'feel' it with his soul sight. It was convincing even to me.

The lich reached out a hand, a greedy smirk on his face, but as soon as he touched the stone, he grunted, as if hit by a sledgehammer.

The fake Soul sent out black tendrils to encircle Kershayne, and the lich screamed.

"Is this what you wanted?" I smiled.

The gem, real and fake, were just a gem to most of those watching, but Thane, Kershayne and I could see its pulsing darkness. It was like a diseased hole in the world, spreading and expanding. It drew in all love, all pity or remorse, so you were left with a darkness like its own inside you. One that hungered. It left you fear, though. Your one morsel of humanity. It loved that emotion, fed on it.

Kershayne's fear made him drop the fake relic and run. He kicked Thane away and spurred his horse wildly, tearing east, toward the warmth of the sun. Even the dead craved an antidote to the First Soul's despair.

And that was only a reflection of the real thing.

I knew why it was getting harder for me to control the First Soul. When I'd tamed it beneath the ocean in Faellion, I'd fed it love, but Thane claimed my heart now. It was hard to find anything left to give it. I feared the real relic would soon realize how vulnerable I was. I feared its reaching darkness, not some illusion, swallowing me, and I had no idea what that meant. I suspected losing myself to the First Soul was far worse than death.

Duane and his crew fought the remaining risen soldiers Kershayne had left behind. Jorg and Gormless crushed and smashed, while Duane and Grim separated heads from shoulders with precise blade work. Still, it looked like it might take a while.

"Stop," Thane told them, and the risen crumpled at his command. Without Kershayne controlling them, they succumbed easily, thanks to Thane's knowledge of necromancy.

I gave them final peace by tearing the chained souls from their lifeless bodies. The souls' light flowed into my hands, my palms glowing a brilliant green for all to see, before I set them adrift, now free to find their way to the Lands of the Dead.

After that, I felt all eyes on us. Duane's blade was levelled on Thane. "What are you, really?"

17 THE BORDER BETWEEN

I didn't like how they looked at us, not just Thane but me.

Duane was most distrustful of the Elf King wearing a half-Solhan guise, but the others gaped or stared at my hands, and I realized they hadn't seen my battle on the bridge and the full extent of horrors I was capable of. Grim and Gormless feared me, and I thought Duane must as well. How could he not? But not Jorg, I noted, for he smiled at our victory, blissfully ignorant of any tension. He must see Duane threatening people all the time in his role of 'accountant' because he was blasé about that too.

The tension increased as silence stretched out, and I wondered what I could say to wipe the fear off their faces. The First Soul had its own solution.

Make these fools around you bow. Kill them and move on to better playmates. Gods and demons await over the horizon. Let me taste of them, it demanded.

No. Patience, I said.

I had no love to spare to ensure it obeyed me, so I gave it visions of Kershayne and Lili, the Gaunt Man and giant spiders, liches and frightening Unmentionables ... all the Dead God's minions defeated and shivering in fear beneath the Soul's dark shroud. The detail of my imaging transfixed the relic until it quieted, satisfied with a promise.

I started, as if I'd been dreaming, suddenly aware they were still staring at me.

Thane nodded to me. "Tell them."

"Put the knife down," I ordered Duane. "It's useless against him anyway."

He raised an eyebrow. "Go on."

"You know who he is."

Duane shook his head. "I know King Fharen, and this is not him. Whether he's wearing pureblood glamour or revealing his half-Solhan 'taint' as his rivals at court call it, his behavior is all off. Hilja knew it too."

"She thinks I have Fharen be-spelled. Does that explanation suit you better?"

"She might believe that, but I know you, Eva. You hate Fharen. The truth, please."

"The truth is, you have met him before, like I said. You've seen him behind Erick's eyes and Conrad's. I told you his name when we rescued Bell from that train, and you were there at the cave in, when he and Gypsum took me through the portal."

Duane paled and took a step closer, his blade now a thrust away from Thane's chest. "Get away from him, Eva."

I stepped in front of Thane, the knife dimpling the fabric of my cloak. "I didn't understand before. He doesn't want to hurt me. He's been protecting me. He and Lili want different things. Thane is only a portion of the Dead God, and he has turned against the greater part of Himself time and again to save me. I trust him. I love him."

"The Dead God?" Duane swayed, and I think he finally understood how mind blowing my first encounter with Thane had been.

"Nonsense," the goblin cut in. "I have travelled with this man and Eva for some time in Faellion, and there was no evidence of god-like powers. He is deluded, the poor creature."

Doctor Ghunnan pulled a magnifying tool from his waistcoat and promptly examined Thane's eyes, practically climbing him to reach; he also used the tool to measure the thickness of his cheek skin with a pinch that made Thane say, "Ow," and smack the doctor's hand away. The goblin's dismissal of the situation, and Thane's ordinary reaction eased the tension a bit.

Duane still didn't put his blade away. I looked down at the sharp steel, close enough to end me and everything with me, if I let him.

Then I looked Duane in the eyes and let him glimpse my soul in them. All of it, from street urchin days when I let him lead to now, where I had more dead than he did weighing on my soul. He could not help but see I had changed, and that Thane was not the one to be afraid of.

Duane had strength in his soul too, stubbornness to match mine, but he threw up his hands and stepped back.

"There's no talking sense to you, Eva. I hope you know what you're doing."

"I do. And if you don't like it, you can go back to Highcrowne now. You should."

"Someone has to protect you from yourself."

Duane tapped Grim and Gormless on the shoulder and said, "Let's get back out there and watch the perimeter."

Knowing what Thane was had left Grim's expression, well, grim, and he seemed ready to brave wild forest over Thane's presence. Gormless was his usual easygoing and obliging self. Jorg followed them, looking confused.

When they were out of sight, I pushed the goblin off Thane, who had remained frozen, watching the stand-off.

"That's enough examination," I told the doctor, summoning a lighter tone for my own benefit. "And don't think I didn't notice your absence earlier when we faced risen. What have you been up to?"

"Hiding, of course," the goblin said, "but I used the time to devise a more effective weapon for our next encounter."

He dug around in his massive pack and pulled out some form of modified crossbow. I could see the brass pieces and goo-filled vials he'd added to it. It didn't fire bolts, either. He picked up a stone from the ground, loaded it into what looked like a mini catapult on the top of the machine, and said. "Look over there."

He indicated the pile of bodies left by the battle. He sighted on a dwarven corpse, the poor fellow's skull cleaved long before he was killed again by Jorg, or whoever had managed to behead him.

The goblin flicked a switch. A line of goo, no wider than a thread, fed out of a vial along a copper wire and ignited the stone the doctor had placed in the crossbow. By 'ignited', I mean the stone was suddenly engulfed in green and yellow flames. The modified crossbow sent the stone flying, which struck with a loud bang. The headless dwarf, along with the pile of defeated risen, was engulfed in a green bonfire.

"Incendiary projectile," the doctor said with a satis-fied smile that showed off rows of needle teeth.

"That would have been more useful earlier," I pointed out.

"There will be a next time," he said knowingly. "Plenty more opportunities." He collected a pocketful of stones from the ground.

He was right.

The Avian returned some time later, when we were on the road again. "The lich is headed toward the wall," he said, making no apologies for fleeing.

Roosal had hollow bones, so I understood his reluc-tance to fight, but I was disappointed by his lack of magical prowess.

I saw a vision of him dead, Calka sobbing and begging for my forgiveness.

Stop. I told the Soul.

It stayed quiet, playing innocent. The visions faded, but my ire didn't.

"Are the tales I read growing up all lies?" I asked Roosal.

He flinched, as though I'd struck him with the accusation. "What did those tales say?"

"That Avians are immortal, older than the Serpent's Ribbon, and that their magical protections will guard the Three Kingdoms until the end of time. I've seen you in action, or lack thereof, and am seriously wondering if my brother mistakenly filed those books under 'history' instead of 'fiction'."

"No. They were not lies. I left to fetch this," he said, changing the subject. "You will need it."

He pulled an object from thin air, much as the fairy could appear out of nowhere. A demonstration of his power to quell my doubts?

It was a golden birdcage etched with Avian symbols and glowing with magical goo. It was small enough to fit in my pack—if I removed all my food. I didn't feel inclined to accept the gift, so asked, "It's pretty, but why, exactly, do I need it?"

"Thane's ability to hide the relic's presence with elvish glamour diminishes. I sense its presence, as Kershayne did. This is another way to conceal it as we travel among enemies."

It looked ancient. I wondered if Avians had built the cage long ago to, literally, cage the First Soul's power, at least until they reached the prison they'd built for it in the mountain. They'd been unable to get the relic from its Keeper, however, and so never had a chance to use it. If it could help shield the Soul, especially as Thane was failing, then I did need it.

"Thank you. Ah, I see it has a loop, so I can carry it on my belt."

I undid my belt pouch, and before I could think too much about it, shoved the whole pouch inside the cage, including the First Soul. I slammed the tiny barred door shut with a clatter.

I thought I'd been crafty, casually locking it away, along with its new trick of temptingly dark visions. But the First Soul laughed in my mind.

I am no songbird to be so easily tamed. For my song shapes your very soul into my likeness.

The goo on the cage glowed, the runes flaring with power, but then the gold bars melted away, along with my belt pouch and everything inside it. Even my fire sparker became a twisted lump of iron.

I stamped out the flames in the grass before they could spread, and when the smoke cleared, the gem that was the First Soul, and the white Avian feather from Calka, were all that remained.

It had even melted my house keys.

I put the feather in my hair and tucked the relic into my shirt, so that it rested against my chest. It was only warm now, not burning, and seemed to purr like a cat.

That's better, it said, triumphant.

Roosal hung his head. "It was untested. I'm sorry I cannot offer you more protection." With that, he took flight again, circling above us like a crow waiting for something to feast on.

"Eva, I will try harder," Thane said, putting a hand on my shoulder.

He concentrated, sweat beading on his brow like when we crossed Lili's army in Faellion.

"Stop," I said. "It's not working. Save your energy for when we reach Solheim and all Lili's minions are after us."

Whether the First Soul was winning or not, time was running out.

"Let's go."

We followed the rail line east, patches of track destroyed in the brief war, but it offered a clear path. Two days into our journey, though, we had to veer into the deep forest in search of our doorway, and the going was slower. The hills grew steeper, and I spurred everyone on, aware of the timing I'd given Hilja and the Highcrowne army.

To spare the donkeys his bulk, Gormless walked alongside Jorg, the giant man looking diminutive next to the truly giant grall, while Grim and Doctor Ghunnan shared the freshest mount. The goblin complained about the thug's knife handles poking his back, while the thug complained about the goblin's new crossbow in his face. Duane ranged out ahead on foot, wary of more ambushes like Kershayne's.

I was tired of a bony spine poking into my behind, despite layers of blanket and saddle, and dismounted. The donkey almost stomped my foot again, so I left it with Thane, telling him to give it a lecture about watching where it put its hooves.

I sought Duane out.

I didn't know why I cared what he thought. He was always moody, but since he'd learned who Thane really was, he'd been colder than usual. If he wasn't going to head back to the city where he belonged, then I needed to make sure he wouldn't turn on Thane or me at a bad moment. More enemies than I could count lay ahead, and I didn't need more among us.

He slunk quietly among the trees, unnoticeable to most, but my soul sense showed me where he was as clearly as it showed me squirrels in their nests and mice scurrying about in the bushes. I walked loudly up to him, tree branches crunching, and he winced.

"Scouting is usually a silent activity," Duane pointed out. "And solitary."

"I thought you were here to save me from myself, not scout," I said. The arrogance of him. Unfortunately, with the First Soul messing with my mind, I might need saving, just not by him.

"Will you listen when I say Thane is bad news and should be the one you leave behind?" he asked. "Will you listen when I say drop that relic the Avians and Ulric are up in arms about? Consign it to a bottomless well, anything?"

"It's not that simple."

"It never is."

"The First Soul is on the run from the Devourer, a Primal god, who will chase it down whether it's hidden in a deep, dark Avian cave or across the universe, and everything around the relic will get gobbled up along with it. That means all of us."

"Yet, we're taking time out to go against the Dead God too? You convinced Hilja and the others who are hungry for an end to war, but you didn't convince me. The puzzle pieces don't fit."

"Glad I don't have to convince you then."

"Because I don't matter?"

"I didn't say that. Listen, the Dead God was summoned to do Lili's bidding, but Thane tells me it's in His interests as well. He wants to 'watch over' Solhan and human souls. That means harvesting us ahead of the Devourer's coming. A mercy."

"Being harvested like a pumpkin is not my idea of mercy."

"Mine neither, which is why we use the First Soul to get rid of Him, then we can figure out what to do about the Devourer."

I was lying from my soul, believing every word I said, because my plan depended on it. He wasn't convinced.

"This is worse than your usual bad ideas."

"You have something better? You know how to banish the Dead God and the Devourer?"

"I'm no 'chosen one' or 'key' or whatever, but I do know about being in a scrap with two thugs bearing down on me, one of them a troll, and the only thing to do is dodge. Then run," he said.

"And live to fight another day. I get it. But we have no place to run, so I say we kick them in the teeth."

"Now, that sounds like Eva."

"I didn't before?"

"Sometimes of late ... you remind people more of ... Ilsa."

He knew how much I'd always hated my twin, and he'd winced when saying her name, probably expecting me to punch him. Bell had said something similar. I didn't hit him, because I was beginning to worry that so many people saying the same thing could only mean it was the truth. I didn't feel like myself.

"I'm going now," was all I said. "Give us more warning next time you spot a necromancer."

After that, Thane and I walked beside our donkeys, nearly dragging them up the hills, and my heart beat wildly. I wanted to go faster, leave the animals behind, but there was more climbing ahead of us. We'd tire and need to ride them again.

Even if we hadn't been slowed by the terrain, the doctor needed to stop every fifteen minutes and use his gadgets. He kept mumbling something about it all being "very strange."

What was strange was the relic against my breast. More than strange, terrifying. Its dark coils were beginning to reach in and wrap around my heart.

Avian cage or elvish glamour, all have failed you, it said. *My power is yours, and you are mine. It is unstoppable.*

The Soul was like a creeping disease consuming me. I couldn't fight it, because it was inside me.

"I can carry it again," Thane offered. He sensed my struggle and wanted to shield me, but it was too late.

"There's no point. And ... I think it would hurt you." Since the battle for Highcrowne, the First Soul, which was already a handful, had become decidedly more dangerous. "With your glamour and Roosal's gadgets failing, we need to find some way to get me and the relic to Solheim undetected. I'm thinking about too many things at once, and nothing is coming to me."

The doctor had been listening in. "I do believe the doorways will allow us to arrive at speed, and if this gem or whatever you call it is a homing beacon of some sort—and you insist on carrying it instead of discarding it—then speed is our only means of evading capture."

"But the doorway in the old temple leads just to the other side of the wall," I reminded him. "How do we travel overland to Solheim 'at speed'? The plan was to move stealthily, while the Highcrowne armies act as a distraction."

"Plans, like hypothesis and experimental protocols, must, from time to time, change, my dear."

"What's changed?" I asked warily, fearing the answer.

The goblin tapped the silk hat he wore, and the brass lenses and detectors fastened atop it clanked together heavily. "My devices are telling me strange and interesting things. The usual doorways have shifted, and there are many more doorways much closer to us now, as well as the possibility of others which lead more directly to our final destination."

He put too much emphasis on the word *final*, which, once again was less than encouraging.

"I thought new doorways required impossible amounts of energy?" I said.

"These are not new. They've become unanchored from their normal locations."

"How do we know they are even navigable anymore?" Thane asked.

"We do not, but I'm burning to experiment," the doctor said, smiling.

"We don't have the luxury of experimentation," I said. "I need a path to the other side of the wall, but the closer to Solheim the better."

"I shall find our way. Never fear, my dear."

I did fear. We could fail and die … or succeed and die.

My best case scenario put us so far beyond the wall there were no Highcrowne guards, no magic, and no bargains to protect us. Once again, I realized how close the enemy had always been, with nothing but the

Compact—nothing but fine print and tradition and handshakes between gods—to hold the hordes back.

"I suppose we don't have a choice," I said. "Lead on."

I would trust the doctor's dispassionate logic, even as I trusted myself less and less.

The 'doorway' Doctor Ghunnan led us to was not as grand as the first one I encountered. That doorway had been the center point of an ancient, ruined temple. This one was a nondescript tree, in a forest of trees.

"How can you tell where the portal is?" I asked.

"Science. And my improved navigation device will allow us to traverse without fail."

He took off his silk hat and put a copper pot on his head. The lenses on it were thicker than those on his previous hat and hooked to tubing filled with Avian goo. As impressive as all the glowing bits were, it was still a pot.

"Time to leave the donkeys," the goblin pronounced.

I was overjoyed and jumped off mine at slightly the wrong angle and had to roll to avoid twisting an ankle.

Duane helped me stand after I came to a stop. "That's why I prefer to be on foot," he said.

"You wouldn't if you were wearing these." I showed him the heel that had been added to my boots by invisible elves working in the palace. I'd tried cleaving the heel off with my sword, but elvish cobblers were mages of a sort and took pride in ensuring their work was unbreakable. I wondered if it was retaliation for ordering them around.

I dusted myself off and ran a hand across the rough bark of the tree Doctor Ghunnan was staring at. "I can't feel any 'door'."

Lenses whirred and clicked into place over the goblin's left eye. He blinked and said, "More to your left. The other left. Perhaps you should allow me? Oh no, now your fingers are jammed in there. The angle of entry must be just so." The doctor sighed and put the pot on my head.

It was heavy and smelled of acid. I closed one eye to look through the series of lenses dangling before me.

The tree was there, and I could see where my hand ended, caught in some invisible place, but on top of it were throbbing circles of light, red and deep blue, alternating in a hypnotic pattern from one location. The lights were coming from the portal we sought, which appeared as a straight line cut in the world. I could see my hand was bent over and caught, as it would be in a crevice. But as I edged to the left, I saw the line widen into a doorway, and my hand came free. It looked like a door into blackness, perfectly rectangle, and seemed to change its shape depending on the angle. It was thinner from the sides, but approached the right way, straight on, a person could pass easily.

"Oh," I said. His funny pot hat was useful after all.

"I should go first," Doctor Ghunnan said, "and scout the way."

I was intrigued and wanted to go, but I was also wary of catching the Dead God's attention if I spent too much time in the Void between portals.

"Find us the shortest path," I reminded him, as I handed the heavy pot over.

"Indeed. That is often the trick." He straightened his lenses then stepped through without hesitation.

The rest of us gathered to watch. Not that there was anything to see but a tree. Still, Jorg held his breath. Thane's soul echoed my worries about the Dead God detecting our approach, and even Duane had given up his reflexive wariness of Thane and stood beside him, staring at the spot where the goblin had disappeared.

I took advantage of the moment to catch everyone off guard, saying, "When he comes back, you're all staying here."

"What?" Jorg took a shocked step back that made the ground rumble.

Grim spat and sheathed his blades. "Good. I've had enough of green growing things, so I won't be twiddling me thumbs here. I'm going back to Highcrowne now."

Gormless put a hand on his shoulder, which was the only thing that kept him from slinking back the way we'd come. "Listen to what Boss says."

I knew Duane was the one to convince. "I don't want any of you coming through this doorway," I told him. "There are dark things within and on the other side, worse than that lich. As much as I hate it, it will take magic, and none of you have any."

"I've been around Ulric long enough to know magic is never all you need. But..." he looked at Thane "...you're convinced you know what you're doing. See you later."

Duane gestured to the others to follow, and they did without complaint. Not even Jorg demanded to stay and protect me.

After they disappeared in the undergrowth, the grall's thunderous footsteps a distant rumble, I narrowed my eyes. "What are they playing at?"

"Perhaps you are not accustomed to being obeyed, my love?" Thane was grinning ear to ear from my reaction. He could sense my strange frustration over not having to fight for it.

That was true, but I also knew Duane, and I knew he wasn't acting out of obedience to me or Ulric. He was crafty.

"The goblin returns," Thane said, pointing at the tree.

The doctor was back, furiously adjusting his eye-
piece and changing out lenses. "Where has everyone
disappeared to? Do I have these settings right?"

"I sent them away. Let's go before they come back.
Where's Roosal? We need his protective net."

The goblin shook his head, gizmos rattling. "As I've
said before, my dear, we do not. Speed will serve us
better than superstition."

"Very well."

I almost shoved the goblin through the doorway, I
was in such a hurry, but Thane sensibly paused to
grab the saddlebags, so I helped, slinging one over my
shoulder. Weeds got tangled around my legs, and I
nearly tripped through the Portal after Thane and the
doctor.

I wished I could send Thane away as well—who
knew what fate awaited him for his betrayal—but I
needed him.

The Void was as I remembered it, a black so thick
it could smother you. My soul sense told me it was
alive. Alive with the potential of creation, but also
with the travelling sparks of souls searching for the
Lands of the Dead or living souls wandering like us,
only too distant for us to call out to them. They might
as well have been other stars in the night sky.

"Stay close," the goblin warned.

"Just hurry," I insisted.

The First Soul's black halo took on a brown and
purple cast in the Void, like something diseased.

I hadn't sensed the Dead God yet, but Thane's soul was bright here, his glamour unable to shield it. I thought the relic's power was what I needed to hide, and it was a beacon as I feared, but not the only one.

"He still believes I serve Him," Thane said, trying to reassure me.

"Lili and Kershayne knew better, so don't think Him ignorant."

The goblin followed a snaking path, avoiding obstacles only he could see with his contraption. There was no ground, but we weren't floating, either. Each step felt like I was sinking into a feather bed.

My feet sunk into nothingness, and I slowed, trying unsuccessfully to tear them away.

"How much farther?" I asked the doctor.

He reached out and peeled apart the blackness, like opening a curtain. The colorful world outside was blinding.

I stumbled forward, shoving Thane and the goblin through the portal ahead of me.

The drop was farther than I expected. I landed on Thane's legs, and he hissed with pain before I managed to roll away.

The groundcover was thick grass, rather than the brambles of the forest, so we had travelled some distance.

My foot was still caught on something. A vine. I tried to tear it away from my ankle and discovered that beneath a few stalks and leaves was an almost invisible silk thread. It cut into my finger, drawing blood. I followed it one direction and found it attached to my belt. I used my blade to cut myself free. I followed the other end, wrapped my hands in leather, and pulled like a fishing line. Duane tumbled out of the portal.

He landed on his feet, as usual.

18 HIDDEN

"**Y**ou followed me. I knew you were up to something," I told Duane, eye to eye. "You are such a liar."

"I never lie. Lies complicate things. Now, you'd best move, because the others are right behind me."

I moved, not because he told me to but because I realized a grall was about to fall on us.

The gang was soon back together. Not that we'd been apart long. Only the setting had changed.

We were in a lush valley, ideal for crops, but instead of the autumn harvest of corn and pumpkins you'd expect to find, there were human-sized, bean-like pods. Exactly human-sized.

"I know what these are," I said, a sick feeling in my stomach. I tried not to think of the abomination, the soul that lurked somewhere below ground in the fungal fibers of the plant's roots. Thinking of it would draw its attention.

"This is why I followed," Duane said. "When the goblin spoke of warped doorways, I suspected…. We should leave now, before we disturb them."

"If they wake, they'd be a formidable force on our side," Thane said.

Thane couldn't take his eyes off the spot where the First Soul nestled against me, and not just because that spot lay between my breasts. I knew he worried about how close it was getting to me, mentally. He wanted all of this over for my sake.

I touched his hand in reassurance. The First Soul, jealous, sent a painful spark along my skin, which arced in blue electricity between us, and I snatched my hand back.

"We may be able to induce them to mature," the goblin said, examining the nearest pod.

"Don't touch them," Duane warned. He nodded to Grim. "Restrain Doctor Ghunnan."

Grim and Gormless moved as one to take the doctor's arms and drag him back.

"What's the meaning of this?" he struggled, baring teeth, and I suddenly worried for the two thugs. Goblins were ferocious, even if the doctor was an anomaly, he was still a fighter at heart.

"Let him go," I ordered, not that I could expect my orders to be obeyed.

"Listen to me for once, Eva," Duane said. "You want to leave these things alone. The doctor needs to find another portal. Better yet, let's start walking and figure this out far away from here."

"It will take me some time to discern what went wrong and find another nearby doorway," the doctor said. "But I need my arms back to do it!"

The two thugs let him go, and the goblin, annoyed, smoothed the creases in his clothes.

"The plant abominations are dangerous, but these are unhatched, so why are you so afraid of them?" I asked Duane.

Jorg stood almost between us, his head swiveling to watch the suspicious looks Duane and I shot one another.

Finally, Duane said, "I'm afraid *for* them. I can't say any more with ... Thane around."

"Why not?"

"Eva, give it a break. Please."

Roosal landed beside us. He hadn't come through the portal, so he must have flown the whole way. That meant he was fast, able to track us, and capable of reaching Solheim before us if he desired. He must not desire to, or at least not alone.

"Your companion cannot speak of these things, because we have forbidden it," Roosal said. "But I concur that we should leave this place as soon as possible. Conduct your calculations away from this valley, Doctor. I can assist."

The goblin grumbled as we climbed hills and entered the tree line. We were over a mile away from the narrow valley where the pods grew before Roosal let us stop again.

I was burning with curiosity. "What can't you tell us?" I looked first at the Avian and then Duane, but neither would open their mouth, or beak as it were.

"Women do not understand the nature of secrets," Grim said.

"So, you were told but not me?" I snapped.

Grim remembered he was speaking to a Solhan necromancer and his eyes widened. "No. I know nothin'. I'm just saying ... never mind."

Duane, unfortunately, was very good at secrets, and he wasn't talking.

Roosal focused on discussions with the doctor, consulting the goblin's instruments, and studiously ignoring me. Was this why he too had been acting strangely when we left Highcrowne?

Avian secrets were the reason we were in this mess. If only they'd done what needed doing centuries ago and got the First Soul away from this world, we wouldn't need to worry about the Dead God and the Devourer bearing down on us.

"Eva." Thane said reasonably, reading my mind or soul as usual. "They may be unwilling to share this secret because of where we are headed and who we must face. Some secrets cannot risk the scrutiny of those able to peer into souls. If you had known before we left Highcrowne, Kershayne would know now too."

I could always extract it from Duane's soul. I just didn't want to look in there. And the Avian's was like a foreign land to me.

Perhaps it was better to drop it.

But it was hard, so hard.

"Fine," I said with a loud exhale. "Where to next, Doctor?"

"I see why we were thrown off course. The paths through the Void have all twisted, as if the fabric of this world has been altered here. We need to move farther away from the hybrid creatures."

I'd have thought the goblin would be dying of curiosity as much as me, but he seemed content to deal with the current puzzle occupying his attention.

We went deeper into the forest, climbing a series of small cliffs to gain altitude, so we could see the distant wall. We kept going until the sun was setting and it was time to make camp. Only then did the goblin say the readings on his instruments were better.

I was exhausted, my legs rubbery and arms shaky. Mountain climbing, wriggling along narrow paths, pulling my way over rocks ... not my favorite way to spend the day. I suddenly longed for Karolyne's café; not the days when I was working there, but when I got to sit in the corner sipping kaffe.

I sighed. I had no choice. "We leave at dawn," I told everyone, lest they thought any of us could rest for long, even me.

I didn't have my fire starter anymore; it was a melted clump along with the remains of my belt pouch. But Jorg made camp for us. He seemed content in these high places, putting his face into the breeze.

"I can smell for miles," he said. "It's good to be away from that valley. Here everything is cleaner. Pure."

He cooked an amazing meal, from nothing it seemed. My pack had emergency kaffe, but he had sausages and dried fruit. I drifted off to the scent of spice and grease. Jorg shook me awake when it was time to eat.

The goblin seemed fueled by sheer scientific enquiry. He buzzed about taking readings until a bowl was forced into his hands. Only Grim seemed as weary as me, so we shared a commiserating look where I forgave him about the women and secrets comment. There was plenty more I could say about thieves like him that went unsaid too.

Thieves like Duane. He and the Avians were sharing secrets. Ulric too. All of it gave me a bad feeling.

I nestled against Thane, and as Lord of Sleep and Death—even if only a fragment of that power—he helped us all rest deeply. Even Duane and Roosal, who shared twitchy looks across the campfire, were soon overtaken by sleep.

It was a mistake. One of us should have kept watch.

The doctor was stolen in the night. He could have run off, but there were signs of a struggle. Dirt and grass were torn up where he'd tried to dig in with his mechanical legs. The gouges in the earth led back into the valley. We followed the trail, and I spotted his brass helmet in the underbrush.

I picked it up. "We could try going on without him. You could find the way, couldn't you Roosal?" I looked around. "Roosal?"

"He was here when we woke," Duane said.

"Perhaps he searches for the doctor from above?" Thane looked to the sky, shielding his eyes from the morning sun.

"Or he's abandoned us again. Avians and their games." I was already tired of them. I'd lost my faith in their kind, and the more I saw their failings, the more I saw only faults. I couldn't believe I'd practically worshipped them. The Unmentionables too. Both had disappointed me.

"What if one of those things took him?" Grim whispered to his boss. Duane quieted him with a gesture, but he saw that I'd seen.

"What things?" I asked loudly.

"Wait for Roosal to return," Duane said. "I'm sure he has this under control."

I lacked faith, as I've said, so I grabbed my pack, stuffed the goblin's helmet inside, and set off along the trail left by the doctor's struggles.

I was going back the way I'd come, but sometimes you had to go back to go forward. Or something like that. I was terrible at sayings.

Thane was right behind me, the boom of Jorg's and thump of Gormless's steps said they were too. Duane could wait if he wanted, but he didn't. Somehow, he'd gotten ahead of me, and he blocked the path.

"Stop, Eva. You don't know how dangerous those things are. If one has slipped Ulric's control…."

"Slipped? What? Tell me."

He clammed up, so I shoved him aside and kept walking. I had the First Soul—nothing was as dangerous as me.

It was much faster going downhill instead of up. As I knew they would, the doctor's tracks led back to the valley and the huge plant pods that reeked of an ancient, alien soul.

Only, now that Duane mentioned my uncle, I could detect his presence as well. It was like he was on a dream walk, where his soul was nearby, projected from elsewhere. But Ulric had spread his soul out thinly, diffusing it over the valley, to restrain the alien plant. That's why I hadn't sensed my uncle's presence before. He was tangled up with the abomination in an unending struggle. The effort must be incredible, and from a distance. No wonder he'd been so exhausted when I saw him.

Thane sensed what I sensed.

"There has to be some way to kill the creature," I told him. "Pacifying it like this can't work forever."

"It's not working, else Doctor Ghunnan wouldn't have been taken," Thane said.

I turned to Duane. "How did it reach so far up the mountain to snatch the doctor? Who else serves the creature?"

"Right now?" he shrugged. "I do."

I drew my sword. Duane backpedaled, lithely darting out of reach, but I wasn't after him. I'd seen the creeper vine moving behind him. It darted at me, and I struck. Either it was too fast, or I moved too slow, and it coiled itself around my good wrist.

The alien plant was covered in stingers that sent an acid burning into my skin. I pushed back with my own magic, and the First Soul reached out its dark tendrils too, grappling with the creature. To others, it must have looked like I froze, staring at the vine wrapped around me, but the vine had stopped too. We were in a contest of wills.

I was surprised it could resist the power of First Soul at all.

Then again, I hadn't unleashed it entirely. I couldn't. A part of me clutched to some sense of control over the relic. I feared it would consume me otherwise. Even now, as I drew on it, I saw its oily blackness all around, like I was swimming in it beneath the sea again, surrounded and drowning in it.

"Stop!" I heard Ulric's voice in my mind. *"Leave this to me, Eva."*

"I can kill it," I said. "End it. I just need to...." I needed to unleash the Soul to do it, but I hesitated.

"You can't kill it," Duane and Roosal said as one. The Avian descended from above and wrapped his fluffy wings around me, and Duane tackled me from the side.

Duane gently stroked the fine hairs of the vine wrapped around my wrist, like a pet, until it loosened its grip and fell away.

When the connection was lost, so was all my progress in the struggle of wills. The contest was over. I growled with frustration. "Why did you stop me? I've seen what this thing does to people."

"This one is different. We have an accord," Roosal said, loosening his wings.

I still had his feathers in my mouth, and I spat them out. "You bargained with it? How many human souls did it want in return? First the Compact and now this. I thought you great and wise, but you Avians are no different from elf slavers, sacrificing others without remorse."

"The Compact was a thing of great remorse." Roosal hung his head, the gooey droplets that were their tears forming in his eyes. "I was with Kerrik and the Unmentionables when it was forged. We spoke to the gods of moon and sun, ancient and powerful. Even speaking to them demanded blood sacrifice. The price was worth it. To buy time for you, Eva. And that is what we do here. Buy time for you."

My fury was like the relic's black cloud, creeping out from my core and shrouding the world around me in it. "How is this on me? I want to kill this thing."

"If you do, you kill us all," Duane said. He looked to Roosal who nodded, and he relaxed, finally free to speak.

"By 'us', I mean humans," he continued. "The Avians took in hundreds of thousands of refugees after the Fortress of Mages fell. General Moore's troops are but a fraction of them. We promised their civilians protection, they and all the others in the Kingdoms not directly protected by Avian magic behind High-crowne's walls. This is that protection."

Duane suddenly looked at Thane. "Get him away. I won't say more with him listening. Then the Dead God, too, will know."

"What I know he knows," I said.

Duane closed his mouth, obstinate. He would not tell me then either.

"I am separate from Him," Thane insisted.

"How is being turned into abominations by this creature 'protection'?" I asked.

"They are not being turned into those things. Their...souls, I guess you'd Solhans would call them,"

Duane said, clearly unsure about believing in something he couldn't see, "are shielded by the plants. That way no one can find them. If we all die and Highcrowne falls—they may be the last humans. Now, do you see why you can't kill it? We can't risk breaking our side of the bargain, and Ulric watches from afar to make sure our terms are kept, and the creature does not spread beyond this valley or seek to consume the people it guards."

"You bargained with this thing?"

Duane had referred to 'you Solhans' and 'we humans', and I'd never heard him talk like that before. I'd never seen him out of the city, either, or believed he could charm a monster plant. He was not the person I thought he was.

"Calka negotiated," Roosal corrected. "And me, with Ulric's help, for the creature speaks your language, not ours."

Solhan? Or the language of souls? I didn't clarify, because each thing I learned was more horrifying than the last, and I didn't want to know anymore.

Still, I asked, "What was promised? Human sacrifices every year from now until the end of time?"

"Only for a century. And only if humanity survives. But we cannot harm it during that time either. We cannot sever their vines or strike their flesh. The price is small in comparison."

I was sickened. Dealing in lives and souls was wrong. Letting this alien thing live was wrong. I knew it was a mistake.

But I did the wrong things and made mistakes all the time. I was as bad as Roosal and Duane.

"Ulric told me there was no other way to shield so many souls from the 'gaze of gods'," Duane said. "Lili's armies, the Dead God, the Risen hordes, even the Devourer are coming at us, and this was the only way to save lives. Bell thought I was collaborating, rounding up refugees in Highcrowne to save my skin, but it was for them. All the men, women and children in those pods are safe, with no fear of starving from war or being killed as collateral damage. They are safe."

I nodded. "We do what we have to do."

I cast about with my gaze until I spotted the doctor's trail again. I found the pod he'd been dragged into. I touched the handle of my Ashur but then remembered the bargain they'd made. I could not cut it.

"Duane," I said, "do your thing and get him out of there. I won't touch that creature gently."

He did as bid, and the giant seed pod opened. The goblin was wrapped in a transparent sack of mucous. It popped open, and delicate tendrils of vines covered in white hairs unraveled, rolling out like a carpet, until the doctor lay at our feet.

He coughed and hacked up mucous, feeling about blindly for his glasses. Another vine handed them to him.

I shivered. The thing was smart.

The goblin shook himself off like a dog, and I covered my face. Great. Now I was disgusting too. The goop on my arm jolted like electricity. It was part of the plant, and I felt that connection to it again. I emptied my water skin washing it off.

When I'd recovered, I saw the goblin had too. He was now examining the pod that had captured him.

"These vines must extend miles to have reached me at the camp. They must be the source of the anomaly. Fascinating."

"Focus, Doctor," I said. "We need to get back to the mission. Can you find another door nearby to enter?"

The goblin shook his head. "We must climb the mountain again."

I groaned.

"There is another way," Roosal said. "Now that we are here and there is no point in secrets, we can use the opening the plant created. This creature disrupts the normal paths through the Void but in a predictable way. Where the edges of this world meet the Void is like the skin of an orange, with each small pore a doorway, and normally, when we traverse the Void, we move along the peel from pore to pore. But this entity has burrowed into our world from elsewhere, creating its own portal. It has twisted the skin of our world to suit it, like a worm or a rot digging in."

"I've never eaten an orange," I said, as such delicacies were rare in the Outskirts, "and now I don't want to. You can see portals and paths with your copper pot, Doctor. Can you map a new route from here, from this 'rot' hole?"

"It has taken me many years to map the corridors through the Void, my dear, and I highly doubt, with the landscape so wildly changed by this disturbance, that I can just cast about and find ... Oh. There it is." He'd donned his goggles as he lectured, and it seemed the first place he looked he'd found what he needed. "With Roosal's explanation I better understand these strange readings. I see the wormhole—a far preferable name to 'rot' in my opinion—which this creature created for its purposes."

"Will it suit our purposes?" I asked. Always hard to keep the doctor on track.

"I'd best explore a bit." He reached into the air and pulled a curtain of sky aside, revealing a line of black. He stepped inside.

"Remember to come back for us!" I wasn't sure he'd heard.

I looked about at the pods and their vines twitching towards us.

"We're not waiting here," I said.

I clambered atop a nearby outcropping of rock that overlooked the spot where the goblin had vanished. Thane and the others joined me, except for Jorg who waited at the base. Roosal was flying again. Avoiding me.

"I am disturbed by these bargains," Jorg said, loud enough for everyone to hear, so I wasn't sure if he was speaking to his 'Boss' or in general. "Seems one danger is traded for another."

Thane agreed. "The security of the moment bought at the price of the future. I—and I have all the memories of the Dead God—have never encountered anything like this plant in our travels from world to world. It smells of a traveler too."

"Traveler?" I asked. "Too? You mean a god?"

Thane shook his head. "Not all who pass through the Void are gods. Ask the good professor."

"What?" The goblin appeared from empty air, dazed, as though woken from a dream or deep scientific reverie. "What year is it?"

"Year? You were gone a few minutes," I said.

He blinked. "Good. Wonderful. Perfect. Alright, let's go then. I found the path. Eventually."

Without the donkeys, we didn't have much to gather. Jorg offered to carry my pack—he already had everyone else's—but I waved him off. "You're an accountant, supposedly, not a pack mule. I really wish you'd turn back. Help Karolyne. I didn't have time, I couldn't ... she needs someone there."

He nodded. "I understand, but you need me more. You just don't know it yet."

The way the First Soul twitched, I knew Jorg was right. Maybe what I needed most of all was not more power but a reminder of who I was supposed to be and what it was all for.

I gave him a hug, and calm settled over me.

I was the first to follow the goblin through the doorway.

It was different from last time, like I was falling rather than floating. There was no wind, but my stomach felt like I was hurtling fast. First down, then I was jerked left, right, and then up again.

I closed my eyes and fought queasiness, seeing only black with patches of bright yellow and orange light. I held the goblin's belt, and Thane held mine. A long chain ran behind him. Without that contact, I knew we'd all be lost. I clutched the goblin tighter, but despite the sensations of movement, there was no danger of losing my grip, for we only shuffled our feet a few steps.

Then the journey was over.

I stepped out, woozy and gasping for breath. I shifted aside before the rest tumbled out on top of me.

The goblin smiled broadly. "Exhilarating. The interdimensional eddies created by that plant creature are clearly disruptive to the normal fabric of space and time as well. I had no idea. When next I return to my studies of it, I must extend my measurements into the Void and other interdimensional spaces."

I wanted to vomit. Instead I looked around to get my bearings, grabbing the rough bark of an ancient tree to catch myself as my head spun. Then the tree caught fire. I heard the crack of leaves exploding into flame, felt the heat, long before I smelled smoke or saw the flames.

I stumbled away from the fire and my back hit cold stone. Great blocks of it extended left and right and high above.

"The wall." I said amazed. "We're here." We'd travelled a few days' journey in a few steps.

Although, I wasn't sure it was a good thing. There was clearly a battle going on. Bolts of electricity arced across the blue sky, and more fiery bolts shot out in all directions. I couldn't spot the mages responsible for the destruction; they were somewhere high atop the ramparts.

I heard the roar of an army, like an ocean, and the pounding of steel on steel, warriors making a raucous music as they fought.

I followed the wall, one hand brushing its stones and hoping it would provide some protection from stray spells sailing overhead. I was wrong.

I found a gigantic hole. A ragged patch of wall had collapsed, forming a small mountain of rubble and dust, footprints having already pounded a path over it.

The wall didn't have gates. It didn't have doors. It was supposed to be impenetrable. Yet, I could see through it. I saw the plain of Solheim on the other side and a fog bank of figures pressed together as armies fought.

Mage fire lit the scene from time to time, revealing Highcrowne's banner, the three ruling races represented by feather, axe, and tower. The Elves' banner was there too: sky blue with golden thread, Hilja's personal banner. And the dwarves' silver crown on black. The enemy too bore a banner: black with a white crowned skull.

"What's happening? Where are we?" I asked.

"*When* is the better question," the goblin said.

19 OUT OF TIME

"W hen?" I shook my head.

"You see," the goblin explained, "the plant creature's wormhole not only allows one to quickly travel physical distances by taking shortcuts through *space*, it also enables travel through *time*. My earlier explorations appeared to last only a short while for you, while they took me many days. I thought I had mapped the correct route, but it appears I was off a bit on the time dimension. Space as well, because we are not as far beyond the wall as I'd hoped. Apologies."

This had to be a nightmare. The wall was falling apart. Highcrowne mages and exhausted soldiers hacked away at undead, but it was like battling an army of marble statues. Fast, deadly statues who could reassemble severed limbs. These were not a lich's creation but the true Risen created by the Dead God. They were unstoppable.

Except for fire.

The battleground was an inferno. In the mages' desperation, they were setting everything around them alight, even their own troops. Dirigibles dropped goblin bombs as indiscriminately, but there were few of them left, their blackened and burning remains scattered everywhere like paper lanterns caught in a hurricane.

That's because the enemy had Unmentionables on their side. I saw Shevic, the blue demon, climbing one of the balloons. She summoned azure flames and ignited the dirigible. It plummeted.

Before it crashed, a swarm of goblin mercenaries launched themselves over the side, spears pointed down, so they could dive-bomb the enemy as they died. Some even had bombs burning in their hands, which exploded on impact, taking Risen in pieces with them.

"Ah," the doctor chuffed proudly. "Good lads. Not many survive two centuries to be as wise as me. Selection. But the hordes who die young often do so spectacularly."

"No." I shook my head at the madness. "This can't be happening. We have to go back."

"I'm not sure that's possible." The goblin spun in circles, adjusting his lenses like mad. "The pathway I took is gone, and I don't see another door. Even if I do find one, it is unlikely to transport us through space-time in the same manner as the one near the plant creature."

"How did the army get here ahead of us?" Grim asked, scratching his greasy chin in confusion.

"Mages." Gormless nodded. "They's fast."

"They weren't meant to attack until we were well across the wall," Thane said. "When the smallest moon was..." He trailed off, as the white orb of the lesser moon visible in the sky was clearly full.

"We moved ahead in *time*," the goblin repeated slowly, as though speaking to children. "They are on schedule. We are the ones who lost time. We could have travelled by donkey the entire way and gotten here sooner, I'm afraid. We're late."

"I knew that," Thane said, sounding a bit defensive.

"Me too," Duane cut in.

I was about to say, "I didn't," but then something burned right through my heart.

I screamed and clutched the First Soul at my breast.

You are where you need to be. Destroy them, it ordered me.

It was right. Plans be damned, people were dying. Highcrowne's army could not stand against the Risen horde long enough for us to reach Solheim now.

I looked down and saw the First Soul had burned its way into my breastbone. Not far from my heart, killing me would be effortless. Easier, better even, to listen to its whispers. The more I listened, the easier it became. Pain receded, and I felt calm. Certain.

"Eva?" Thane said, a nervous quaver in his voice.

I felt him trying to speak to me, soul to soul, as we did so often, but it was like we were suddenly worlds apart. He was as much a stranger to me as all the others following me around, plaguing me with their sentimentality and fear.

I didn't need any of them.

When Thane reached for me, I sent him sprawling with a gesture.

Olyve's lessons about manipulating Void stuff, moving air, transforming matter to fire, achieving anything I wished ... it had all been too difficult, but this ....

Now, thought and struggle were non-existent. Whatever I desired was mine. The First Soul would give it to me. I had never felt so free.

I knew I wanted to face the Dead God, stop Him, but I wasn't sure why.

You want Him and all the other gods at your feet, the Soul told me. *You are tired of weakness. You want to be strong.*

That sounded good.

But there was an army in my way. Risen were slaughtering elves, humans and dwarves. All was annoyance, distraction. They stood between me and

Solheim, and so they had to move. It was as simple as that.

I knocked the army to the ground as easily as I had Thane. Thousands and thousands of people and Risen, like a field of bloody wheat, were crushed against the earth. Those who needed to breathe struggled for air. Those who were already dead struggled to rise and fight as their god demanded, but they were all helpless.

It felt very good.

Until one stood again in the middle of it all. Like an ugly weed sprouting in my rich field. This one seemed familiar, like looking in a mirror. I recognized a spark within it. My spark.

"Conrad," I said. Shaking my head and blinking as though waking up from a dream.

A piece of my soul lay inside him, the bit I had used to animate him, much as the lich's animated their minions. Conrad was no minion, though, he was a man I could have loved, a man who had deserved love. He'd died because of me, and I had done this to him, made him Risen, in a desperate attempt to undo a horrible mistake. That anguish I'd felt, that hope at redemption, all those emotions were caught inside the bit of soul I'd lent him, like fire in amber, preserved.

I suddenly remembered what my uncorrupted soul was supposed to feel like.

This thing lodged inside my breast wasn't it.

Destroy that one first, the First Soul ordered.

I couldn't.

Kill him, the Soul repeated.

I would not destroy Conrad. I had saved him in the only way I could. Now, the reminder of him would save me.

The First Soul wanted me hollow. A mindless vessel for it to control.

"No," I screamed. "No!"

I grasped the First Soul with my fingers, digging into my own skin, and ripped. It hadn't burrowed more than a hairsbreadth into the bone, but even so the pain was terrible as I tore it away from me. I expected blood to pour, but the flesh where it had embedded itself was cauterized, the bone blackened. It smelled of burnt flesh, my flesh, and I gagged.

I held the First Soul at arms' length. I didn't know what to do with it. I felt it burning into my fingers now, trying to fuse with me again, a leach hungrily seeking me out.

I dropped it.

The relic bounced against broken stones from the wall and wedged in a crack of rock. Sunlight hit its diamond facets. It looked harmless again—and alluring.

Why had I thrown it away?

Roosal swooped down from the sky and covered the relic with his wing. I smelled burning, heard him squawk, but then he tore out a handful of his own feathers and let them fall like snow to cover the Soul.

Without it glinting at me innocently, all I saw was its black miasma. A cloud of its putrid power hung over the battlefield.

"Stop," I told it.

With a rush of air, the spell broke. The Risen sprung to their feet. Hilja's banner was next to rise, then all the soldiers from Highcrowne.

Faces turned toward me, but I couldn't see Conrad's face anymore. He was one more enemy among thousands again, my spark within him obscured by the God's.

"Doctor Ghunnan," I said calmly. "Find us a way out of here and to Solheim. Now."

Thane helped the goblin to stand. Jorg, Duane and his goons gave me strange looks, but they set up a cordon around us. I'd made us the center of attention, and all the Risen who had been fighting Highcrowne soldiers now took a step toward us.

"The door we came through is shut. The closest doorway not disturbed by the plant creature is out there," the goblin said, pointing into the middle of the plain.

Thane stepped ahead of us all, walking out to meet the Risen in our way. "I command you to stand aside."

As one, they obeyed, their combined movement sounding like thunder. A path formed, right down their center.

I looked at Thane, and he looked worried.

"Lili and the Dead God will countermand me," he warned. "We don't have long before they're His again. Hurry, Eva."

"Find the doorway," I told the goblin.

He nodded, checking his helmet's readings, and then ran fearlessly into the heart of the battlefield, ignoring the blood-spattered corpses of Highcrowne soldiers who were already beginning to rise at the bidding of Kershayne or some other Solhan necromancer. The doctor may have survived centuries, but he still had that insane goblin lack of fear at his core.

I scooped up the pile of scorched feathers Roosal had left on the ground, the First Soul wrapped inside.

Listen to me, Eva, it whispered over and over in my mind. It wanted to control me, but for now its voice was muffled by Avian magic.

Rain began to fall, droplets beading up on my skin and soaking into the ashen ground. The raindrops came faster and faster, quickly forming puddles, which I didn't bother to dodge as I ran after the goblin.

Jorg was behind me, sending up sprays of gray mud that coated the back of my legs. I hoped the others were running too—because the Risen were turning on us.

The surviving Highcrowne troops had taken advantage of the momentary distraction. Dwarves were shoring up the broken wall in several places, and Hilja rallied the elves to fight and defend the workers.

"Strike the enemy down!" she ordered, brandishing a silver sword. She had on a nice gown as usual, this one adorned with armor plates at the shoulders and breast, but the sword was not ornamental. It glowed blue and sheared through a Risen's neck in one slice.

A group of elves surrounded Doctor Ghunnan as well, holding back the enemy while the doctor checked his lenses and made adjustments.

Thane's command over the dead faded fast, and he was forced to draw the short sword he carried, using it to cleave reaching arms, spear tips, or anything that got in our way.

I fell behind. I'm a terrible runner to begin with, but the First Soul felt leaden.

Jorg lifted me and carried me along, until he suddenly tripped. It was like he'd run into a brick wall at knee height. He tumbled forward and dropped me into the mud. I regained my feet and saw it was no stone wall—Conrad stood there.

I recognized his face, but not the look in his eyes. The spark I had given him, the piece of my soul needed to raise him from the dead, was masked by the Dead God's presence. Guilt had made me raise him before, knowing I had killed him. The guilt was worse now. My mistake staring back at me.

But it was the Dead God who looked out at me from those eyes.

"Eva," His cold, distant voice called from Conrad's lips. He stretched out Conrad's hand. "Come to me."

"I want to talk face to face," I said, taking a step back. "Your face. Not this one."

"You seek to bargain and plead. There can be no new bargains until the first is fulfilled. I was promised a wife—you are to rule by my side."

"My mother made that bargain, not me. My soul was not hers to trade."

"But it was. It is. If you don't like the bargain, then compel her to make another. I see the scion you carry. It brings chaos wherever it goes, a plethora of death, destruction and displaced souls for me to reap. But it is powerful. Unwrap it from its package of mud and feathers and you could command Lili to do anything. You could command anyone."

"Even you? It said I could destroy you."

The hollow laugh that came from Conrad's throat sent shivers down my spine. "The First Soul is mad. Keep listening to it and you will be too. Come to me, Eva."

His presence faded, and once again Conrad was a mindless corpse. He raised a bloody sword that had killed before.

My conversation with the Dead God had lasted only seconds. Jorg was still climbing to his feet. Elves fought back the Risen, while the goblin peeled back a patch of sky to reveal a portal.

And Conrad was just another foot soldier sent to kill me. The Dead God wanted me to join Him, but not necessarily alive. It was my soul that mattered to Him.

Souls sold, blood pacts and marriage contracts signed before I was born…. All that was left for me to do was die.

I dodged instead. Death would not take me today.

In fact, the Dead God had just given me a way out. An answer. But I needed to survive first.

I couldn't draw my Ashur for fear of dropping the feathers blanketing the First Soul and protecting me from its power. I needed both hands.

Thane ran back for me, but mud pulled at his boots. I was mired in it too and couldn't dodge Conrad's next blow.

Time does funny things when you see a sword descending. The metal didn't glint as much as I remembered his sword glinting before. Conrad too had faded, his golden hair now like winter's grass, his skin pale, eyes filmed over. I don't think he saw me. Like an automaton, he struck because that was his purpose now.

I ducked, hoping that would save me.

A shield blocked the meagre light, and Conrad's sword clanged against it.

It was Duane. He'd stolen an elf's shield and wielded it as confidently as any knight.

"Go, Eva," he said. Giving me a shove out of the mud with his shoulder.

Grim and Gormless crashed into Conrad's legs, knocking him over. Duane picked up Conrad's dropped sword to fight another Risen soldier who'd rushed forward, bare claws tearing at the shield like it was foil.

"No!" I thought about using the First Soul and obliterating everything in our way. But it had almost taken me. It had almost made me kill everyone I cared about.

"Go, Eva," he shouted.

Duane was right. There was far more at stake than one life. Even if it was his. I nodded, memorizing the look in his eyes. He believed in me, despite everything.

I ran toward the doctor.

Thane's blade hacked at the Risen pressing in on us, and I jumped through the doorway, which started a foot above the ground.

I thought the Void would be safer than the battlefield, but I was wrong.

20 GHOSTS

The Void is a strange place. Always 'between', it was nowhere. But it was the source of everything. That emptiness, like a blank page, held limitless potential. Worlds had been created from it, gods, even. And monsters.

The Gaunt Man, ravager of souls, was one of those monsters, and he was waiting for us.

I hadn't seen him since Ismerkel. I thought I'd scared him away, but I should have guessed he'd be wherever Shevic, the blue demon was. She'd been shredding dirigibles and wreaking havoc on the battle-field. The Gaunt Man, in contrast, wasn't a fighter, more a spider, waiting for me to get stuck in his web.

"How did you find me?" I asked, carefully trying to maneuver away from him, my hands still clutching the shrouded Soul.

Doctor Ghunnan was distracted as usual, looking for something in the darkness of the Void that was invisible to everyone but him. He didn't seem to notice or care that we had an unexpected visitor, one who could traverse the Void as we did. Maybe the goblin ran into travelers out here all the time. The Gaunt Man was ordinary looking enough—unless you could read souls.

You see, I knew he was worse than Risen. My sense of bad had evolved recently. Death is bad. Death of everything is unimaginably horrifying. But death itself was not an end. Not really.

What the Gaunt Man lacked in strength and downright scariness, he made up for in destructive ability. He ate souls. Not as I or the Dead God did, stripping them away to be reborn in the Halls of the Dead. He simply ate them, like a cracker, leaving nothing but crumbs behind.

"I thought, with Harbinger gone, you could give the relic to me," he spoke politely, as if doing me a favor.

Taking the First Soul away would be a favor, but I couldn't trust him with it.

In fact, I wanted to smash him with my boot. Ravagers like him gave me the same creeped out feeling as a spider, and my instinct was to squash,

"No," I said, taking a step back.

The Gaunt Man grabbed the goblin by his small, green throat.

"Say no again and your friend dies."

Amazingly, Doctor Ghunnan kept looking at something in the Void, oblivious to the threat on his life.

"You'll kill us both anyway," I said, wondering where Thane was. I could use an extra pair of hands.

"Yes, I will," the Gaunt Man said.

"You don't speak to people often," I noted. "Otherwise, you'd know that's no way to bargain."

"I am hungry."

"Do you intend to eat the First Soul?" I thrilled at the thought.

"It is not a real soul. It offers no nourishment. But it is useful."

Too bad.

Thane came through the portal, finally, his boots making a loud squelch as he pulled them free of the gray mud that had delayed him.

I took a step forward.

"Stop right there." The Gaunt Man held his palm toward me. A mouth opened in it, circular and bordered in thousands of hair-like teeth.

One touch was all it would take to eat the shred of soul remaining inside me.

"See me, creature," Thane said. "See what a feast I offer."

Thane dropped the usual glamour he maintained to conceal his own soul, the piece of the Dead God that lay within him. It was bright and hot as fire to anyone with sight like mine. The Gaunt Man had soul sight too, because he squinted, his palm drifting away from me and toward Thane.

I kicked the ravager as hard as I could and heard his knee snap.

He was dangerous but not invulnerable.

Doctor Ghunnan made a strangled sound. I thought he'd finally noticed what was happening, but he was surprised by something else. Something invisible threw him aside.

What now?

Thane and the Gaunt Man grappled. The ravager balanced on one leg, reaching out with incredibly long arms. Thane fought to keep the ravager's hand away from him. I kicked at the Gaunt Man again, but his soul-sucking hand got dangerously close, and I stepped back, shivering at the nearness of oblivion.

"Allow me," an invisible voice said.

No-Thing knocked the ravager's other leg out from under him, and the Gaunt Man crumpled. Still, his hungry grasp stretched towards Thane.

Then No-Thing, a blacker black against the material of the Void, snapped the ravager's hand at the wrist.

He cried in surprise and stared at his limp, dangling limb. "You betray one of your own?"

"The Unmentionables betrayed this world first."

I'd never heard No-Thing speak so emphatically. He had always been the observer, showing vague curiosity from afar. Now he sounded angry.

Then he did something unexpected. Somehow, whether it was magic or something natural to his kind, he made the Gaunt Man fall.

I had taken it for granted that the Void had enough substance for us to stand. Something about the paths, the fractures between worlds, created a path, which we could walk. But that path was fragile. Whatever No-Thing had done made the portion holding the Gaunt Man vanish.

The ravager kept falling until I could no longer see his white flesh against the darkness.

I didn't dare move. I glanced at Thane standing still as me and Doctor Ghunnan.

"You are safe," No-Thing said reassuringly.

He sounded near, so I reached out, feeling only empty air. "You survived Leviathan," I marveled.

"I did."

The goblin was coughing and rubbing his shoulder where No-Thing had pulled him aside, but otherwise he was unhurt.

"Next time, pay attention, will you?" I scolded.

"I was. The Void paths shifted around us, and I knew something was happening."

"You mean No-Thing."

The goblin gave me a look of glee, the curiosity causing the cogs and wheels of his brain to whir almost visibly.

I didn't want to explain about Void Walkers and Unmentionables to someone who didn't even believe in magic, but I could tell the goblin was about to unleash a flurry of questions or spiel of theories.

Fortunately, No-Thing cut him off, saying, "We cannot tarry. The Dead God is watching."

I felt His presence, like a nearby fire with cinnamon scented smoke. The brilliant threads of His soul stretched all around us, each one linked to a Risen corpse under His control on the battlefield we'd just left. I could tell he was busy wielding them at Lili's command, but He was aware of us, of me, and one of those threads was slowly shifting in my direction.

We had no time, not here in the Void or in the world without, because time had twisted and betrayed us, turned against us like everything else.

People were dying on that battlefield, people I cared about. I'd left Duane—killed him as surely as I'd killed Conrad.

I needed to keep moving, so as soon as No-Thing peeled back the Void like I curtain, I hurried through into a world of bright daylight and dust-coated stone.

The goblin gasped. "I did not detect a doorway so near."

"I see more than your eyes or devices can discern," No-Thing explained. "This should set you back on course."

I looked back at the doorway we'd travelled through, but it was gone.

"No-Thing?" I called.

He was gone too.

We stood on a desolate, limestone plain. It was colder than Highcrowne winter, and I shivered whenever the wind blew, for it went right through me like I was a ghost. A few scrubby green bushes were the only living things visible. Low hills in the distance formed an uneven blue line on the horizon.

"Yes," the goblin said. "Even better than I could have managed. We are as close to Solheim as is possible, for all the doorways are blocked in this vicinity."

"The Dead God," Thane explained. "Solheim is His prison. His presence is obstructing the Void and living world alike until He is freed. Even with Fharen's glamours at my command, Lili will sense us here. Let's move quickly."

Dry, cold air chapped my lips as I took the First Soul, smothered in Avian feathers, and carefully placed it in a bag the doctor pulled from one of his many pockets. He had water as well, something I'd left behind in the rush, which I was grateful he shared with me.

I followed Thane, glancing back at the distant white mountains where Highcrowne lay far behind us. The wall where I'd left Duane and too many others to die wasn't even visible.

Then I looked ahead across the vast plain that stretched to the south and east. I'd never seen so much flatness in my life. This frozen desert was the land of my birth, but it was alien.

We walked for an hour before I noticed a black finger rising from the white plain. The jagged structure could have been natural, but it was the only thing like it.

"Is that...?" I began.

"Solheim," Thane confirmed. "We're close. From here, we must wend our way through the karst, not over it. Sinkholes in the limestone can drop a person hundreds of feet to their death. Worse, Lili's watchers can see someone miles away."

He searched the ground and then led us over another low hill. I was shocked to see a series of narrow canyons, like deep cracks in the stony ground. I didn't notice the canyon until we were almost on top of it, its white blending with the white plain. Falling to our deaths sounded all too probable.

"These are everywhere," Thane said. "It is safest to travel through them, rising to the surface only when there is no other path open."

He scrambled down the cliff, holding out a hand to help me when needed, but the canyon wall here was terraced, with layers of sediment in slightly different shades of white and gray, forming natural steps.

"You navigate well despite compass or map," the goblin told Thane.

"I have been here before."

I had as well, but there was no memory of this place. No real memory. There were the dreams.

All my life I'd woken from cinnamon scented dreams filled with laughter and dancing, a faceless multitude of souls, celebrants in the Halls of the Dead. All that remained of my people. Solheim was gone, and only the undying liches, like my mother, who enslaved the cast-off bodies of the dead as their soldiers, remained.

This is what Lili wanted for Highcrowne, Gernwold and Faellion too. A dead world.

The closer we got to Solheim, the deeper my dread grew.

Roosal's feathers blocked the relic better than Thane's glamour had, but still it whispered to me.

And louder than that whisper was the sound of the Dead God … existing, if you could say such a thing had a sound. It was a weight on my mind, in my ears, a cinnamon infusing my skin.

Not since the temple where Gypsum and Thane first tried to capture me had I been this close to Him. And never had I been this vulnerable. There were no portals to escape to, no Olyve to come to the rescue. I hadn't had a chance to ask No-Thing about her, to learn if she even lived.

Thane squeezed my shoulder, sensing my fear, and I took a breath. I focused on the sound of pebbles falling, the taste of white dust in my mouth, rather than cinnamon smoke.

We were at the bottom of the crevasse before Doctor Ghunnan started down.

A flash of gold in the sky caught my attention. Like a metal vulture, it circled above us, growing larger as it descended.

By the time the goblin reached our side, I made out an Avian. Roosal. He wore golden armor made of overlapping feathers. Whether real gold or gilt, I didn't see how he could wear it and fly. Then again, I had no idea how Avians flew to begin with—they were larger than any bird, with wings smaller than a similarly sized wyvern—unless magic was involved.

The goblin had once attempted logical and mathematical acrobatics to explain it, but I hadn't listened, because not even he'd seemed convinced by his arguments.

Roosal perched on the edge of the cliff above, watching with his head tilted to one side.

"How did you find us?" I asked. Still feeling quite lost in place and time from all the jumping through doorways.

"I sniffed out my feathers, and No-Thing helped me along the path."

"And the battle?" I asked, fearing the answer.

"It continues, but only in defense of the wall. The diversion is over, and both Lili and the Dead God turn their attention this way."

"Come down," Thane prompted. "You are visible up there."

"I prefer to maintain a safe vantage," he said.

"Then do not follow too close." Thane warned. He led the way along the smooth canyon floor while Roosal circled high above.

The ground here had a few broken stones and pebbles but was otherwise smooth and powdery.

"You called this the karst? Nanny talked about it when she remembered Solheim, but she never explained what it was."

"A limestone landscape, once the bottom of the ocean. It's now as dry and brittle as sun-bleached bone. It is riddled with hollows and caves, and storms break through the limestone crust easily, creating canyons like these."

"Why is it so cold?" I shivered worse than before, teeth chattering, as the chill seeped deeper into me.

"Nothing to block the wind from the north," he said.

It was more than that. My stomach coiled.

"Lili is here," I said.

Roosal's shriek of warning confirmed the feeling.

"Into the caves," Thane said, taking my hand.

The crevasse we'd been following grew narrower, shadowy, and then I saw the darkest shadow was a cave.

"Why isn't Lili at the wall with the armies?" I wondered aloud.

"Because she knows we want to use the First Soul to send the Dead God away. He's her source of power and she must protect it. She can trust no one else with that task."

"Stop," I said. I dug in my heels, not wanting to go into the cave. The goblin ran into me. He wasn't big enough to knock me down, but I felt brass goggles dig into my back painfully.

"We have to go," Thane insisted.

"She knows exactly where to wait for us," I reasoned.

I tried to back up, but it was too late.

Pebbles skittered down the sides of the crevasse as corpses tumbled down behind us, descending faster than we'd managed because they had no fear of broken necks or bones. There were three, then six, then twelve. Each one stood, covered in white dust, their hollow eyes watching and waiting.

I turned to see what they were looking at, and there she was. My mother. She emerged from the darkened cave I'd feared and stepped into the daylight, her decayed shoulders donning the light like a royal mantle.

"You brought her," Lili smiled, all teeth and no lips.

Thane bowed his head. "I have no choice but to serve."

21 THE END

I tried to move away, but Thane squeezed my shoulders tight.

Soul to soul he told me, *You know I have no choice. She has bound the Dead God and me with a bargain. Only you can break it.*

How? I asked.

Lili threw back her head and laughed. I saw her spine through her throat and had no idea how she could produce such a rich and haunting sound.

"Eva," she said. "My, Eva. Always running away or hiding, but there is no place to run now. You are home. Ulric kept you from me for too long, protected in one of his soul jars, then protected by his power, by

Avians and Compacts and walls. If only Erick had succeeded in defeating your uncle, if Aguragas had killed the Avian queen when I asked ... this reunion could have come so much sooner."

"You are the one who ran in Faellion," I said. Never able to keep myself from poking a stick at a villain.

And Lili was the greatest villain of them all. Summoning the Risen, stealing silver crowns and ordering assassinations. It had all seemed like activities happening around me, but it had all been because of me.

"You want to give me to the Dead God and complete your ritual?" I said. "Then let me go to Him now. Release me."

She clucked a tongue that no longer existed, the sound more like the rattle of a crow.

"You are *mine* to sacrifice for *my* reward. You die here and now."

"No," I retorted. "You fear what I—the key, a keeper's daughter—wielding the First Soul can do when I face the Dead God on my terms. You are afraid for your precious bargain."

Roosal's feathers still muted the First Soul's call, but I heard it whispering.

Power, my beloved. I am power. Claim me.

I saw the whip of black shadow extend from Lili's hand, and I pulled free of Thane, wiping feathers away from the First Soul as I did.

Yes, the relic exalted.

There was no time for doubt. Lili frightened me. Her life-stealing shadow frightened me. I reached for power as someone drowning would reach for land.

The First Soul had me believing I could smash Lili like smashing a mosquito, but it was more like grappling with a snake. I had power and little understanding how to use it, while her mastery made the lesser power at her command formidable.

The first arc of green lightning from my hands, which had been good enough to squash werewolves, missed Lili and obliterated the hill behind her.

She smiled, just before an avalanche of limestone and granite covered her and the cave entrance.

"Let's go another way," Thane said.

I recoiled from him. "Whose side are you on?"

"Yours. In my heart. But I am compelled to obey Lili's direct commands. Keep me away from her, please."

The First Soul liked his pleading tone. *He is beneath concern.*

I turned my power on the Risen filling the crevasse. A black fire consumed them, like the icy shadow my mother wielded, this fire of the relic's creation was like the Void, twisted into a semblance of fire. Where the weapon the First Soul had given Lili stole life, this one destroyed the dead. It consumed them in darkness until they were nothing but black ash upon the ground.

The face of one Risen after another melted away, and I could not help but think about so many lives lost and how all this began with Lili accepting dark gifts.

I didn't want the power the First Soul gave me, and I hesitated. The shadowy flames dying down.

The Dead God's voice issued from all the corpses I'd left intact, their words a chorus: "Eva."

I ran up the hillside and turned to see Thane helping the goblin. I grabbed the doctor's hands and pulled him up beside me.

"You shouldn't be here," I told him.

"I'm beginning to believe you're right, Miss Thorne. But I've come too far to abandon you."

Impatience turned to a swell in my chest. I had friends I did not deserve.

I helped Thane over the rise as well, wondering at my foolishness for trusting him, but he had warned me this could happen, that Lili could compel him. He had told me the truth, and for that reason I still trusted him.

I followed where he led, and soon we reached another small canyon, the dark shadow of a cave entrance at its base.

Swarms of Risen dotted the plain all around, but they kept their distance.

"The Dead God isn't attacking. Why?" I asked.

"Lili is distracted and failed to give Him a direct command to kill you," Thane said. "He wants to be free. In the past, that meant your death to fulfill Lili's bargain. Now, He sees another way."

"You're in contact with Him right now, aren't you?"

He nodded. "This way."

There was a narrow hole at the bottom of the crevasse, which opened out into a wider cave far below.

I slung my legs over the precipice, feeling for purchase. I skid and reached out, catching the goblin and pulling him down with me. White limestone billowed up in clouds to choke and blind us. We plunged down the natural slide, no way to slow our descent, but the slope levelled out and we landed gently.

I felt Lili's chill presence draw nearer. I left Doctor Ghunnan and Thane behind and took off running down a dark passage, following the scent of cinnamon.

Usually, there was enough starlight or distant gleam from lamps for my Solhan eyes to adjust, be it a dungeon or underground sacrificial altar room. I've spent time in both. This was an old-fashioned cave, and as soon as I was away from the glow of the entrance, I was blind.

Was this how humans felt at night?

My breathing was loud in my ears. I listened for the sound of falling stones as I shuffled my feet. There could be a precipice near me, and I wouldn't know.

I heard Thane or someone slide down the slope behind me, followed by the sound of a spitting snake. I jumped then realized it was the sound of flint and striker scratching against one another. Sparks exploded in the darkness, and Thane held a burning torch, which danced and flickered as he hurried to catch up.

I could feel Lili. Feel her fury.

Turn around, and I will lay her low at your feet, the First Soul told me.

"No, I must reach the Dead God."

Yes. I will destroy Him for you.

Since I'd dropped the feathers, I'd lost my wariness of the relic and placed it inside my shirt again. It was warm there, burning into my skin, burrowing deeper.

"Eva?" Thane had been talking, the torch ahead of me now, and he held out his hand. "This way. Hurry."

I didn't take his hand, but I took the torch. Fire was comforting, light and warmth, and I needed it to push back the dark.

The fog in my mind terrified me. I desperately needed to do something, but I couldn't remember what it was. It was like being in a dream so real you struggled to recall your waking life. Was this what losing your mind felt like?

The relic burned deeper into my breast, and then I worried, was this what losing your soul felt like?

"Left now," Thane instructed.

He navigated not by landmarks, as there were none I could see, but by his connection to the Dead God. I had it too. The scent of cinnamon grew stronger.

The natural caverns gave way to limestone-washed corridors, painted in blues and reds. Solhan art adorned the walls. The city fell just over twenty years ago, but these looked ancient.

The colors were brighter than I had expected from the somber nature of every Solhan I'd ever met, but the way the symbols were written.... They shifted in my soul sight. The red and blue writing looked more like veins and arteries, and together they formed an image of death in my mind's eye.

The level tunnel sloped up and became steps. A few here, another few there, so that we slowly rose above the ground. Well past ground level, we continued up into what had to be a building. A tower.

We were ten stories above the ground before the first window allowed me to see that we had ascended through the ruins of Solheim into its tallest spire.

The ancient city that had filled my dreams looked as new and alive as it must have been when I was born. Limestone-washed walls were painted in visceral colors, illustrating war and death.

People teemed through the streets. You could imagine them going to work, browsing the markets ... except their eye sockets were black, set in white, boney faces, and their ragged clothes were stained with the ichor of their deaths.

A city of death.

"We are all trapped here," a familiar voice travelled down the stairs in a cloud of warm cinnamon smoke. "But see what release I give them."

The image of the city shifted, and I recalled the day I'd killed Erick. How Thane's black shadow form had appeared and held me, and how I'd been connected to the Dead God then. Every breath of cinnamon drew us closer together. On that day, He had showed me a ballroom filled with laughter and dancing, filled with the souls of all those trapped within Solheim.

He showed me more now. The whole city was alive, truly alive, more ecstatic than ever they had been in life. Dancing and playing, while behind that image I saw their corpses swaying like dried corn husks in the wind.

"It's not real," I said.

"It's the only thing that is," the God insisted. "Come closer, Eva. I will show you."

I clutched the First Soul at my breast again, and Thane said, "Careful, Eva."

It was too late for that.

I climbed more flights of stairs, following cinnamon scents in my mind, seduced by a glowing image of afterlife.

The First Soul quivered in expectation of the confrontation ahead, of my promise to unleash it fully. To give myself to it.

Thane tried to hold my hand, but I dropped it and the burned-out torch as I ascended.

I began slowly, one hesitant step at a time, then I forgot about everything except the next step, until I was moving faster and faster. Running so fast my chest ached, but I didn't know if it was from the exertion or from the relic digging its way deeper into me.

I stopped when I reached the rift chamber. It was like a lighthouse, with glass-filled arches all around. Green light poured from a crack in the Void and spilled out through the windows. In the flood of light, I made out a ceremonial altar, once white limestone, now stained rust brown with old blood.

Lili was there. She'd gotten ahead of us because she knew this decayed city, its secret ways, and she knew exactly where we'd be going. Plus, she could teleport. Not fair at all.

She'd been bent before the altar, praying. At my approach, she rose off her knees and turned to me. A skeletal smile beneath black locks and tattered veil.

"My child. At last." One hand held an ancient bronze dagger, stained like the altar, and the other was clawed, her skeletal fingers twitching as she summoned her magic.

This was it. What my whole life had been leading up to. I was going to die here today.

Sacrificed by my mother, joined to the Dead God, or claimed by the First Soul the moment I unleashed it to destroy her. One of them would kill me.

I'd survived so much. Part of me dared to hope I'd figure a way out of this, that I would not be anyone's or anything's pawn—that I'd belong only to myself.

It must have been that small rebellion of hope that cleared the fog the First Soul had laid over my mind enough to hear it: Ulric's voice carried on an Avian's shriek. I saw Roosal circling outside one of the arched windows, far above Solheim.

"Remember, Eva," Ulric's voice said.

I remembered how ragged and strange Ulric had looked in that Avian sanctuary. A failed trap for the First Soul. I remembered the Devourer then, the real enemy. And why I was here.

I held out a shielding hand against my mother's advance.

"Stop," I told her. "I will join Him, but not like this."

"Eva," Death said my name, and His Soul was a hundred-fold brighter than Thane's.

Intense, burning. I wanted to turn off my soul sense but couldn't. It was how He spoke to me. Everything was mine to take, if I wanted it. Rule by His side in the Lands of the Dead and fear nothing. See Viktor and my father and all my lost loved ones. No one would ever be lost to me.

His hooded form appeared within the rift of light and he reached out to me. His cinnamon breath filled me, His hot soul burned me, and I think I would have said yes to anything He asked. But fear shivered beneath my skin.

"The Devourer is coming," I told Him. "Search my soul and you'll know what I say is truth."

"I know it," He said. And the warm cinnamon feel of Him turned hard and cold like frozen marble. A sarcophagus in the snow. Was Death afraid? Or Angry?

"You know what draws the Devourer?" I asked.

"I do."

"Take it from me, please."

"A bargain must be fulfilled. I cannot break it ... unless you free me. Come to me."

There was only one way to do that, and that was to die. At least my soul would be intact, but life—the breath in my body, the thumping of my heart, the thoughts churning through my mind—I could not give up so easily.

And there was something else. A tiny spark I had not acknowledged, not even to myself, but it was there, and it meant I could not surrender to Death.

A child grew inside me. Thane's child.

"I will not sacrifice *her* as my mother sacrificed me," I told the Dead God.

My only choice was to kill Lili, which required the First Soul. It would destroy me in the process, but my body would live. As would the spark that had no true name yet, and whose life was not mine to give.

If the cost required was my soul, already bartered and battered, then so be it.

I turned to Lili and said, "Your machinations were for nothing. This is where it all ends."

My mother smiled, her shriveled lips, thin as wire, pulled back revealing yellowed bone.

"Return to me," she said. "I will wield you as you were meant. Together, we will rule over the corpse of this world."

I thought she was speaking to me, but then the relic in my breast burned hot. She was speaking to it.

I put my hand over my heart to cage the First Soul, which I felt tearing away from me. But I didn't call on it. I summoned my own power. The power that had destroyed Erick, consumed Ilsa's soul long before Harbinger took the last trace of it, the power that had killed and raised Conrad.

"Taste me," I whispered. "My power is far greater than hers." I opened myself to the First Soul then, letting the black ink of its aura stain my pores, seep into my muscles, into the core of my power.

It consumed me.

And in the hollow shell that was left, darkness entered. The dark, limitless power of the Void.

Lili's gaping expression made her appear more skeletal than ever. She lashed out with a whip of black shadow, but this time the First Soul was my shield.

No. I was the First Soul.

I was more than protecting myself, I was claiming all that was mine. All the creations who came after me, all the weak and pathetic beings who crawled, mewling, out of the Void and filled up existence.

I would poison it all, and when the Devourer finally caught up with me and tried to expunge me from creation, It would discover all the souls chained to me, and I would be larger and stronger than It had ever imagined. The girl called Eva was a powerful vessel, but I would not stop there. I would take a god's soul next. Then another's and another's....

Lili of Solheim had no more part to play in my plans. She had created Eva for me, and now she would be rewarded with oblivion. I reached out and grasped her shadow magic like a comrade. It was mine, and I absorbed it back into my darkness.

Lili had opened herself to me already, and it was like breathing to absorb the last bit of soul infused into her undead flesh. She was all mine now, and she crumpled. Not even the Dead God could save her.

"God of Death." I snickered in Eva's voice. "So many beings tremble at your name, when they should tremble at mine."

"Do you have a name?" The Dead God asked, His voice a boom of command.

I made Eva's voice boom in return. "Not giving me a name was my creator's greatest mistake. I cannot be stopped without one. No matter how many of my servants It devours, no matter how far and long It hunts me, I will triumph. And you will help me."

I reached out for the Dead God's light. So strong, so full of souls. All the countless souls He guarded in the Halls would be mine when I consumed Him.

Eva was my conduit to the Dead God, and with Him, I would have all I needed to stand and face my creator.

I grasped the Dead God's reaching hand and sighed. Eva soaked in His light as easily as she had soaked my darkness into her.

The First Soul's darkness. Mine... Its....

"Eva," Thane said, coming up behind me and touching the arm I held out.

What a fool. "Eva is no more."

"You're wrong. Lili gave her soul in marriage, and it is mine. I claim it." Thane and the Dead God's voices spoke as one. "Eva Maleca Aisa Thorne, I claim you."

He knew her true name. Of course.

That fool Lili had insisted on summoning her god, on making her bargain with Him for eternal life, not realizing how much more power I could give her. Or maybe she had guessed that I would not give her any-thing, but take everything instead?

That the First Soul would betray her.

I felt Eva squirm inside me, like worms in my stomach.

I had swallowed her, but she was not gone. Like a lump of flesh not yet digested.

I vomited, physically trying to be rid of her, but what came out of my mouth was darkness. A torrent of myself. She tore the reliquary from her breast and tossed the gem on the floor. I felt myself drawn back into its crystal lattices, compressed once again into its prison.

No.

"Yes," I said.

I, Eva, said.

The First Soul was furious. Its black tendrils reached out for me, refusing to give me up.

"We don't have much time," I told the Dead God. I looked into the shadow of His face, surrounded by blinding light, and I swear I saw Thane's face there.

I clutched Thane's hand, reassuring myself he was beside me. We were connected soul to soul again, and he knew everything I was going to say.

"A child?" Thane whispered.

I nodded.

"Eva." It was Thane's voice, tender, but it came from the Void, from that huge shadowy figure of Death, and I shuddered.

"You can't have me," I told Him. "I killed her and broke Lili's bargain. I will not be your bride. And I will not let the First Soul have me either."

"It was a mistake to send part of me away," the Dead God said, his voice still Thane's.

He looked at my Thane, and Thane looked back at Him. I felt their connection, soul to soul, and it grew impossibly bright, searing my soul sight, so I had to look away. I held Thane's hand—Fharen's hand—and I felt the difference beneath his skin. He was far more than my Thane. Much more.

"He's mine," I said, clutching Thane tighter, knowing it was pointless.

"You are my demise," the Dead God and Thane said as one. They both looked at me, and it was the same being, a single soul looking into mine. "I was foolish to send a part of me away to grow, to be human, elf, Solhan …. To feel alive. It is my undoing, or a true beginning. I know not which. All I know is that I am Thane and I am Death. We are one. I love you, Eva, and I will do anything for you."

"Then help me."

The First Soul's tendrils had stretched far, encircling themselves around my ankle now, sharp needles of darkness trying to dig themselves in again.

I chanted to myself over and over, *I am Eva, I am Eva* … fighting to hold on.

"Give the First Soul to me," the Dead God's voice boomed now with Primal authority. "You defeated Lili, holder of my chains, and so now I am yours to command. Send me away with it."

"It's too late to run," I said. "The Devourer is coming."

"It cares only for The First Soul. This world means nothing to It. We will face the Devourer and draw It far away from here."

"How can anything face the Devourer? Even you?" I asked, feeling a pain in my chest that was far worse than the ache where the First Soul had scorched my breast. "It swallows worlds."

"Death cannot die," Thane and the god said as one. "Send me away."

Tears streamed down my face as I shook my head at Thane. "You and He are one?"

"Yes," they said. "We were one, then separate for a time, now joined once more. I am still me."

It was strange hearing Thane's way of speaking issued in the Dead God's voice, and I got whiplash looking from one to the other.

"Sending you away means both of you?"

"Yes."

"I can't do this alone." I put one hand on my stomach, the child within too small to be felt with anything but my soul sense.

"You can," they said.

Thane leaned in and kissed me. "Although I will miss this."

My lips trembled against his, not even the fiery warmth of his kiss able to dispel the chill that had seeped into me.

The First Soul's black tendrils coiled themselves tighter, reaching up my leg, and I felt my knee about to buckle.

Eva, it said angrily.

I pulled away from Thane, looking once more into the face he'd worn longer than any other for me, but beyond that to his soul. And I saw how his soul stretched on and on, one with the Dead God's. I gazed into both of them, into Him, and I knew He did this for me.

"Goodbye." I reached down and snatched up the relic as I would a viper. Its smoky tendrils twisted around my wrist and reached for my heart this time.

I placed the gem in Thane's hand and commanded Him, "Go. Take the First Soul from this place and destroy it if you can. Protect this world from the Devourer."

Thane and the Dead God bowed their heads at the same time. "As you wish, My Love."

Thane stepped into the portal from which the green light shone, his shadow merging with that of the god's.

I felt love in that light, a longing to stay.

But also fear, as the First Soul entangled itself with them, grappling them for power.

I wanted to run to them, to help, but just as I took a step forward the doorway vanished.

Light was gone. Sound was gone. I couldn't sense anything anymore. I stood in the ruins of a dead city, all alone.

Epilogue

I found the goblin doctor locked behind a door at the base of the tower. Thane had done it to save his life, but the doctor was not happy.

"Other than a strange locking mechanism that defies every device at my disposal, I have yet to encounter anything remotely supernatural in this place. Diseased 'risen' specimens of course, but no god."

"He was here. You missed Him. And it was necromancy that barred this door. I used my blood to open it. No key or lockpick would ever have worked."

He *hmphed.*

I felt strange, arguing with the goblin automatically, while the greater part of me was floating, watching all of this from afar.

Had it all happened? Had the First Soul nearly destroyed me? Had I used it to kill my mother? Had I ordered the man—the god—I loved to draw the Soul and the Devourer away? Would He ever return to me?

Had I kissed the father of my unborn child one last time? Had I?

I couldn't remember, and so I kept walking, deaf to whatever Doctor Ghunnan was saying. I wasn't even sure this was me. Or that I ever would be me again.

I saw a barred door at the base of the tower and opened it, stepping out into Solheim's main plaza.

Sunlight burned down through the cloudless sky, gilding my white breath, the light a painful contrast to the chill inside me.

Solheim looked ancient and decayed, cracked stone buildings and pavers as far as I could see. It had died long before its people were consumed by Lili's quest for power.

The square was full of corpses, as I had seen from above, but they had collapsed. The ground was piled with them. Up close they were unrecognizable as people, desiccated mummies with the barest outlines of human features remaining. Their faces were skulls, their frayed clothing more substantial than the sinews holding their skeletons together.

I should have been terrified. These were Risen, and they could easily stand up and tear me to shreds, but I was numb. I walked among them heedless, despite the doctor's shouted warning.

"Come back inside, Miss Thorne. These plague victims can behave quite erratically."

They didn't move. Their eyes were gone, so no gazes followed me, no arms reached out for me. There was no reaction when I climbed the highest mound of them, leathery skin against my fingers. The fingers of my right hand. I couldn't feel my left. It was as dead as they were.

I wanted to be as curious about it all as the goblin was. He took a tentative step among them, then boldly examined one after another with his instruments. I wasn't curious. I wasn't anything.

I wanted him to examine me. To explain this hollowness inside. My breast felt as empty as these creatures with nothing left but ribcages.

My soul felt ... gone. My soul sense was gone too.

I couldn't read the goblin. I couldn't look to see if the ghosts of these Risen were still chained to their lifeless bodies or if they had moved on.

Not having that unwanted power anymore should have been a relief, but it wasn't. I felt as though I was missing a part of me, a hand or an eye. I was lessened. It didn't matter, because I was missing even more than that.

Thane was gone.

I took an automatic step, and then another, until I reached the top of the mound of dead in the center of the plaza. I stood tall and took a breath. Cold sunlight beat down so fiercely I'd soon be bleached and dried like the bones all around.

A welcome shadow blocked the light, but it passed too quickly, circling round and round until Roosal landed beside me. Another shadow came, another Avian. Kerrik I think it was.

"Let us carry you," Roosal said.

"Why didn't you do that before?" I asked, wanting to be angry, annoyed, anything, but my words, like my movements, felt automatic. There was no soul in them.

"The void paths were the safest way to evade Lili, as she cannot access them. We would have had to fight her flying creatures, and stealth seemed the better option."

"I didn't avoid her in the end. I killed her."

The Avians didn't react to the dangerous tone that crept into my voice. They put their magical cords around the doctor's and my waists and lifted us by the shoulders high into the air.

I remembered soaring like this with Olyve, and I wondered where she was. She hadn't come to my rescue. No one had. I'd done what had to be done, but I couldn't help wishing there had been another way.

We reached the battlefield at the wall, and dead were everywhere. Most of them still walking.

How?

I saw the older corpses had collapsed, just like those in Solheim, but the newly dead were another matter.

There were too many of them for Kershayne and the remaining necromancers to control, and The Dead God's creations took days to rise.

Then I figured it out. He was gone. I'd sent Him away before He could take their souls to the Halls of the Dead. They were trapped between life and death and so could not die. They wandered aimlessly, as I had in Solheim, as though they, too, were dazed by His departure.

My connection to Him had stretched thin as He disappeared into the Void, and then snapped. He was beyond my reach. Maybe the goblin's portals could find Him, but I doubted it. The Dead God—who was also my Thane, one and the same—had drawn the Devourer away from this world. For me. For love.

I saw Shevic's blue corpse among the restless dead, along with scores of elves and dwarves. Too many had died here.

The remnants of Highcrowne's army had retreated behind the hastily repaired wall, and they continued to shore it up from the other side.

"Stop," I told Roosal. "Set me down."

Something had stirred in me. An urge to know what had become of my friends. Were they among the dead, or the dying?

Roosal obeyed, and I found myself standing in a camp filled with wounded. They lay scattered everywhere, and I stopped to tend one after another.

Healing was beyond my abilities, but I could hold a wound, change a bandage, close a set of eyes....

At last I found someone I recognized. Captain Uanal sat, leaning against a rock, exhausted.

"Where is Queen Hilja?" I asked.

Where was Jorg and Grim and Gormless ... and Duane? I suddenly needed to know, but Hilja was the best place to start.

The captain waved towards the mountains. "Highcrowne. There's a kingdom up for grabs. You want to stay here and help with the clean up?"

I wanted to find my friends, but if Hilja was maneuvering in the halls of power, then Walz and others would be too.

"I'm sorry," I said, handing him the pile of bloody bandages I carried.

I didn't know where the goblin had gone. I'd been sleepwalking, and even he felt like a dream. Elves seizing control of Highcrowne, though, would be a nightmare.

"Roosal," I called, wondering if I'd sent him away, but he circled down, a black spot in the blue sky that grew into the familiar bird man.

"I need to reach the Council chambers now. Thane ... Fharen is gone, and it all depends on Hilja and Calka and—"

"—King Harley. I know," Roosal said calmly, picking me up again by my shoulders. "Let us continue our journey."

I remembered this view from the last time I'd crossed the wall, rescued by Olyve's massive dragon claws.

I asked Roosal about her, but all he said was, "There has been no sign. Shevic and the ravager were her captors, and they are dead."

"I'll have to find her," I mumbled absently. But I had a hard time remembering Olyve, whether she was a friend or someone I should be frightened of. Dragon godmothers weren't clear cut at the best of times, and the fog in my thoughts didn't help.

I stumbled out of Roosal's grasp on the Avian mountain, and for once my thoughts cleared.

The magic of the place made all beings wiser. I wondered if that's why Ulric did not try to impose his massive and formidable presence upon me or Queen Calka.

They both stood calmly looking at me.

"It's done?" Calka asked.

"The Dead God took the relic and will draw the Devourer away."

"You're certain?" Ulric asked.

"Thane will make sure of it." Thane and the Dead God were one person now, but it was Thane who I knew, loved and trusted. And I had sent him away.

"Let us hope neither He nor the Devourer return," Calka said, and I felt a ball of pain in my chest, something else to push the fog of shock away. "We have a reprieve at least. We must use it wisely."

"Then speak before the conclave," I told her. "Force Hilja and Harley to abide by the deal Fharen struck with the humans. Dead still walk beyond the wall. It isn't safe. Highcrowne must remain a sanctuary."

"I cannot force them," Calka said, "but you can convince them. Bring your arguments to the conclave, and I will ensure they are heard."

"My arguments? Why would anyone listen to me?"

"You are the one who defeated the Dead God."

I had. But that's not what I'd wanted in the end.

He was not the true enemy. He never had been.

I thought on that as the Avians readied themselves in their finest shiny stones.

Had the enemy been Lili and her lust for dominion over a dead world? Had it been the First Soul, seeking love and vengeance on its creator? Or had it been all of us?

Solhan arrogance, including my uncle's, unleashed the First Soul and the Dead God. That chain of events led to the fall of Solheim and the human kingdoms—and to my brother's death. Lili could not have done it alone.

Solhan arrogance and lust for power had been Ilsa's undoing as well, sending her running into Harbinger's dark embrace.

I'd had my part to play. Believing I was better than all of them, I turned my back on necromancy, which made me weak and unprepared. I'd been lucky, but I would never be so weak again. This time I would act before it was too late.

I was surprised Ulric did not show interest in the conclave. He stayed behind in the Avian sanctuary to watch over the Abomination and the deal they had struck to save humanity. Could he release those cocooned humans now? I supposed it depended on if the Three Kingdoms was a sanctuary. It depended on me.

Roosal carried me down the mountain, but I made him take me to the Outskirts. Free of the Avian's soothing magic, I fought off the shock that threatened to overwhelm me once again.

In the filthy streets of my home, among the grime and spilled blood leftover from the civil war and invasion fought across the muddy ground, I summoned all my arguments for the Conclave.

I touched the shoulders of goblin workers digging for scraps in the sewers, sought out scattered clumps of humans, my hands raised in peace, and I even tried to reason with Bell and Gas, only to have General Moore put them both in irons so they could not usurp his authority and interfere. At last, I went to see Bert and Reginald and their new king, who was still in awe and a little afraid of me.

So, when I marched an army of the dispossessed upon the Central City it was no surprise the EEPs barred our way. Harley's presence alone was not enough to get them to stand aside, so a goblin gas bomb was required.

No one died, and no one wielded weapons. When more EEPs came to surround us in the royal gardens, I went up to them and asked to see Hilja. They said Governor Walz had her under his 'protection'. I translated that to mean she was a prisoner.

Harley and his wolves were a blur as they swept elven soldiers away, throwing and locking them in the nearest tower.

I found Hilja in a tower as well, but she was not imprisoned so much as defending. Her supporters had every door and parapet heavily guarded. I saw her moon like face shining down from the highest window, and I told her, "It's safe to come out. Calka has called a Conclave, and you should be there."

"I will be there presently," she reassured me.

My army waited to escort her, and we flooded into the Assembly chambers en masse.

Governor Walz was there with his own army. I could see Hilja's mistake had been leaving so many of her loyal troops behind on the battlefield to repair and defend the wall. It was the right thing for a ruler to do, but the wrong thing for a power-hungry crown scavenger.

"I thought, with the Dead God beaten, you and your kind would return to Solheim," Walz told me.

I didn't have the First Soul to defend me against his glamours anymore. I couldn't read his thoughts and desires, and I couldn't even summon an impressive display of green magic to frighten him.

But I didn't let my weakness show—I was a better Solhan than that. Instead, I slowly walked across the massive chamber and joined him on the dais, so we wouldn't have to shout at one another.

"My kind will return," I whispered, then louder I said, "but these defenders of Highcrowne, its slaves and workers, its muckrakers and smiths and bakers ... these are the people the Crowns must answer to now, for without them—"

"—without them, the machine stops." It was Seneschal Ernest who'd spoken. He walked beside Hilja and joined me on the dais.

"You've left your tower," Walz said, smiling to see her exposed.

The small army on the dais with him twitched as one, the motion creating a loud metallic noise like a coordinated military parade.

Did he intend to assassinate her in the middle of the Crown Assembly? I didn't think that was Walz's style, being the master manipulator. Or had things changed?

"Prince Gallan is alive and on his way," I reasoned, knowing he was the only real challenger to Hilja's authority now. Walz must have made himself the prince's minion.

"A mistake," Hilja mused, pursing her perky lips. "I should have killed my betrothed instead of unmanning him, metaphorically. It seems he still has his followers."

"While yours were decimated on the Solhan plain," I finished. "Sorry about that. Our timing was ... off."

I knew it was not the best moment, but I couldn't help asking her, "And those I left behind. Duane...?"

"I do not know Mister Rose's fate."

I didn't blink. The numbness inside was complete.

I turned to Governor Walz, undistracted by the glinting armor of the hundred or so elven soldiers arrayed behind him, and said, "Prince Gallan will be too late, and you haven't apologized to my friends for imprisoning and starving them. I think King Harley has something to say about that."

The dwarf touched Bert and Reginald's emaciated shoulders as he walked slowly through the crowd I'd brought in my wake. But by the time he climbed the few steps to the top of the dais, he'd transformed into a werewolf and stood there, towering over the elf.

Walz and the others had silver weapons and were unafraid, but then coils of rope descended from the ceiling.

Each rope was golden, no more than a few threads thick, but laced with green goo, and so they moved of their own accord. Fast as striking vipers, they wrapped themselves around soldier's sword arms and around Walz's neck. The cords tightened, pulling guards off their feet to dangle in mid-air, and Walz turned red as the cord tightened around his throat.

Queen Calka descended from the darkness of the high rafters as silently as the ropes had. She stood, feathers bristling, beside Hilja and the wolfish Harley.

"I called this assembly and did not invite you onto the dais, Governor Walz. Begone." With a wave of her hand, the cords carried the elves out of the chamber, through the high doors, and out into the Central City somewhere beyond my sight. Walz had been turning redder and redder, fighting for breath, and I didn't care one way or another if Calka released him before he choked to death.

The Three Crowns took their seats, the Elf Queen and the Dwarf King flanking the Avian. Was Calka's throne just a bit bigger than theirs as well?

Their calm expressions made the rabble I'd roused settle down and take whatever seats they could find. There were more than enough, as most of the elf nobles had fled to country estates in Faellion and most of the dwarven Matriarchs still had not returned from Gernwold. There were a few though, Baroness Syla among them, her ornate veil raised for the Assembly, and she gave me a nod. I had no idea what she meant, and then I realized I was the only one standing and that all eyes were on me.

I sidled towards the edge of the dais, but Calka's high voice screeched, like a call to order, and then she sang out: "All those Assembled here this day, listen. Hear the words of Miss Eva Thorne who has borne witness to the banishment of the Dead God, and whose wisdom this Assembly and we Crowns should heed."

Now Calka nodded to me, and I couldn't get the word 'wisdom' out of my head. I didn't have any. Wise was not a description anyone would attribute to the headstrong and ill-prepared Eva Thorne. Still, no one laughed, and the massive hall remained silent.

I stood taller, summoning memories of my deportment lessons from finishing school days, but then I sighed and sagged. Who was I kidding?

"The Dead God is gone," I said. "But that is not entirely a good thing. I was wrong about Him. We all were. He hoped to save our souls from the Devourer, and He now draws that greatest of all enemies away for our sake. I know the Devourer is a Solhan god, but you all have a similar name for It, do you not? The Sun-Eater is the elvish translation, or the Swallower of Stone and Fire in dwarvish. The truth is … we came closer to destruction than we ever imagined."

I let the murmurs die down before I continued. "The Devourer feels like a fairy tale, I know. All you know is the suffering you've endured, the people you've lost. And you will only be satisfied with vengeance. The necromancer who controlled the Dead God and unleashed Him upon the Human Kingdoms, Lili of

Solheim, is dead. I killed her. But that offers little solace, does it?"

I felt a deep ache in me around Lili, my mother, that was too abysmal to see clearly or understand. I didn't try. I plunged on with my speech before the grumbles of agreement rose too loud.

"You want real vengeance, don't you? Against Governor Walz for imprisoning you and your loved ones, against humans for fouling your pristine city, against dwarves for their allegiance to a traitor queen.... As far as we know, the Three Kingdoms holds the last living people on this world. Can we really afford to kill our neighbors anymore? Can we? Solhans are not good at forgiveness, and I will not ask it of you. Do not forgive those who have wronged you and do not forgive my people either. We had a role to play.

"Remember instead.

"Remember the evils that others so easily commit, so we are watchful of them repeating. Remember those you have lost, even as you rebuild your homes and bring your remaining friends and family together. Remember that the Devourer came a hairsbreadth from taking all of it. Remember to love again. Remember to move on.

"And so, I ask today that we all remember. That we remember the promises made to General Moore and his people, to Harley and his. Let us embrace we few who remain, and all those who have built Highcrowne, our neighbors, whether they be goblin, grall, elf, dwarf, werewolf or Avian. Let us move on by coming together as one free people. Our pain came from fighting one another instead of the true enemy. Let us never make that mistake again. Let Highcrowne be the home of free people, who defend one another from the darkness without. For there is darkness still clawing at our walls. The newly Risen are directionless without the Dead God, but they are still out there. We must remember that. And we must protect one another."

There were so many familiar faces in the crowd. Bert and Reginald, Syla, Captain Uanal, Doctor Ghunnan … but I couldn't help remembering all the faces I didn't see. Bell and Duane, Jorg and Gypsum. I ran out of the hall and left them all to either listen or ignore my words.

I was tired. I needed to go home.

When I reached my brother's old house, where Nanny and Little Viktor still hid behind formidable protective spells, it didn't feel like my home.

I saw Nanny through the window. She read to Little Viktor as he sipped some awful soup she'd made. He managed to swallow, and only dumped a little out into the planter when she wasn't looking. Something she read was funny to him, and he laughed, looking over the book to point and ask a question. The grim Nanny was aglow with him, as she'd always been with his father.

I didn't know why I'd come back.

I'd told everyone they needed to band together and protect Highcrowne, but that was because I no longer could. It was up to them now.

There was nothing for me here.

I didn't go inside to say goodbye. I'd said those already, to everyone. I didn't even long for my favorite sweater or my good boots. I had my Ashur still, and the pack I'd carried to Solheim. I refreshed my canteen with water from the well outside Karo's, where I'd always dawdled before my shift.

I saw the cafe was under repair. The boards had been removed, the hurtful words erased, and Karolyne had left crates of spoiled food out front for the goblins to scavenge.

I hadn't seen Karo when I gathered my mob, her red hair would have been easy to spot. Was she avoiding me? Was she ashamed? I couldn't imagine what for.

I dug a few dried crusts of bread from the refuse and filled my pack. I thought I saw the curtain shift, but I couldn't be certain, and the door was securely locked.

Just as well.

I was not in the mood for friends.

My only other friend was locked in a stone prison, perhaps to be executed for her treason.

I couldn't save Gypsum. I shouldn't save her.

I couldn't feel anymore. I'd said some words for Calka and the others, just what they needed to know, and now I was empty. I couldn't feel to save myself.

There were few guards at the Outskirts gate, and they looked outward, wondering what new horrors might come their way. None stirred when they saw me leave. One less refugee to feed.

When the Avian had carried me, it had been quick and warm. It was not warm on foot, especially where snow drifted across the shattered rail line. There would be no locomotives to help me on my way. No stages either, for the coach house was deserted, horses long gone. I found canned food and some old blankets to warm me. They were heavy, and so I trudged through the snow slowly, picking up my feet and taking one step after another.

I stopped when I got tired, building a nest in the snow to keep me warm, a fort in a snow drift as I'd done sometimes as a child whenever the snow drifted in the Outskirts too high and fast for the goblins to clear.

I walked and slept and ate. All of it slowly, without purpose. I felt hollowed out, and I wondered if the First Soul had chewed me up. Was this what it felt to be a crumb? A haunt, the barest echo of a living soul?

I thought I might have been headed to Gernwold. I'd grown up there as much as Highcrowne. Really grown up. But my feet carried me past that fork in the rail line.

I scavenged and survived, although I couldn't recall why. Weeks past, and it was deep winter, when no one should be travelling anywhere, that I arrived at the wall.

Had this been my destination?

A larger, more permanent camp was built in its shadow. I had seen dirigibles passing overhead in my travels, like floating clouds. They must have been transferring soldiers back and forth, building materials, provisions.... The wall looked impregnable once more, the camp a fort, and the scent of fire and warm food pulled me in like a siren's call.

I warmed myself by the fire in what looked like an inn's common room, filled with tables and comfortable chairs. Someone brought me soup: A goblin, I was surprised to see. I squinted, wondering if I could recognize the good doctor in disguise, but this one was too young.

"Eva Thorne," he said.

Was that my name? I'd forgotten everything as I walked, which had been the blessing of it.

"Yes?"

"I was there when you spoke for us. No one knews where you went. They searched. Very mysterious."

"I was coming here. It looks like you managed the trip more quickly. And is that a Highcrowne guard uniform you wear? No mercenary leathers?"

He stood tall. "I is a Citizen. No more elvish armor, dwarven armor, no goblin leathers or human ... whatevers it is humans wear. We is all of Highcrowne and all free. Thanks to you."

"No more slavery?"

"Forbidden. Every kind, whethers born to it or not. Faellion still resists. They say there might be war over it, but not now. Peoples is still licking their wounds. And all refugees is now Citizens."

I, Eva Thorne, was finally a citizen in my homeland.

"Good," I said. They had listened. But for me, it all felt too late.

"What other news from Highcrowne?" I asked.

"Humans from the south gone back to they's homes around the Fortress of Mages, not just the soldiers but lots a civilians. Lots a humans from Highcrowne too have come back. They'd been hiding in some valley, can you's believe it?"

I could. It was not what the goblin imagined, and I wondered if those poor people, entombed by the abomination, had any recollection of it, or had Ulric erased the memory from their souls? I hoped he'd spared them that. Those to be sacrificed in future to appease the plant creature would not be so lucky, though. A century of sacrifices had been promised. The dark bargains never ended. Why did no one understand it was never worth it?

"Where you going?" he asked me.

"I don't know. Maybe I'll stay here ... or move on."

"There's not many places where dead not in the ways."

"True in more ways than you imagine."

I was reluctant to give up warm food and a hot fire, and so I did stay. For days, I wandered the camp like a revenant.

I found a near deserted hospital tent, certain all the wounded had been ferried back to Highcrowne by dirigible, but one of the beds was occupied.

The figure's arms and legs were in plaster casts. As I drew nearer, I realized another cast encircled his torso. The face was bruised but recognizable. Duane.

I pulled up a chair and sat beside him. I didn't want to wake him if he was sleeping, but it seemed I needn't have worried.

An elvish nurse saw me and came over, saying, "He hasn't woken since the war. It's good if someone speaks to him. Do you know him?"

"Yes. What happened? Why haven't mages been able to heal him? Or was he deemed unworthy of a mage's exertion?" Anger rose in me, and the heat of it felt good.

"Mister Rose was tended to by the Queen's own healing mage, but to no avail. We believe a necromancer or another of the strange beings on the battlefield that day cursed him. His broken bones are mending on their own, if slowly, but there is an injury to his back, and we dare not move him until he is as recovered as he will ever be."

As he will ever be. That didn't mean back to normal. I felt a tightness in my throat, another emotion stirring the cobwebs of numbness.

I'd left him behind. I had done this to him.

"Can you give us some time?" I asked. The elf nodded and left the tent.

I was reluctant to disturb the silence, but I cleared my throat and said, "I hope Jorg is alright. I didn't see him in Highcrowne. There's a lot of people I didn't see. You among them. But you're alive. You need to get better now. Highcrowne is much changed. You won't know the place when you go back, but you need to go back. Wake up and go back."

I took his hand, and the usual furnace of his body heat was smothered by ice.

Ulric had never taught me to heal, and neither had Olyvandra. All I'd ever learned was death. But whatever power I'd once wielded was cold anyway, cold like his hand, cold like a sarcophagus that had locked my true self somewhere inside, and I could not summon it.

I spent ten more days in camp, each one of them beside Duane's bed, talking about whatever I could think of. I'd never been good at idle conversation, so I told him about Solheim and what I'd seen there. I told him about my guilt over what I'd done to him and all the others I could not save. I told him about the child growing inside me and how I had no idea what I should do next.

Then one day, before I even sat down, I saw a flutter of eyelashes. An expression of pain crossed his features, and his brow, much less bruised than before, furrowed into taut lines.

I fetched the nurse, who fetched a mage. The elf was armored and must have been taken from guard duty on the wall. Power flowed from his hands in waves of golden light, and Duane suddenly sucked in a deep breath.

"I managed to heal him this time. We must get these contraptions off him." He and the nurse removed the casts using a mixture of hammers and magic, and when the one came off his chest, his breath was even deeper.

"Where...?" he croaked, his eyes half opened.

I took a step back.

"What did you do?" the mage asked me.

"Nothing." I could do nothing.

I hurried from the tent, found my bag, which I'd already restocked with supplies, donned a borrowed jacket and set off before the mage asked more questions I couldn't answer, and before Duane woke enough to hunt me down and look me in the eyes.

I couldn't face him now. I couldn't face anyone.

During my first days at the fort, I'd scouted a section of damaged wall that had been repaired with sheets of steel rather than stone. I went there now, found the tools I'd hidden nearby, and pried open a doorway. I shut it as best I could from behind and stood upon the Solhan plain.

I looked east, toward a cold and distant horizon. There was no more Dead God calling me, no more pull toward that place, but I couldn't help thinking about Solheim's once haunted and empty streets. About the empty place where Thane had vanished into the Void. That emptiness felt like home now, more than Highcrowne could.

I took a step, but then saw dark shapes move. They had been lumps upon the battleground, like all the other discarded armor and debris that littered the field, only these were not debris.

The dead still walked without Death to shepherd their souls away.

Crossing the wall had been a mistake.

I took a step back, but then memory welled in me.

It was Thane's voice, his soul's voice, entwined with mine the last night we spent together in Highcrowne.

"You know all I know," he'd said to me then. He'd given me everything when we danced.

Like remembering the go-cart Viktor had built and I'd ruined as a child, crashing it down the street, I remembered instants that were not forgotten, only difficult to reach. The knowledge Thane had given me was buried, but it was there when I knew to seek it out.

I knew the secret ways through the karst that riddled the Solhan plains. I knew how to avoid dead and living alike. I could find my way to the hidden tunnels and the Chamber of Inner Seeing if I wanted.

No. I would never return there, not unless Thane returned. But Solheim did call. The karst called, and even more vast emptiness beyond that. There was so much of the world I'd never set foot on, never seen. Thane had travelled it all, and the memories he'd locked inside me could help me find what I sought. Whatever that was.

I crossed the battleground one careful step at a time, and the dead that shuffled toward the sounds of my footsteps were blind things, their eyes torn out by vultures already. They reached out for me, almost as if seeking my help.

A spark stirred inside me. It connected with their spark, their trapped souls, a puppeteer's strings reaching out and pulling on their bones and sinews.

My power was not lost, simply huddled like a frightened animal inside me, frightened the First Soul would steal it away. I was in there somewhere too. Power and I were one, and I reached out, feeling the dead dance to the song inside my mind. The song Thane's gramophone had played, which reverberated through my memory.

I walked unhindered, the dead moving out of my path with a languidness that matched that unheard melody.

I saw Grim and Gormless dancing to my tune, and I stopped, breath caught in my throat.

There was no one to shepherd their souls away. Without the Dead God to escort them, there would be no end to their wandering. I tried to remember how it felt to tear souls from their tormented shells, to release them to the Halls of the Dead, but that power eluded me. It was a memory, as were they.

"Goodbye," I told them, and I walked on.

I saw more faces I knew. Too many. But not Conrad's at least. I knew he was out there somewhere, my spark sustaining him, but seeing him now would have been too much to bear. The loss had already gone beyond my imagination.

I had loved Thane, truly loved, and I gave it up too easily. I failed him worse than I'd failed Duane.

What was left but regret?

And all these dead. Like me, they wandered through this empty place, through the karst, and if I could not save them, at least I could leave them the peace of it. For it was peaceful.

With the quietude of death all around, I could finally hear the new soul within me. She lived, and I gave her a secret name....

THE END

Eva will return if you want her to. Email us at author@lorelclayton.com and tell us you want more!

Did you enjoy this series? Please leave reviews. They are hugely important for authors to be noticed, so we can sell more books and keep writing.

Authors' Note

Thank you to everyone who waited patiently for this fourth Eva novel. There's been two years in between this book and the last, because life gets in the way. But writing is the best part of our lives, and so you can expect many more books from Lorel & Clayton (hopefully faster than this one). We plan to stretch out into other genres we love, such as Military Sci-Fi, Cyberpunk, as well as more Young Adult Fantasy featuring new characters. But we have so many ideas for future Eva novels, and we will start writing them sooner if you tell us you want more. And tell your friends how much you loved this series! Your recommendation, your words, carry great power. We need you to help keep Eva's story going.

Until next time...

Subscribe at http://www.lorelclayton.com for updates on forthcoming novels, free novellas, and other interesting stuff (i.e. random musings)!

ABOUT THE AUTHORS

Lorel and Clayton were teen sweethearts, brought together by a fierce love of books (and hormones). Despite being married for 30 years, they are still madly (the perfect adjective) in love and still writing. As writing partners, they meld logic, creativity, and genres. Fantasy, science-fiction, mystery, horror, steampunk, thriller, romance, classics ... they read them all, and if they can mix them they will!

Still reading? Want to know more?

Lorel has a PhD in molecular biology and Once Upon a Time did cancer research before turning to the dark side (aka marketing), but she uses her powers for good, helping to raise funds for charity. She loves books, movies and animals, and would gladly spend all day with a cat on her lap and the wind in her hair (Conan reference there), while tapping out a story on her keyboard. Or maybe a movie script. With coffee of course. And lots of chocolate!

Clayton is an artist and has recently tackled digital painting, mostly because there's a hyperactive eight-year-old boy running around the house (their gorgeous son, in case you were wondering if that's normal). Clayton is severely dyslexic but loves books and storytelling. He adds vast imagination and a discerning ear for effective prose to their creative collaboration, not to mention the book cover art.

Born and raised in the Western United States, they traveled to Sydney, Australia in 1997 and never left, finding the sunshine and beaches of "Oz" too irresistible. Look them up if ever you're Down Under.

CONNECT

Website: www.lorelclayton.com
Twitter: @lorelclayton
Facebook: www.facebook.com/AuthorLorelClayton/
Goodreads: www.goodreads.com/Lorel_Clayton